W. E. B. GRIFFIN
ZERO OPTION

ALSO BY W. E. B. GRIFFIN

HONOR BOUND
HONOR BOUND
BLOOD AND HONOR
SECRET HONOR
DEATH AND HONOR
  (and William E. Butterworth IV)
THE HONOR OF SPIES
  (and William E. Butterworth IV)
VICTORY AND HONOR
  (and William E. Butterworth IV)
EMPIRE AND HONOR
  (and William E. Butterworth IV)

BROTHERHOOD OF WAR
THE LIEUTENANTS
THE CAPTAINS
THE MAJORS
THE COLONELS
THE BERETS
THE GENERALS
THE NEW BREED
THE AVIATORS
SPECIAL OPS

THE CORPS
SEMPER FI
CALL TO ARMS
COUNTERATTACK
BATTLEGROUND
LINE OF FIRE
CLOSE COMBAT
BEHIND THE LINES
IN DANGER'S PATH
UNDER FIRE
RETREAT, HELL!

BADGE OF HONOR
MEN IN BLUE
SPECIAL OPERATIONS
THE VICTIM
THE WITNESS
THE ASSASSIN
THE MURDERERS
THE INVESTIGATORS
FINAL JUSTICE
THE TRAFFICKERS
  (and William E. Butterworth IV)
THE VIGILANTES
  (and William E. Butterworth IV)

THE LAST WITNESS
  (and William E. Butterworth IV)
DEADLY ASSETS
  (and William E. Butterworth IV)
BROKEN TRUST
  (and William E. Butterworth IV)

MEN AT WAR
THE LAST HEROES
THE SECRET WARRIORS
THE SOLDIER SPIES
THE FIGHTING AGENTS
THE SABOTEURS
  (and William E. Butterworth IV)
THE DOUBLE AGENTS
  (and William E. Butterworth IV)
THE SPYMASTERS
  (and William E. Butterworth IV)
THE DEVIL'S WEAPONS
  (by Peter Kirsanow)

PRESIDENTIAL AGENT
BY ORDER OF THE PRESIDENT
THE HOSTAGE
THE HUNTERS
THE SHOOTERS
BLACK OPS
THE OUTLAWS
  (and William E. Butterworth IV)
COVERT WARRIORS
  (and William E. Butterworth IV)
HAZARDOUS DUTY
  (and William E. Butterworth IV)
ROGUE ASSET
  (by Brian Andrews and Jeffrey Wilson)

CLANDESTINE OPERATIONS
TOP SECRET
  (and William E. Butterworth IV)
THE ASSASSINATION OPTION
  (and William E. Butterworth IV)
CURTAIN OF DEATH
  (and William E. Butterworth IV)
DEATH AT NUREMBURG
  (and William E. Butterworth IV)
THE ENEMY OF MY ENEMY
  (and William E. Butterworth IV)

AS WILLIAM E. BUTTERWORTH III
THE HUNTING TRIP

W. E. B. GRIFFIN

ZERO OPTION

PETER KIRSANOW

G. P. PUTNAM'S SONS
NEW YORK

PUTNAM
— EST. 1838 —

G. P. PUTNAM'S SONS
Publishers Since 1838
An imprint of Penguin Random House LLC
penguinrandomhouse.com

Library of Congress Cataloging-in-Publication Data

Names: Kirsanow, Peter N., author. | Griffin, W. E. B.
Title: Zero option / Peter Kirsanow.
Description: New York: G. P. Putnam's Sons, 2024. | Series: Men at war
Identifiers: LCCN 2024003347 (print) | LCCN 2024003348 (ebook) |
ISBN 9780399171222 (hardcover) | ISBN 9780698164611 (e-pub)
Subjects: LCSH: World War, 1939–1945—Fiction. | Assassins—Fiction. |
LCGFT: War fiction. | Thrillers (Fiction). | Novels.
Classification: LCC PS3611.I769845 Z35 2024 (print) | LCC PS3611.I769845
(ebook) | DDC 813/.6—dc23/eng/20240202
LC record available at https://lccn.loc.gov/2024003347
LC ebook record available at https://lccn.loc.gov/2024003348

Printed in the United States of America
1st Printing

W. E. B. GRIFFIN
ZERO OPTION

Eight Germans armed with Karabiners were charging toward Canidy with astonishing speed. He sighted the one in front and squeezed the trigger of his M1911. The round struck the lead German squarely in the chest and he dropped to the ground as if a trapdoor had opened beneath him. The others kept charging without pause, firing as they ran.

Canidy fired four rounds to give himself cover, rose from the ground, and ran in the direction of the dock. The air snapped around him as the Germans fired a volley of rounds after him. Canidy broke through a bank of thornbushes into a clearing and saw Fulmar, Kapsky, Matuszek, and McDermott no more than seventy-five meters in front of him along the bank of the canal. Fifty meters north of them sat the Njord, the Thorisdottir twins standing on deck, fists on hips.

Canidy spun and fired three more rounds at the pursuing Germans, dropping one of them on his face. The other six stopped, aimed, and fired several rounds. One grazed Canidy's left shoulder, spinning him sixty degrees to the left. He grimaced, gathered himself, and fired a round that went wide but caused the pursuing Germans to dive to the ground.

Canidy catapulted himself off the ground and sprinted toward the dock, zigzagging as he went. He could see Fulmar, Matuszek, McDermott, and Kapsky at the dock beginning to board the boat and Kristin raising her Gevarm to her shoulder. Seeing a weapon raised in his direction, Canidy immediately dove to the ground as Kristin fired several blind rounds at the Germans, causing them to drop to the ground for cover once again.

Canidy instantly popped back up and resumed sprinting, the effort producing a piercing sensation in his wounded shoulder. He heard the air snap inches from his right ear and a millisecond later saw Matuszek pitch forward and disappear onto the deck of the Njord. Canidy turned, fired toward the Germans, striking one in the throat, but without slowing the charge of the remainder. He emptied his weapon firing at the five remaining Germans, turned, and resumed running toward the dock.

Again, the air snapped above him and his eyes locked on the dock and the boat, where Fulmar and McDermott were struggling to assist an exhausted professor onto the vessel—all three presenting prime targets to the Germans.

Canidy shouted, "Move! Move! Move!" and leapt onto the dock and turned just in time to see the five Germans slow to a halt forty meters from the dock. For Canidy, the next ten seconds seemed to grind almost to a standstill and unfold over minutes rather than seconds. As Fulmar and McDermott lifted Kapsky onto the deck, the Germans trained their rifles at the boat. Everyone but Matuszek and Katla Thorisdottir was exposed on either the dock or the deck. Professor Sebastian Kapsky, the mathematical genius who possessed the keys to geopolitical hegemony for the next several generations, was being held upright on the deck of the boat by Fulmar and McDermott, displaying his back to the Germans as if it were a bull's-eye.

Even as Canidy thrust himself toward Kapsky to knock him to the *ground he knew it was too late. He and Kapsky, along with Fulmar and McDermott, would be shredded by Karabiner rounds.*

As he drove himself against Kapsky, Canidy heard a rapid succession of gunshots. Crashing into Kapsky, Fulmar, and McDermott, he braced for the sickening impact of the rounds. All three fell to the deck of the Njord as Katla drove the boat away from the dock up the canal.

But there was no pain. No blood. Not even a moan.

Canidy and Fulmar, lying together on the foredeck of the boat, stared at each other in astonishment, astonishment that they were both alive, astonishment that Kapsky, whom they had rescued and extracted from Nazi-dominated Poland, was unharmed.

They remained prone on the deck waiting for another volley of shots. None came.

CHAPTER 1

The eyes of the Oberstleutnant stationed behind the desk in the anteroom to the office grew wide with awe as the door opened.

The most important and imposing figures in all of the Wehrmacht had at some point during the war walked through that door: Guderian, Jodl, Keitel, Blomberg, Rommel—even Himmler and Göring. At some point each had reason to meet with Vice Admiral Wilhelm Franz Canaris, chief of the Abwehr. The Genius. Each of the figures was powerful and impressive in his own right, commanding vast military or political resources. But none, save perhaps Rommel, had a reputation as storied as the man who had just walked through the door.

SS Obersturmbannführer Otto Skorzeny would be impressive even to those who were oblivious to his many exploits that had bedeviled the Allies since the advent of the war. The commando's muscular six-foot-four-inch frame conveyed the attitude and physicality of the superb natural athlete he'd been before the war, as did the four-inch scar that spanned his left cheek—the consequence of a fencing duel while at university in Vienna. So consequential had his covert missions been that it was claimed that when British general

Bernard Law Montgomery and his staff were poring over the detailed maps of Operation Husky—the massive July invasion of Sicily that had engaged nearly two hundred thousand Allied troops as well as more than seven thousand ships and aircraft—he had scanned the German troop, tank, artillery, and aircraft positions and asked his subordinates just one question: "But where is Skorzeny?"

The Oberstleutnant glanced at the large black-and-white wall clock above the door. All visitors to Canaris's office were expected to arrive five minutes prior to the scheduled appointment. No exceptions, no matter the visitor's importance. In most cases, those who were late were required to reschedule. Skorzeny, however, was precisely on time.

Skorzeny presented himself before the Oberstleutnant and said affably, but with standard Teutonic decorum, "Obersturmbannführer Skorzeny at Herr Admiral Canaris's pleasure."

The Oberstleutnant gestured deferentially toward one of the two chairs to his right. "Yes. The admiral awaits. Please be seated until the appointed time."

Skorzeny smiled. "I prefer to stand."

At precisely 2:05 p.m. the Oberstleutnant cleared his throat, rose from behind his desk, and opened the door to Canaris's office. Skorzeny proceeded through the door and saw Canaris seated behind a small, highly polished desk completely devoid of paper, pens, or memorabilia.

Skorzeny stood in front of Canaris's desk. Even at attention the commando looked relaxed and composed. Nazi Germany's intelligence chief placed the memorandum he was holding on the mirror-like desktop and gestured for the commando to take a seat in one of the three high-backed chairs that formed a semicircle around the desk. Skorzeny bowed slightly and then sat in the middle chair. Canaris said nothing for several seconds, his thick white eyebrows forming a canopy over his penetrating eyes—their gaze appearing to look through and beyond anything they were directed toward.

Most found the gaze unnerving. Skorzeny simply smiled.

Canaris spoke softly and precisely.

"You have been briefed?"

"Only, Herr Admiral, that the mission in question concluded without obtaining the objective."

"That was an understatement, whoever briefed you. Were you informed of the nature of the objective?"

"I was told that its purpose was to obtain strategically critical scientific and mathematical data," Skorzeny replied.

Canaris nodded. "Again, quite an understatement. Who briefed you?"

"Oskar Brecht, Herr Admiral. It was clear he was being quite reserved in his brief."

"As he should be," Canaris said appreciatively. "The item to which Brecht was referring was being sought by the British, Americans, and Soviets, as well as by us. Each power considers the item to be of paramount importance to the outcome of the war as well as the postwar balance of power."

"May I ask, Herr Admiral, who has obtained this item?"

Canaris's gaze became even more intense, almost searing. "You understand, Skorzeny, that this information and the manner in which we've obtained it is known only to the Führer, Reichsführer Himmler, Reichsmarschall Göring, and me?"

"Fully understood, Herr Admiral." Skorzeny narrowed his eyes, but kept his face relaxed. "Upon pain of death."

Canaris smiled coldly. "Precisely. Even with your understanding and assurances I am constrained to tell you only *who* obtained the information, not *how* we know they obtained it."

Canaris stopped speaking for several seconds, seemingly to think through his next words. Although his office was the most secure location in all of Germany, he spoke in a hushed tone. "The Americans and British believe they have it in the form of the very professor who developed it: Sebastian Kapsky. But, actually, the Soviets have it." Canaris paused. "More precisely, the Soviets believe they *will* have custody of it imminently, in the form of the professor's notebook. Shortly after obtaining the information, whoever has it will have strategic dominance during the balance of the war and likely for decades thereafter." Canaris's jaw tightened. "They will be the world hegemon."

Skorzeny straightened. "Forgive my presumptuousness, Herr Admiral . . ."

Canaris waved dismissively. "No, no, Skorzeny. You are often two steps ahead. Please go on . . ."

Flattered but sober, Skorzeny said, "Again, at the risk of being presumptuous, I conclude that you would like me to somehow retrieve the information from whoever possesses it." He tilted his head. "Either by seizing Kapsky from the Americans, or his notebook of formulae from the Soviets. Or both."

The normally taciturn Genius permitted himself a barely perceptible smile at Skorzeny's confidence and nonchalance. "That, Obersturmbannführer Skorzeny, would be the most audacious operation in the history of modern warfare. Perhaps the most spectacular since the Greeks breached the walls of Troy with a wooden horse."

Skorzeny agreed. "The difficulty, of course, is in the logistics," he noted clinically. "Finding and seizing the mathematician, presumably somewhere in Britain or America, and finding and seizing his notebook of formulae—and any copies that may have been made—presumably someplace in Eastern Europe . . ." He seemed to concentrate on a spot on the ceiling. "Obviously, it would be difficult. Many will die. But it *can* be done. The most serious, and *perhaps* insuperable, problem is that it cannot control for any copies of the notebook that the Soviets may have made before we seize it."

Canaris nodded. "Your analysis is quite sound. But we calculate that the probability of copies being made before acquisition of the notebook is low. Our information is that the notebook will be or already is being conveyed to Moscow by a Major Taras Gromov. Our sources do not have his precise location at this moment, but it is calculated that he should be within thirty kilometers of Tallinn. We estimate that it will take him between ten to twelve days to deliver the notebook to OKRNKVD chief Aleksandr Belyanov in the Kremlin. Once in Belyanov's possession it will likely take a substantial amount of time to make copies, even if each of the characters in the formulae is legible and decipherable. I am advised that their scientists will endeavor to render each and every character of the various formulae with painstaking precision so that there will be no error, not the slightest deviation or misinterpretation. It must be flawless."

"What is the estimate, Herr Admiral, for how long that will take?"

"Given current battlefield deployments, as noted we calculate it will take Gromov between ten to twelve days to arrive at the Kremlin and another fourteen days—in shifts working twenty-four hours a day—to make and verify precise copies."

Skorzeny smiled. "Splendid. The logistical challenge remains daunting, but provided we are given accurate information regarding the whereabouts of the item, I assess the operation as feasible."

Canaris leaned forward. "You are exceptionally confident in your abilities, Skorzeny."

Without a trace of arrogance or hubris, the commando asked, "Forgive me, Herr Admiral. Should I not be?"

You have no reason not to, Canaris conceded to himself. Skorzeny had proven himself capable of executing the most audacious of missions, all while making the British and Americans look like fools. The mission would be impossible for all *but* Skorzeny. "What of acquiring Kapsky? How do you assess the probabilities of accomplishing that?"

"Clearly, that is far more problematic, both in terms of planning, timing, and actual execution," Skorzeny replied. "Kapsky likely is many thousands of kilometers—nearly a hemisphere—away from the notebook."

He paused, gazed for a moment at the floor, and then shrugged. "Assuming reasonably reliable intelligence and planning, the execution will be difficult but feasible."

Canaris assessed Skorzeny's demeanor for several seconds. The commando appeared clinical and sober, with no discernible trace of hubris or arrogance. Canaris pressed a button on the underside of his desk and the Oberstleutnant immediately appeared at the door. Canaris gestured toward Skorzeny. "Provide Obersturmbannführer Skorzeny with the Washington briefing packet."

The officer retreated and reappeared within seconds holding a dark brown expandable folder and handed it to Canaris. The Genius scanned the packet's contents and nodded to the Oberstleutnant, who turned and quickly left the office, closing the door behind him.

Canaris held up the packet. "You will study this on your way to Washington, D.C."

Skorzeny nodded. "I assume I am to depart immediately."

"The *U-124* is at Kiel. It will disembark at six in the morning the day after tomorrow and will take a little more than a week to convey you to the coast of the American state of New Jersey. You will be met there by Heinz Waltz, who will assist in every aspect of discharging your mission."

"Which is . . ."

"Bring Dr. Sebastian Kapsky here. Or, failing that, kill him."

CHAPTER 2

Washington, D.C.

0955, 17 August 1943

William "Wild Bill" Donovan's displeasure with meeting in the East Room was plain on his face. The spy chief, short silver-white hair neatly trimmed, was stocky but fit, his countenance that of a bulldog, as was his attitude toward lax security.

The East Room was too open, too accessible. Voices had a tendency to carry and echo, even when muted. Despite the fact that most everyone in the White House carried some level of security clearance, Donovan didn't trust anyone he hadn't known for at least ten years, and damn few of those.

A meeting of this sensitivity should be conducted in the War Room, located on the ground floor of the White House between the Diplomatic Reception Room and FDR's physician's office. Only a handful of individuals even knew it existed: Prime Minister Winston Churchill, General George Marshall, Admiral William Leahy, and, of course, Harry Hopkins. Not even FBI director J. Edgar Hoover or Eleanor Roosevelt was aware of it.

Donovan knew that Secretary of War Henry L. Stimson, seated across from him at the long, polished table, detested meeting in the East Room as well, but no one could discern it from his cool demeanor. The quintessential statesman, with an aloof but proper manner, the reserved Stimson believed in protocol. Certain things just weren't *done*—such as discussing clandestine operations in a cavernous room in which even quietly spoken words seemed to hang for seconds before dissipating into the air like cigar smoke. Stimson tilted his head toward his friend. "Has he been briefed at all about the outcome?"

"No. He wants to hear the whole story all at once, like a kid who doesn't want you to spoil the tale beforehand by telling him just a bit."

"Well." Stimson agreed. "It *is* a damn good story."

Donovan nodded. "Damn fine operation. If you had asked me at the outset what odds I'd give to a successful conclusion, I would have honestly said five to ten percent."

"I *did* ask you for odds. And I recall you said zero to five percent."

Donovan shrugged. "Hell, I'm surprised I was that optimistic."

Harry Hopkins, ubiquitous aide to President Franklin Delano Roosevelt, poked his head into the doorway. "The President asked me to relay that he apologizes for his tardiness but he should be with you in no more than five minutes."

Donovan turned to Stimson as Hopkins withdrew. "What do you make of him?"

Stimson thought for a moment. "Extremely efficient. Seems almost to run this place. The President apparently regards him as nearly indispensable. Why do you ask?"

"Too much of a busybody for my taste. Every time I turn around, he seems to be right over my shoulder."

"That's precisely what a commander in chief needs," Stimson said.

"I suppose."

Donovan had been a member of the Fighting 69th National Guard Infantry Regiment from New York in World War I. He was awarded the Medal of Honor after he continually exposed himself to enemy machine-gun fire to reconstitute his platoon and lead them in multiple assaults against the enemy, refusing to be evacuated despite his numerous injuries. He had little patience for those he perceived as perennial office staff, regardless of how valuable their contribution.

President Franklin Delano Roosevelt wheeled himself into the room in the wooden chair he had had specially fitted with wheels. He was pushed superfluously from behind by Laurence Duggan, Harry Hopkins's aide, who placed him at the head of the conference table before retreating from the room and closing the door. FDR's face bore a mischievous grin, causing the ivory cigarette holder clenched between his teeth to tilt upward.

"Why the sour faces, gentlemen? Is it because your Republican brethren seem to be dwindling toward extinction?"

"Given the overabundance of Democrats, Mr. President," Secretary of War Stimson said, "it's peculiar that you had to resort to us as your most critical appointments in a time of war."

FDR threw his head back and laughed. "And thank God, too. Not only do you know what you're doing, but you have the perfect sense of humor for the situation." The President paused to insert a fresh unfiltered Camel into his cigarette holder, light it, and place the holder into its rightful place in the left corner of his mouth. "Now, Bill, give me the *Reader's Digest* version of your magnificent operation to save the world from totalitarianism. An operation regarding which—let the record show—I had more optimism than you, you eternally pessimistic SOB."

Donovan grunted. "History shows pessimists are almost always vindicated in the end."

"Apparently not this time, thank God." FDR chuckled. "So tell me of this most unexpected success. Don't leave out any important details."

"Before I get started, Mr. President, how's Jimmy?"

Donovan, who on March 24 had been promoted by FDR to Brigadier General William Joseph Donovan, USA, had a fondness for the President's son, who had been temporarily assigned to the OSS. Now a major in the Marine Corps, James Roosevelt II had been awarded the Navy Cross in the Makin Island Raid.

"Jimmy's just fine and sends his respects. Now, tell me about the miracle in Poland."

Wild Bill, who had earned nearly every martial honor the U.S. could confer and who was not given to elaboration or long narratives, endeavored to keep it brief. "Mr. President, this was the first OSS operation—indeed, the first *U.S.* operation—of its kind, and I have specifically commended all involved in the report I forwarded to Mr. Hopkins."

FDR gestured for Donovan to continue.

"Canidy, Fulmar, and the Brit McDermott were conveyed from Gotland to an insertion point just east of Danzig to locate and extract Dr. Kapsky before the Nazis or Soviets got to him. Upon discovering a corpse that we believed was Kapsky, we concluded we were unsuccessful. However, we later learned that, in fact, the SS had secured a document from such corpse, which document ostensibly contained the mathematical formulae for advanced weaponry that would afford its bearer strategic superiority for the foreseeable future—"

"That would be an understatement," Stimson interjected.

Donovan continued. "So we revised the operation, requiring Canidy and Fulmar, along with McDermott, to retrieve the document from the Abwehr—at 76 Tirpitzufer in Berlin."

"By God, a hopeless mission. Suicide," FDR said.

Donovan dipped his head in acknowledgment. "Many of our operations could be termed such," he conceded. "But this one almost certainly so. Nonetheless, we had no options, so Canidy and Fulmar—"

"And McDermott," FDR added.

"—and McDermott were conveyed across the Baltic to Poland by our contract transporter, the Thorisdottirs. From there they were to go to Tirpitzufer, get the document, and return to the U.S."

FDR smiled. "Upon hearing this in retrospect it sounds even more absurdly impossible."

"*Impossible*, Mr. President," Donovan agreed. "But that is why you so shrewdly approved creating the Office of Strategic Services."

"Flattery is an indispensable component of our relationship, Bill." FDR winked. "Please continue to remember that."

Donovan continued. "At some point they disobeyed orders—"

"*Exercised remarkable initiative*," FDR corrected.

"—and, instead of going to Tirpitzufer—admittedly a suicide mission—they went back into Poland and found Dr. Sebastian Kapsky himself. He wasn't dead after all."

"You're leaving out the good stuff, Bill," FDR interjected, traces of both disappointment and irritation in his voice. "Your report alludes to what must have been several remarkably heroic acts on the part of both Canidy and Fulmar—evading, outfighting, and outsmarting the Nazis, particularly that rather odious fellow, even by SS standards, Maurer."

Donovan didn't mask his surprise that the President of the United States knew such details. "Konrad. That's Standartenführer Konrad Maurer."

"Yes, Maurer. A monster. Vicious. How do such people exist on the face of the Earth?"

Donovan knew that the President had a particular fascination with Major Richard Canidy, who months earlier had sabotaged a German cargo vessel carrying nerve gas. Previous to that he had smuggled scientists from behind enemy lines to work on the Manhattan Project. He'd also uncovered German germ warfare capabilities. But the Kapsky operation was the most spectacular. FDR had heard some in his administration refer to Canidy as a "loose cannon," but Donovan staunchly supported him—in part because of Canidy's "calculated recklessness" in approaching seemingly suicidal missions.

"Canidy killed Maurer," Donovan said. "And with the assistance of Fulmar and McDermott safely conveyed Kapsky through Nazi-occupied territory to the Baltic coast, where the contractors conveyed them by boat to Gotland. They are resting there, awaiting orders, while Kapsky will be transported to Newfoundland on his way to Washington, where he will be debriefed by Oppenheimer and eventually collaborate with Einstein and Fermi as part of the Manhattan Project. An *enhanced* Manhattan Project."

"The contractors, I understand, were quite striking. From Iceland . . ."

"The Thorisdottirs," Donovan acknowledged.

"Sisters from Iceland?" the President added.

Donovan nodded dourly, without elaboration.

The President waved smoke from his face. "Well, Bill, if you're not going to indulge my adolescent appetites, tell me when we can expect dividends from Kapsky."

"Mr. President," Stimson interjected, "Dr. Kapsky is resting in Gotland. As you might imagine, the escape was quite arduous. We have sent a physician to monitor him. He's severely exhausted and was dangerously dehydrated. We expect he will be cleared to be flown to the U.S. within forty-eight to seventy-two hours. When he arrives he will stay at the Mayflower for several days, where he will be debriefed by some of my men before his Oppenheimer and Fermi meetings."

Laurence Duggan appeared at the door and cleared his throat. The three men looked in his direction.

"Mr. President, Mr. Hopkins asked me to inform you that the majority leader is waiting outside the office for your nine forty-five meeting."

Roosevelt nodded and waved Duggan away. "Excuse me, gentlemen. Alben Barkley's support of the Revenue Act may be incomprehensible, but he is, after all, a fellow Democrat. Sorry for not seeing you out, but perfunctory partisanship awaits." Roosevelt snapped his fingers as he recalled another matter. "I will need to speak to you about Tehran. Stalin insists on meeting Winston and me there. His purpose is transparent, although one can hardly blame him. Hitler is hammering him in the western portions of his country and he desperately needs us to open a European Front to relieve the pressure. In his place I would be insisting on a meeting as soon as possible also, though I'd never admit it to Uncle Joe."

Roosevelt grinned with his cigarette clenched between his teeth. "Excuse me, gentlemen, but as I noted, partisanship necessarily trumps statesmanship."

CHAPTER 3

Major Richard M. Canidy, United States Army Air Force, opened
an eye and scanned his surroundings: a gray eight-by-twelve room
with cinder blocks for walls and a floor made of concrete. A single
caged lightbulb hung from the low ceiling over his cot. The MIT
honors graduate in aeronautical engineering who had logged more
than three hundred fifty hours of flying time in P-40B fighters defending supply lines along the Burma Road with General Claire Chen-
nault's Flying Tigers momentarily thought he was in a Japanese prison.
On the other side of the cramped room was an identical cot where
First Lieutenant Eric Fulmar, United States Army Infantry, lay nearly
inert, the only sign of life the slight, rhythmic expansion and contrac-
tion of his chest as he breathed. Two M1s were on racks next to him.

Although lean and energetic, Fulmar's looks were a distinct contrast to Canidy: blond hair, blue eyes, and Nordic features, courtesy
of his German father. They'd known each other ever since Fulmar's
mother had sent him to St. Paul's School in Cedar Rapids, Iowa,
over which Reverend George Crater Canidy, Ph.D., D.D., presided.
Fulmar's father was a German citizen and his mother an American
actress.

Everything in the windowless room was gray, including the small table and chair at the foot of Fulmar's bed, along with Canidy's physical exhaustion, which slowed his ability to orient himself. His brain felt sluggish, as if mired in a bog.

He hadn't the slightest idea how long he'd slept, although experience suggested the prickly sensations indicating his left arm had gone to sleep meant he'd been motionless for hours.

Random memories began to sprout in his brain cells and migrate to the synapses, where they became more coherent and chronological. He was safe in a small bunker appropriated by the British Royal Marines near the southern coast of Gotland along the Baltic. British sergeant Conor McDermott and the genius Polish mathematician Sebastian Kapsky were in an identical room across the hall.

Grizzled *Armia* commander Matuszek, who'd assisted them in spiriting Kapsky past hordes of German troops and Waffen SS, had left for Great Britain shortly after their arrival.

Canidy checked the wall clock. He estimated he'd slept more than ten hours since they'd been conveyed across the Baltic by the Thorisdottir twins—the six-foot Nordic goddesses contracted by the OSS to insert them by boat into northern Poland and then extract them upon completion of the mission.

During the journey Kristin Thorisdottir had tantalized him with hints of pleasures to come. Just as he had fallen asleep, she and Katla had returned to the dock to square away their vessel before well-deserved R and R. The plan formulated by Canidy, Fulmar, and the sisters was to spend some time together in London after the two OSS operators had been debriefed.

"So, we agree that Kristin is yours and Katla's mine?" Fulmar asked.

Canidy glanced at Fulmar, who was lying on his back on the cot to his right. "Not our call, Eric, but they were giving off fairly clear signals that that is their intention, too."

"Just confirming," Fulmar said. "Honestly, that's my preference also. Kristin scares the hell out of me. The imperious ice goddess."

Canidy smiled. "She's a goddess, all right, but she melted a bit on the way over here. There's a damn volcano underneath."

"Are they still at the dock?"

Canidy rose on his right elbow. "I expect they'll be back pretty soon. They've got to be almost as hungry as I am." He sat up and swung his legs over the side of the cot.

"Let's wake up McDermott and the professor, get something to eat, and get the celebrations going. Hell, everyone left us for dead. Instead, we're coming back heroes. Can't wait to see the look on Wild Bill's face when we deliver the Holy Grail."

The two operators rose slowly, stiff from the brutal exertions of the last few days. Canidy, big-boned, with broad shoulders, stretched his arms overhead, while Fulmar twisted tentatively from side to side.

"Nothing a couple of fingers of Dewar's won't cure," Fulmar observed. "But I think I'll go with a gallon or two of coffee first. Then, maybe toast."

Canidy nodded. "Good call. I have to get something solid in my stomach. I want to be properly fueled for whatever escapades the ice goddesses have planned for us. Hell, they're used to cavorting with Vikings. We need to vindicate American manhood. We've got to keep the American flag—as it were—flying."

"Raise it high and keep it up." Fulmar nodded, shuffling toward the door.

Canidy opened the door to the room across the hall. Kapsky and McDermott were sprawled on their respective cots—McDermott face down and Kapsky face up. "Get up, you lazy buggers," Canidy said loudly. "A day of celebration and debauchery awaits. We don't leave for East Moor for forty-eight hours, and I, for one, don't intend to waste a single moment of our time here. The order of battle, as declared by Lieutenant Eric Fulmar, is coffee, toast, and Scotch. Each in copious amounts."

McDermott opened his right eye, then his left. He looked skeptically at the pair for a moment, then sat up and grinned broadly through the thickest mustache in the British Army.

"Aye, sounds like a plan. Although for my purposes I suggest we skip the coffee and toast and go straight to the Scotch, perhaps with a bit of bannock. There will always be time for coffee and toast; there's never enough time for Scotch or bannock."

Canidy nodded. "Well said. Must be from some Scottish fable." He looked over at Kapsky still lying on his bed. "Tough journey for the professor. Hell, it's been a tough couple of *years* for the professor. He got some painkillers from the Thorisdottirs. The medic who met us at the dock told me to let him sleep as much as he needs. We're just supposed to make sure he stays hydrated. A doctor will be here soon to check on him."

Canidy clapped McDermott on the shoulder. "How are *you* feeling, champ? Ready to be knighted by King George?"

"What about you and Eric?" McDermott asked. "How many medals and ribbons will your Mr. Donovan pin on your chests?"

"I haven't really thought about it and I really don't care. I do know that none of us is going to have to pay for a single damn drink for the rest of the war."

"Hell," Fulmar snorted, "I doubt we'll have to pay for a single damn drink for a long time after that. And, I suspect, we'll be even more popular with the ladies than we are now."

"Not sure about you when it comes to the ladies," Canidy replied. "Heroism can't cure ugly. And you, my friend, rank highly in the latter category on three continents." He turned toward the door. "Come on, let the professor get his rest and let's get some food. Did either of you notice any food in the kitchen when we came in last night? Is there a mess somewhere on the compound?"

Fulmar pointed left. "There's a pantry down the hall that way," he said. "I was too tired when we got in last night to check for food."

Canidy proceeded only a few steps down the hall before being met by a short, alert-looking physician. "Who the hell are you?" Canidy asked.

The man grinned and extended his hand. "Neville Smythe, Royal Army Medical Corps. I'm here for my two-hour check on Professor Kapsky."

"You've been checking every two hours?" Canidy asked.

"Indeed," Smythe replied. "And despite my best efforts, made quite a thorough racket. Needn't have worried, though. I suspect I could have discharged a pistol in here and not caused any of you to stir one damn bit."

Canidy moved to the side to permit Smythe to pass. "Don't mind us, Doctor. Go about your business. We'll be in the kitchen. Just let us know how the professor is doing before you leave."

Pausing in the narrow hall to permit Smythe to enter Kapsky's room, the three continued into the pantry and immediately rifled through cupboards in search of food and coffee.

"Pleasant enough fellow, that Smythe," McDermott said as he retrieved a loaf of rye bread and moldy cheese from a cupboard. "Had the distinct air of someone used to being considerably smarter than most people he meets."

"I'd be surprised if he weren't smarter than *everyone* he meets," Canidy said. "I'm pretty certain Mr. Churchill sent the very best doc the Brits have to look after our good professor. Only the very best of everything for him, and"—Canidy smiled broadly—"only the very best for the astonishingly courageous and impossibly handsome operators who, along with Fulmar, rescued him."

McDermott located a cutting board, placed the bread and cheese on top of it, and began rifling through the counter drawers for utensils, when Smythe reappeared.

Canidy raised his eyebrows. "I *told* these guys you were probably really good. When is the professor going to wake up and be ready to travel?"

Smythe hesitated a moment. "Not for some time, I'm afraid. If at all." In a hushed tone laden with tension, he explained, "He's in a coma."

Canidy, Fulmar, and McDermott stared at Smythe in silence.

"My orders were to be sure that he's in perfect physical condition. We'll need to convey him to the airstrip for transport to East Moor," Smythe continued. "We've the ability to only provide rudimentary medical care here."

Canidy pushed past Smythe and stepped rapidly toward Kapsky's room, followed by the other three. Kapsky was reclined at a forty-five-degree angle to the headrest, Smythe having propped several cushions behind the mathematician's head and upper torso.

"His breathing is normal, if somewhat shallow," Smythe informed them. "His heartbeat is regular but weak."

"He went through hell during our escape, barely able to walk the last couple of miles," Canidy said, his eyes fixed on Kapsky.

"He passed out at one point from exhaustion. Hell, he'd gone through hell evading the Germans for nearly two years before that.

But coming here on the boat across the Baltic he was *okay*—ate plates of herring and bread, drank lots of water, even some beer. He walked off the boat and up the hill to the lorry that drove us here. On his own power. Was pretty chipper . . ."

Smythe knelt next to Kapsky's cot and placed two fingers on the right side of his neck. "Was he given any medication last night?"

Canidy looked to Fulmar and McDermott. Each shrugged ignorance.

"Why?"

Smythe placed his left ear close to Kapsky's mouth and nose before rising and turning to the three. "This isn't due to exhaustion. And it doesn't appear he has any wounds resulting in trauma or loss of blood. The indications suggest the coma was drug-induced." Smythe glanced back at Kapsky. "Rather tall chap. I'd say he weighs about eighty kilos. Could you lift him—"

"The notebook," Fulmar interrupted. "Where's his notebook? The one with all the crazy symbols and equations and stuff? The one Hitler, Churchill, and Roosevelt moved heaven and Earth for? He never let go of that thing. He brought it off the boat last night. I saw it. He had it." Fulmar's head turned rapidly from left to right, scanning the room as he spoke. "Check the cot, check the covers, check the room . . ."

McDermott knelt, pulled up the covers, and started running his hands swiftly over the sheets, while Canidy frisked Kapsky. "Nothing." He frisked Kapsky again. *"Nothing."*

McDermott's head was on a swivel, searching the small room. "Not in here."

Smythe stood by, bewildered, as Canidy pointed to Fulmar. "Eric, check the kitchen—the pantry—whatever the hell it is."

Fulmar turned quickly and disappeared down the hall as Canidy and McDermott repeated their search of Kapsky and the room. Smythe stood flush against a wall, out of the way. Fulmar appeared less than thirty seconds later.

"Nothing . . . Nothing. It's not here."

"Damn it!" Canidy shouted, startling Smythe. "Damn it!"

"Are we sure he had it with him when he got off the boat last night?" McDermott asked. "Are we *sure?*"

"*Hell yes,*" Canidy said. "I gave it to Kristin Thorisdottir minutes after we set sail and told her to put it in a secure compartment until we got here. She gave it back to the professor when we docked. I *saw* her do it. I *saw* him carry it off the boat."

Canidy looked to Fulmar and then to McDermott. The same look flashed simultaneously in each man's eyes. Instantly all three operators bolted past a startled Smythe, out of the room, down the short hall toward the kitchen pantry, and out of the cottage.

The three descended the grassy two-hundred-meter slope toward the boulder-lined coast at a full sprint, the athletic Canidy and Fulmar abreast, with McDermott trailing by several meters.

Less than ten seconds later the dock and shoreline came into full view past the boulders. Canidy, Fulmar, and McDermott each came to an abrupt halt, chests heaving, as they scanned the dock, shoreline, and waters along the coast. No ships; no boats. Nothing on the horizon except whitecaps and a few gulls gliding across the water's surface. After several seconds, Canidy bent at the waist, put his hands on his knees, and whispered to himself, "Damn Thorisdottirs. Damn them both to hell."

CHAPTER 4

Wolfgang Schmidt prized precision more than anything—other than, perhaps, his life. Exactitude was imperative in his craft, but Schmidt was precise in all things, from the time he arose each day—5:30 a.m.; to the scheduling of his two meals—6:00 a.m. and 6:00 p.m.; to his weight—seventy-five kilos measured at 5:45 a.m. every day; to the amount of water he consumed daily—four liters. Every one of the short white hairs on his head was brushed perfectly into place. His white lab coat was spotless and pressed. Every single beaker, scale, and test tube in his immaculate lab was clean, polished, and arranged for maximum efficiency. The slightest speck of dirt, hint of dust, or smudge of any kind anywhere in his work area was an abomination to be rectified instantly.

Schmidt prized perfection in planning, construction, mechanics, movement, and execution. And that was why, among all the individuals he'd encountered during his tenure as the Abwehr's specialty armorer, he respected the man who had just stridden into his lab more than anyone else—even more so than the Genius himself.

Schmidt had first met Obersturmbannführer Skorzeny in early 1942 while the latter was recovering from wounds suffered at Yelnya.

He and Schmidt showed a revulsion for what they perceived as unnecessary carnage to accomplish inconsequential military objectives. Skorzeny believed massive deployments of men and matériel were counterproductive relics of primitive war fighting. Both men believed military objectives could be achieved with more intelligent and precise deployment of troops. A few highly trained soldiers, properly outfitted, could—with sophisticated intelligence, surgical strategies, and precise deployment—achieve objectives faster and more effectively than whole divisions of armor and infantry. Fortunately, both Wilhelm Canaris of the Abwehr and Walter Schellenberg of the Sicherheitsdienst agreed. Canaris and Schellenberg charged Skorzeny and Schmidt with developing a special operations unit unlike any that had been seen in warfare—the Waffen SS Sonderverband z.b.V. Friedenthal.

The men in the unit were selected for their superior intelligence, adaptability, athletic ability, and sheer martial ruthlessness. Just a few of Skorzeny's men, properly supplied with Schmidt's unique devices and weaponry, could accomplish more than an entire battalion. On the other hand, given the high-wire tasks undertaken by Skorzeny's unit, the slightest defect in Schmidt's equipment could mean disaster.

Schmidt dispensed with the *Sieg Heil* salute, grasped Skorzeny's hand, and shook it vigorously. "I had not heard you were back until a few hours ago. You just returned from Iran, yes? I trust the operation was successful and that cur Stalin is still cursing your name?"

Skorzeny was mildly surprised Schmidt knew of Operation François, but grinned and said nothing.

"I also understand that the absurd marionette Il Duce may need to be rescued soon," Schmidt continued. "Why the Führer thinks that idiot is worth a moment's concern escapes me." Schmidt tilted his head, a sly expression on his face. "But I understand that the king removed Mussolini and replaced him with Badoglio. It's only a matter of time before they execute that fat bastard. So it's only a matter of time before the Führer directs you to perform your next magic trick."

Skorzeny smiled and said nothing.

"But that's not why you're here. You are here because you have been assigned another impossible task. Admiral Canaris has informed you that such task is to assassinate Dr. Sebastian Kapsky, and I am to provide the weapons and equipment to allow you to perform that task."

Skorzeny continued smiling, saying nothing.

"And, if I may note, such task, even for one as gifted as you, my talented friend, is nearly impossible. Suicidal, in fact."

Skorzeny remained silent, but his expression shifted from bemusement to skepticism. The change was not lost on Schmidt, who grinned broadly.

"Of course, the Great Skorzeny can accomplish *any* mission. That is what you are thinking, correct? Send Skorzeny to America—to its capital city, no less—and have him execute a man that all of the Great Powers believe holds the key to military and geopolitical dominance for generations to come. A man so heavily guarded that ten divisions couldn't penetrate. Such is but a simple assignment for the Great Skorzeny; what the Americans call 'a walk in the park.' Correct?"

Skorzeny chuckled, indulging his friend.

"I am sorry to dash your visions of even greater glory for the Great Skorzeny," Schmidt said, "but you are not embarking on that mission anytime soon. Perhaps ever."

"I assume you have received information to which I am not privy?"

"You assume correctly." Schmidt said. "You saw Admiral Canaris earlier today?"

Skorzeny nodded in return.

"Whatever plans you discussed, whatever directions you were given, have changed," Schmidt informed him.

"But I met with him about five hours ago."

"Events and circumstances move quickly in war, my friend. Plans even more so. Of all people, *you* know that."

Skorzeny ran the fingers of his right hand through his hair. "Yes, but these were not ordinary plans, ordinary objectives."

"Very true. I was given an overview of the same plans to permit me to begin working on logistics. I, in fact, may have been given more details than you.

"The original plan was for you to travel by U-boat to the American coastline, insert off the northern coast of the state of New Jersey with two of our agents, and then motorcar to Washington, D.C. Our information places Kapsky under heavy guard at a fairly grand hotel called the Mayflower. It was there that you would execute him. But if I understand what Admiral Canaris suggested quite obliquely, the Führer has plans for you that eclipse by several orders of magnitude the assassination of Dr. Sebastian Kapsky."

"My friend, nothing can be that important. You know the importance of Kapsky. Everyone seeks him."

"Yet despite that, the Abwehr did not in the first instance send *you* to acquire Kapsky. Instead, they sent Standartenführer Konrad Maurer."

Skorzeny agreed. "Maurer has always been reliable and effective."

"But he wasn't *you*," Schmidt said. "Tell me you would not have secured Kapsky."

Skorzeny shrugged. "I cannot know. I understand the Americans sent exceptional operators to acquire Kapsky."

Schmidt waved Skorzeny off amiably. "No need for modesty. We all know your abilities. Saying you can jump three meters high is not bragging when you have jumped four meters several times before." Schmidt began walking toward a large glass display case in the rear of the lab. "Follow me.

"In accordance with his usual practice, Admiral Canaris has given me as little information as possible, the least amount necessary to fulfill whatever assignment he has in mind for you. It will take some time to engineer some of the equipment you will need—indeed, I have yet to be given more than a rudimentary description of the operation."

"I understand you to say these were the Führer's plans?"

"Forgive my imprecision. They were 'plans' in the broader meaning of the term. It would be more accurate to say the Führer had changed the *objective*. The *plan* will be designed by you."

"And what is this objective?"

"All I have been told at this point is that it will involve the targeted but considerable killing of our enemies . . ."

Skorzeny smirked dismissively. "I can do that."

"Demonstrably so. But, my friend, it is far more than that. I've not yet been given the details, but I am blessed with a certain wisdom that comes from experience and proximity to individuals who think on a global scale."

Skorzeny smiled again, leaned toward his trusted friend, and whispered, "You mean, Wolfgang, on a *megalomaniacal* scale."

Schmidt gave Skorzeny a disapproving look and whispered, "Be careful. You may have the Führer's favor, but . . ."

Skorzeny put his hand on Schmidt's shoulder. "I am sorry. I do not mean to cause you discomfort. But I am having difficulty comprehending what could possibly be more important than the Kapsky operation."

"We will know the details soon enough. But at 76 Tirpitzufer it is believed that nothing of this scale or daring has ever been attempted, let alone done, before."

CHAPTER 5

The waves crashing onto the rocky coastline masked the sound of NKVD major Taras Gromov's footfalls as he crept behind the two partisans engaged in idle chatter as they faced the sea, Pattern 1914 Enfield rifles slung over their shoulders. They were earnest and vigilant, but not a threat to Gromov or his objectives. Nonetheless, they were an impediment, however slight, and Gromov dealt with impediments much like most dealt with used tissues—he disposed of them unceremoniously.

Drawing silently within two meters of the pier, Gromov determined to dispatch the slightly larger partisan on the left first. It was always better to eliminate the biggest impediment before addressing the lesser concerns. Of course, size didn't necessarily correspond with who posed the greater challenge, but absent any other evidence, size was the most useful gauge.

Gromov moved silently behind them, the sounds of the ocean's waves obscuring any random noise he might make. He seized the larger partisan, wrapping his right arm around his neck and viciously snapping it backward with such force that the sound of bone cracking was audible above the surf.

Gromov released the larger partisan, whose lifeless body collapsed to the ground. He instantly thrust the middle three fingers of his left hand at the smaller boy's windpipe, causing his eyes to bulge with shock as he struggled in vain to get air. As the smaller partisan began to sink to the ground, Gromov seized the boy's rifle and beat his head multiple times with its stock until there were no signs of life in his body.

Gromov swiveled his head about, checking for any witnesses. The coast was desolate, save for sand, rock, and several dense rows of pine that began not far from shore. He decided to make constructive use of his time by concealing the bodies of the two boys within the tree line on the remote chance that someone might happen along while he waited for the *Njord*.

By the time he had completed the task a few minutes later, he spotted an indistinct structure on the horizon. He estimated the distance to be five to six kilometers. He retreated to within the tree line and watched the structure become larger and more distinct. At its current pace it would approach the shore in approximately twenty minutes.

Despite the fact that there were no other people in sight, Gromov grew increasingly anxious as the vessel drew near. His eyes darted about almost incessantly along the coastline and tree line. Surely, whoever had given the two slain boys their orders hadn't sent them to guard an area in which no one ever set foot.

Gromov's timing was fairly accurate. The twenty minutes felt, however, more like an hour.

When the vessel was within a kilometer of shore, its vector shifted toward the pier. A few minutes later, someone on deck flashed a light several times in a repeating pattern. He did not understand the pattern but surmised it was to signal that the vessel had arrived.

Gromov emerged from the tree line and looked up and down the shore and into the water for any people or vessels in the vicinity. They'd chosen well. There were no signs of other human presence in sight.

He walked cautiously toward the pier. By the time he got there, the boat was close enough that even in the murky gray light of pre-dawn he could distinguish Katla Thorisdottir standing on the bow, hands on hips.

The *Njord* closed to within a few meters of the end of the pier. Gromov pulled himself onto the pier, walked to the end, and leapt onto the bow. Katla greeted him with a brief hug.

Gromov held her with both hands at arm's length. "Any problems?"

Smiling, Katla nodded. "No, it went more smoothly than even we had anticipated."

Kristin, Katla's twin, approached holding a package. Kristin and Katla were identical in almost every respect: nearly six feet tall, ice-blue eyes, white-blond hair that cascaded to their respective waists. The one respect in which they were different was that Kristin was almost completely sightless.

Gromov released Katla. "That is it?"

"Yes, Kapsky gave it to us for safekeeping."

"The Americans, the British, did not hold it *themselves*?"

"They trusted us." Kristin drew close to Gromov and kissed him lightly on the lips. "We gave them no reason not to. We had reliably conveyed their soldiers to their destinations multiple times."

Gromov shook his head in disbelief.

A sly grin on her face, Katla added, "And their leader was en-thralled by Kristin."

Gromov instantly struck Kristin with his left hand and swiftly drew his Tokarev TT-33 from his belt, his right hand holding it within inches of Katla's forehead. Both sisters stood rigid with terror.

"Provoke me at your peril." It was a growl, not a sentence.

Her wavering voice apologetic, Katla said, "I did not—"

"Quiet," Gromov warned. After several seconds, he returned the weapon to his waistband and stood silent for a moment. His shoulders sagged slightly.

"An overreaction," he acknowledged. "Of course, any man would find either of you attractive, not just Canidy. But be aware that I had several opportunities to kill him and his team and did not do so, only because it served our purpose. But on the remote chance I ever encounter him again, I *will* kill him, if for no other reason than your provocation here and now."

No one spoke for several seconds. Gromov's tone turned conciliatory. "You've performed well, both of you. Please do not take my reaction as an indication we do not respect and value what you have accomplished." He turned to Kristin, his expression remorseful. "It was stupid of me to allow our personal relationship to affect our professional relationship. The value of what you have done is worth twenty divisions. In truth, it cannot be quantified."

Gromov paused and lowered his head, the closest the assassin could come to an act of contrition. "The compensation was as agreed? It was adequate?"

The sisters nodded. "We now are quite wealthy," Kristin said, her nearly sightless eyes conveying no emotion.

"And the professor?"

"He was exhausted, dehydrated, and in considerable pain. During the crossing to Gotland we supplied food, water, and the aspirin with the stipulated dosage of malonylurea."

"The others on the vessel—their suspicions were not aroused?"

Kristin shook her head. "Not at all. Aspirin is not suspicious. Moreover, we had just rescued them. They were enormously grateful."

Gromov smiled.

"After we docked he was able to walk to the cabin," Kristin continued. "Afterward, he lay in bed and he was completely unresponsive, but they acted—rationally—as if he were merely exhausted."

Gromov nodded. He stood silent for several moments as if contemplating what he should say. The Thorisdottirs thought he appeared apologetic.

"I must go," Gromov said after several seconds. He stepped toward Kristin and kissed her briefly. "Someone will be in touch."

Gromov turned and walked to the end of the pier. Less than a minute later he had disappeared into the trees with Dr. Sebastian Kapsky's notebook.

Katla turned to Kristin. "It is some way to Moscow. Someone along the way is going to die a grisly death."

CHAPTER 6

Dick Canidy stared at Dr. Sebastian Kapsky while Dr. Neville Smythe checked the professor's pulse once again as he lay in the cargo hold of the de Havilland Albatross. Seated on a bench across from Canidy were Fulmar and McDermott. They were on a runway, all headed to East Moor.

Smythe had quickly determined that the relatively rudimentary medical facilities on the island were insufficient to address Kapsky's condition. They needed to get Kapsky to Great Britain, but had needed to message Stewart Menzies, chief of the Security Intelligence Agency, for an adequate transport to convey them. Such transport had arrived less than twenty minutes ago and now was preparing to depart.

Twelve hours ago, Canidy, Fulmar, and McDermott had each been contemplating a hero's welcome. The three had been assigned a task everyone had assessed as imperative but impossible: infiltrate the Abwehr and retrieve a document prepared by a presumed deceased Dr. Sebastian Kapsky, a document that had the capacity to affect the geopolitical balance of power for decades. The team hadn't merely accomplished the objective; they'd surpassed it. They'd located Kapsky himself, with the bonus of discovering that the Abwehr was in possession of a *bogus* document: Kapsky had prepared the document for the specific purpose of misleading the Germans into believing they had the keys to global hegemony. The operation was by far the Office of Strategic Services' greatest success of the war. Everyone from Roosevelt to Churchill to Stimson, and, perhaps most important, legendary OSS chief Wild Bill Donovan was ecstatic. Canidy, Fulmar, and McDermott had not only survived; they'd far exceeded anyone's grandest expectations. Theirs was a future of decorations, drinks, and dames in abundance.

And then suddenly it had all imploded.

The courage, cleverness, and sheer endurance they'd displayed in finding and rescuing Kapsky in the midst of massive German troop concentrations was for naught.

Now the trio was returning with an unconscious Kapsky, one who—according to Smythe—might never awake. And Kapsky's notebook containing the actual keys to global hegemony had been stolen by the Thorisdottirs, who were on their way to deliver it to either the Germans or, more likely, the Soviets—for what no doubt would be a titanic financial reward. The mental and emotional whiplash of the last few hours had rendered each of them nearly catatonic with dread.

For his part, Canidy feared facing Donovan most. Explaining failures or mistakes to a superior was never pleasant. But explaining a failure of this scale to a perfectionist who had earned nearly every medal his nation could confer was not merely unpleasant. It was ruinous.

The strategic calamity was matched only by the humiliating manner in which it had occurred. They'd been outwitted and duped by the Thorisdottirs. Not because of some elaborate scheme, but because they'd suspended their fundamental baseline skepticism or, as Donovan would simply say, they'd been astonishingly stupid.

Stupidity during war or in spycraft often had grave outcomes. But this time it wasn't the death of a comrade or the disclosure of a position. Rather, it was the potentially catastrophic loss of strategic advantage in the war and for decades to come.

"What do we say to Donovan?" Fulmar asked in a whisper.

Canidy, hunched over and looking at the floor of the cabin, shrugged and quietly asked, "What *can* we say?"

"Sorry for making the biggest screwup of the war?"

Canidy ran the fingers of his right hand through his hair, sat upright, and exhaled. "Hell. Of the war? That might be an understatement."

McDermott, also hunched over, sat up and attempted to rationalize. "Gentlemen, we should keep in mind that *we* did not select the Thorisdottirs to convey us to and from Poland. We did not locate them. We did not vouch for them. *Our superiors* directed us to them. We did not have a reason or the means to investigate or be suspicious of them."

Canidy smiled weakly and patted McDermott's shoulder. "Nice try."

Fulmar's chuckle was devoid of mirth. "Unfortunately, that's not going to work with the guys we work for. And it shouldn't. Kapsky should have never left our sight under any circumstances, and one of us should have had custody of the notebook at all times."

"Didn't see it coming at all," Canidy conceded. "I admit I wasn't at all thinking that the Thorisdottirs would somehow betray us. Hell, they've made the run across the Baltic for you Brits several times. And for us once before. They put themselves at risk getting us out of Poland. No one would have . . ." Candy rubbed his forehead. "What the *hell* do we say to Donovan?"

A British corporal appeared in the compartment.

"Pardon, sirs. You are Major Canidy, Lieutenant Fulmar, and Sergeant McDermott?"

"We are," McDermott replied.

"Just received a message from SHAEF. Sergeant McDermott is to remain on board for the flight to RAF East Moor. Canidy, Fulmar—you're to stay in Gotland pending further orders."

The corporal withdrew from the plane. The three looked at one another for several seconds before Canidy spoke. "Well, I don't know what that means. But it can't be good."

CHAPTER 7

"Give me your damage estimate in one minute or less."

FDR sat comfortably behind a large heavy desk in the Oval Office. Donovan preferred this desk to the *Resolute* desk, located in the President's office on the second floor of the White House residence. Donovan had heard that someone on the White House staff, probably Harry Hopkins, was making arrangements to move the *Resolute* desk to the Oval Office. The *Resolute* desk, some maintained, was more fitting for the most powerful office in the land. It was ornately carved and had a storied past, having been crafted from wood taken from the HMS *Resolute*, a British vessel that had been trapped in ice in the Arctic Circle until it had been rescued by an American whaler. Donovan thought that the *Resolute* desk was too fancy: An American President should perform his work behind a plain desk, a modest one. He wasn't a king, after all. Although, if FDR kept winning consecutive elections, he might begin assuming the trappings of one. Donovan tilted his head deferentially to Stimson, seated to his right.

Stimson sighed. "Mr. President, I am not being evasive when I say the damage is incalculable. It cannot, in truth, be calculated. At last report Kapsky is in a coma and may very well be dead as we speak. The volume containing his work, his calculations, is gone, and we must assume it is—or soon will be—in the hands of the Soviets."

"Why do you say the Soviets? Why not the Germans?"

"Mr. President, the Thorisdottirs rescued our team from Poland with the Germans in close and furious pursuit. Had the women intended for the Germans to acquire the notebook, and Kapsky for that matter, they would have simply left our team, Kapsky, and his notebook to be captured by them."

"I see." FDR nodded. "Then, assuming the Soviets have or are about to acquire this notebook, what is the assessment?"

Stimson straightened and spoke stiffly. "The Soviets are our allies . . ."

The President smiled sardonically. "Only Donovan and I are present, Henry. No need to recite the current geostrategic postures as a preamble."

"It does, however, make a difference in the near-term outlook, Mr. President. We understand from Fermi, Oppenheimer, Goddard, and others that Kapsky's work was nearly a generation beyond where they are today. *A generation.* If the Soviets are able to capitalize on Kapsky's work, they could—no, *would*—in short order attain an almost insuperable strategic advantage over every other major power, including the United States. In the short term they will be able to defeat Nazi Germany and bring the war to a conclusion. But they would have strategic superiority over the West." Stimson paused. "Mr. President, Stalin is indeed our ally . . ."

Roosevelt's face took on a pensive look. "But he is not our friend. He is as vicious and megalomaniacal as that man in Berlin. And there is a fair likelihood that one day Uncle Joe will become our biggest concern." The President looked to Donovan. "Bill, is there a way for us to know whether the Soviets have the notebook at this moment?"

Donovan scowled. "I'm afraid not, Mr. President. We have precious few assets in the Soviet Union. Dissidents, mainly. And they tend to have a very short life span in that country. I asked one of our logicians to do some math, however. We assume the two sisters—the Thorisdottirs—left Gotland sometime before three forty-five p.m. Gotland time. The departure window is imprecise, but it would have been in approximately an eight-hour block when our operators were asleep. If we assume they were headed toward the closest non-combat landfall to the Soviet Union, they could have arrived anytime from one to nine a.m. Soviet time, which is approximately five p.m. yesterday to one a.m. today, our time." A frustrated look crossed Donovan's face. "But hell, Mr. President, we don't honestly know. They could have gone in any number of directions. They could even still be at sea. But for our purposes, it's best to simply assume that the Soviets already have the notebook and have begun deciphering it."

FDR shifted in his chair, his irritation plain on his face. "Bill, how could that *happen*? It's enough we've got to contend with the Wehrmacht. Now, even if we beat them, and then the damn Japanese, we've got *Uncle Joe* looming in the future?"

Both Stimson and Donovan sat frozen in embarrassment. FDR had never remonstrated with either of them. Donovan had begun to respond when FDR raised his hand. "Sorry to both of you for that display. It was unseemly and uncalled for. You and your men have performed miracles, especially during this operation. Going in, we had given them zero possibility of success. It was an actual real-life suicide mission. They were to go to 76 Tirpitzufer to get a docu-

ment that was just a small summary of the Kapsky notebook. Somehow, they survived by disobeying orders, evading the SS, finding
and rescuing Kapsky himself—and then, implausibly, conveying
the man through Nazi-occupied Poland to safety." He looked down
contritely. "And here I am complaining. That, gentlemen, is not a
suitable performance for a commander in chief."

Donovan shook his head. "Respectfully, Mr. President, I disagree. You have every right to be irritated. Even furious. The OSS is
charged with getting things done. Well, the fact is we didn't get it
done in this case. True, Canidy, Fulmar, and their British counter-
part, McDermott, performed brilliantly . . . until they didn't. I'll be
damned if I try to evade responsibility. Nor will I allow the Office
to fail this country." Donovan leaned forward, the muscles in his
square jaw tensing. "We *will* set this right, sir. The Office will set
this right."

The President fixed Donovan with a stern gaze for several seconds and then chuckled with childlike delight. "Gracious, Bill. You
can be downright terrifying at times." Roosevelt's eyes twinkled
mischievously as he turned to Stimson. "You Republicans tend to
view your jobs as life-or-death propositions. On the other hand, we
Democrats"—Roosevelt paused as he retrieved his cigarette holder
from his desk, inserted a Camel, and lit it—"tend to approach matters in the way one approaches a tennis match—volley and serve, serve
and volley. There will always be another game, another set, another
match."

Donovan sat back in his chair, ramrod straight. "Respectfully,
sir, I don't know what the hell that means."

FDR pointed his cigarette holder at the secretary of war. "Henry,
tell him what that means."

Stimson turned in his chair toward Donovan and said in a patrician voice wholly unsuited for colloquialisms, "It means, Bill, *lighten up*."

Donovan blinked uncomprehendingly. "Damn it, Mr.—"

"Franklin . . ."

"Damn it, *Mr. President*, the scientist with the keys to the balance of power for the next century is in a coma and Stalin is about to acquire the means to use those keys—if he hasn't already. I don't for the life of me understand how you can be so flippant. Sir."

"Well, for one, I was told a few moments before you arrived that Georgie Patton and his Seventh Army just arrived in Messina, ahead of the insufferable Field Marshal Bernard Law Montgomery." FDR's face radiated with delight. "Not only is that both a marvelous tactical and strategic victory but it means, more importantly, that the prime minister of Britain won't be crowing for the next six weeks about the bravery and martial superiority of his Eighth Army."

FDR noticed Stimson shift uncomfortably in his seat. "What's on your mind, Henry?"

"Mr. President, we may have to address some issues with General Patton in short order."

"Issues? What sort of issues?"

"George Marshall—by way of Ike—brought to my attention a couple of personnel issues involving Patton."

Roosevelt waved dismissively. "Whatever they are, I'm sure Marshall will handle it appropriately. If we had a couple more Georgie Pattons, this war would come to a swift conclusion. He may drive us all crazy, but he *fights*." FDR paused, arranging his face in a show of mock horror. "By God, I believe I've just praised a Republican general by paraphrasing a Republican president praising another Republican general who would later become a Republican president himself."

Stimson, portrait of patrician rectitude, continued. "Mr. President—"

"When did we become so formal, Henry?" FDR knew full well that when it came to matters of decorum and protocol, Stimson spoke formally. The President, however, enjoyed needling the secretary of war.

"Mr. President, I do not disagree with your assessment of Patton's manifest talents, but I believe Marshall's options are limited. We cannot have our general officers striking enlisted men."

FDR raised his eyebrows. "Is that what happened? Are we sure of that?"

Stimson nodded. "There were multiple witnesses to each incident. Credible witnesses. Doctors, nurses . . ."

FDR interrupted. "Well, as I said, he must have had compelling reasons, not to mention the unimaginable stress of Operation Husky. My goodness, a random slap in the midst of intense battle jeopardizes our finest fighting general? What have we come to?"

"Nonetheless, and respectfully, Mr. President," Donovan interjected. "Patton may be a genius, but there's the—"

The President warned Donovan off. "As I stated, I'm sure Marshall will handle it and do what's appropriate." Flicking ash from the end of his cigarette, he muttered, "I can't believe I'm defending this man while you two hard-asses are calling for his head . . ."

"Not his head, Mr. President . . ." Donovan said.

"All right. May we continue with the matters at hand?" FDR picked lint from his trousers while thinking. "In your estimation, might it be worthwhile to have Canidy and Fulmar locate the Thorisdottirs and retrieve the notebook? They're already in the general area and may have an idea as to the route they may have taken. In addition to which, they know what they look like."

"Mr. President, I've given orders that Canidy and Fulmar stay in Gotland pending further instructions," Donovan began, trying not to sound patronizing, "but the Thorisdottirs could be anywhere within a fifty-thousand-square-mile area, perhaps more. They might even be in the Soviet Union. Having Canidy and Fulmar search for them probably wouldn't be feasible."

"Yes," the President said reluctantly, a tinge of embarrassment in his voice. "I suppose that wouldn't be feasible. Well, then, what do you suggest? What do you propose?"

"Mr. President," Donovan replied, "even though sending Canidy and Fulmar after the notebook wouldn't be feasible, or at least would yield a vanishingly small probability of success, we assess that it may actually be our only option. Professor Kapsky is in a coma from which he may never emerge, and even if he does, there is no assurance he'd be in any condition to re-create his prior work. And if he could, he would be starting from scratch. Who knows how long it would take? The Soviets would have a nearly insuperable head start."

Stimson added, "I'm afraid, sir, that we've been dealt a very bad hand but have no satisfactory options other than to play it. Meanwhile, Stalin has his own troubles, which troubles have a high probability of making all of this moot even before he can capitalize on Kapsky's notebook."

"Yes," FDR agreed. "Especially since the fighting around Kursk escalated. Stalin's been pressing relentlessly for us to open a Western Front against Hitler to relieve the pressure. I'm sure that will be his sole focus at the conference he's pressing for in Tehran." FDR looked at Donovan. "What do you suggest, Bill?"

"Mr. President, we're presently gathering all the available intelligence from sources in the Baltics. As you might imagine, *reliable* information is sparse. But as soon as we have enough to responsibly deploy Canidy and Fulmar, I recommend we send them after the notebook. As you've said, they're 'in the area.'"

FDR nodded.

"A long shot," Donovan conceded. "But it's our only shot."

FDR sighed. "Very well. Gentlemen, keep the details of this among us and your two operators only. Regardless of the low probability of success, I don't want the Soviets to know that we're undertaking this operation, which may have little to do with the present war but everything to do with the next, and perhaps final, one."

There was a quick rap at the door to the Oval Office. Donovan turned to see Harry Hopkins's head and neck as he cracked open the door.

"Mr. President, Speaker Rayburn is here for your nine thirty appointment."

FDR nodded. "Thank you."

Hopkins disappeared as he closed the door. FDR looked at Donovan.

"My word, have you no control whatsoever over your *orbiculares oculi*?"

Donovan looked at his former Columbia Law School classmate with incomprehension. "Your facial muscles, Bill," FDR explained. "Anyone closer than Dupont Circle could see you don't have much regard for Harry, but do you have to display it so vividly?"

Donovan shrugged. "I really don't have an opinion of him."

"Not everyone can win the Medal of Honor, Distinguished Service Cross, Distinguished Service Medal, Silver Star, Purple Heart, and—what else did you earn? The Little Sisters of the Poor Potluck Ribbon? Look, Bill," FDR explained. "Hopkins didn't serve in the

Great War because he had a bad eye, not because he's a coward or unpatriotic."

"I didn't say a word, Mr. President."

"The man's damned talented—my principal advisor on nearly everything. So show him just a little courtesy, all right?"

"Yes, Mr. President. Respectfully, it's not so much Mr. Hopkins but that Duggan fellow," Donovan said, referring to Hopkins's aide. "He seems consistently underfoot."

FDR sighed in mock exasperation. "Geez, Bill. We're fighting a world war on two fronts and you're preoccupied with minor irritations."

Donovan agreed. "That, sir, is because minor irritations, left unaddressed, have a tendency to become major problems."

CHAPTER 8

Canidy and Fulmar had exchanged their goodbyes with McDermott in the jocular manner of those who have faced death together:
equal parts needling, bravado, mirth, and respect. Each had a feeling they'd see one another again before the end of the war. The two
American operators had an uneasy feeling that the reason they were
instructed to remain in Gotland had to do with impending official
sanctions for their unforgivable failure to secure Kapsky and the
notebook. Neither of them outwardly betrayed the anxiety each
felt, but both understood the scale of the disaster.

Back at the cabin they engaged in random small talk as they ate
a desultory meal consisting of the remains from the *Njord*'s galley:
bread, sardines, and beer. Canidy occasionally glanced at the cabin
door as if expecting Donovan to burst through and give them a
dressing-down for the ages, complete with ceremonious ripping off
of any insignia or badges of rank. An hour after their return to the
cabin, Fulmar said, "Hell, I don't know about you, but this feels too
much like we're just waiting to be sent to the gallows." He rose from
the kitchen table and began walking toward the short hallway leading to the bedroom. "You never know when you'll get another

chance to eat or sleep. I'm not missing out on either just because we're waiting for Donovan to drop the ax."

Fulmar stopped upon hearing a short rap at the door, which opened to reveal the same corporal who had conveyed the order that the two Americans remain in Gotland awaiting further orders. He held a small brown envelope in his right hand.

"Major Canidy, Lieutenant Fulmar, I am instructed to convey this to you." He placed the envelope on the table, nodded deferentially, and withdrew, shutting the door behind him.

Canidy and Fulmar looked at each other with apprehension for several seconds before Canidy said, "Well, I suppose that's from Wild Bill, giving us the day and time for our appointment with the guillotine."

Fulmar picked up the envelope, opened it, and read the contents.

"Well," Canidy said, "when's the execution?"

Fulmar, continuing to stare at the message in his hand, didn't respond.

"Well?"

A stunned look on his face, Fulmar handed the document to Canidy and said, "I estimate not long after we get to the Soviet Union."

CHAPTER 9

Major Taras Gromov, like most Russians, expected hardship in any and every endeavor. That included making the journey from the Estonian Baltic coast to Moscow. He was both elated and cautious upon discovering an unoccupied ZIS in a copse of trees a few kilometers east of Pärnu. A remnant of war. It was a wreck: multiple dents and scratches, missing a door, and with an unknown amount of fuel. But it was operable.

Gromov determined to drive the vehicle as far as it would go. He drove slowly, averaging under thirty kilometers per hour as he traversed the eastern edge of the Wehrmacht fronts, toward Moscow. The truck ran out of fuel in a relatively isolated area of the Tver Oblast. Gromov secured Kapsky's notebook inside his waistband at the small of his back, covered it with his shirt, and began walking south. The weather was pleasant and, although he wouldn't otherwise be in a hurry to get to Moscow, he moved at a brisk pace. His immediate objective was to avoid any complications that would delay or prevent him from delivering the notebook to the Kremlin.

Though Gromov was not normally given to nervousness or tension, the closer he drew to Moscow, the more anxious he became. He was conveying an item that was perhaps the most consequential object in the entire war. He had acquired it using his strength, determination, guile, and wit. When first given the assignment by Belyanov, he was told that its successful completion would merit the Order of Lenin. He fully understood that only Stalin himself could confer that honor, one that virtually guaranteed status, respect, and perhaps even a measure of wealth. Even Belyanov would have to accord him a degree of deference. Indeed, Belyanov had never executed an operation remotely as consequential as securing the Kapsky notebook. Given that Lavrentiy Beria valued usefulness and loyalty in his subordinates above all else, Gromov arguably was the most valuable person in the entire NKVD.

At the moment, however, Gromov was one of the hungriest persons in the Tver Oblast. He'd eaten nothing but blackberries in the last thirty-six hours, and there didn't appear to be anything edible in the expanse of grassy fields that looked to Gromov indistinguishable from the seemingly endless steppes of Novosibirsk Oblast, where he'd grown up.

He could see a few edifices to the southwest. Not enough to be a village. Most likely a cluster of farmhouses. Food and water would be there, perhaps even a mode of transportation. He had rubles to compensate whoever resided on the farmland—likely peasants who might have assumed occupancy after the kulaks were eliminated. In this region, fifty rubles would purchase a feast for dozens. If he was fortunate, perhaps there would be a vehicle—a GAZ or an automobile of some type that he could commandeer to go as far as it could take him. He knew the prospect was unlikely. Motorized vehicles of any sort were a luxury out of the reach of most in this area.

Forty-five minutes later, Gromov was close enough to discern that the edifices consisted of three houses, two small barns, a well, and an outhouse. Fencing enclosed a few pigs and chickens. A rotting shack housed what appeared, to Gromov's surprise, to be a GAZ automobile. Caked with dried mud, it sat at the end of a short patch of grass.

An old man emerged holding a Mosin rifle at waist level. He appeared to be in his late sixties or early seventies, thin and sinewy. His forearms, laced with bulging veins, seemed outsized for the rest of his body—the product of a lifetime of manual labor. His eyes appeared rheumy—the product of a lifetime of vodka consumption.

Gromov raised his hands to chest level, palms outward. "I am a simple *Krasnoarmich* in search of food. Can you help?"

The old man regarded Gromov through squinting eyes. "You are a deserter."

Gromov shook his head. "I am on duty. I am on my way to Moscow."

The man snorted. "You have quite a journey ahead of you, then."

Gromov motioned for the man to lower the weapon. "Yes. But it's manageable if I have some food. Can you help?"

The old man kept the rifle trained on Gromov. "I do not know you. Why would you be here and alone if you are on duty? You are either a criminal or a deserter."

Gromov nodded. The man was old but not a fool. A lone individual, dozens if not scores of kilometers from the front, didn't fit the description of a soldier. "I have a special mission," Gromov explained. "Please lower your weapon. It may discharge accidentally."

The man raised the bill of the Mosin slightly, training it on Gromov's chest. "Do you think I do not know how to handle myself?"

Gromov smiled genially. "No, no, friend. Like anyone else, I simply do not like having a firearm trained in my direction. I have had accidents with firearms. No matter how proficient one is, something may go wrong. I prefer not to be at the other end of it if it does."

The man did not move. Gromov continued, "I have traveled from the Baltic—Estonia—on a special assignment to Moscow. I've eaten little on my journey. I still have some distance to travel. I can pay you for food."

The man continued to train the rifle on Gromov, but there was a barely perceptible relaxation of his muscles. "I was a Wachtmeister in the tsar's war," the old man said skeptically. "A single soldier does not travel from Tallinn to Moscow."

"I am not regular Red Army."

The old man squinted and looked Gromov up and down slowly. "What does that mean, not regular Red Army?" Before Gromov could respond, the man asked, "NKVD?"

Gromov hesitated to respond. The old man continued.

"NKVD and SMERSH have killed many. Stalin's executioners. Not just kulaks. Many, many peasants." The man cocked his head toward the expansive fields. "It was not always like this," he informed Gromov, referring to the unpopulated surroundings. "Killed or starved. No difference. Stalin wanted us gone. We are gone."

"I do not work for Stalin."

"But you are NKVD. Did you not kill kulaks?"

"No," Gromov lied.

"I do not believe you."

"I cannot help that, friend. But I am simply a patriot who has a mission for the Motherland. I cannot fulfill that mission if I starve."

The old man looked Gromov up and down again. "You have no weapon?"

Careful so as not to startle the man, Gromov pointed to the sheath sewn into the back of his collar. "Only this."

"Show me."

Gromov slowly moved his left hand to the NR-40, withdrew it from its sheath, and then returned it.

The old man was silent for several seconds. "You are an assassin for Beria," he declared.

Gromov, suspecting from the man's tone that he'd lost friends or family to Beria's men, replied, "I *am* an assassin. But not for Beria. I am a patriot."

"My family were patriots. My friends were patriots. It did not matter. Beria had them slaughtered."

Gromov shifted his stance. The old man was sober and lucid and calm. But that didn't preclude him from shooting Gromov. A display of empathy was in order.

"We have all lost people to Beria, friend."

"You have lost family? To Beria, not the Germans?"

"Yes," Gromov lied.

"I do not believe you. You strike me as a person who would not abide the killing of your family members."

Gromov raised his eyebrows. "Who would? But not all have the courage or capacity to act. At least not immediately. Opportunities are few." He lowered his hand slowly.

The man pointed the rifle at the dirt. "How much money do you have?"

"Enough. How much food do you have?"

"Never enough." The old man put his right arm through the rifle strap, slung the weapon over his shoulder, and turned toward the farmhouse door. "Come with me."

Gromov exhaled, climbed up three steps onto the rotting porch,

and followed the old man into a small kitchen that smelled of ma-
nure, yet was exceptionally tidy and clean. There was a small table
with two chairs, shelves lining the walls with dishes and pots, and a
washbasin next to an entrance to a hallway leading to the rest of the
modest abode.

The old man set the rifle in a corner, reached into a cupboard
next to the washbasin, and retrieved a basket with several loaves of
hard bread. He placed the basket on the table, then reached above
the cupboard and pulled down a bottle of vodka. He turned to
Gromov. "I have water also, but I must pump it from the well. We
have had something of a drought, so it would take some time to
produce enough to fill a cup." The old man's eyes flickered as he
remembered something. He produced a black kettle from inside the
washbasin. "I forgot that there is tea. Not much. But better than
vodka for a long journey."

"A matter of perspective, I suppose."

The old man shrugged indifference. "I do not understand what
you mean." He lifted the kettle for display. "But there *is* water."

Gromov placed ten rubles on the table. The old man's eyes grew
large. "No, no. Too much. That is too much." The old man grabbed
the money and extended his hands to Gromov, who refused it emphatically.

"It is fair compensation, friend. You cannot even spare what you
have offered me."

The old man dropped his hands to his sides. The look on his
face suggested he believed Gromov was testing him.

"Please," Gromov insisted. "Take it. It was provided to me for
circumstances just such as this."

The old man refused with a sharp shake of his head, a peasant who believed punishment awaited those who freely accepted good fortune. Gromov seized the old man's wrist and forced the money into his hand. "This is *your* money. From where do you think the tsar gets it?"

A frightened, almost wild look came into the old man's eyes, as if mention of the tsar would, like an incantation, invoke Stalin's actual presence. Gromov held his wrist more tightly and pressed the money into his palm. "It is your money," he repeated with a reassuring smile.

His eyes fixed on the old man, Gromov sensed a presence directly behind him. In a single motion he drew the NR-40 from its sheath, spun swiftly to his right, and with his right hand slashed a diagonal arc across the throat and chest of a man standing behind him.

The old man recoiled in horror, his open mouth unable to summon the cry stillborn in his chest.

Blood spurted across the room, splashing against Gromov, the old man, and much of the kitchen floor. The victim remained suspended in the air, like a marionette after its strings had been cut, before collapsing into a formless heap.

Gromov examined the carnage. The victim appeared to be another old man, unarmed, his frail physique posing no threat. Gromov realized that the alien feeling he was sensing was remorse. He had acted instinctively. No thought, just the natural consequence of superb reflexes and incessant training. He was protecting the notebook at the small of his back, a notebook that was producing an impressive body count.

Gromov turned back to the old man, whose mouth was agape and whose face was otherwise frozen in horror. After a moment, his jaw began quaking and he looked up at Gromov with eyes wide. He said simply, "You have killed my only friend."

Gromov cast his eyes to the floor. "It was not my intent," he said. "I reacted in the manner I was trained. I reacted to eliminate a potential threat to the mission."

"You murdered Yaron," the old man informed him, his voice a mixture of anguish and disbelief. "He was my only friend. Everyone else is dead. I have no one. No one is left. They are all dead." The old man stared at Yaron for several seconds, then looked up at Gromov and said almost clinically, "I must clean the blood off the floor and walls, dig a grave, and bury him."

Gromov said, "I will do it. It is my responsibility." He bent down and grabbed the dead man by the arms. "Show me where he should be buried."

Without responding, the old man walked out of the house to the east side of the rotting shack housing the GAZ and pointed to the ground. Gromov could discern at least two small mounds bearing no grave markers in the same plot.

The old man retrieved a shovel from the shack and handed it to Gromov. The ground was relatively soft, and within twenty minutes he'd excavated a six-by-three-foot hole almost four feet deep. He looked at the old man, who stared back with indifference. Without ceremony, Gromov dropped the body into the grave and covered it with dirt. When he was finished, the old man said, "I will die soon also."

Gromov withdrew all but five rubles from his pocket and extended it to the old man.

"What is this? Payment for my friend's life?"

"Four hundred rubles. For the bread, the water, and the auto."

The old man stared at Gromov's hand for several seconds, then shrugged and took the money. "I never in my whole life have had so much money. What will I spend it on? And for what?"

Gromov pointed to the GAZ. "Petrol?"

"Enough for twenty kilometers from Moscow."

The pair walked into the house and the old man handed the basket of bread and kettle of water to Gromov, who placed both on the table and consumed a piece of bread as the old man watched.

"What will you do?" Gromov asked.

"There is nothing to do. The Gypsies will be by sometime soon. With the rubles I will buy something that will help me pass the time until I die."

Gromov picked up the remaining loaves of bread. The old man slid the bottle of vodka across the table toward Gromov, who put it to his lips and took two swallows before handing it to the old man. "What is your name?"

The old man drank long and slow from the bottle. "Anatoli."

"I will remember," Gromov said, and walked out the door.

CHAPTER 10

"I expected there would be consequences to our screwup, but I never expected it would be exile to Siberia," Canidy said to Fulmar as they stood on the dock imagining the journey to the Baltic coastline near Rågervik, Estonia.

"Really, we should be grateful Wild Bill's sending us there as opposed to the gallows."

Canidy sighed. "That's still a possibility, you know." He stomped his foot on the wood. "Damn it. How the hell did those women do it? How did we let them do it?"

"Lesson learned. Never trust twin Viking goddesses who have nerves of steel."

Canidy chuckled wryly, shaking his head. "First time in my life I've ever been taken for a ride by a woman, and it turns out it could end up affecting the entire damn war. The entire war."

"Look at it this way, Dick. There's not a man in the world who wouldn't have been taken in by Kristin. Or Katla. Six foot. Legs to here. Those eyes. I would have given either of them Delaware if they'd asked."

Canidy stomped his foot on the dock again. "I can't imagine

what the hell Wild Bill's got planned for us. The Soviet Union? How are we going to get a damn notebook out of a country with the largest landmass and the largest military force in the world? A country whose leader is a bloodthirsty paranoid who thinks anyone he hasn't known since birth is an enemy of the state?"

Fulmar shrugged. "We knew going in that Kapsky was important. Remember, the original plan was to infiltrate Berlin and get his documents from the Abwehr." He laughed, a sardonic look on his face. "At least this time we're supposed to infiltrate an *ally*."

Candy shook his head in disgust. "What a screwup. Still hard to comprehend." He took another look across the sea, half hoping to see the Thorisdottirs' vessel, the *Njord*, sailing toward shore. "Come on. Let's get back to the cabin. We wouldn't want to be late for our briefing on how we're supposed to commit suicide. Again."

CHAPTER 11

Churchill had directed that they meet in the War Room for no other reason than he was already there from a previous meeting. It didn't hurt that it also was a fitting place to have a cigar, the aroma of which penetrated the mahogany table and chairs and hung in the room for days after the last was extinguished.

Stewart Menzies had requested the meeting two hours ago, indicating that Commander Ian Fleming had an important update on the Kapsky operation. Fleming was flamboyant and creative to the point that an observer unfamiliar with his behavior might doubt his veracity. But Churchill had long ago determined that Fleming's colorful narratives were almost invariably accurate and contained some of the most vital intelligence of the war thus far.

Two light raps at the door were followed by Churchill's security ushering in first Menzies and then Fleming. As usual, Naval Intelligence officer Fleming was dressed in civilian clothes punctuated by his trademark bow tie. Menzies, who invariably looked as if he had stepped from the front page of an Eton alumni magazine, was dressed in a perfectly tailored black suit, white shirt, and spotted azure tie. A blue kerchief peeked from his left breast pocket and he held his beloved bowler cradled between his left elbow and hip. "Apologies for the late notice, sir," Menzies said, "but I thought it imperative that you be briefed on the latest developments regarding Dr. Kapsky."

Churchill regarded them from his high-backed leather chair positioned at the head of a horseshoe-shaped mahogany table. A large color-coded map of continental Europe with troop placements hung behind him. "You two seem to have become an item," Churchill said. "Prior to the Kapsky affair I was given to believe you rarely spoke to each other." He waved them toward two chairs to his left. Menzies sat nearest to Churchill, with Fleming to Menzies's left.

"Before we begin, Stewart, how goes the Gerry codebreaking?" A mischievous grin grew on Churchill's face. Menzies had been obsessed with deciphering the German codes, enduring frustrating setbacks each time a breakthrough appeared imminent.

"Sir, I grant we have been tantalizingly close to what we believed would be a breakthrough several times. And indeed, Turing and Welchman have had several. The overall endeavor, however, has sometimes been frustrated by slight but clever running adjustments the Gerries have made. It is not, after all, without reason that Canaris is called 'the Genius.'"

"What of Gaither?" Churchill asked.

"He's still working on them, too," Menzies answered. "At this point primarily as a counter to German penetration of *our* codes. The damn Gerries are indefatigable in that regard, but not more so than Gaither. Clever fellow."

Churchill pointed to a row of cigars peeking from Fleming's breast pocket. "I assume those are for me? Tribute from the villain?"

Fleming smiled and retrieved two cigars, extending them to Churchill and Menzies, respectively. "Romeo y Julieta, sir, I believe is your preference."

"Indeed," Churchill agreed as he reached for one of the cigars. "A civilized people cannot conduct proper business without tribute to vice."

Fleming pulled out a cigarette holder and displayed it to Churchill for permission. The prime minister nodded, his jowls quaking. "From that place in Grosvenor, I presume?"

Fleming nodded in return. "A Turkish blend, probably with a bit of Balkan thrown in for spice. It cannot be exceeded."

Fleming produced a strike match. Churchill and Menzies extended their respective cigars toward Fleming, who lit each before lighting his cigarette. The stoking ritual was followed by a full minute of silence as the three drew deeply upon their tobacco.

Churchill's eyebrows arched. "Splendid," Churchill declared. "Although incomplete without a snifter of Hine."

"I shall endeavor to bring some along next time." Menzies smiled. "Although I was given to believe, sir, that you preferred a different cognac."

"Prunier," Churchill acknowledged. "Not a preference, just a difference. A bit of variety sharpens the senses." He shifted the topic. "What news of Dr. Kapsky? After everything that's happened, please do not tell me he's expired."

Menzies deferred to Fleming for response. "No, sir, he has not."

"Where is he?" Churchill questioned.

"RAF East Moor."

Churchill grunted. "Do the physicians have any hope he'll survive? At least regain consciousness long enough to provide the essentials of his work?"

"Well, sir," Fleming responded, "it appears he's regained consciousness."

"Splendid. What is that physician's name? Dr. Neville Smythe? Know the family. Please tell him splendid work, will you?"

"To be precise, sir, it wasn't Dr. Smythe who revived Dr. Kapsky in midflight from Gotland."

"No?" Churchill asked.

"No, sir," Menzies explained. "It appears a Sergeant Conor McDermott—"

"Sergeant McDermott," Churchill muttered. "Why do I know that name?"

"Sir," Menzies responded, "McDermott was the chap we sent to Germany to retrieve the Kapsky documents."

Churchill nodded as he exhaled a cloud of blue-gray smoke. "Yes. Forgive me. We must see that he is appropriately decorated. Absolutely splendid chap."

"He is," Fleming resumed. "McDermott became somewhat concerned—'frustrated' may be a more appropriate word—that Dr. Kapsky was showing no signs of response as Dr. Smythe was ministering to him on the flight from Gotland. Kapsky's condition appeared quite grave and Dr. Smythe was exercising great prudence in treating him."

"Understandably so. I take it he had been briefed on Kapsky's importance?"

"Indeed," Menzies assured him. "Not specifics, of course, but he was given to understand that Kapsky was indispensable to the war effort."

Churchill pointed his cigar at Fleming. "Continue."

"Yes, sir. As noted, McDermott became somewhat concerned with Kapsky's failure to respond to Dr. Smythe's ministrations and decided to employ what he termed a 'universal battlefield dressing.'"

Churchill leaned forward and took the cigar out of his mouth. "You're joking."

"No, sir," Fleming said. "To Dr. Smythe's horror, it appears Mc-Dermott poured a container of cold water on Kapsky's head and cuffed him about the face a bit."

The prime minister placed the hand not holding his cigar on the armrest and stared at Fleming, mouth partially agape. "I assume that if it did not produce cardiac arrest in Dr. Kapsky, it certainly did so for Dr. Smythe."

"Sometimes the old ways are the best," Fleming observed. "Mind you, while he is stable, Kapsky remains in critical condition. The ultimate resolution remains in doubt. But he woke long enough to convey something quite intriguing."

Churchill interrupted. "You say he is at East Moor?"

"Yes, sir. The facilities there are more than sufficient until the physicians clear him to be conveyed to London. Although he's surprisingly stable, they do not want to place stress upon him just yet by moving him on ground."

Satisfied, Churchill made a rolling motion with his cigar hand. "Please continue."

"It seems McDermott's actions revived Kapsky for a few moments, and he—not surprisingly, given his prodigious mental acuity—*winked* at McDermott and motioned for him to draw near—"

"For God's sake, Commander, dispense with playing Arthur Conan Doyle and get to the rub . . ."

"Evidently, Kapsky had determined he had been poisoned or

otherwise incapacitated by the Thorisdottirs so that they could abscond with the notebook." Fleming's face displayed a look of awe. "Well, you will recall that when Dr. Kapsky was evading the Germans in Poland he prepared documents bearing false calculations in order to lead them to believe they had acquired the real thing."

The prime minister's mouth fell open. "No . . ." Churchill said. "He did it *again*? With the damn notebook itself? It's fake?"

"Not quite, sir," Fleming responded. "The notebook is genuine. But, according to Kapsky, essentially indecipherable. It's coded in such a way as to be gibberish to anyone but him. He inserted a number of expressions that are nothing but rabbit holes, and the genuine expressions are coded in a way he believes will nonetheless take even someone at Kapsky's level—say a Kurchatov or Artsimovich—*years* to understand."

"So it will take the Soviets years to understand, and years to deploy, weaponry based on his work?"

Fleming nodded. "That's precisely what he says. In the meantime, Kapsky can provide the West with a significant head start based on his work."

Churchill gazed past the blue smoke surrounding his head. "Do we have any estimate as to how long it will take before Stalin knows the notebook will require decryption?"

Fleming shook his head. "Not with precision, sir, but McDermott was of the impression it will take months before they can even conclude the decryption will be a long, slow slog."

Churchill smiled approvingly. "And what of Kapsky?"

Menzies said, "It will be a while before we know, sir. He responded to McDermott's expert medical intervention, but that was momentary."

Churchill puffed pensively on his cigar for several moments. "On balance, we appear to be in a better position than we believed a few hours ago. Of course, everything is relative." He placed the cigar in the ashtray at his side. "Thank you for the briefing, gentlemen. I will inform our cousins across the way."

CHAPTER 12

Donovan had been reviewing OSS field reports from various European stations when he received a call from the President's private secretary, Grace Tully, graciously requesting Donovan's return to the White House for a 5:00 p.m. meeting with the President. She promised the meeting would be brief, which, by Roosevelt standards, could mean anywhere from one minute to five hours.

Donovan, like any spy chief, prized confidentiality and discretion. He was therefore irritated to learn that this time the meeting would be held in the Map Room.

Donovan's irritation grew when he was met inside the west entrance by Laurence Duggan, who escorted him to the Map Room to await the President's arrival. Sensing Donovan's displeasure, Duggan remained silent, and Donovan was mildly surprised to find FDR waiting for him upon reaching the destination. The President grinned with delight.

"I truly enjoy seeing you nonplussed, Bill. Ever since we were in law school you've almost always looked as if you fully expected whatever transpired." FDR looked behind Donovan to see Duggan, who was standing at the door. "You may leave us, Laurence. Thank you."

Duggan disappeared as Donovan sat in the chair closest to Roosevelt. "Being here a second time today can only mean bad news. Disastrous news."

"Bill, you always expect bad news."

Donovan shrugged. "That way I'm never disappointed."

"Then you'll be chagrined to learn I've gotten some splendid news from the prime minister. It's news that normally would be conveyed from, say, Menzies to you, but Churchill believed this information to merit principal-to-principal notice."

"My feelings aren't hurt, Mr. President."

FDR smiled. "Indeed. Have they ever been?"

"Not that I can recall."

"Just as I thought. Well, to get straight to it, the prime minister relates that what we perceived as a debacle this morning seems to have evolved into an imminent victory." FDR paused theatrically. His law school classmate waited patiently, indulging the President's penchant for theatrics.

"Professor Kapsky is alive and in their custody and has confirmed that the documents seemingly everyone has been searching for are so heavily encrypted as to be virtually useless to Uncle Joe— at least for quite some time. Furthermore, Kapsky, provided he recovers, should be able to provide us with the essence of his work in due course."

Donovan responded approvingly. "That *is* good news, Mr. President. How long before Kapsky can provide us with 'the essence of his work'?"

"The PM couldn't provide a precise estimate. It will take days, if not weeks, for their physicians to be sure Kapsky can return to work."

"That's a relief. My men, then—"

"Are out of a job for now."

"They were thoroughly briefed on their insertion into the Soviet Union. Their second suicide mission in as many months."

Roosevelt leaned forward in his wheelchair and patted Donovan's knee. "And I think they deserve a heck of a lot of credit, even from a tough old bastard like yourself. Yes, they permitted those boat ladies to get the best of them—from your description I suspect they would have gotten the best of all of us—but they really did something extraordinary in finding and extracting Dr. Kapsky from hostile territory in the midst of the greatest land battle in history. This nation needs men like that. We won't have many of them if we punish the few that exist."

"True," Donovan agreed. "But good superior officers are like good football coaches. You can never let your most talented players think they're special. That applies double to the likes of Canidy and Fulmar. They are cocky SOBs—"

"*Not* at all like their boss," Roosevelt chided.

"—who need to be kept in check for the next mission."

"Which, in a way, brings me to the second reason I've asked you to return. We've received another communication from Stalin. He's throwing more than a million men into the meat grinder at Kursk. I understand hundreds of thousands have been killed over the last three weeks alone. He's lost over a thousand tanks there and who knows how many aircraft. He's been insisting on the meeting in Tehran for several weeks now, where both Churchill and I know he's going to press for the opening of a Western Front against Hitler immediately.

"We will still have the meeting. Averell Harriman and Harry Hopkins, at minimum, will accompany me. Perhaps Hap Arnold or Leahy. Churchill no doubt will have General Brooke and Admiral Cunningham. Stimson insists we be prepared for a Soviet delegation consisting not only of the likes of Molotov, but a sizable intelligence contingent from the NKVD."

Donovan nodded vigorously. "Mr. President, I've prepared a plan to deploy approximately two dozen OSS operators to counter any Soviet shenanigans. We should expect the Soviets to pat us on the shoulder with the left hand while robbing us silly with the right."

"My thoughts exactly," FDR agreed. "And toward that end I was thinking that perhaps your Canidy or Fulmar—perhaps both— might accompany our delegation?"

The master spy hesitated. "Mr. President . . ."

"No doubt Stalin will have his best agents—NKVD, SMERSH— there. As you said, Bill, the Soviets will be trying to rob us blind. It strikes me that in such an environment we would want—what did you once call Canidy? 'A reckless but effective SOB'?"

Donovan rubbed his forehead. "Yes, Mr. President. I think I did call him that. My concern, however, is that he might very well do as much damage to us as to Stalin."

Gotland, Sweden

1730, 18 August 1943

Canidy could tell from Fulmar's face that he was puzzled but relieved. Canidy felt the same way. Both of them were prepared to insert into the Soviet Union after being betrayed by the Thorisdottirs, but neither believed they had much chance of getting out alive under any circumstance, let alone getting out alive with the notebook.

Donovan had indicated that other plans involving them were in development. He did not elaborate. But neither Canidy nor Fulmar could imagine any possible operation that was more likely to result in their deaths than either the one they had just completed or a foray into the Soviet Union. Any other operation would be a walk in the park by comparison.

The GAZ was slow and uncomfortable, but, of course, vastly superior to walking. Gromov would be at the Lubyanka within hours.

The Order of Lenin. That was what Belyanov had said would be awarded Gromov if he secured Kapsky. Gromov had effectively accomplished that objective. He had secured Kapsky's notebook, and the Thorisdottirs had killed Kapsky. The Soviet Union had the prize.

Gromov understood that the Order of Lenin was not Belyanov's to give. But the magnitude of securing Kapsky's work was such that Lavrentiy Beria, and perhaps even Stalin himself, would take note. Gromov was not one given to daydreaming, but an honor of such magnitude conferred numerous and inescapable benefits. He was determined to take advantage of each and every one.

CHAPTER 13

"Obersturmbannführer Skorzeny for Vice Admiral Canaris."

The startled Oberstleutnant looked up from his desk to see Skorzeny towering before him. Skorzeny had entered the office without making a sound. The Oberstleutnant was rattled. He glanced at the clock over the entrance door. Skorzeny was precisely on time.

"Yes, Herr Skorzeny," the Oberstleutnant babbled. He gestured toward the chairs along the wall to Skorzeny's right. "Please have a seat."

"I prefer to stand."

"Yes, of course. I recall." The Oberstleutnant fidgeted with paperwork and office supplies for the next few minutes, flustered in the presence of the storied commando.

The Oberstleutnant rose from behind the desk and at precisely 11:30 a.m. opened the door to Vice Admiral Canaris's office and announced Skorzeny's presence. He then opened the door wide, signaling Skorzeny to enter.

Skorzeny walked in to find a wry expression on the Genius's face. Canaris motioned for Skorzeny to take a seat, and he did.

"Did Schmidt inform you?" the Genius asked.

"He did, Herr Admiral. But he only stated that I am not to go to Washington, D.C., as discussed. Obviously, that raised several matters . . ."

". . . none of which he was at liberty to discuss," Canaris finished. "More accurately, little of which had been confided to him. Schmidt is a good man, but there are obvious matters to which he is not privy."

"Respectfully, if I may ask, Herr Admiral, such as?"

"The deliberations of the Führer."

Skorzeny sat up rigidly. "My orders come directly from the Führer?"

Canaris's piercing gaze answered the question. "You may still, at some point, be ordered to Washington. But not for a while. And not related to Dr. Sebastian Kapsky. The Führer has more immediate concerns. He has identified you as the person to remedy them." Canaris grew quiet for several seconds for effect.

Skorzeny remained silent, resisting the urge to ask what those concerns were. Canaris was impressed.

"The first operation relates to Italy," Canaris said.

"The invasion of Sicily by the British and the Americans?"

"Not directly. You have heard that the king ordered Prime Minister Benito Mussolini arrested?"

"Of course."

"The *carabinieri* have been moving Mussolini about with some frequency, so it has been a challenge for us to know his location from moment to moment, which is the reason they are doing it . . ."

". . . in order to prevent loyalists from freeing him."

A shadow seemed to pass over Canaris's features. "But more so to prevent enemies from killing him. Not because the new Italian government is concerned for Mussolini's life, but because they do not wish to create a martyr. They also know, if they have any sense, that we will not permit the Italians to simply join with the Americans and British in support of the Sicily invasion or any invasion of the mainland. Toward that end, they want to be sure we do not return Mussolini to power."

Skorzeny immediately grasped the purpose of the meeting. "So, the Führer would like me to free and protect Mussolini."

Canaris nodded. "I fully understand that there has never been an operation like this before," he said. "I understand the Americans are fond of calling such actions 'suicide missions.' He is guarded—Mussolini is—by hundreds of well-trained and equipped troops. Moreover, the place where he is being held is near a heavily armed garrison. The planning, logistics, execution, and extraction . . . each will be an unparalleled challenge."

Skorzeny remained silent. Canaris watched as Skorzeny's face went from expressionless to calculating to a broad, unabashed smile. "You find this humorous? A 'suicide mission'?"

Skorzeny shook his head and attempted without success to suppress his grin. "Apologies, Herr Admiral. I happen to concur with the American description. Extracting Mussolini is, indeed, a suicide mission."

The normally unflappable intelligence chief stared at Skorzeny with incomprehension.

"It's just that I am honored—and admittedly somewhat flattered—that of everyone in the entire Wehrmacht, the Führer would think that I have even the remotest chance of executing this operation."

A grave look covered Canaris's face. "The Führer has been well briefed. He has been advised and fully understands that he is sending you and your men to an almost certain death." He paused and regarded Skorzeny once more. "But it is more than the honor and the flattery, isn't it, Skorzeny?"

Skorzeny continued to smile as Canaris examined his face with incredulity. "The assignment's very impossibility is what excites you so much, isn't it? And that you actually believe that among all of the soldiers in the Wehrmacht—indeed, in the entire world—only *you* have even a one-in-ten-million chance of executing it."

Skorzeny appeared as if he were struggling not to break into un-bridled laughter. "You are correct, Herr Admiral."

"Impressive. Perhaps astonishing."

Still smiling, Skorzeny said, "You mentioned, Herr Admiral, that the Mussolini operation was the first of two the Führer has for me. May I ask—presuming I somehow survive the first one—what is the second mission?"

A dark expression settled on Canaris's face. "One that is exceedingly more dangerous than the first."

Bendlerblock

1236, 19 August 1943

Wolfgang Schmidt, having already been briefed by Canaris, was expecting Skorzeny, who approached with a smile.

"I presume you have already been briefed?" Skorzeny asked.

Schmidt curtly responded, "The broad outlines." He then grinned. "I suspected when you appeared you would have a smile on your face. This sounds like the operation of a lifetime, perfectly suited for you, my friend."

"The Führer himself ordered that I lead the mission," Skorzeny said.

"Who else would he choose?" Schmidt asked. "I am sure you are not surprised he selected you."

Skorzeny shrugged. "Perhaps not. But nonetheless, it's an honor to be entrusted with an operation so audacious."

Schmidt raised an eyebrow, searching for a better description. "'Audacious' is one way to describe what you are to do. 'Suicidal,' my friend, is another. And perhaps more accurate. I'm sorry to say that I have few clever gadgets or tools to heighten the probability your mission will be successful. Or lower the probability you will be torn to shreds."

Skorzeny clapped his friend on his right shoulder. "I am confident that you do have such equipment or can direct me to some. My team needs only a few items from you, chief among which is something that approximates the size and weight of a Luger, but with a magazine capacity of an MP forty."

Schmidt's eyes widened. "Concealable, but with what? Thirty to forty cartridges?"

Skorzeny nodded. "We likely will be operating clandestinely among civilians as well as Italian, American, and British troops for portions of the mission. We do not wish to reveal ourselves by carrying heavier weaponry. It must be concealable under ordinary clothing yet have sufficient capacity to engage a sizable opposing force."

"You have good timing and fortune, my friend. I don't have to craft such a weapon because Heereswaffenamt recently commissioned Schmeisser to design something that meets your description. With a minor bit of adjustment, it should be precisely what you need."

"Splendid, although we must be able to carry several magazines unobtrusively."

"The weapon is chambered for a nine-millimeter round with a thirty-two-round magazine."

"Can you increase that?"

"More than thirty-two rounds?"

Skorzeny looked gravely at the other man. "It may literally sound like overkill to you, Wolfgang, but I do not wish to have to change magazines in the midst of a fight. Fractions of a second feel like hours under those circumstances."

"I shall see to it, my friend."

"Excellent."

Schmidt stroked his chin. "Your most pressing need will be transport. You will need to insert rapidly and stealthily. I'm not sure I can assist you there."

Skorzeny smiled confidently. "No need, my friend." He placed his arm around Schmidt's shoulders. "I have an idea."

CHAPTER 14

Both Canidy and Fulmar dropped to their knees and braced themselves with the palms of their hands on the ground as their lungs heaved, attempting to inhale as much oxygen as possible.

Canidy had persuaded a reluctant Fulmar that they shouldn't sit around waiting for Donovan to give the order to proceed to what any rational actor would conclude was near-certain death in the Soviet Union. They should work out their nervousness with strenuous exercise, which had the added benefit of conditioning them for what would likely be a physically arduous operation ahead. The last two hours had consisted of scores of push-ups, dozens of fifty-meter sprints, hundreds of sit-ups, and a twelve-kilometer run along the rocky shoreline.

For most of his life, Canidy had despised exercise and held in contempt those who used it to try to improve their physiques. He considered those who did to be little more than muscular narcissists. He had been blessed with a superior natural physique, one that, even without improvement, was sufficient for his purposes. In childhood, Canidy had had a natural male rivalry with Fulmar, whose physique—though Canidy would never acknowledge it—was even more impressive. So he'd begun exercising, and liked the results. Then, in preparation for a unique operation behind enemy lines, Donovan had required that he go through an intense physical regimen similar to that developed by then Lieutenant Colonel Robert Laycock of the British No. 8 Commando Unit. It was unlike any military training ever developed, designed for an individual soldier who was expected to perform as a self-contained one-man unit—as a guerrilla, saboteur, and spy. It was created for combatants who depended upon speed, stealth, adaptability, and sheer ruthlessness to discharge their missions. It suited Canidy perfectly.

Canidy straightened slowly, still heaving. Between gulps of air he said, "We're going to leave damn fine-looking corpses."

Fulmar stood erect. "Or," he huffed, "if we're not so lucky, we'll be the prettiest prisoners in all of Siberia."

The pair turned as they heard footsteps racing downhill toward the shore. It was the corporal. He came to an abrupt halt just in front of them, caught his breath, and said, "Urgent communication for you two from Washington." He then resumed panting.

"And?" Canidy asked.

"You are to stand by for further orders."

Canidy rolled his eyes. "We should urgently *stand by*? What the hell does that mean? Who's the clown who gave that genius order?"

"Colonel Donovan."

Canidy fixed the young corporal with a piercing look. "You didn't hear me say that."

"Say what, sir?"

Canidy turned to Fulmar and pointed to the corporal. "Quick study. We should get up to the airstrip. Sounds like we're about to be sent to our doom."

CHAPTER 15

Donovan was the first to arrive in the Map Room, followed less than a minute later by Stimson. Donovan let his displeasure with the location be known.

"I have known this man for decades, and although I do disagree with him on everything but the color of the sky, he's damn shrewd. That's why, for the life of me, I can't understand his lack of discipline regarding communications."

"That's because this is the White House, Bill, for God's sake," FDR said as Laurence Duggan pushed his wheelchair to the head of the table before departing. "If this place isn't secure, no place is. And, by the way, the stick that's been wedged between your buttocks since law school now seems to be cemented firmly in place."

The typically taciturn Stimson chuckled. Donovan appeared unamused.

The President smiled. "Something must have agitated you, Bill. I've seen you more frequently in the last day than I have Eleanor."

Stimson and Donovan said nothing.

FDR raised his eyebrows. "Well?"

Donovan dispensed with preambles. "Hitler is planning to extract Mussolini from Italy, Mr. President."

Roosevelt nodded as if the information were a matter of course. "I suppose that should not be surprising," he said pensively. "But, clearly, we mustn't allow Mussolini to command in exile. This is reliable information, Bill?"

Donovan nodded.

"Should I ask the source?"

Donovan shook his head curtly.

"What do you gentlemen recommend?"

Stimson spoke first. "Mr. President, any extraction could compromise the war effort. It's difficult to gauge the extent to which Mussolini would inspire and command loyalists who would continue to battle against the Seventh Army. But as long as he has a protected command, this must be countered."

FDR looked to Donovan, whose massive head bobbed in agreement. "Our information is that Hitler is sending a specialized unit under the command of his most proficient commando to extract Mussolini and take him to safety—probably to Germany itself. This likely will happen imminently. We must move rapidly."

Roosevelt said, "I agree. Precisely how would you act?"

With a determined look on his face Donovan said, "Canidy and Fulmar, sir."

"The two you have in the doghouse?"

"They remain our best."

FDR's eyebrows arched. "Evidently so . . ." he remarked. "Nonetheless, do we have anyone that may be staged nearby?"

Donovan shook his head. "I've concluded that Canidy and Fulmar are the best of the closest."

FDR paused for a second. "This is your business. I'll leave it to you. They're in Gotland? That's the closest?" FDR dismissed his own question with a shrug and asked another. "But is this a matter that can reasonably be handled by two men?"

"No number of men could 'reasonably' handle this, Mr. President. We're going into heavily defended enemy-held territory. The logistics challenges even for a larger force would be serious. This type of operation is contingent on stealth and speed. The bigger the force, the less stealth and speed."

Donovan, noticing the President looking over his shoulder, turned to see Harry Hopkins and Laurence Duggan standing at the door. Hopkins pointed to his wrist, though he wore no watch.

"Apologies. Time, Mr. President. Your meeting with Henri Hoppenot . . ."

"Who?" FDR asked mischievously.

"The French ambassador . . . I mean, the 'delegate from the French Committee of National Liberation.'"

Roosevelt winked at Donovan and Stimson, waved Hopkins and Duggan off, and returned his attention to Stimson and Donovan.

"I must be going. What do you need from me, gentlemen?"

"Just your approval, sir," Stimson replied.

"On a matter such as this, I would have thought you two would exercise your own discretion."

"No, sir, on a matter such as this, things are highly likely to go south fast. And if they do, a former head of state with millions of supporters will die. And if he dies, that could galvanize a massive resistance that could affect the course of the war. I'll be damned if I get hung for making that call."

CHAPTER 16

Aleksandr Belyanov, chief of the Otdel Kontr-Razvedki, the dread OKRNKVD, strode regally down the long hall toward his office on the fourth floor of the Lubyanka, trailed by two bodyguards carrying PPSh-41 submachine guns.

The bodyguards were partly for protection. Someone who had put thousands of his countrymen to death, often in horrific fashion, needed round-the-clock protection. But they were mostly for effect. Belyanov believed a person in his position needed to intimidate, to project power. Commanding people to slaughter thousands of their own countrymen, sometimes including their own family and friends, required unquestioned obedience. Belyanov believed the most reliable—or at least the simplest—way of ensuring obedience was terror.

Belyanov's face appeared serene. His chin was tilted slightly upward in regal fashion, as if the world's concerns were beneath him. In truth, he was highly agitated. A nervous *Kursant* had interrupted his dinner at the apartment of a beautiful young woman to inform him that an urgent encrypted message had arrived for him and required his immediate attention. The subordinate stressed that it was not he but a Podpolkovnik who had determined this required Belyanov's immediate attention.

When he came to the entrance of the office, the bodyguard trailing to his right sprang forward to open the double doors for him. Belyanov was immediately met in the outer chamber by the Podpolkovnik, who wordlessly extended to him a small sealed envelope. Belyanov took the envelope, nodded, and entered his private chamber. He read the contents of the envelope and immediately called his boss, Lavrentiy Beria.

76 Tirpitzufer, Berlin

1845, 19 August 1943

There was a short, sharp rap at the door as the chief of the Abwehr was trying to alleviate his headache by rubbing his fingers in a circle at his temples. The rap conveyed urgency.

Canaris sighed. *Everything* was urgent. "Yes."

The aide approached briskly and handed him a sealed envelope. "Apologies for the interruption, Herr Admiral. Oberst Mann directed that you should receive this immediately."

Canaris took the envelope, thanked the aide, and dismissed him with a nod toward the door. The Genius opened the envelope, scanned its contents, and immediately reached for one of two telephones on the credenza behind his chair.

Gotland, Sweden

0349, 20 August 1943

Canidy and Fulmar had been standing by, though without any particular urgency, since the young corporal had relayed Donovan's message over twelve hours earlier. After their run, they took turns washing the sweat off with cold water in the large gray metal tub in the rear of the cabin. They ate a wretched meal consisting of objects that purported to be potatoes that they found stored in a small cooler behind the cabin. The remainder of the time was filled with sitting at the kitchen table telling lies and exaggerations, starting with their childhood exploits together and moving on to romantic conquests. When one began drifting off to sleep, he'd be momentarily jarred awake by a particularly salacious detail offered by the other.

The stories slowed and gradually ground to a halt a couple of hours before dawn, each having fallen asleep seated at the table with their respective heads resting on their folded arms. Both were in a deep sleep when Canidy opened an eye upon hearing something. A second later the kitchen door exploded inward, splinters of wood driving throughout the kitchen ahead of two massive, fast-moving objects.

Dazed, Canidy instinctively fell to the floor and rolled away from the objects. Not as quick, Fulmar was struck forcefully by one of the objects, propelling him off his chair and several feet across the room. The small room became a swirl of black and gray as both Canidy and Fulmar crawled and sprang upright. Canidy threw himself blindly at one of the contorting forms, feeling the painful impact of a shoulder against his ribs. The glint of metal slashing downward toward his skull prompted him to collapse to the floor—

barely avoiding impact. He then thrust himself upward toward the attacker. Center mass. The top of Canidy's skull struck under the attacker's jaw, whipping his head backward nearly to his shoulder blades. A geyser of blood shot from the attacker's mouth as he crashed to the floor onto his back. Canidy dove toward the man's arm, which was still grasping the knife, and wrenched it from his grasp. With both hands he plunged it repeatedly into the attacker's neck and chest until he lay still. Canidy immediately looked up and saw Fulmar, knife in hand, kneeling in an expanding river of blood. The second attacker lay on his side, blood pouring from a gaping hole in his throat.

The two regarded the grisly scene for no more than two or three seconds before both spun on their heels, reacting to the possibility that there might be other assailants. Fulmar moved in a crouch toward the side of the splintered door, looked furtively outside, and slowly moved to the porch. Holding his breath, Canidy followed, knife at the ready.

After a couple of minutes of searching the surroundings, they satisfied themselves that the attackers were alone and returned to the kitchen. "Donovan sure can't say we haven't been standing by *urgently,*" Canidy said dryly.

The kitchen floor resembled that of a slaughterhouse. Blood continued to flow from the two bodies and covered most of the floor. Canidy whistled and shook his head. "We were fortunate, my friend. Look at the size of those guys."

Fulmar spared a quick glance at the corpses before kneeling between them and searching their pockets.

"Nothing. No other weapons."

Canidy pointed to the inside of the right wrist of one of the corpses. "What's that? Looks like a sword and a mask."

Fulmar examined the tattoo. "Brandenburgers. It means that they're *very* bad men."

"You're not telling me anything that didn't become abundantly clear about two minutes ago."

"German commandos. Highly trained, very tough. Usually used for reconnaissance and sabotage. Often detailed to the Abwehr," Fulmar explained.

"English, please."

Fulmar stood. "Nazi military intelligence. You were right. We were damn lucky. They should have made short work of us."

The two looked at each other for several seconds, analyzing, calculating. Canidy exhaled. "Do you have any idea how they—"

"None," Fulmar replied, shaking his head emphatically. "Not at all. But we better get an idea, *fast.*"

CHAPTER 17

The lunchtime crowd at Old Ebbitt Grill was lighter than usual.

Donovan, spotting the secretary of war sitting at his usual table, approached the bar and ordered two doubles of Macallan. The bartender, who'd served both men regularly over the years, handed them to Donovan almost simultaneously with the order. A drink in each hand, Donovan proceeded to Stimson's table, kicked the free chair back, and sat, sliding Stimson's drink over to him. Stimson nodded acknowledgment and downed a spoonful of crab soup.

"Change of plans, Henry."

Stimson looked up from his bowl. "Am I permitted to finish my lunch?"

"By all means," Donovan replied. "You'll be relieved to know this won't require any action on your part."

"I can't tell you how much I welcome that news."

Donovan adjusted himself in his chair. "Henry, you've long since learned that merely because something doesn't require any action from you, doesn't necessarily mean it's not concerning."

"Indeed I have. Sometimes the things that require no action on my part are the most bothersome, or even frightening. I learned

some time ago that it's better to be the captain of a boat in a hurri-
cane than a sailor confined belowdecks. The captain may be frightened, but at least is aware of the danger and has a measure of control
over his circumstances, however futile. All the sailor has is sheer
terror."

Donovan exhaled. "Each day that passes in this damn war shows
me that no matter what I think or do, I don't control anything."

Stimson looked up from his soup, sat back in his chair, and read
Donovan's face. "What's the bad news?"

"More concerning than bad," Donovan said quietly.

"Concerning in the big-picture sense?"

"Downstream, definitely," Donovan acknowledged, rubbing his
head. "Canidy and Fulmar were attacked last night."

"Were they killed? Wounded?" Stimson asked.

"No, they're all right."

Stimson looked puzzled. "This *is* war, after all. Is there a reason
you find this noteworthy?"

"Very few people knew where Canidy and Fulmar were, Henry.
Damn few. They were taken by surprise. They should be dead."

Stimson looked about before resting the spoon in the bowl and
leaning forward. "You believe Canidy and Fulmar were specifically
targeted?"

Donovan nodded. "I do."

"For God's sake, Bill. I know you're paid to be paranoid, but two
men on an obscure island in the Baltic in the middle of the largest
military conflict in world history were specifically targeted? How
would you possibly know or even suspect that?"

"The attackers were Brandenburgers."

Stimson blinked incomprehension. "What's that?"

"Nazi military intelligence, generally directed by the Abwehr."

Stimson's face turned grave. "The *Abwehr* dispatched intelligence officers to kill Canidy and Fulmar?"

Stimson studied the bowl of soup for several seconds, then looked up at Donovan. "That implies Canaris has the knowledge, reach, and wherewithal to send assassins to kill two American officers whose location is known to only a few people in the world."

"The Abwehr must have determined their deaths were imperative," Stimson said. "But why?"

"As I see it, only two plausible reasons. And even those are a bit far-fetched: retribution for securing Kapsky, or to prevent interference in their plan to rescue Mussolini."

Stimson removed the napkin from his lap and placed it on the table. "That suggests, Bill, that the Abwehr knows who Canidy and Fulmar are—that Canidy and Fulmar are the ones who rescued Kapsky, or that Canidy and Fulmar were charged by the American President with compromising the Genius's Mussolini operation."

"We need to ask how they would know any of that," Donovan said. "And we need to ask how they could move so fast."

The two most serious men in Washington, D.C., stared at each other for several seconds, each assessing the possibilities. Stimson spoke first.

"I know he's your man, Bill, but the improbabilities—the speed in which the Germans had to have reacted . . . It's as if Canaris was right there when these things happened."

"What are you suggesting, Henry?"

Stimson raised his palms as if warding off an attacking dog. "I am suggesting we have to consider how it is that something to which only a few are privy could have gotten to German intelligence so quickly. Could it have come, for instance, from Eric Fulmar? He is, after all, half German."

Donovan's neck swelled and the veins bulged. An intimidating sight even to Stimson.

"Eric Fulmar has put his life on the line multiple times for this country," Donovan hissed. "He has outwitted and outmaneuvered the Germans so often, I've lost count. Hell, he has *killed* more Germans than ninety-nine percent of the soldiers in the entire U.S. Army." Donovan inclined his massive head forward. "And, mere hours ago, *he* was the subject of an assassination attempt by the Germans." He exhaled, leaned back, and settled himself. "No, Henry. Please engage that legendary intellect of yours and tell me precisely how you could imagine Fulmar is, in actuality, a German agent. Because if he is, he's the most inept double agent in the history of warfare."

Stimson remained unflappable and analytical. "Bill, I readily concede this is your area of expertise. And this is your man. All that I am suggesting is that everything you've just recited clearly makes him the least likely person to be a German agent, yet at the same time, the most effective." Stimson shrugged. "You know very well how cunning Canaris is. Mind you, I am not saying Fulmar *is* a German agent. I'm merely suggesting that it would be unwise to foreclose that possibility."

"Henry," Donovan said, his voice firm but conciliatory. "It may seem like you've been secretary of war to the last thirty presidents or so. I respect, and have always respected, your opinion enormously. But everyone is entitled to be catastrophically wrong on something. This is your turn."

"You'd agree, however, that this was a worthwhile, even necessary, exercise nonetheless. Right? The best way of teasing out something this important is to subject it to rigorous analysis, don't you agree?"

Donovan rose.

"The President wants Canidy and Fulmar to be in Tehran for the Big Three conference, if it happens. Not for protection but for counterespionage. He suspects, as do I, that Stalin will salt the place rotten with spies. And he thinks, based on their past performance, that Canidy and Fulmar will drive those spies crazy."

He reached into his pocket, pulled out his wallet, and placed several bills on the table to cover Stimson's tab. "Stalin is our ally, but he's more devious than Hitler. The Soviets will be trying to steal anything they can. We'll need Canidy and Fulmar to counteract the Soviet spies. And make sure the President comes back alive."

Donovan patted Stimson on the right shoulder before proceeding to the door and into the hot, humid Washington afternoon, pausing on 15th Street to stare absently at the Treasury Building as he nervously rubbed his head.

CHAPTER 18

Nervousness was not a sensation with which Gromov had great familiarity. He rarely experienced nervousness generated by fear. In fact, he couldn't readily remember an occasion when danger had produced nervousness. He had experienced nervousness as a result of delay or impatience, but very little.

The anticipation of meeting Lavrentiy Beria, however, made Gromov nervous, although he became conscious of it only because he noticed his fingers drumming rapidly on the Kapsky notebook resting on his right thigh as he waited on the bench in the outer chamber of Beria's office. Gromov had expected Belyanov to accompany him to the meeting. After all, Gromov reported to Belyanov, who was the one who had given him the mission of acquiring Kapsky and/or the notebook. And Belyanov was notoriously scrupulous about maintaining hierarchies, as well as accruing credit for the successes achieved by his subordinates. Acquiring the notebook was a momentous success, especially since Kapsky was out of commission.

Belyanov had told Gromov that he would receive the Order of Lenin if he successfully secured Kapsky and brought him to the

Soviet Union. Gromov didn't necessarily believe that, but it was clear that he would be grandly rewarded were he successful.

The Americans and Germans had also been hunting for Kapsky, and the Americans had prevailed. Although the Americans had been as talented, innovative, and aggressive, Gromov had been smarter. Unbeknownst to the Americans, who believed the Thorisdottirs had been engaged to provide them with transport across the Baltic, Gromov had engaged the twins—for a significant fee—to work for *him*.

The Thorisdottirs were smart and crafty, but Gromov had understood that their otherworldly beauty was the feature that would ensure the success of the plan. It had dulled the senses and instincts of the Americans sufficiently that the Thorisdottirs were able to poison Kapsky and abscond with his work.

Gromov had won. And both Stalin and Beria had taken notice.

A tall, severe-looking woman of indeterminate age entered the outer chamber and sat at the desk just outside the door to Beria's office. With a stern look on her face, she folded her hands atop the desk and informed him, "Comrade Beria will now see you."

Gromov felt a charge of anxiety and excitement as he stood, the notebook grasped lightly in his right hand, and strode through the massive, heavily padded doors to Beria's office. He was momentarily disoriented upon finding himself not in Beria's office but in a small vestibule with a second set of padded doors. Unaware of the appropriate protocols, he momentarily pondered whether he should announce himself before proceeding through the second set of doors, but decided to simply enter and take his chances—something he would not have done without the armor of the notebook.

Gromov was a bit surprised, in fact disappointed, upon entering Beria's office. The space was as large as, if not larger than, he'd expected, but it was considerably less grand than the ornate furnishings and appointments Russians expected of their tsars. Nothing adorned the walls save a large portrait of Marshal Joseph Vissarionovich Stalin to Gromov's right, the eyes of which appeared to follow Gromov as he approached the massive but plain desk behind which sat the chief of the most feared secret police organization in the world.

Lavrentiy Pavlovich Beria—master of horrific purges, engineer of the Katyn Forest Massacre, and the effective warden of the millions rotting in the Soviet gulags—sat ramrod straight in a large black leather chair and watched expressionlessly as Gromov approached to within a meter of the desk. His pate was bald to the crown of his skull, in a way that created an aura of cunning and calculation. His cold, colorless eyes seemed reptilian behind the small rimless spectacles that sat on the bridge of his nose.

Major Taras Gromov, assassin of hundreds who had experienced terrors and horrors witnessed only by a scant few, felt his mouth go dry and his windpipe constrict. Uncertain of the protocol, he simply stood at attention, eyes fixed on an imaginary spot on the wall behind Beria's chair.

"Sit, Gromov."

Gromov did as directed, placing the notebook atop his knees.

Wordlessly, Beria held out his hand. Gromov extended the notebook to Beria, who balanced it in his hand, considering its weight. "It is not very heavy for something that would dominate the world."

Gromov said nothing. Beria placed the notebook on the desk and considered Gromov.

"I wished to meet you. Belyanov has briefed me. I, in turn, have briefed Joseph Vissarionovich," Beria said coolly. "Impressive, Gromov. Quite impressive. Comrade Stalin concurs."

Gromov struggled to contain his exhilaration. He pursed his lips to restrain the possibility of a grin.

"Belyanov suggested a promotion may be in order," Beria said. "There is also the matter of the appropriate decoration." He stared at Gromov for several uncomfortable beats. "Have you completed your report?"

"Yes, Comrade Beria. I provided it to Comrade Belyanov this morning."

"It is not a formality, but it is a formality. Not a precondition, but it is a precondition," Beria said. "There are certain honors only Comrade Stalin may bestow."

Gromov bobbed his head in understanding.

Beria again stared wordlessly at Gromov for several seconds, which felt to Gromov like minutes. The silence was broken by Beria tapping his fingernails on the desktop.

"Belyanov has not told me the number of your kills, although he notes you have a reputation for modesty in that regard." A macabre smile formed on Beria's face. "What, precisely, is your number of kills?"

"I have not kept a tally."

"Belyanov told me that would be your response. I understand that as of very recently it was eighty-eight."

"More than that now."

"You know precisely how many you've killed," Beria asserted. "What is the figure?"

"Precision is difficult because of the nature of the latest operation," Gromov explained. "But, likely, ninety-four."

Beria nodded slowly, absorbing the statistic. "I ask, Comrade Gromov, because you are being considered for another assignment that requires a number of specific qualities and talents to perform. The principal talent, of course, is killing, a talent you've exhibited both deftly and flamboyantly. But despite your demonstrated competence in this regard, and this most recent achievement, you are not automatic." Beria leaned back in his chair and steepled his fingers in front of his chin as if in prayer. "Dyachenko now has one hundred eighty-one kills. Ilyin has two hundred fifteen."

Gromov nodded. "So I've been told. As I have noted to Comrade Belyanov, Dyachenko and Ilyin are snipers. They kill only from afar."

"True," Beria agreed. "But why should the distance from which they kill concern me?"

"Respectfully, Comrade Beria, perhaps it shouldn't. I do not presume to know how you contemplate the assignment be executed. No assassin dictates the manner of death. It is true that many, perhaps most, targets can be eliminated with a bullet, close or far. But not every kill can be choreographed to the assassin's preferences. Weather, geography, bodyguards, obstructions, and unexpected factors can have a say."

Beria looked at the other man coldly. "I assume Belyanov has covered what I am about to ask. Your kills were all during war?"

"Mostly."

"Any children?"

"No."

"Women?"

"Two."

Beria's eyebrows arched in mild surprise. "You do not strike me as someone who kills women."

"It occurred during the latest assignment. It was not my preference and not premeditated. One does what is necessary to complete the assignment."

Beria smiled more broadly. "You had some assistance in this latest matter, I am told. What were their names?"

"Kristin and Katla Thorisdottir. Sisters. Twins."

Beria's eyes narrowed. "They are reliable?"

"Very much so. Very brave, *very* smart."

"Now very rich. We expended a considerable sum to engage their services, although given the results, we would have happily paid much more." Beria paused as if deciding how much he wished to reveal about the contemplated assignment and the Thorisdottirs' possible role in it. "It may be necessary, or at least helpful, to employ them once again. The operation being planned will require a fair degree of misdirection and deception. They appear to excel at that.

"We should engage them relatively soon. The preparations for this operation should begin as soon as possible. You know how to contact them?"

"Yes," Gromov lied.

"Splendid. Do so immediately. This endeavor must be planned to the last detail. Nothing can be assumed."

"Understood."

Beria stared at Gromov. Although his eyes conveyed malevolence— and he knew his eyes conveyed such—he was feeling magnanimous.

"Your patience is commendable, Gromov. I am unable to discern any anxiousness on your part despite the fact that you must be waiting to learn whether you will receive recognition for your extraordinary work."

"I expect nothing, Comrade Beria."

"Strangely, I believe you. You expect nothing even though you deserve something. And you do deserve something substantial. You deserve, at minimum, a promotion, which will become official after the usual bureaucratic machinations; but I can inform you that as of this morning you are no longer Major Gromov, but Colonel Gromov."

Gromov nodded curtly.

"That is relatively immaterial, Gromov—*Colonel* Gromov. More important—much more important—is that Comrade Stalin recognizes you as the type of man needed for an assignment he believes to be of unmatched importance. As he put it to me, this is the most crucial single undertaking of the war to this point." Beria paused for effect. It accomplished its purpose.

Gromov sat forward in rigid attention. "May I ask the assignment, Comrade Beria?"

"It is two tasks, Gromov, but one overall assignment." Beria purposely fell silent. He enjoyed casually tormenting Gromov, tormenting anyone.

After several seconds, Gromov asked, "Yes?"

"The first task is formidable and by far the most consequential of your storied career, the most consequential of anyone's career. It is the predicate upon which the overall mission is based. We assess that without its successful conclusion, the assignment will fail."

Gromov shifted impatiently in his seat.

"The Americans," Beria said. "The ones that you so cleverly outmaneuvered. Despite your outwitting them, we assess they are quite resourceful and formidable, and, as such, likely will be an impediment to the overall mission."

Gromov's eyes narrowed as he strained to comprehend how, even with the formidable resources of the NKVD, its chief would determine that these two specific Americans would be an impediment to a Soviet mission.

Beria noticed Gromov's expression and smiled. He leaned back in his chair and folded his hands across his chest. "Major Richard Canidy. Lieutenant Eric Fulmar. Kill them."

CHAPTER 19

Skorzeny drained the last drops of Göring-Schnapps from the bottom of the stein before he placed it on the table. For at least the twentieth time in the last few months, he reached into his trousers to attempt to pay the tab, and for at least the twentieth time in the same period, the enormous man in his late sixties, proprietor Klaus Brecht, shook his head sharply. Brecht had directed each of his employees that under no circumstances was Obersturmbannführer Otto Skorzeny ever to pay for anything at the establishment. Each time Skorzeny frequented the pub, the ritual was the same: the commando would order a beer, occasionally accompanied by a schnitzel, and when he was ready to leave he would attempt to pay, only to be rebuked by Brecht for insulting him. Skorzeny would shrug, thank the man, and, when Brecht turned to tend to another customer, put several reichsmarks under the stein and leave quietly and quickly. Brecht had the decency to neither return the money nor even mention it at all the next time Skorzeny returned.

Skorzeny stood to leave—waving to Angelica, the supernaturally buxom blond barmaid who somehow was conveying three large pitchers of beer to a nearby table without spilling a drop—when he saw Wolfgang Schmidt enter the establishment, pausing to allow his eyes to adjust to the light. Schmidt spotted Skorzeny and, as he approached, motioned for him to sit back down.

Schmidt sat next to Skorzeny and raised a finger to signal the barmaid for a stein, which arrived seconds later. Schmidt waited until no one was within earshot and said, "You are still going to Italy, my friend."

Skorzeny arched his eyebrows. "Information truly travels fast. I suspect this comes directly from 76 Tirpitzufer?"

Schmidt took a sip of beer and nodded. "The two Americans appear to have survived, but the decision was made that that was far from enough to adjust our plans."

Skorzeny studied Schmidt's face for several seconds. "And you think an adjustment should be made?"

"Plans must always adjust to changing circumstances. My devices and equipment must always adjust to changing circumstances."

Skorzeny sighed. "I have no argument with you, but the circumstances have not radically changed. The operation is going to be an extremely hazardous one, regardless. The additional impediment of the two Americans does not render it that much more hazardous such that the operation must be postponed or scrapped."

"Ordinarily, my friend, I would agree with your assessment." Schmidt rubbed his jaw. "How well did you know Standartenführer Konrad Maurer?"

"I believe I understand where your argument leads," Skorzeny replied. "Maurer was charged with finding Dr. Sebastian Kapsky and bringing him to 76 Tirpitzufer. The Americans beat him."

"The very Americans who have been selected to keep Mussolini secured. How well did you know Maurer, my friend?"

"I knew him by reputation only." Skorzeny shrugged. "I understand he was tough, smart, and driven. He was considered to be a rising star with unlimited ambition." Skorzeny paused. "I know what you're driving at, my friend. He was a formidable opponent for the Americans, yet they beat him."

Schmidt grasped Skorzeny's forearm for emphasis. "He was not simply a formidable opponent. By every measure he should have been an indomitable opponent. Intelligence, strength, sheer ruthlessness, and the resources of not just the Abwehr but the entire Wehrmacht behind him. The match was being played on our ground. We controlled the roads, the rails, the seaways, the air. Maurer had hundreds of thousands of troops at his disposal, and the Americans had nothing but Polish resistance, *Armia*. Yet they secured Kapsky, not he."

Skorzeny smiled appreciatively and placed his right hand on Schmidt's shoulder. "I understand. Thank you for your assessment, or perhaps I should say *warning*." Skorzeny signaled to the supernatural barmaid. "But you know as well as anyone that Standartenführer Konrad Maurer had a titanic weakness." Skorzeny changed the subject the instant the barmaid appeared next to him. He held the thumb and index finger of his right hand a few centimeters apart. "*Eine Schnaps, bitte.*"

The barmaid flashed a blinding smile and proceeded to the counter. The two men watched her retreat before Schmidt asked, "And what do you think I know about Maurer's weaknesses?"

"That he had a matchless self-regard that rendered him blind to his opponents' strengths—particularly their cleverness. Maurer believed he was smarter than anyone, a belief that is the essence of stupidity."

Schmidt sat back in his chair and gestured toward Skorzeny. "And what of your own self-regard? The Great Skorzeny has less self-regard and confidence than Konrad Maurer?"

The barmaid returned, bent to place the schnapps on the table before Skorzeny, and then arched her back slightly as she stood erect, causing her bosom to appear as if it might explode from the confines of her dress. Skorzeny handed her ten reichsmarks and waited for her to flash the obligatory seductive smile and retreat before he answered Schmidt.

"Confidence in one's preparation is not the same as confidence in one's abilities, my friend. Some have such confidence in their abilities that they neglect not just their own preparations but the preparations of their adversaries. Standartenführer Konrad Maurer underestimated the preparations of the Americans."

Schmidt slapped the tabletop with his right hand and erupted with a booming laugh. "And the unmatched Skorzeny will never underestimate the enemy?"

Skorzeny cocked his head to his right. "I do my best not to. I hope I am smart enough never to do so. In the present case I have already read everything Tirpitzufer has on Major Canidy and Lieutenant Fulmar. I found them talented, but more than that." Skorzeny searched for the right word. "They are *fascinating*. You are aware that Fulmar's father is German?"

Schmidt winked. "Then you maintain Canidy and Fulmar will not compromise your operation?"

Skorzeny slid the schnapps over to Schmidt. "I do not make guarantees. But the probability of a successful extraction of Mussolini will not be diminished by Canidy and Fulmar."

Schmidt raised the schnapps glass appreciatively to Skorzeny. "And what if they do—interfere?"

"I will kill them," Skorzeny replied matter-of-factly.

Schmidt tilted his head back as he downed the schnapps. Exhaling, he placed the glass on the table and rasped, "No need for you to do that, my friend. The Genius leaves nothing whatsoever to chance."

CHAPTER 20

William Donovan never left anything to chance. It was for that reason that he selected Robert Grasso to travel to Gotland to convey
the message to Canidy and Fulmar.

Grasso was a six-foot, 220-pound, twenty-three-year-old block
of muscle, sinew, and brains who had the heart of a lion but the left
leg of a flamingo, a consequence of muscular atrophy produced by a
severe football injury at Yale. He couldn't run and could barely walk
more than one hundred meters before he needed to sit for a minute
or so until the pain in the deformed leg subsided. Despite that, he
retained the physique of a circus strongman due to a punishing regimen of push-ups, pull-ups, sit-ups, and squats. The initial progno-
sis by the Yale team physician was that, with time, Grasso's gait would
return to some semblance of normalcy, but he would never run again
and walking would always be accompanied by pain and stiffness.

Nonetheless, Grasso was a Bulldog. And Bulldogs weren't lightly
deterred by mere pain and disability. So with brains, determination,
and persistence—and the intervention of a Babylonian history professor who sporadically performed strategic analysis for the OSS—he
had gotten an interview with William Donovan himself. Donovan

agreed to the interview thinking he'd quickly and perfunctorily perform the favor for the professor and then move on to more serious endeavors, but to his mild surprise the earnest Grasso impressed him as someone who had the ineffable qualities of a star. So upon hiring him for the Office, Donovan gave Grasso a variety of tasks and assignments of increasing complexity and responsibility. And Grasso performed each almost precisely to Donovan's liking.

The current task was to brief Canidy and Fulmar in Gotland about the Mussolini situation. The attempt on Canidy's and Fulmar's lives had made Donovan uneasy about the integrity of communications with the two operators, so he commissioned the reliable and trustworthy Grasso to personally convey the information to the pair. Grasso, of course, seized the opportunity as if he had been commissioned to personally vanquish the Third Reich.

Grasso arrived at Gotland shortly before 8:00 p.m. wearing a white cotton shirt, a tabinet jacket, and black corduroy pants. He carried an M1911, holstered under the jacket at his right hip. He carried Donovan's instructions in his head.

He'd been told he'd find Canidy and Fulmar "waiting urgently" and "in a decrepit cabin near the south shoreline" and to exercise caution approaching the cabin, as the pair were likely more than a little skittish.

Grasso followed the directions precisely, and when he got to within fifty meters of the cabin he shouted out Canidy's and Fulmar's names and identified himself. Seeing no one and getting no audible response, Grasso raised his hands above his head and approached the cabin slowly—partly because he didn't want to alarm Canidy and Fulmar and partly because the walk to the cabin had produced aching spasms in his withered left leg.

He'd taken barely a dozen steps when he saw someone who fit

the description he'd been given for Fulmar emerge from the front door of the cabin.

"Identify yourself."

Grasso stopped and yelled, "Bobby Grasso, OSS. I was sent by Col—" Before he could finish Donovan's name, Grasso felt the M1911 being pulled out of its holster from underneath his jacket. He spun around to find the weapon pointed less than two feet from his face by Dick Canidy. Grasso raised his hands chest high and repeated, "Bobby Grasso, OSS. Colonel Donovan sent me."

Canidy trained the weapon directly at Grasso's forehead. "Prove it. Identification, please."

Grasso looked momentarily bewildered. "I don't have any, Major. I'm civilian OSS, not operations. You know that I'm not supposed to carry identifying documents in the field."

Canidy gave Grasso a derisive look. "In the *field*? Did you just get out of school?"

"As a matter of fact, yes."

Canidy felt inclined to roll his eyes, but kept the M1911 leveled at Grasso's forehead. "Don't tell me. Harvard, right?"

"Yale."

"Even worse. Why the limp?"

"Football injury."

"What's the team nickname, Grasso?"

"Bulldogs."

"See the irony?"

Grasso smiled. "Played for the Bulldogs, now working for the Bulldog."

"When did you graduate?"

"Nineteen forty-two."

"What was your record senior year?"

Grasso's jaws tightened.

"Well?"

"One and seven."

"You guys stunk."

Grasso shrugged. "Can't argue with that, Major."

Canidy handed the M1911 back to Grasso and motioned for him to put his hands down. "Come on inside, Grasso. Have some coffee. But watch your step. Not all of the blood is completely dried."

Seeing the puzzlement on Grasso's face, Canidy added, "Don't worry, not anyone you know. We had some visitors earlier. That's probably why we've been graced with a visit from you. Donovan's notoriously paranoid about leaks and such."

As the pair neared the front door of the cabin, Canidy pointed to Fulmar. "Grasso, meet Fulmar. Fulmar, Grasso." The two nodded to each other and all of them proceeded into the kitchen.

Fulmar pointed to a coffeepot sitting on the woodstove. "Coffee?"

"You bet. There was none on the plane."

Canidy snorted in mock disgust. "Barbaric." He gestured toward the chairs arrayed around the wooden table. Grasso stepped around a puddle of congealing blood and took a seat. Fulmar placed a cup of coffee in front of him.

Canidy gestured toward Grasso. "Our visitor has been sent courtesy of one Wild Bill, who has suddenly developed an aversion to risk previously held only by us mere mortals. So the guy with more medals than an entire ring of the Pentagon sent Bobby Grasso— former Yale football player on a lousy Yale team—to tell us something Donovan doesn't want the damn Nazis to ever have an inkling about." Canidy turned with eyebrows arched to Grasso. "That about right, Bobby?"

Grasso laughed. "That's about right, Major. Colonel Donovan told me that the message is for your ears only."

"From memory?" Canidy asked.

"Maybe why I was chosen," Grasso admitted. "I'm supposed to have an unusually good memory—while in school I memorized part one of *The Epic of Gilgamesh* in two readings."

Canidy winked at Fulmar. "This guy is going to be fun to work with."

"I don't know him well enough to be certain, but Donovan seemed to be seething about the attack on you here and he appears to suspect that our communications aren't completely secure, that they've somehow been intercepted."

Canidy glanced at Fulmar. "I'm not sure he was seething about us getting attacked, Bobby. But obviously, the Germans picked up on something—"

"They appeared to pick it up *immediately*," Fulmar added. "The Brandenburgers got here in no time. So, the Germans learned where we were, developed a plan of attack, and then dispatched Brandenburgers who had to come across the Baltic from—probably Poland."

Grasso looked pensive. "And they must have come here by boat, which would have taken some time."

Canidy slapped the top of the table. "Except, Bobby, we looked up and down the coast and couldn't find any vessels. Nothing. So somebody conveyed them across the Baltic, dropped our would-be assassins off—and then went on their merry way back to whatever hellhole they came from. And not only did they move fast, but they must have had a pretty good familiarity with this place and the surrounding waters."

Grasso nodded agreement, picked up the cup of coffee, and downed it in a single gulp. Canidy and Fulmar looked on.

"You're going to go far in this business, Bobby," Canidy re-marked. "I never met a soldier, airman, sailor, or Marine that didn't drink a gallon of coffee per day who was worth a damn. Probably evaporated your epithelial cells, though."

Grasso chuckled and planted the cup on the table like a Viking slapping an empty stein on a *veizla* table.

"Epithelial cells?"

Canidy winked. "Went to MIT, my boy. While you Yalies were goofing off with Chaucer and Milton, we were studying the hard stuff."

Grasso chuckled. "Checkmate. By the way, how was your foot-ball team at MIT?"

"Go to hell. But if I were you, I wouldn't be so sure a team with a one-and-seven record was actually playing anything resembling football."

Fulmar rolled his eyes. "As fascinating as I find this pompous duel of pretentious alumni from overrated colleges, perhaps we should talk about whatever it is Donovan sent Mr. Grasso four thousand miles to tell us."

Canidy rolled his eyes in turn and waved toward Fulmar. "Krauts. All precision, all seriousness, all the time."

"Fulmar's *half* German," Grasso said.

"You read his service file?" Canidy asked.

Grasso looked at him slyly. "His OSS file. Before I left. Yours, too. I have to say it was really impressive. I'm hoping my leg gets good enough that I can do some of that . . ."

"Because you think it will get you laid?"

Grasso grinned. "Hell yeah, that's part of it."

Fulmar drummed his fingers impatiently on the table. "Matter at hand, please?"

Canidy gestured dismissively toward Fulmar and said to Grasso, "Ignore him. Nothing would help get *him* laid."

Grasso nodded deferentially toward Fulmar. "Colonel Donovan instructed me to inform you that you will be going to Italy. He believes the Germans are going to try to rescue their ally."

"*We're* supposed to go to Italy?" Fulmar asked. "Isn't that what Patton's Seventh Army is in Sicily for?"

Grasso shook his head. "To be more specific, Donovan says you two are going to prevent the Germans from extracting Benito Mussolini from Italy."

Canidy gave Fulmar a puzzled look. "I suppose I've been too busy grappling with Nordic vixens and Nazi assassins to keep up with current affairs, but why the hell do they have to 'extract' Mussolini?"

"Donovan says that Patton's defeat of the Germans and Italians in Sicily is starting to tip some dominoes. He thinks the Italian Army may be on the verge of switching allegiances to the Allies against the Germans. If Donovan believes that's the case, surely the Germans believe it. In fact, it's already happening, very quickly. Pietro Badoglio, who replaced Mussolini, started secretly contacting Eisenhower and then imprisoned Mussolini so he couldn't rally the Italians behind the Germans. Our intelligence says Badoglio's moving Mussolini from prison to prison so his supporters can't find him and break him out. Right now, we think he's on the island of Ponza, southwest of Rome in the Tyrrhenian Sea—a vacation spot for the wealthy. But there's also some evidence he's under extremely heavy guard on Maddalena, near Sardinia. Hundreds of troops and *carabinieri* are surrounding him to prevent that from happening. You two know better than I do that Donovan likes to play things close to the vest, but he thinks the Germans believe if they can extract

Mussolini from prison—and from Italy—his followers will remain allies with the Nazis."

Canidy rubbed the top of his head and exhaled. "I'm glad I don't have to figure out the big picture. Donovan always looks around three corners at the same time. So, the Italians are defecting from Hitler. Therefore, Hitler needs to extract Mussolini to rally the Italian fascists to remain allies of Germany." Canidy pointed his index finger at Fulmar and then at himself. "Just what is our role here again?"

"Prevent that from happening. That is, thwart any attempted extraction of Mussolini by Hitler's forces."

Canidy and Fulmar looked at each other, each with an expression of skepticism. Fulmar nodded to Canidy to express what he knew they were both thinking. "Look, Bobby," Canidy said, "I'll do whatever Donovan tells us to do, but I have to say, this sounds . . . *nuts*. I mean, hell, there are a thousand issues here. I don't even know where to begin . . ."

"I do," Fulmar interjected. "It's all superfluous, overkill. Mussolini is already surrounded by hundreds of guards on an island. The addition of Dick and me isn't going to make that island any more secure than it already is." He extended his hands, palms up, and shrugged. "What does Donovan expect us to do?"

"What he says you guys excel at—throwing a monkey wrench into any German extraction operation. Complicate things. Screw up their plans so the operation crashes and burns . . . Donovan says you guys are the best at doing just that."

Canidy rubbed his chin. "Yeah, well, I'm not so sure he meant that as flattery . . ."

"No, he actually did," Grasso said earnestly. "He said if anyone can do it, it's you two. In fact, you might be the *only* ones capable of doing it."

Canidy glanced at a grinning Fulmar and then looked back at Grasso. "Do they offer ventriloquism classes at Yale? Donovan's manipulating you like a dummy—flattering us through you."

Grasso's torso shot forward. "No, no, no. He was sincere. Really. Besides, you know Colonel Donovan better than I do. Has he ever resorted to flattery before? Hell, he's the boss. Does he even *need* to?"

Fulmar looked at Canidy. "Kid's got a point. Also, remember that we just screwed up the biggest mission OSS ever conducted—the Kapsky mission. Not really a good time for unmerited praise."

"I just can't get used to flattery from Wild Bill Donovan, regardless of his motivation." Canidy shook his torso as if warding off a chill. "It just seems wrong."

The three sat silently for several moments. Then Fulmar said, "Well, then, I'm sure Donovan has a team that's studied this and put together a plan. An island fortress protected by hundreds of guards. I'm not sure what Dick and I are supposed to do to thwart the Nazi plans. Seems like geography has done a better job of doing that than we could ever hope to. Are we supposed to go there and mill around until some Germans show up, stick out a foot, and trip them?"

Canidy raised his hand as if he were a third-grade student in class. "By the way, how does Donovan think the *Germans* are going to get onto the island and get Mussolini out? Didn't we just beat them in Sicily?" He gestured toward Fulmar. "I mean, admittedly, we've been pretty occupied recently—too occupied to pay close attention to current events—but didn't we just send a couple thousand ships to that region? Operation Husky? Can't they just form a . . ." He searched for the appropriate term.

"Blockade," Fulmar interjected.

Canidy snapped his fingers. "Right, a blockade, a cordon, a phalanx—whatever the hell squids call it. Germans can't get in. Mussolini can't get out."

Grasso hunched his shoulders. "Again, Colonel Donovan gave me the orders. I've got to believe he's thought of every contingency. Hell, you know how thorough he is, for God's sake . . ."

Canidy studied Grasso's face, then turned to Fulmar and cocked his head questioningly. Fulmar gestured with his hands held palms up, as if to say, *What the hell? Why not?*

Canidy stared at Grasso for several seconds and then exhaled. "If Donovan sent you here because you can memorize *Gilgamesh* in two sittings, I'm guessing the plans for this can't be written on a cocktail napkin. Let's not spend any more time debating the merits of this. Donovan wants us to do it, we do it." Canidy looked to Fulmar, who nodded concurrence. Canidy continued. "To be honest, I think Donovan concluded that we're so mortified by what we allowed to happen in our last assignment that we'll crawl naked over red-hot coals to successfully complete any assignment he gives us."

"What's the plan, Bobby?" Fulmar asked.

"A C-54 plane will arrive on the island tomorrow morning to take you to an airstrip in Malta. All of the munitions and equipment you might possibly need will be aboard the plane. You'll be met there by Franco Giglio of the *Resistenza*, who will supply you with the necessary equipment . . ."

There was a subtle vibration in the cabin followed by a change in air pressure. Canidy and Fulmar didn't comprehend what their optic nerves were transmitting to their respective brains for at least a second. As they watched, blood, bone, tissue, and fabric exploded from the left shoulder of Grasso's jacket, propelled by several

7.92×57-millimeter rounds from an unseen weapon somewhere outside the walls of the cabin. The impact of the shot threw Grasso off his chair and onto the floor. Canidy and Fulmar dove next to him as multiple rounds splintered the kitchen door, Canidy immediately crawling as rapidly as possible to the M1 resting against the pantry door.

Fulmar pulled his M1911 from the holster at his right side and fired three shots in the direction of the incoming fire at the same time as a grimacing Grasso fired his weapon in the same direction.

Several more rounds splintered the door, which burst open shockingly to reveal a large figure clad entirely in black brandishing a Karabiner at his shoulder. The figure immediately careened backward as he was struck by several rounds fired by Canidy, Fulmar, and Grasso. Even before the black-clad figure's body hit the floor, another figure—also clad entirely in black—materialized in the doorway and fired several rounds at Fulmar and Grasso, who rolled on the floor in opposite directions to avoid the fire, which abruptly ceased. The left side of the second attacker's jaw had been sheared off by one of two shots from Canidy's M1. He fell to the floor, lifeless eyes staring at Grasso.

Before either Canidy or Fulmar could react, Grasso leapt up and limped toward the door with his weapon held at eye level. He fired two shots as he disappeared into the night.

Canidy and Fulmar each cursed as they rapidly crawled with their weapons toward the open door. The air cracked above their heads as they reached the porch and heard Grasso shouting with rage. The sound of several shots from Grasso's weapon was followed by more shots receding into the damp darkness.

Canidy and Fulmar looked at each other as they knelt on opposite sides of the door. Canidy nodded and each rose in a crouch, weapons at the low-ready. Canidy first, then Fulmar. They heard two more shots from a Karabiner before Canidy moved from the doorframe onto the porch, followed by Fulmar a fraction of a second later. Both hit the deck, weapons trained forward. Each swept his weapon from left to right, looking for Grasso and any attackers.

Canidy spotted a muzzle flash approximately fifty meters in front of them, accompanied by a curse that sounded like it had come from Grasso. Less than two seconds later came another volley of shots followed by an agonized groan.

The last thing Canidy and Fulmar saw was the silhouette of a black-clad figure outlined by a muzzle flash approximately thirty meters in front of them appearing to throw something before melting into the darkness; and the last thing Canidy and Fulmar heard was the ominous thud of an object landing inside the doorway to the kitchen.

CHAPTER 21

Colonel Taras Sergeivich Gromov strode confidently down the corridor until he came within ten meters of the highly polished oak double doors to the most frightening room in the Soviet Union. Or at least Gromov perceived it to be so. He'd never been inside those double doors, although he'd imagined the room's appearance on more than one occasion. Usually, his imagination had portrayed his entry into the room as a moment of triumph. He'd performed some great feat that had merited a summons to the chamber for recognition and commendation. His imagination had not been vivid or detailed; it merely rendered a vague, watery image of rich ornateness suited for imperial ceremony, suited to honor the Hero of the Soviet Union, Taras Gromov.

Yet when he came within five meters of the tall twin doors, Gromov—the man who had executed the stunning operation to secure the Kapsky documents, assassin of scores of enemies of the Motherland—felt a piercing spike of anxiety. For although Gromov intimidated nearly every person he'd ever encountered, on the other side of the double doors sat the three most intimidating men in the entire Soviet Union, perhaps even the entire world. And there was no predicting how any of them would behave. Between them they'd ordered and executed the extermination of millions of people—from the great and powerful to the weak and powerless.

They were OKRNKVD chief Aleksandr Belyanov; head of the People's Commissariat for Internal Affairs, Lavrentiy Beria; and premier of the Union of Soviet Socialist Republics, Joseph Vissariono-vich Stalin himself.

Nonetheless, Taras Gromov's eyes and carriage remained those of a predator. Despite the fact that he wasn't physically remarkable, he appeared to the world as one whose purpose in life was to lo-cate prey and kill it, quickly and unceremoniously, without any in-crease in heart rate. Though his face was placid, most people marked him as a killer on sight.

An officer opened the large, highly polished double doors to the room. Stalin was seated at the end of a long marble table, Beria to his immediate left and Belyanov to his right. Bright rays of sun-shine beamed through the tall windows to the right, sparkling off the mammoth chandelier hanging over the center of the table.

"Enter," Belyanov commanded. "Sit."

Gromov sat at the end of the table opposite the three, who stared at him for what seemed like minutes. The only sound was the tick-ing of a mammoth grandfather clock in Gromov's periphery.

Gromov's chest tightened. As the seconds passed, he became unsure whether he was expected to say something, a salutation or introduction. The hairs on the back of his neck stood straight.

Mercifully, Belyanov broke the silence.

"Comrade Stalin wished to meet you. Both to congratulate you for your momentous victory in obtaining the Kapsky document and to discuss the magnitude of your upcoming mission."

Stalin stared at Gromov, saying nothing.

"Comrade Stalin notes that you will be awarded the Order of Lenin upon your return from Tehran. Congratulations."

Gromov nodded appreciation. Stalin continued staring at Gromov, saying nothing.

"You also will be awarded a newly established decoration, which shall be first commissioned upon your successful return: the Order of Victory. You shall be its first recipient, Colonel Gromov. It is reserved for marshals and generals only. Congratulations."

Gromov nodded once again. Stalin stared, saying nothing.

Belyanov continued. "Finally, should you succeed in your assignment but not return, you shall be awarded Hero of the Soviet Union posthumously."

Stalin continued to stare, saying nothing.

"You understand the gravity of the assignment, Colonel Gromov. The outcome of the assignment will affect the outcome of the war," Belyanov concluded.

Gromov nodded. Stalin stared.

Beria cleared his throat. "Good luck, Colonel Gromov. Should you fail, you may not wish to return. You are dismissed."

CHAPTER 22

Canidy's eyelids fluttered open and he was immediately met by a dull ache in his arms, shoulders, and chest.

As he rose from the cot, his head felt as if it were made of lead. A thin film seemed to coat his eyes until he blinked several times. Still, his vision remained somewhat blurred for several more seconds.

The cast of the light streaming through the small window indicated it was midmorning, perhaps nine or ten o'clock. He'd been sleeping between nine and ten hours a night for the last several weeks, something he couldn't remember doing since, perhaps, childhood. It irritated him. For most of his adulthood he'd been able to get by on five to six hours of sleep. Although he enjoyed occasionally sleeping more than eight hours when circumstances permitted, he believed anything more than that or doing it more than once or twice a month was a waste of life.

Standing erect, he took an inventory of stiff joints and aching muscles. There were fewer than last week and the pain wasn't nearly as severe. He tested his right knee—still grotesquely discolored—repeatedly placing weight on it and then bending it back and forth as he stood on his left leg. It seemed looser than yesterday. It wasn't one hundred percent yet, but it was serviceable.

Canidy smelled something familiar yet out of place. He retrieved his trousers from the chair next to the cot, balanced himself, and slowly put them on before crossing the hallway to Fulmar's room. Canidy opened the door and asked, "Is that *yours?*"

Fulmar raised his head from the cot, eyelids fluttering. "What the hell are you talking about?"

"Get up, you lazy sack of shit. It's got to be at least nine o'clock already. That sadistic sergeant major will be down here any minute to inflict his daily torture regimen. You don't want him stomping in here catching you looking like Sleeping Beauty. He's likely to slap you silly and kick you a few times in the ass until you get your butt outside for daily torture." Canidy paused and sniffed the air. "Is that yours?"

Fulmar sat up on the edge of his cot. "Is *what* mine?"

Canidy tilted his head back and inhaled. "Don't you smell that?"

Fulmar yawned, rolled his neck, and spread his arms, stretching his chest. "I smell someone in desperate need of a bath."

"And I always believed a person couldn't detect their own body odor."

Canidy turned, stepped into the hallway, and sniffed the air again before proceeding toward the kitchen.

Fulmar rose slowly from his cot, taking an inventory of aches and pains in the same fashion as Canidy. He heard Canidy shout something unintelligible.

Fulmar walked briskly but stiffly toward the kitchen in time to see Canidy exchanging shoulder punches with a large, bluff Scotsman sporting one of the largest mustaches in Christendom. The

Scotsman paused only to exchange punches with Fulmar before embracing him heartily.

Fulmar pulled back, scanned Sergeant Conor McDermott's broad, ruddy face, and laughed. "What the hell is your ugly ass doing here?"

Canidy purposely punched McDermott's still unhealed arm, impressed but not surprised that the Scot didn't even wince. "I would say it's good to see you, you old goat, but hell, with Fulmar here, you two make the island uglier by a factor of eight or nine, at least."

Rather than respond with another insult, McDermott simply laughed and punched Canidy's right shoulder hard enough to interrupt his laughter.

Canidy rubbed his shoulder, pointing to a dish with slices of what looked like bread soaking in some kind of liquid. Next to the dish was a bottle. "What kind of breakfast is that?"

"A Clan McDermott special. Not suited for your unsophisticated palate."

Fulmar announced, "I smell alcohol."

"Alcohol?" McDermott scoffed. "Mere alcohol? By God, I'm in the presence of heathens."

"Hell, if it's not alcohol, what is it?"

McDermott pointed to a bottle sitting on the counter. "That, my dear unreformed barbarians, is a bottle of Glenfiddich, the finest single malt Scotch whisky ever produced by mortal man."

Canidy screwed up his face and feigned disgust. "And you're soaking bread in it? Is *that* what's in that dish?"

McDermott spread his arms wide and looked up at the ceiling. "Have mercy on my soul for I am truly surrounded by primitives.

They're likely to boil me alive before consuming me whole." He looked back down at the two Americans. "Bannock."

"What the hell is that actually?" Canidy asked.

McDermott shook his head. "If you have to ask, you're not worthy of consuming it."

"No danger of that happening." Canidy laughed and embraced McDermott. "We swore they'd put you out to pasture. What misfortune brings you here?"

"Commander Ian Fleming prevailed on a fellow by the name of Winston Leonard Spencer Churchill, grandson of the seventh Duke of Marlborough." McDermott cocked his head to the side. "Heard of him?"

Pointing at McDermott, Fulmar turned to Canidy. "He's obviously pretty taken with himself. I think we're supposed to bow or curtsy. Maybe both."

"Not necessary," McDermott said. "But it *would* assure that you are at least somewhat civilized."

"All right," Fulmar said. "Why *are* you here?"

McDermott's face sobered a bit. "How much did they tell you?"

"Who?" Canidy asked.

"The docs, the mountebanks, Donovan, anyone?"

"Not much more than we already remember. Some German commandos had the audacity to attack us. The second time we were so attacked, Bobby Grasso, who had been sent by Donovan to brief us on an upcoming operation off the coast of Italy, charged out into the night to fight the attackers. Eric and I went out after him. We know he was killed, but he must have done some damage to the attackers. Otherwise we wouldn't be standing here talking to you. Don't remember much more than that. I do know that someone repaired the front porch, door, and kitchen. We've been here since then."

"The Italy mission," McDermott said. "I don't expect you to tell me what that was about. But it's not hard to figure out what Donovan wanted you to do."

Candy rolled his eyes. "Oh really, wise guy? Donovan sent Grasso here for the express purpose of informing us about that operation without the Germans—or anyone else—finding out about it. No messages intercepted, no conversations overheard. But the Scottish genius who soaks bread in Scotch for breakfast has figured it all out?"

McDermott shrugged, tugging on one end of his mammoth mustache. "It wasn't too hard if you keep up with current events, of which, obviously, the fine medical folks your armed forces have stationed on this island have neglected to keep you abreast. Or to be fair, they probably have little interest in the kind of developments that keep the brows of the likes of Fleming and Donovan permanently furrowed."

"Well, they haven't told us much more than there's a war still going on and that we took a pretty nasty hit."

McDermott studied the pair's faces. "You did indeed. You both were in dreamland for some time. I asked about you. They didn't want to tell me anything—I understand they have rules about such things, but my goodness, after what we went through together you would think they'd make an exception."

Candy snorted. "Hell, welcome to the club, Conor. They haven't told *us* much about our medical conditions, either, other than we got some pretty nasty concussions."

McDermott exhaled. "That's an understatement. Anyway, I prevailed upon Commander Fleming to provide me with as much detail as possible. I'm sure he checked with General—Colonel—Donovan to get clearance with the medical people here." The creases at the corners of McDermott's eyes that conveyed nearly perpetual mirth disappeared. "You had quite a shock. A Gerry M24 went off near you or not far from you. The docs said it was close enough that both of you could have—maybe should have—been killed. Your concussions weren't trifling. You were out for some time. They said it would take you a while to remember, to 'reorient'—whatever that means."

Candy chuckled wryly. "You're sure these aren't British docs? They have a gift for understatement. I'm still trying to fill the gaps in my memory and I get headaches that come and go several times a day."

Fulmar nodded concurrence. "I think I'm back to normal, that I've collected all my thoughts and memories, and then I remember something that's been missing. That happens daily. Sometimes a few times a day."

"In that vein," McDermott continued, "one of the things you may have forgotten—or maybe they didn't tell you in the first place—is that your aborted operation in Italy may have contributed to the successful execution of the German operation you were tasked to prevent."

McDermott's last statement was met by blank stares from Candy and Fulmar. McDermott nodded that he understood.

"Don't worry, gentlemen. There were no operational breaches. After all that's happened it wasn't hard for me to figure out that Donovan had directed you to go to Italy and somehow help secure Il Duce. Hell, I'd be surprised, and not a little disappointed, if Menzies and Fleming hadn't cooked up a similar plan for Major General Laycock's commandos to execute. Were it not for the beating

I took on our Kapsky operation, I should think I would've been at the center of it. At least I bloody well hope so."

Canidy tilted his head back and exhaled toward the ceiling. "Lord, if you figured out what we were up to that easily, Fulmar and I were sitting ducks."

McDermott shrugged. "Well, also, keep in mind who is on the other side."

"The Genius," Fulmar said.

"He probably knew what you two blokes were tasked with doing before you did," McDermott said with a mirthless chuckle.

"They tried to hit us *twice*," Canidy informed him. "I mean, one attack right after the other. I still can't figure out how in God's name they could do that."

"And do it so fast," Fulmar added.

Canidy's brow furrowed and he rubbed the back of his neck. "There's something very wrong going on here. Very wrong. Donovan figured that out right away. Sent Grasso here to minimize the probability of a breach. Yet . . ."

". . . yet I wish I wasn't the one to give you the bad news." McDermott hesitated. "But since it seems you haven't been told, the Germans *did* get Mussolini out of there."

Canidy and Fulmar stared at McDermott slack-jawed. Canidy whispered. "Holy—"

"Nothing holy about it," McDermott interrupted. "It's been in all the papers. Movietone reels, too. Hell, Hollywood *wishes* they could come up with a story like that."

Irritated, Canidy asked, "What do you mean? What kind of story?"

"Hitler's been playing it up since it happened. Hell, Goebbels couldn't have come up with a more perfect piece of propaganda: the superiority of the German intellect; the cunning, daring, and ruth-lessness . . ."

"You're saying that the damn Nazis actually pulled Mussolini out of there? Off of that island—what was it? Ponza? In the Tyrrhe-nian Sea?"

"Actually, he'd been moved from there to a place in the Gran Sasso mountain range. *Seven-thousand-foot elevation.* Guarded by hundreds of *carabinieri.* A fortress. Impregnable."

"Holy . . ." Canidy whistled. "How in the hell did the damn Nazis pull *that* off?"

"Hitler's got some supercommando—I kid you not, that's what the news reports call him—by the name of Skorzeny. Obersturm-bannführer Otto Skorzeny. The Krauts are playing this bloke up like he's Errol Flynn. Six foot four, tremendous athlete, daring and crafty, genius-level intellect, with the proverbial nerves of steel. Movie star good looks, to boot."

"That's not their Errol Flynn," Fulmar said dryly. "Sounds more like their Dick Canidy. Or at least what Dick Canidy imagines himself to be."

McDermott and Fulmar chuckled. Canidy shot them a scorch-ing look that reduced the volume of the chuckles only slightly. "Once again, how the *hell* did the damn Nazis—the German Errol Flynn—pull this off? How the hell does one get a former head of state off a heavily guarded, fortified mountaintop? Didn't at least *one* of the hundreds of guards see them coming from ten miles away? Wouldn't the guards have mowed down any Germans even *approaching* the mountaintop?"

McDermott picked up a piece of well-soaked bannock and took a bite. "Gliders," he said simply, yet with a hint of awe.

Canidy's head cocked backward. "What?"

"Gliders," McDermott repeated. "No one heard or saw Skorzeny coming because he and his SS commandos—barely more than a dozen—came in on DFS gliders. They *glided* one hundred and twenty kilometers over the Albans, then over the Gran Sasso d'Italia mountains. No engines. Completely silent. And death-defying. Skorzeny's commandos stunned and disarmed the hundreds of armed guards surrounding the edifice. They disabled all of the guards' communication equipment and held them, flabbergasted, at gunpoint. After doing so, Skorzeny radioed in a small plane. They took Mussolini onto the plane, packed in the SS commandos, and were on their way to Vienna, barely able to take off because of the weight. By all rights, they should have crashed into the side of a mountain, but . . . they made their way to Vienna. Goebbels is milking this to death, although frankly, he really doesn't have to. Cecil B. DeMille couldn't have scripted something like that. Impossible."

"Fortune favors the bold," Fulmar said quietly.

"And sometimes the bad," Canidy added.

He shrugged. "So we're out of a job. Except you wouldn't be here stuffing your ugly mug with"—Canidy pointed to the bannock soaking in Scotch—"*that* godforsaken combination. For breakfast, no less."

McDermott grinned. "For someone with such limited intellectual capacity, you do seem to eke out remarkable insights on occasion." He sat down. "I'm here to supervise your preparation for going to the conference between Churchill, Roosevelt, and Stalin in Tehran, Iran, at the end of next month. I may even be accompanying you there if the PM approves."

Fulmar frowned. "Preparation?"

McDermott nodded. "Look at you two. Even for Americans,

you two are physical wrecks. Colonel Donovan and Commander Fleming want you in Tehran. That means Roosevelt and Churchill want you in Tehran. From what I gather, they want you to act as a counterweight to Stalin's secret service, who, despite being an ally, will undoubtedly be up to no good. They'll be spying on us, so we'll be keeping them in check. Maybe do some spying of our own. Friendly, of course."

"So you're going to inflict yourself upon us again?"

"Inflict? I'm here to make sure you Americans don't bollocks things up as you are wont to do—*especially* you two."

"The conference is not for another month," Canidy said. "What are we supposed to do until then?"

"We'll know the full details soon enough. I understand that we'll be transported there in advance of the conference, but until then you two are to concentrate on rehabilitation. You're a sorry sight, you know.

"Donovan, by way of Commander Fleming, has ordered me to supervise your rehabilitation to get you back to fighting trim, as it were. I'm afraid our superiors think this could be something of a physically challenging mission."

Canidy smiled broadly, followed by Fulmar and then McDermott, who began laughing almost maniacally. Canidy and Fulmar followed suit. The laughter continued for a full thirty seconds before Canidy said between gulps of air, "*This* is going to be a physically challenging mission? Physically challenging? Compared to the Kapsky mission? We have *never* had OSS missions as tough."

Tears welled in McDermott's eyes and he pounded the table with his fists. Fulmar had to brace himself against the counter. "Well, traveling across half of Poland, evading Panzer machine-gun fire and bloodthirsty SS Totenkopf was a day at the fair, after all."

McDermott wheezed between gales of laughter. "I rather enjoyed the exercise. It would be quite nice if my arm were not shredded, my eardrums would stop ringing from that 7.5-millimeter tank ordnance, and I could get a spot of sleep without sitting bolt upright every hour, screaming from the nightmares about that bloodthirsty SS Standartenführer who was the size of Frankenstein's monster."

"Or the MG 34 machine-gun fire," Fulmar added. "Or the blasts of—"

"I think that's about enough of a stroll down memory lane," Canidy interjected. "No doubt, we had a pleasant little journey extracting Kapsky. But I get it. The assignments we had *before* we extracted Kapsky were challenging, but not nearly as physically demanding. We took a hell of a physical beating in Poland, so our superiors want us in Olympic condition for Tehran. Like we've got to match the Russkies. Some of those Ivans look like they're made out of blocks of carved granite. So." Canidy exhaled, placing his hands on his hips. "When do we start?"

McDermott grinned once again. "As soon as I finish my bannock."

CHAPTER 23

Gromov's usual imperturbability had been shaken by the flight from Tallinn to the crude RAF airstrip on a rocky volcanic archipelago in the North Atlantic midway between Norway and Iceland. He'd sat in the medevac cabin of a Lisunov Li-2 that rattled as if the wings would fall off at any moment. They'd hit several pockets of turbulence off the Scandinavian coast, one of which was sufficiently violent to cause Gromov to inadvertently bite his tongue. The noise in the cabin was deafening and gave him a pounding headache. The pilot had to twice abort the approach to the short landing strip at Vágar Air Base because of a vicious crosswind.

By the time he'd boarded the G-5 class torpedo boat that would take him to Iceland, he was in a dark mood. He was a soldier—a colonel. Not just a colonel but one on the verge of receiving the Order of Lenin and possibly the Hero of the Soviet Union. He was not a deliveryman—he was a peerless assassin. His job was not to run errands, but to kill.

After the turbulent flight he was at least mildly grateful that the North Sea was relatively calm. The boat sliced through the water at forty knots. They had an extra tank of fuel, so he conservatively estimated they should arrive in Iceland in ten to twelve hours.

When Beria had handed him the duffel bag filled with more than one million dollars in American currency, he untied one end and peered inside. There were packs of bills sorted by various denominations, the largest of which depicted a man named "Franklin" on one side and "Independence Hall" on the other. One hundred American dollars. A recess of Gromov's mind imagined absconding with the bag to some remote location where no one would ever find him. Someplace always warm. Financed by a sum that vast he would have a good chance of never being found.

But not good enough. He might get away for a while, perhaps even a few years. But eventually they'd find him. He would be sitting in a cantina or lounging on a beach and a soulless SMERSH assassin from Novgorod or Tbilisi would approach from behind and fire two rounds from a Tokarev TT-33 into the back of his skull. SMERSH would find him. They *always* found their quarry.

So the fantasy was fleeting. Gromov had a duty to discharge. Glory and fame—perhaps even riches—would follow. He would receive the highest honors that the Motherland could bestow; in fact, he'd already been assured of at least one.

Gromov was a killer, an assassin. But he was foremost a patriot.

Gromov kicked the duffel bag at his feet. Beria had not given him direction as to how to disburse the money to the Thorisdottirs. He had opined that the sisters would demand fifty thousand rubles to convey information of an assassination plot to the Americans, but the manner of payment was not discussed. Was Gromov to hand the money over to the Thorisdottirs upon their acceptance of the assignment? Should it be delivered only upon its successful conclusion?

Gromov realized that the failure to provide payment instructions was not an oversight or a mistake. It was deliberate. Beria had placed his trust in Gromov's judgment. Remarkable. Gromov was far too experienced and cynical to rush to any conclusions, but this was an extraordinary act by someone with a deserved reputation for controlling the tiniest details of any operation. Beria would never trust Belyanov to exercise such discretion on an item of this magnitude. Fascinating.

Gromov spent little time pondering the manner of payment. He trusted no one, not even the provably reliable Thorisdottirs. He would pay them one-quarter of the total upon acceptance of the assignment and the balance upon receipt of demonstrative evidence that the assassination plot had been conveyed to Canidy and Fulmar. Beria had said he would, somehow, know when it had. Gromov had no doubt that he would.

Vík í Mýrdal, Iceland

0730, 17 October 1943

The lower pitch of the boat's engines as it slowed woke Gromov, who had drifted into a slumber, the fantasy of absconding with more than a million American dollars still playing in his mind. He oriented himself and looked off the starboard bow to see a stunning verdant landscape surrounding the village of Vík í Mýrdal, the beach forming a crescent in front of the village consisting of black sand and pebbles. To the rear were impressive rock formations that ascended into the mountains and glaciers beyond. Waterfalls descended from the rock formations, disappearing behind the village. Just beyond the beach were numerous fishing boats that sat on wheels. Yet there were no docks to be seen. The fishermen simply rolled the boats into the ocean and, upon returning, landed on the beach and rolled the boats back onto land.

The captain of the vessel, looking perplexed, informed Gromov that they'd arrived. "There's not a dock in sight."

"Proceed a bit farther," Gromov instructed, pointing forward. "There should be a small dock within a kilometer, perhaps two."

The captain peered ahead and proceeded, hugging the jagged coastline. Within five minutes they saw a small dock. A fishing vessel bearing the name *Njord* was moored on the side opposite them. A small dwelling sat approximately two hundred meters inland.

"There," Gromov said. "Moor on the opposite side of the dock."

The captain did as told, and a few minutes later Gromov was walking toward the dwelling, which was much larger than it had appeared from the sea. Gromov held his Tokarev in his right hand and carried a bag with 1.2 million in American dollars in his left. When he closed to within twenty meters of the front door, he stopped.

"If you shoot me," he shouted, "the crew on that boat will strafe your beautiful home with heavy machine-gun fire before launching a ROFS-132 rocket directly at your front door." A few seconds passed before the front door opened. Both Thorisdottir sisters emerged with a smile, surprising Gromov. Given their last interaction he expected there might be a bit of friction. Katla, her smile broadening, pointed at the bag. "Beware of Russians bearing gifts."

"What makes you think I have a gift for you? Perhaps I've come to have you wash my laundry." Gromov placed the Tokarev in his shoulder holster.

Kristin, appearing to gaze at the torpedo boat, said, "You are here because you have a task of some importance for us. Perhaps even more important than the last one, although I cannot imagine any task rising to such a level." She moved to the side of the door. "Well, whatever it is, you are not going to discuss it in the open air, even if there's no one within two kilometers. Come in."

Gromov sprang onto the porch and followed the sisters into a relatively spacious front room appointed with several pieces of fine furniture. A large armoire containing fine china sat behind a low table, on which there was a silver tray of pastries.

"You were expecting someone?"

Kristin shook her head. "A neighbor. A somewhat elderly woman who lives in the village and maintains our home when we are fishing—or otherwise away—enjoys the pastries. She stops by often when we are not away . . . fishing."

Gromov nodded approvingly. "A very nice place. And away from conflict. I am somewhat surprised, however, that the Thorisdottir residence isn't besieged by Viking suitors."

The twin sisters sat on two French provincial–style chairs. Katla gestured for Gromov to sit in a similar chair opposite them. He placed the bag on the floor next to him and sat.

"I will not waste your time," Gromov said. "The torpedo boat cannot idle forever." Gromov opened the bag and displayed the cash. "This is for you."

Katla arched her neck to peer into the bag. "American dollars," she informed her nearly sightless twin. "I estimate a very large sum." She glanced from the bag to Gromov. "For us?"

Gromov tilted his head to the side. "Perhaps. How much were you paid for the last assignment, if I may ask?"

"Two hundred fifty thousand American dollars," Kristin replied.

"You're quite wealthy."

"We were very happy with the compensation, yes."

"That was a very complex, dangerous, and arduous operation," Gromov said. "You took great risks. Your lives were in great peril throughout, so you were compensated accordingly."

"Then, based on the size of that bag, whatever task you have for us may be something of a suicide mission," Katla said.

Gromov smiled and shook his head. "Not at all. In contrast to your previous operation, this one is much simpler and safer. In fact, as opposed to the Kapsky operation, this one entails little, if any, risk of physical harm."

Katla again craned her neck to peer inside the bag. "Then why the large sum of currency?"

"Because of the importance of the assignment."

Kristin arched her eyebrows, incredulous. "More important than securing the Kapsky documents?"

"Indeed."

"Impossible," Kristin said.

"You might think so, but there are matters afoot that will have a direct effect on the outcome of the war, and our allies—the Americans and British—need to be focused. They must concentrate on such matters in a way they have not done to date."

Kristin leaned forward slightly. "Our allies need to concentrate on matters? I should be forgiven for being so cynical, but do I understand you to say that our allies are to be manipulated somehow to share the perspective of the Union of Soviet Socialist Republics—that is to say, Comrade Stalin?"

Kristin's question reminded Gromov that he was dealing with two extremely bright and knowledgeable people. Little escaped their attention or understanding.

"What benefits the Soviet Union necessarily benefits its allies," Gromov said. "But sometimes our allies do not appreciate that what happens on the Eastern Front controls the ultimate outcome of the war. The battles on the Eastern Front are titanic, not just in comparison to the battles in France or Italy or elsewhere—but in comparison to all the battles in human history. If Hitler is successful on the Eastern Front—more specifically, in the Soviet Union, the largest landmass in the world—he will have access to our vast resources, *lebensraum*, and a buffer against invasion."

Kristin shifted her right thumb, pointing at Katla and herself. "What does that have to do with us?"

"Let me be direct. We—the Soviet Union—would like you to convey to our American and British allies that we are in peril—"

"I am fairly confident they already know that," Kristin interjected.

"*Imminent* peril," Gromov explained. "They need to know that Hitler is planning a decapitation strike on the Allied heads of state." He paused and waited for a reaction. Both Kristin and Katla looked slightly perplexed, with a hint of skepticism.

"To be clear," Kristin said. "By 'decapitation strike' do you mean destroying the military leadership of the respective countries? The officer corps? Killing their generals and such?"

"A bit more ambitious and serious than that," Gromov replied.

"Civilian leadership?" Katla asked. "How far up?"

"All the way up," Gromov replied. "Stalin, Churchill, and Roosevelt."

The sisters looked at each other. The room was silent for several moments as Gromov permitted them to absorb the information. Kristin shifted in her chair, pondering the implications. "How reliable is this information?"

Gromov shrugged. "As reliable as you make it."

The brows of both sisters furrowed in consternation. "No riddles, please, Gromov," Kristin said. "What, precisely, do you mean by that?"

"In approximately one month, there will be a conference in Tehran, Iran, attended by Stalin, Churchill, and Roosevelt, the purpose of which is to determine Allied strategy in the war as well as the contours of a postwar world. As is self-evident, that conference will be one of the most monumental in the entire history of the world."

"And at such conference, Stalin, Churchill, and Roosevelt would be assassinated?" Kristin asked, incredulous. "The leaders of the most powerful nations, save perhaps Germany and Japan, on Earth?"

Gromov folded his hands under his chin and nodded. Katla and Kristin said nothing for half a minute until finally Katla spoke. "If you—the Soviets—know this, I assume the British and Americans are also aware?"

"They are not," Gromov responded.

"And why not?" Kristin asked. "Haven't you told them? And if not, why not?"

Gromov smiled. It was predatory. "You always know the right questions to ask, Kristin." Not to leave her out, Gromov turned to Katla. "And you, too, Katla. I am sure both of you have concluded what the assignment must be."

Katla looked at the bag again. "That is much more than one hundred thousand American dollars. Precisely how much is it?"

"One million two hundred thousand dollars. Several times the compensation for your role in acquiring the Kapsky documents."

"All of that is for us?" Kristin asked.

"It is," Gromov confirmed.

"One point two million for a role I assume we are to play at the conference in Tehran. Whatever you have in mind for us undoubtedly is of exceeding significance," Kristin said, drumming her fingers on the armrest. "One point two million dollars. A sum that large can only be for the taking of a life, or lives."

"We sail. We fish. We convey personnel and cargo," Katla recited, stabbing the armrest with an index finger for emphasis. "We do *not* kill."

"The sum, which I agree is quite large, is not for killing anyone," Gromov assured them. "It is for conveying information."

Both of the twin sisters skeptically asked, "Information?"

"Information and information alone. All you are to do is convey to the British and Americans that Hitler plans to kill their leaders at Tehran."

Kristin smiled. It was a cold and cynical smile that Gromov decided made her appear impossibly beautiful. "No one pays one million dollars for conveying such information—for *conveying any* information." She sighed. "What is the true objective, Gromov?"

"The true objective," Gromov replied with a hint of false indignation, "is to inform our allies that our respective leaders are in peril."

"Of course," Kristin agreed in a mocking voice. "No one could be expected to convey such information for any smaller amount. Stalin, for example, could not send a message to Churchill warning him that the NKVD had uncovered a sinister Nazi plan to kill the Big Three at their upcoming meeting. Understandably, that *would* be a burden."

"It is not about *who* could convey the information. Almost anyone could do that. It is about who would be believed by the recipient." Gromov sat forward. "The British and Americans understand the situation the Soviet Union is in. They know very well that Comrade Stalin wants the British and Americans to attack the Germans from the west, thereby relieving pressure in the east. They have not, however, acted with any sense of urgency, and it appears they are unlikely to open a Western Front on the timetable Comrade Stalin desires."

Kristin sighed cynically. "So it is Stalin's belief that Churchill and Roosevelt would move with greater urgency and dispatch if this became personal, and that Hitler revealed he observed absolutely no norms or conventions of civilized warfare."

Gromov clearly approved of this analysis. "That is, indeed, part of the calculation. But the real impetus for attacking Hitler from the west sooner rather than later will be the populations of America and England. Ordinary people. Citizens. Especially Americans. They understandably will be outraged not just by Hitler's evil but by his audacity. The supreme insult of having the *audacity* of attacking America's President. Americans would *never* tolerate that. It is part of their cowboy mentality."

Gromov leaned back in his seat and remained silent. There was nothing else to say. As his grandfather used to say, "The shoes have been sold."

Although they were identical twins, Kristin, older than Katla by six minutes, always took the lead. "You had little doubt we would agree. Therefore, you expect us to begin right away. Which brings us to the details . . ."

"You'll be paid three hundred thousand American dollars now, and the balance, nine hundred thousand dollars, upon completion of the assignment."

Kristin and Katla simultaneously said, "That is acceptable."

Gromov grinned, reminding Katla of why her levelheaded twin had been drawn to him. He was a soulless killer, but he possessed a frightening magnetism. She shivered slightly, unsure if it was due to the assassination plot or the large sum of money at her feet.

"And how are we to pass along the intelligence? What, precisely, are we to say, and to whom?"

Still grinning, Gromov said, "Yes, of course we will discuss that.

But first, might we mark the occasion? Is there no vodka in this dwelling?"

"At this time in the morning?"

"Why not?"

"No vodka. Not since the prohibition ended."

Gromov said, "But wasn't that several years ago?"

"True," Kristin said. "But there is a war, after all. Imports are running behind demand. We do have Brennivín." She turned to Katla. "And a fair amount of shark?"

Katla nodded, rose, and disappeared, returning mere seconds later with a bottle, three glasses, and a plate covered with shark flesh. She placed the tray on the coffee table. Gromov filled each glass with Brennivín and the three held their respective glasses aloft for a second before simultaneously consuming the contents.

Gromov returned his glass to the tray. "Quite good. Now, as for execution of your task. The details are few and simple. You have considerable discretion as to precisely how you complete the assignment, but the essence is as follows: you will sail the *Njord* to Gotland—"

The sisters simultaneously asked, "What?"

Gromov spoke slowly and deliberately. "You will sail to Gotland and inform Major Canidy and Lieutenant Fulmar that Hitler is sending assassins to Tehran to kill Roosevelt, Churchill, and Stalin."

"Who developed this plan?" Kristin asked in an incredulous voice. "This is guaranteed to fail. Canidy is more likely to shoot us on sight than patiently listen to our story. Then, when we tell him the story, the likelihood will become a certainty."

"We were without any doubt the greatest and most acute failure in his life, let alone career," Katla protested. "He would sooner sleep with two vipers in his bed than allow us within one hundred meters of him. Let alone believe anything we tell him." She threw her hands up in exasperation. "I will gladly take the sum of money in that bag. I will take substantial risks for such a sum." She shook her head emphatically. "But I will not risk my life for a mission that has absolutely no chance of succeeding; that is *unquestionably* destined to fail; that is madness."

Gromov raised his hands to dampen their protests. "Everything you say is completely logical." He nodded sympathetically. "But we assess Canidy's—and Fulmar's—ultimate reaction will be precisely what we want.

"That is, they will inform their superiors—their Colonel Donovan—that your source within the Abwehr told you that Hitler has commissioned German intelligence to assassinate Stalin, Churchill, and FDR in Tehran.

"There are several reasons for this," Gromov noted. "To me, the most rational is that they could not risk *not* telling Donovan that Hitler plans to assassinate the Allied leaders. They could not readily sit on that information any more than they could sit on hot coals. That is a category of information that *must* be forwarded, regardless of source, because of the magnitude of the consequences if the information is accurate and it is not forwarded.

"Moreover, although your initial reaction—that they would discount any information coming from the two women who betrayed them—would, in fact, be *their* initial reaction, within a fraction of a second they would conclude that no person on Earth who had betrayed them as you had would have the audacity or the stupidity to attempt a *second* deception. A second *titanic* deception."

Katla read her twin's face. She knew Kristin's thought processes as well as her own. "Even so, given that he has assessed us as self-interested mercenaries, why would we tell them about such a plan? Why travel to Gotland? What, as the Americans say, is in it for us?"

"That is actually the easiest part. At least two things. Since he's concluded you are self-interested mercenaries, act like it. Hint at the possibility the United States might provide a reward, *a substantial* reward, for critical information you have in your possession. But also make clear that you are motivated by the oldest reason in the world—revenge. Tell them that I not only rejected Kristin but that I struck her, viciously. I trust you with how to best use that."

"It also has the virtue of being true," Kristin said caustically.

Gromov lowered his head slightly. "It is, and I am genuinely remorseful," he said. "I concede that you have no reason to believe that I am sincere. I hope nonetheless that you will understand that my actions were due to the pressures of the Kapsky operation."

"That is no excuse. Even if it were, we do not believe or forgive you," Katla said, looking at Kristin. "But we will address that another time."

"We will take the assignment," Kristin said. "Not because we believe you are contrite, but because of the sum involved. Your terms, however, must be modified."

Gromov appeared genuinely surprised. "Modified? In what way?"

To Kristin the bag looked like a gray-green smear at Gromov's feet. She pointed at it and said, "We shall require the full amount in advance."

Gromov's head recoiled slightly. The demand surprised him. It wasn't like them.

"You have the money," Kristin continued. "It is right there. It is not as if you have to gather the sum. And you have our commitment. We will do as asked. We have never failed to do as asked. We have agreed to discharge the assignment. You agreed to compensate us for same. Now."

Gromov stared at Kristin for a moment and found himself mildly amused. Her demand didn't anger him; it entertained him. Only the three men he'd met within the large chamber in the Kremlin would have dared to speak to him that way. He shrugged, pushed the bag toward Kristin with his right heel, and chuckled. "Why not?"

Katla rose from her chair and sifted through the packets of bills bundled in denominations of twenties, fifties, and hundreds. She turned to Kristin. "I believe it is all there."

"When do we begin?" Kristin asked.

Gromov slapped the armrests of his chair with both hands. "As soon as we finish the Brennivín."

CHAPTER 24

Sweat appeared to burst from Canidy's pores and ran toward his soaked T-shirt as he finished his twentieth forty-meter wind sprint, even with Fulmar, who doubled over in dry heaves as soon as they came to a halt. They'd been working out since 7:00 a.m.: a five-kilometer run along the craggy shoreline, followed by seemingly incessant ten-repetition sets of push-ups, pull-ups, and chin-ups—the latter two exercises performed off the branch of a pine tree near the cabin. All "supervised" by McDermott, who enjoyed the spectacle while sitting on the cabin porch nibbling on Scotch-soaked bannock.

"Again!" McDermott shouted between bites.

"Go to hell!" Canidy responded between gasps for air.

McDermott burst into a gale of laughter and took another bite.

Canidy and Fulmar turned and sprinted forty meters in the opposite direction, staggering the last ten meters before again hunching over, hands on knees. Canidy turned and looked at Fulmar, whose face was crimson and drenched in perspiration.

"I thought we were going to some damn conference in Tehran," he gasped. "I must've missed the Movietone reel about the Olympics being staged there."

Fulmar took several gulps of air. "Donovan's punishing us for the notebook fiasco. This has nothing to do with Tehran."

"Or physical rehabilitation. Hell, I feel worse now than I did when I woke up from the grenade blast."

"Again!" McDermott shout-laughed.

Canidy sucked in a lungful of air. "No!"

"Again!" McDermott insisted. "Or I'll tell Commander Fleming, who'll tell Colonel Donovan."

"Go ahead. What's he gonna do? There aren't any other idiots who will do this."

"Again!"

Fulmar looked at Canidy. "Loser buys beer."

They took off again, staggering across the finish line, even with each other.

"We both get a beer," Canidy wheezed. "Then we beat the crap out of McDermott and take his Scotch."

Looking north over Fulmar's shoulder, Canidy spotted a jeep carrying two soldiers coming over the hill from the direction of the airstrip. The vehicle came to within a few meters of where Canidy and Fulmar were standing, and a lanky colonel got out, returned Canidy's and Fulmar's salutes, and extended his right hand. "Colonel Dennis J. Barbato," he said, pumping Canidy's hand once, then Fulmar's. "No more disturbances, I trust?"

Canidy turned and gestured toward the shoreline behind him. "Not since we almost got blown to Sweden. How many snipers do you have positioned along the shore?"

"A half dozen. They're not snipers; they're guards."

Canidy winked and grinned broadly. "Somebody needs to tell them that. I don't think a single one of them has taken his eye off his respective foresight since you positioned them there."

Barbato laughed. "Somehow, they've gotten the impression that you guys would buy a case of Schlitz for the first guy to hit a German soldier in the forehead."

"We never said that," Canidy objected. "That would be unbecoming of an officer. We said the first guy who hits a German soldier in the forehead would probably deserve a case of Schlitz."

"Well, Colonel Donovan was pretty hot after the second attack. He insisted you get the VIP treatment."

Canidy shot Fulmar a skeptical look. Fulmar rolled his eyes.

"What?" Barbato asked. "You don't believe me?"

"We believe he ordered snipers all right. But not for Germans. For us," Canidy said.

"Well, you've got to admit, for the Genius to send two teams—one after the other—to kill you is pretty remarkable. And it was equally remarkable they didn't succeed. OSS confirms that the attackers were Brandenburgers. They may not be quite as invincible as reported, but they're still damn lethal."

"I won't be upset if they don't pay us another visit," Canidy said. "What brings you to our lovely neck of the island today?"

"Colonel Donovan continues to insist that messages must be delivered personally. He said that you should be prepared to leave for your destination imminently."

"When is imminently?" Fulmar asked.

Barbato shrugged. "Apparently he trusts only a handful of people with the specifics and I'm not one of those people. He wanted to alert you so that you'll be prepared to depart at a moment's notice."

"Did he provide *any* information?" Fulmar asked. "Did he give you a range? Means of transport? Orders?"

Barbato shook his head. "Just be ready to go. The order could come as soon as the next hour. I suspect when it does, you'll get the specifics."

Canidy and Fulmar looked at each other. "Is that it?" Fulmar asked.

Barbato peered off into the distance. "He said one more thing."

Canidy and Fulmar stared at Barbato expectantly. He looked conflicted.

After a few moments Canidy said, "Well, what in hell did he say?"

Barbato rubbed the back of his neck as if he were trying to solve a puzzle. "He said, 'From this moment forward, trust absolutely no one, including each other.'"

CHAPTER 25

The Oberstleutnant found it remarkable that the most celebrated man in Germany adhered to the Genius's protocols and arrived precisely five minutes before the meeting. Obersturmbannführer Otto Skorzeny acted no differently than he had before he'd become a worldwide legend. In fact, he acted no differently than he had before he'd become a German legend. He observed all protocols of military decorum, yet never asserted privileges of rank and remained affable without compromising military discipline.

The Oberstleutnant, however, was thrilled to be in such proximity to the man of the hour. He would recite the minutest detail of his interaction with the famed hero of the Gran Sasso Raid to his family and friends: *Of course* Skorzeny was a longtime friend. Yes, he occasionally asked for advice. No, he didn't ask for *specific* advice on how to execute the operation, but that was only because the Oberstleutnant had offered advice before the mission. Advice about what? Well, I cannot discuss details but, well, the use of gliders to stealthily approach the mountain and surprise the guards? That wasn't something he'd necessarily considered on his own, if you understand my meaning.

"Obersturmbannführer Skorzeny. Please take a seat and I will inform Admiral Canaris of your arrival."

The receptionist rapped twice on the door to Canaris's office, opened the door a few centimeters, and peered inside. The receptionist turned and gestured for Skorzeny to approach and enter.

Skorzeny stood at the entrance, waited for Canaris to wave him in, and then stepped before the highly polished desk on which absolutely nothing save for a small black envelope sat. Canaris gestured for Skorzeny to sit.

"As a preliminary matter, Goebbels is a very talented 'publicist,' but his explanation of your extraordinary heroics in Italy is somewhat excessive."

"I agree, Herr Admiral. It is not military."

"Nonetheless, you deserve the accolades. Splendid performance, Skorzeny."

"Thank you, Herr Admiral."

Canaris chuckled. "I'm afraid that is the conclusion of today's pleasantries." He reclined slightly in his chair before continuing. "We have another operation for you. Far less challenging than your previous one. In fact, perhaps your least challenging of the war."

"Yes?"

"There have been discussions within the Oberkommando der Wehrmacht about a planned meeting between Churchill, Stalin, and Roosevelt to take place sometime soon. The exact time and place have not yet been established, but we expect to know soon.

"It is our assessment that the formal meeting will be primarily *informal* and inconsequential, but the secondary and tertiary meetings among the respective staff will have great significance. The plans for the conduct of the balance of the war will be debated and sharpened. Consequently, considerable intelligence could be gleaned from the communications of support staff and their ancillary meetings.

"This is not the type of operation to which we would assign someone such as you. Indeed, the Führer is somewhat conflicted. Security for such a meeting will be extraordinary. He prefers not to expose our most famous soldier, a hero of the Reich, to unnecessary risk in the conduct of a nonmilitary operation, but staff correctly pointed out that Obersturmbannführer Otto Skorzeny, famous or not, is the best, and an operation involving the heads of state of our principal adversaries demands our best."

Skorzeny sat without expression. He quickly surmised what he would be asked to do. As audacious as such an operation would be, he anticipated Canaris was going to state that Churchill, Stalin, and Roosevelt were to be assassinated.

"The location of the conference," Canaris continued, "has not yet been confirmed, but we expect it will be Tehran. You will go there several days before the conference accompanied by Brandenburgers."

Skorzeny nodded. The Brandenburgers were highly proficient operators-assassins. He'd worked with them on two previous missions—both successful. "If I may ask, Herr Admiral, how many?"

"I do not have a final figure yet. But the preliminary figure is, perhaps, a little more than a dozen."

Skorzeny raised his eyebrows. His surprise was obvious to Canaris.

"You anticipated a different mission, I suspect," Canaris said with a smile.

"A dozen Brandenburgers is an excessive number to execute the mission I had anticipated," Skorzeny noted.

The Genius stared at Skorzeny as if attempting to read his mind.

"You would not need more than a few assistants, even to carry out such a mission against the so-called Big Three. There would be—of course—immense logistical and tactical hurdles to overcome, but they would not be irresolvable. You could, under the right circumstances, execute such a mission with the assistance of . . . how many?"

"One, perhaps two."

"Do you believe you could successfully accomplish such a mission?" Canaris asked pensively.

"Respectfully, Herr Admiral, what I *believe* is irrelevant. I *know* I could accomplish such a mission."

"I believe you could." Canaris nodded. "Assassination of the Big Three is, however, not the objective. The objective is intelligence gathering. Each of the Allied heads of state will have entourages with them."

Canaris picked up the black envelope from the desk. "There is a second component to your assignment in Tehran. This component is better suited to your peerless skills." He retrieved two photos from the envelope and held them in front of Skorzeny. They were of two men standing near a cabin on a bluff above a shoreline. The photos appeared to have been taken from a distance, but the focus was clear.

"We have information that these two will be deployed to Tehran about the same time as the conference of the Big Three. They have posed significant problems for us recently and promise to continue posing problems. We have directed two teams of Brandenburgers to eliminate them. Unsuccessfully."

Canaris extended the photos to Skorzeny and then pressed a buzzer on the underside of his desk. The receptionist opened the door instantly. Canaris indicated toward Skorzeny. "When he leaves, kindly give Obersturmbannführer Skorzeny the files on Major Richard Canidy and Lieutenant Eric Fulmar."

The receptionist nodded crisply and closed the door. Canaris said nothing, allowing Skorzeny to commit the photographs to memory. Having done so, Skorzeny extended the photos back to Canaris. "I understand that I should kill them?"

Canaris again held the photos before Skorzeny. "They likely will be performing a function similar to yours: gathering intelligence, performing counterintelligence. Watch them. Collect information. Observe and report. You'll be given the order to kill them at the appropriate time."

CHAPTER 26

Canidy and Fulmar both were hunched over, hands on knees, gasping for breath. Despite the cool, damp breeze wafting over the bluff overlooking the Baltic, rivulets of sweat poured off their foreheads and drenched the green cotton shirts McDermott had "requisitioned" from the airstrip.

"You're right," Canidy huffed. "This has nothing to do with preparing for the Tehran operation. This is Donovan's way of punishing us for the Kapsky debacle." Canidy took several gulps of air before resuming. "He's got us training for the Olympic decathlon here. I haven't run this much since . . . Hell, I've *never* run this much."

Fulmar stood erect and tilted his head back to face the sky, mouth agape. "Enemy intelligence agents are always required to run from the scene of the crime whenever they steal secrets. It's in the secret agent handbook. They're all very fast. We need to be able to catch them."

Canidy pointed toward the cabin, where McDermott stood grinning. "Look at that Scottish jackass having the time of his life over there. I swear—he makes just one smart remark, just one joke at our expense, and I'm decking him."

Canidy noticed the thick veins bulging from his forearms and biceps. Prior to the Kapsky operation he'd always believed exercise needed a purpose beyond merely improving one's physique; otherwise it was mere vanity, and vanity was not for real men. But when he found his physique transformed by the grueling regimen Donovan imposed, he conceded to himself that he liked the results. He'd been blessed with a splendid natural physique, but in rare moments of introspection conceded that Fulmar's was a bit better. Not necessarily enough for the casual observer to discern, but his keen competitive instincts compelled him to punish himself to the point where there was no appreciable difference in their musculature. And during the operation to extract Kapsky from Nazi-occupied Poland, his improved strength, speed, and endurance might have made the difference between escape and capture, life and death.

And, he imagined, it wouldn't hurt with the ladies. He'd always had the look of an Errol Flynn or Clark Gable, but now he had the physique of a Jim Thorpe or Johnny Weissmuller.

"When you're finished admiring yourself, you may notice that our friend from the airstrip has returned," Fulmar said.

Canidy looked farther inland and noticed the jeep with Sergeant Kevin Wood bouncing over the landscape toward them. "How much you want to bet it's another update from Donovan?"

"No doubt. Probably going to tell us to run ten more miles and straight into hell."

The jeep came to a halt within a few yards of Canidy and Fulmar and Wood hopped out and saluted.

"There's no Olympics this year," Wood said. "You can take the rest of the afternoon off."

"Did Donovan say that?" Fulmar asked.

Wood grinned. "Donovan wants you to run five more miles and do five sets of twenty push-ups."

Canidy pointed petulantly at McDermott resting on the ground near the cabin's porch. "Why doesn't Commander Fleming make *him* run? Are we expected to haul his fat, bannock-fed ass around Persia?"

"Take it up with Churchill. In the meantime you need to be prepared to go to Iran."

"When do we leave?"

"Looks like no later than seventy-two hours from now. More likely forty-eight. That's what I came here to tell you."

"Another poor sap was dropped off today solely to tell us, 'Hey, you guys are supposed to be ready to go right away.'"

"You'll fly a C-54 into Malta, refuel, and then go to Tehran. We've taken the liberty of packing bags for each of you with items provided by OSS. Weapons, equipment, and the like."

"Where's that sap? Why didn't he come to tell us himself?" Fulmar asked.

Wood turned and pointed in the direction from which he had come. "Probably because we told him that if someone you guys didn't recognize comes over that hill, you'll shoot them."

"Honest answer."

"You'll get a briefing sometime before you leave," Wood continued. "Probably from another poor sergeant who has to fly across the Atlantic just to tell you not to use the latrines in Tehran."

"Donovan plays to win. And he doesn't make the same mistake twice," Canidy said. "If that means he has to send a sergeant to tell us when to take a piss, he'll do it."

The sergeant rubbed the back of his neck. "Yeah, I heard they gave him the Medal of Honor, DSM, and DSC?"

Canidy's face turned grave. "Nobody *gave* him anything. He

earned the Medal of Honor, Distinguished Service Cross, Distinguished Service Medal, a Silver Star, and a shitload of campaign medals and ribbons. Toughest, bravest SOB you'll ever meet. But the thing to remember about Wild Bill is that he's got even more brains than balls."

The sergeant stared silently for several seconds at Canidy in amazement. "Seriously? He earned all those? And you report to him? You've really got to respect and admire a boss like that."

"'Respect' and 'admiration' aren't quite the right words. 'Fear' is. I'm scared shitless of him."

Canidy noticed Wood looking over his shoulder toward the sea. Canidy turned to see a vessel about a quarter of a kilometer off the coast. He squinted and his shoulders dropped in disbelief. "Eric, tell me that's not a mirage."

"If it's not a mirage," Fulmar replied, "it has to be a ghost ship. They wouldn't dare come within a hundred miles of this place."

Canidy clenched his jaw and walked quickly toward the cabin, torso pitched forward as if to ram into a wall. Wood watched with a puzzled expression as Canidy disappeared into the cabin, emerged seconds later with an M1911 in his right hand, and appeared to ignore a question from McDermott. His face and neck flushed red with anger, Canidy stopped next to Fulmar, whose face still registered disbelief. Fulmar glanced at the weapon and said, "Don't kill them until they tell us everything they know about everything."

Canidy nodded and spoke slowly. "This weapon's not for killing. Not immediately. It's for compliance."

Canidy and Fulmar strode toward the shore as Wood concluded it was a good time to get back to the jeep rather than be a witness to whatever was about to occur. By the time they'd reached the edge of the dock, the *Njord* was close enough that they could see Kristin Thorisdottir at the helm, literally navigating almost blindly, with her twin sister standing at her left side.

Katla acknowledged them with a single wave. Canidy cursed. Fulmar spat. Each was angry at the Thorisdottirs, but perhaps more so with himself—both because they had been deceived and outwitted by the sisters, and because, despite the titanic betrayal, Fulmar and Canidy remained captivated by the twins' extraordinary beauty. Each woman stood erect, with avalanches of white blond hair cascading down to their waists. When Canidy first met Kristin he had instantly concluded that she had the longest hair, longest neck, and longest legs he'd ever seen on a woman. At the time he'd thought her piercing ice-blue eyes conveyed intelligence and a regal aloofness. Now he believed they conveyed cunning and calculation.

Kristin shut off the engine and maneuvered the starboard bow of the *Njord* toward the dock. Katla tied the boat off and the four stared at one another, Canidy and Fulmar implacable and the Thorisdottirs anxious. "You've got bigger balls than me. I'll give you that," Canidy growled. "I'm going to kill both of you. Make no mistake about that. But first you're going to tell us the whole story. And for every sentence, word, inflection, or punctuation mark that I don't like, I'll shoot an arm, leg, hand, or foot until you're dead or I'm out of bullets."

The sisters nodded, uncowed. "We expected as much," Kristin said. "Actually, we expected you might fire on us before we were even moored."

"Go to hell with your damn expectations." Canidy raised the M1911 at Kristin's head. "No one gives a damn about your expectations. Give us the story. Then we'll find out if I shoot you in the head or in the gut. Pray it's in the head."

The sisters wore identical genuine expressions of fear. Unsatisfactory. Canidy wanted them to feel nothing less than terror. "The story," he demanded. "Prolong your worthless lives a couple more minutes. Give us the story."

"Money," Kristin said, voice quavering. "The Russians gave us two hundred fifty thousand dollars to deliver the equations. SHAEF, on the other hand, was paying us just a thousand per transport. We transported five teams of Brits and we transported you twice. That's seven thousand, only four thousand of which had been paid by the time we transported you. The Russians gave us two hundred fifty thousand American dollars to get the notebook. One hundred thousand *in advance*.

"We assessed that since the Americans, British, and Soviets were allied against the same enemy, in the end, *which* ally gained possession was immaterial. But Katla and I would be far richer if the Soviet ally got the equations. An *ally* would have the equations. The enemy would not."

Canidy's grip on the M1911 tightened, but his trigger finger remained next to the trigger. "When I kill you I won't know if it's because you stole the Kapsky notebook or because you're lying weasels. If you really believed that it made no difference which ally got the notebook, why did you poison Kapsky? Why did you try to ensure that *only* the Soviet ally would have the benefit of Kapsky's work?"

"I do not understand. What do you mean, 'poisoned'?"

Canidy's face became flushed with fury. "Kapsky nearly *died*, you worthless . . ." He paused for a second. "Whatever you gave Kapsky put him in a coma, nearly killed him. Why did you do *that*?"

Kristin blinked several times and plaintively extended her arms, palms up. "Again, because we were *paid* to give the notebook to the Russians. And as for poisoning Kapsky, we were given a vial of fluid by an NKVD major, our contact. He told us it would render whoever consumed it unconscious. We were prepared to put it in all of your drinks so that we could take the notebook and be far out to sea by the time you regained consciousness and realized the notebook was gone. But we were only successful in getting Kapsky to take some tainted aspirin that we had slipped him."

Canidy's jaw jutted forward. He became more enraged with each sentence she spoke. But what enraged him most was that he didn't know if his anger was due to losing the Kapsky notebook or to being duped by Kristin—seduced, in part, by her beauty. *He* duped women. Women never duped *him*. Canidy squeezed the trigger of the M1911 and fired into the ground. Fulmar started; neither Kristin nor Katla flinched. Canidy raised the weapon toward them again.

"Why are you here?" he asked. "Apologizing? Asking for forgiveness?"

"No," Kristin said. "Perhaps, however, we are here to make amends for our duplicity. Although we believe our actions helped the Allies as a whole, we regret our duplicity."

Canidy lowered the M1911 to his side. "You sailed all the way from—wherever you were—to apologize? You really do think we're idiots. You expect us to think any garbage that comes out of your mouths isn't a colossal lie? That you're not trying to manipulate us again?"

"I do not have any expectation other than for you to be skeptical. Rightfully so. Nonetheless, we have information, if you believe it, that you likely will consider highly important. In fact, of critical importance. Perhaps more important than the information in Professor Kapsky's notebook."

Fulmar chuckled sardonically. Turning to Canidy and gesturing toward the sisters, he said, "I don't know why you don't believe this, Dick. They sailed all the way from"—he turned back to Kristin—"where did you sail from?"

Kristin shook her head. "You wouldn't know it. Someplace in Iceland."

"Someplace in Iceland. All the way here. Probably a good— what? Twelve hundred miles?"

"Approximately eighteen hundred fifty kilometers," Katla said.

"I can see that," Fulmar said, nodding, his voice full of sarcasm. "When I feel guilty I usually take a quick trip through the North Sea and the Baltic. Give a friendly wave to Admiral Dönitz's six or seven hundred U-boats patrolling the vicinity. Cheers me right up."

"Relieving ourselves of guilt is *a* reason we came here," Kristin informed them. "But it is not the only reason. We're certain the information we have is important. It's consequential to the war and beyond."

Canidy's face flashed disbelief. "Look, the more you talk, the less credible you sound. Quit while you're ahead. I don't believe that you sailed all this way just because you feel guilty, to give us information because you want to make amends. Turn your boat around and go home."

"We didn't sail here to make amends and give you information. We came here to make amends and *sell* you information."

Both men seemed unconvinced. Canidy pointed at Kristin and turned back to Fulmar. "Do you believe this woman? She's going to make amends by *selling* us information. The woman who stole information from us now wants to sell us information." Canidy clearly needed more convincing. "Since you felt so bad that you sailed all the way here, you *must* be giving us a break off the sales price for the information, right? What's your price?"

"One million American dollars."

CHAPTER 27

Skorzeny found Schmidt hunched over one of the many long tables containing vises, microscopes, beakers, and precision tools that lined the perimeter of the laboratory. Hearing Skorzeny's footfalls, Schmidt looked up and adjusted the glasses that had slid down the bridge of his nose. He saw that his friend was sporting a self-satisfied smile, something rare for the famed yet modest SS Obersturmbannführer.

Skorzeny examined the metal tube lying on the table in front of Schmidt. It looked like a small telescopic sight, but he knew that objects in Schmidt's laboratory were not always what they seemed.

Schmidt frowned. "Be very careful, my friend. It may look like a telescope, but it has a dual purpose."

"Is that so? I am astonished," Skorzeny said without a hint of sarcasm, thereby making the sarcasm unmistakable. He walked over to the bench next to Schmidt, where there was a silver metal orb the size of his fist, and tossed it in the air, caught it, and then juggled it as if he couldn't control it.

"If I drop this, it will explode, yes?"

"Why don't you walk away twenty paces and find out for yourself?" Schmidt said nonchalantly.

Skorzeny gently placed the orb back on the table. "It *is* an explosive," he said. "What is so special about it that it is in your laboratory?"

Schmidt grinned slyly. "I am not at liberty to disclose that, even to the Great Skorzeny." He wiped his hands with a cloth and handed it to Skorzeny.

"What do you expect me to do with this?"

Schmidt shrugged. "Just a precaution. The object you just handled may have an unforeseen side effect. Unlikely, but it is new and I have yet to subject it to the usual protocols."

"But you allowed me to handle it without warning?" Skorzeny said, rubbing his hands vigorously with the cloth.

"I have had a difficult time finding suitable rodents on which to test the object."

Skorzeny threw the cloth at Schmidt's face. "I suspect you have already been briefed. And likely much more thoroughly than I."

"Yes. I have been briefed. Markus and Roland have been preparing a kit for you. Nothing exotic. This seems to be a relatively straightforward assignment. No gliders, miniature communication devices, or the like."

"Splendid. The less the better. Any weaponry?"

"You will *not* be taking the orb," Schmidt said. "But you have your requested variety of pistols." He opened a drawer in his table, displaying a variety of firearms. Walther P38, Walther PPK, Walther PP, Luger P08. "Everyone I outfit demands just *one* of these." He sighed. "Why do you insist on several?"

Skorzeny answered with a question. "Why do you have so many different instruments, beakers, and tubes of different sizes and shapes?"

Schmidt held up a finger, remembering another item. He bent down and picked up a semiautomatic pistol with a wooden stock from a shelf below the table's surface.

"Why you continue to insist upon this mystifies me," he said, handing the weapon to Skorzeny. "Mauser C96. Absolutely no one requests this anymore."

Skorzeny picked up the weapon, feeling its weight. "Not so. Some in both the Luftwaffe and Kriegsmarine still carry them."

"What is so attractive about such a seemingly unwieldly weapon?"

"The 7.63-millimeter cartridge, my friend. When something *must* be stopped, this Mauser will stop it."

Schmidt slapped the table. "From my understanding of the general nature of your assignment, I should think you would perhaps like to have a sniper rifle." He walked to the nearest wall, which sported an array of weaponry. "My recollection is that you've employed one of these to reasonably good effect in the past." Schmidt unhooked a Mauser 98 from the rack and placed it gingerly on the table before Skorzeny, who picked it up and felt its weight and balance. He shook his head.

"I do not think an occasion will present itself to use this."

Schmidt frowned. "Am I mistaken? I understood part of the operation involved, for lack of a better word, the assassination of an American OSS agent."

Skorzeny chuckled. "Do they tell you *everything*?"

Schmidt tilted his head to the right. "How else am I supposed to properly outfit you and your men?"

"It is unlikely that circumstances will permit for use of the Mauser. I doubt the agent will be at a predictable and specific time and place that permit assassination at range. Besides, even if that were the case, I think I would prefer a Mosin-Nagant."

"A Soviet rifle?" Schmidt asked indignantly. "Inferior."

"Vasily Zaitsev would disagree. So would the ghosts of the scores of troops we lost at Stalingrad to his Mosin-Nagant. And our young and prolific sniper on the Eastern Front, Allerberger? I understand even he is using a captured Mosin-Nagant now."

"Inferior," Schmidt repeated, unpersuaded. "When will you be departing for Tehran?"

"They did not tell you that?" Skorzeny smiled.

"Not yet."

"Very soon, I gather. Within a few days. In the meantime, you know where to find me."

"*Turnhalle?*"

Skorzeny grinned as he clapped his friend on the forearm and turned to leave.

"It is unbecoming of someone of your stature, Skorzeny. What is the obsession with fitness?"

"It is an obsession with survival," Skorzeny replied as he walked away. "After all, Spencer said 'the fittest survive.' I aim to be *the* fittest."

The mammoth hall was empty and dark save for a solitary light near the far door. A corkwood track ran the perimeter of the interior, approximately two hundred meters in circumference. Various items of exercise equipment were neatly arranged inside the perimeter. Some were exotic; most were simple. Skorzeny used none of them.

Skorzeny believed he'd escaped several encounters with death or dismemberment because of his sheer physicality. He was a superb natural athlete—strong, fast, and agile—but his distinguishing attribute was his drive. He had a nearly limitless capacity to push his endurance beyond that of anyone he'd ever known. And his threshold for pain was legendary among all those with whom he'd served. He sometimes wondered whether that was the reason he'd take risks most would never even contemplate. A high tolerance for pain, he thought, produced a greater tolerance for risk. And his willingness to take risks most would never dare had elevated him to heroic, if not near-mythic, status.

So Skorzeny began the pain by running on the sloped cork track for nearly a full hour. He wasn't precisely sure of the distance, but estimated he covered approximately fourteen kilometers.

A fair warm-up.

Skorzeny walked around the track once before dropping to the floor and performing fifty push-ups. He rested on his hands and knees for thirty seconds before doing fifty more. He repeated this cycle three more times before shifting from thirty-second breaks to sixty-second breaks. He performed four more sets of fifty push-ups, rose, and ran another two kilometers. Hands on hips, he walked until his breathing and heart rate slowed to normal. He then walked to the east end of the hall in order to sprint to the west end—approximately seventy meters. Just before he began his first sprint, a group of nine or ten boisterous Brandenburgers entered the double doors on the west end. They didn't notice Skorzeny until they were in the middle of the hall and one of them stopped abruptly.

"Skorzeny."

The group stopped and stood slack-jawed, staring at Skorzeny. The shortest of them, an Obergefreiter with reddish blond hair, said, "We did not mean to disturb you, Obersturmbannführer Skorzeny. We did not know you were here." He gestured toward the group. "We often come here at this time, but we shall leave if you wish."

Skorzeny studied the group slowly and said, "Not at all. There is plenty of room for all. I was nearly finished."

The Obergefreiter said, "As you wish, Herr Skorzeny."

Skorzeny turned to leave, but stopped abruptly and said, "In fact, there is one thing you may do for me."

The group straightened. Skorzeny examined each of them. All appeared athletic and fit. One stood taller than the rest, taller even than Skorzeny. He was an Obergefreiter with short blond hair and a square jaw and was heavily muscled. Skorzeny estimated he weighed at least 110 kilos. He wore a silver Close Combat Clasp on his upper-left breast.

"What is your name?" Skorzeny asked.

"Obergefreiter Heinz Wagner, Herr Skorzeny."

"Obergefreiter Wagner, I have a somewhat peculiar question."

"Anything, Herr Skorzeny."

Skorzeny nodded at Wagner's Close Combat Clasp. "Weapons or hand-to-hand?"

"Both, Herr Skorzeny."

"Casualties?"

"Three. Two killed, one wounded."

"Where?"

"Kessel von Demjansk, Herr Skorzeny."

Skorzeny smiled in appreciation. "Tough. Very tough. Impressive."

"Thank you, Herr Skorzeny."

"I wonder, Obergefreiter Wagner, if you might indulge me. You see, it has been several weeks since my last operation . . ."

Every one of the Brandenburgers broke into a knowing grin.

". . . and I have not had an opportunity to train properly since then. I suspect my next assignment could involve a bit of hand-to-hand. The probabilities may be low, but it is always best to be prepared for that which does not happen than to be unprepared for that which does."

Each of the Brandenburgers nodded agreement with their idol.

"Accordingly, will you accommodate me in a bit of close quarters? Three falls? Just a minute or two?"

"It would be my honor, Herr Skorzeny. I assume no head strikes?"

"All strikes are permissible. Hold nothing back, please."

The eyes of every one of the Brandenburgers grew large. This promised to be something to tell their children and grandchildren.

"Herr Skorzeny, permission to remove my tunic?"

Skorzeny agreed and watched as Wagner removed his jacket, revealing shoulders that resembled small boulders, and handed it to the red-haired Obergefreiter. Wagner rotated his arms and cracked his neck from side to side before bending into a grappler's stance. Skorzeny, standing casually, turned to the Obergefreiter. "Call the signal."

The Brandenburgers formed a semicircle five meters in diameter around the combatants. Each wore the eager look of anticipation of a ten-year-old at Christmas. The Obergefreiter raised his right hand over his head, paused, and said, "*Beginnen.*"

Wagner, obviously hoping to establish a legend, immediately lowered his right shoulder and charged Skorzeny, who pivoted on his right heel like a matador, slamming his left elbow into the back of Wagner's skull as he passed. Although his face contorted with pain, the giant remained standing and immediately turned to face Skorzeny, who instantly drove his right fist into Wagner's forehead, followed by a left uppercut into Wagner's jaw, causing a jet of blood to erupt from his mouth.

Skorzeny stepped back, permitting Wagner to regain his bearings. The other Brandenburgers shouted encouragement to Wagner, whose facial muscles were rigid with determination.

Skorzeny rapidly closed to within a meter of Wagner, feinted right, and jabbed the three middle fingers of his left hand into Wagner's neck just below his right ear. Wagner's eyes bulged as he gasped for breath while Skorzeny jammed the heel of his right hand under the giant's chin, snapping his head backward with enough force that the back of his skull became parallel to the floor.

Wagner groaned, collapsed to his knees, and fell forward onto his face, blood from his mouth forming a pool around his head and neck. The elapsed time from the moment he had charged Skorzeny until his head crashed onto the gymnasium floor: seven seconds.

Skorzeny knelt beside Wagner, whose half-open eyes were bloodshot and glazed, and placed a hand under the giant's nostrils to check his breathing. He looked up at the other Brandenburgers, who appeared awestruck.

"He will be fine, but he may have fractured facial bones. He may also have some difficulty breathing until his windpipe heals. But there should not be any hemorrhaging or permanent trauma."

Skorzeny rose and adjusted his collar. "We will, obviously, dispense with the additional two falls. Kindly extend my thanks to Obergefreiter Wagner when he regains consciousness. He is a creditable opponent—lasting longer than expected."

Skorzeny turned and walked toward the exit. The Brandenburgers watched in stunned silence as he disappeared through an exit. No one moved or spoke until the red-haired Obergefreiter shook his head as if trying to clear a daydream, and croaked, *"Mein Gott."*

CHAPTER 28

Canidy, Fulmar, and McDermott stood in the field between the coast and the cabin, out of earshot of the Thorisdottirs. Each had an identical expression: disbelief trending toward uncertainty. Canidy's expression and posture were the most skeptical. His arms were folded across his chest and his jaw muscles flexed as he ground his teeth.

Canidy kicked the dirt. "We can't believe a thing those two snakes say about anything. If they told me my name is Dick Canidy, I'd go back and check my birth certificate. Twice. They're the liars responsible for the biggest screwup of our respective lives—a screwup that could have been one of the most consequential of this damn war. Now they come back and casually tell us that out of remorse and the goodness of their blessed little hearts, they want to tell us something that *itself* promises to be the most consequential thing of the war." He snorted with derision. "And all they ask in return is 'one million American dollars.'"

Fulmar's expression conveyed a mix of anger and indecision. "I've got to admit, I've never before thought of doing the slightest physical harm to a woman, but right now . . ." His voice trailed off as he composed himself. "Look, at some point those two witches will pay for their crimes. But right now, it seems to me we've got a decision to make."

Canidy chuckled sarcastically. "To maim or to kill?"

"Dick, I know you're thinking exactly what I'm thinking." Fulmar turned to McDermott. "And you, too. Yeah, we're definitely in a pickle, but we don't have many options . . ."

Canidy kicked the dirt again. "Are you actually thinking about going to Donovan with their proposition? A million dollars for a fairy tale from the most devious women on the planet? Donovan would have us certified. The term 'he doesn't suffer fools gladly' was coined because of one William Joseph Donovan."

Canidy and Fulmar watched as McDermott sighed and walked into the cabin. Canidy took a deep breath. "In the last couple of months, we've been shot at by Panzer IVs, MG 42s, Karabiner 98ks, and Lugers." He pointed toward the *Njord*. "None of those were remotely as dangerous as those two."

Fulmar grinned. "The great Dick Canidy's ego . . ."

Canidy's response was vehement. "No, no, no. That has nothing to do with it. This has to do with putting us between a rock and a hard place, each of which is closing in on us. If we don't go to Donovan with this and it turns out whatever information they have is as consequential as they claim, we're screwed. And more important, the Allies are screwed. If we *do* go to Donovan and he gives us one million dollars for this and it turns out their information is false or inconsequential, our careers are over—and not just our military careers—"

"The third possibility," Fulmar interjected, "is that we go to Donovan with their information and it turns out to be just as accurate and consequential as they claim . . ."

". . . and we win the damn war. We each get so many decorations on our chest that we can't stand up straight, and Cecil B. DeMille makes a movie about us," McDermott said, returning from the cabin with a bottle of Glenfiddich in his left hand and three glasses cradled between his right arm and rib cage. He handed the bottle to Canidy, distributed glasses to him and Fulmar, retrieved the bottle, and poured two fingers in his glass and each of theirs. Then he poured two fingers more. He raised his glass in salute. "Sometimes you just need to make a damn decision. And this invariably helps." He downed the contents in one swallow. Canidy and Fulmar followed suit.

Canidy exhaled forcefully and nodded. "Well, it certainly helps with procrastination."

Fulmar rubbed the back of his neck. "I'd trust them more if they didn't look like they'd just descended from Valhalla. They know their looks compromise our judgment. *We* know their looks compromise our judgment. Even if everything they say is one hundred percent accurate, even if they hadn't screwed us before, we can never be confident in our decision, whatever it may be."

Fulmar held his glass toward McDermott, who poured another shot for each of the three.

"I'm *not* going to Donovan without more information," Canidy said after downing the second shot of Scotch and exhaling. "They've got to give us something. A taste of whatever information they have. It has to sound credible. And they have to know they aren't getting a million dollars for *anything*."

"How can you be sure, Dick?" Fulmar asked. "What if it *is* that important?"

"They could have a formula for immortality and Donovan's not giving them one million dollars for it," Canidy replied.

"How much will he give?" McDermott asked.

Canidy cocked his head and shrugged. "Hell, I don't know that he'd give them anything. But first things first. The Thorisdottirs need to convince us that we should even approach Donovan. That's the first hurdle. Then we decide if we go to Donovan. Donovan decides how much the taste is worth and how much he pays for the entire story."

Fulmar nodded. "We better move right away, though. If the information is even close to being as important as they claim, we can't waste time." He handed his empty glass to McDermott. "I'll go get the women and bring them back to the cabin." He shook his head. "All I know is this better be legitimate this time. If it's not, I'll kill them as soon as I find out it's bull."

Kristin and Katla sat next to each other on one side of the wooden kitchen table. Canidy, Fulmar, and McDermott sat across from the sisters, their torsos leaning forward as if they were going to interrogate them. Canidy thought the sisters looked contrite, a realization that increased his skepticism. He reminded himself that their looks were not merely tools but weapons.

"The first thing you should know is that—"

"—you do not believe anything we have to say," Kristin finished. "You made that clear at the dock, just as we made clear we understand your skepticism."

"The *first* thing you should know," Canidy continued, "is that there is no way we're going to go to our people with a proposition that involves anything close to a million dollars. The second thing you should know is that you could tell us the precise location of the

Holy Grail and we wouldn't give you one million dollars for that information."

"Major Canidy," Kristin said amiably, "we appreciate that you don't have the authority to make any commitments. It is uncomfortable for you to go to your superiors—especially after your credibility has been compromised—with information from the very individuals responsible for such embarrassment."

Both Canidy and Fulmar flushed, not from embarrassment but from anger. "Be careful what you say and how you say it," Canidy hissed. "You two may think you're clever—hell, I'll concede that you were clever enough to betray us—but you should understand that your continued existence depends entirely on our good nature."

Kristin straightened in her chair as if she were a student remonstrated by a teacher, causing her breasts to strain against the fabric of her cotton shirt, something Canidy, Fulmar, and McDermott pretended not to notice.

"What will it take, then?" Kristin asked.

Canidy looked puzzled. "What do you mean?"

"What will it take to demonstrate our goodwill?"

"Please be serious," Fulmar interjected. "There really isn't anything that you can say to demonstrate your goodwill after your betrayal. You simply need to tell us enough of what you know to convince us it's something worth taking back to our people."

"And what do we get in return?" Kristin asked.

"A price," Canidy replied. "Our superiors will assess what you've told us—its veracity and importance—and give us the price they're willing to pay for the whole story."

Kristin turned to Katla, who nodded. Although Katla appeared to her to be an outline in fog, Kristin discerned her sister's intent.

"Reasonable enough," Kristin said. "Will you give Katla and me a moment to discuss what we can tell you and still . . . what is the phrase . . . maintain some leverage?"

"Take your time," Canidy said. "We'll be outside."

The three men rose. Before following Canidy and Fulmar out the door, McDermott pulled two glasses from the cupboard, put them on the table before the Thorisdottirs, and placed the bottle of Glenfiddich next to them. "You may find this helpful to decision-making." He winked and trailed Canidy and Fulmar out the door, closing it behind him.

The three men stepped off the porch and walked thirty meters from the cabin. They huddled in a semicircle.

"I'd say that went rather well," McDermott said.

"How so?" Canidy asked.

"You didn't maim or kill them. Admirable restraint."

"What in hell could this be all about?" Fulmar said. "To even *ask* for a million dollars?"

"We'll find out soon enough," Canidy said, staring at the cabin. "But even if it's worth telling Donovan, we have a problem."

"What problem?" Fulmar asked.

"Donovan's still transmitting all messages by courier because he's concerned that the Germans are somehow intercepting our communications. Even if the Thorisdottirs' information is worth telling Donovan about, someone's got to travel to Washington to do it."

McDermott shook his head. "If it comes to that, I can transmit the information. Commander Fleming hasn't stopped using telephones or cables. I can get the message to him and he can get it to Donovan."

Fulmar disagreed vigorously. "No way. Donovan would still have our heads for circumventing his directive. You absolutely do *not* try to be clever in evading his directives. He'll nail us to a tree if we pull that kind of stunt."

McDermott waved his hand dismissively. "Not to worry. All we need to do is alert him to the fact that we have vital intelligence—that is, if what the Thorisdottirs tell us actually is vital—and allude to the general nature of it. I'm sure he'll make arrangements for us to somehow convey greater detail. That's what he does."

Canidy put his hand up. "We're getting ahead of ourselves. Let's just see what they say and take it from there." He twisted his torso from side to side to stretch.

"I'm still not over the urge to kill them," Fulmar said, as if talking to himself.

Canidy agreed. "I was thinking just that when they were talking."

"But that's not all you were thinking . . ."

Canidy said nothing.

"Hey, I had a few stray thoughts in there, too," Fulmar conceded. "But it only makes me angrier—at them for deceiving us and at me for being duped."

McDermott inspected Canidy's and Fulmar's faces. "Both of you may no longer be fools, but you're still liars. I caught your faces in there. Both of you would have jumped at the chance if they let you."

Canidy laughed. "And you wouldn't?"

"We Scots have far more personal discipline than you Yanks. Legendary. Especially when it comes to women. A Yank sees a beautiful woman and he immediately loses all powers of rationality and discernment. Scots, in contrast, become suspicious."

Canidy looked incredulous. "Rationality and discernment? This, from a Scot who eats cardboard soaked in alcohol for breakfast?"

"That is not a breakfast peculiar to Scots," McDermott protested in defense of his countrymen. "That is peculiar to my clan and my clan alone."

Katla appeared at the door of the cabin. "Gentlemen, would you join us?"

The three returned to the cabin and took their seats. "What do you have that we can take back to our superiors?" Canidy asked brusquely. "Something worth a million dollars?"

Kristin replied, "The Soviet NKVD has an informer deep in the Wehrmacht. His information over the last two years has been unerringly accurate: troop deployments, munitions capabilities . . ." She stopped and cast her nearly sightless eyes directly at Canidy. "Tell them that the outcome of the war will be determined by the events of the next few weeks," she continued. "And that the Germans will likely win."

CHAPTER 29

By the time the secretary of war was ushered into the Map Room by Laurence Duggan for an 8:15 a.m. meeting with the President, William Donovan had had almost twenty minutes to shake his head, scowl, and grumble to himself about the location of the meeting. Before Stimson could even utter a "good morning," Donovan looked up and hissed, "This is no damn way to run a country in wartime. Our allies have secure rooms in which to conduct confidential meetings, wartime strategy. Yet here we are, the most important and powerful of the Allied powers, conducting a meeting between the President, secretary of war, and head of the Office of Strategic Services next to the front entrance of the most recognizable building in the country."

Stimson patted his friend on the shoulder, sat at the conference table on Donovan's right, and waved his hand at the maps of the European and Pacific theaters displayed on the opposite wall. "This is, after all, where the President and his staff are briefed about the progress of the war, Bill. Besides, no one comes through the front door of the White House."

Donovan jabbed his right index finger toward the windows as if firing a gun. "What about the windows facing the North Lawn?"

"No one can see in here, Bill."

"I'm not so sure. Our Professor Moriartys are working on a system that would permit specialized scopes to penetrate window dressings. We have to assume the Germans and the Japanese have similar capabilities."

Stimson clapped his friend on the shoulder. "I would be damned surprised, Bill, if the Germans and Japanese have anyone who could outwit you."

Donovan grunted. "We have to assume that each of them has ten people who could outwit me and my staff. That's precisely what my job is, Henry. To think like they think and then try to stay one step ahead. Or at bare minimum, keep up with them and counteract what they do."

The normally serious Stimson smiled. "I don't see anyone peeking in the window, Bill. There's no one in the hall. Relax."

Stimson's reassurance had the opposite effect. "We're not paid to relax. We're paid to be damn alert, damn smart, and damn tough. We'll spend nearly fifty billion dollars on the war this year. We estimate the Germans are spending nineteen billion reichsmarks. You better believe both of us are spending at least a portion of that on peeking through windows or finding ways to peek through windows."

A look of disgust came over the patrician Stimson's face.

Donovan said, "Henry, you may like to maintain that civilized nations do not engage in such tawdry activities, that civilized men do not act like brigands and pirates. But the Germans and the Japanese don't play by gentlemen's rules and neither can we."

Stimson raised his chin. "Bill, I've been secretary of war to a Republican president and a Democratic president, and secretary of state to one Republican president. More than almost anyone, I am quite familiar with what is required to win wars. I am merely saying that the United States of America should not succumb to the depredations of imperial and dictatorial states."

"We're not succumbing to anything, Henry. We're just keeping up."

The two men looked to the entrance as Laurence Duggan opened the door wider for the President to wheel himself in. His demeanor was pleasant, verging on jovial, and an unlit Camel protruded from the cigarette holder jutting from the left corner of his mouth. Both Donovan and Stimson rose halfway from their respective chairs.

"Go ahead, Bill," FDR taunted playfully. "Give me hell for the location of the meeting."

"I've said my piece before, Mr. President."

Roosevelt came to an abrupt stop on the opposite side of the long table. "You have. And I wouldn't tolerate less from my chief spy. Now, what have your assistant spies rustled up that requires my attention?"

Donovan tried to summon his most contrite expression, but he still resembled a bull about to burst out of its stall.

"Mr. President, Major Canidy and Lieutenant Fulmar—"

Roosevelt held up a hand and Donovan immediately stopped speaking.

"The same Canidy and Fulmar who were sent on what I believe you termed a 'suicide mission' to get Professor Kapsky out of Poland. Am I right?"

"That's correct, Mr. President."

"And they succeeded, against all expectations. Right?"

Donovan nodded. "That's right, Mr. President. They extracted

Professor Kapsky. But I am duty bound to remind you that they almost lost Kapsky due to the perfidy of two of our confidantes."

Roosevelt removed the cigarette holder from his mouth. "Bill, you needn't recite the record as a form of mea culpa. Your boys did a spectacular job but were betrayed. How many times a day does betrayal occur in war, particularly a war of this magnitude? Daily? Hourly?"

"Yes, Mr. President," Donovan conceded to his law school classmate. "The betrayal, however, was one that could have affected the geopolitical balance of power."

"Understood." Roosevelt agreed amiably. "But it didn't."

"Nonetheless, Mr. President, I prefaced my response to your question about Canidy and Fulmar with those facts because the betrayal is integral to what we need to decide."

Intrigued, Roosevelt gestured for Donovan to continue.

"Canidy and Fulmar were approached by the same individuals, the two contractors we used to convey our operators across the Baltic, the same contractors who poisoned Kapsky and absconded with his notebook."

Roosevelt's eyebrows arched and he put the cigarette holder back into the left side of his mouth. Speaking around it, he confessed, "I'm surprised your boys didn't shoot the two on the spot. What possessed these two ladies to proverbially return to the scene of the crime?"

"Ostensibly contrition, Mr. President. And, of course, money."

"I believe the part about the money. I have a bit less confidence that it was at all motivated by contrition."

"Indeed, Mr. President."

"Well, Bill, let's get right to it. How much money are they talking about?"

"A million dollars, Mr. President."

Roosevelt slowly removed the cigarette holder from his mouth again. "What?"

"Their price for revealing certain information is one million U.S. dollars."

"One million dollars?" Roosevelt asked incredulously. "Have we ever paid even remotely close to that for intelligence?"

Donovan and Stimson, who knew how much Roosevelt enjoyed intrigue, jointly said, "No, Mr. President."

Roosevelt stared silently at the wall behind the two for several seconds before finally saying, "Because I know you two weren't born yesterday and because I know how smart each of you is, I assume you've assessed that request in the same way I have."

Stimson glanced at Donovan, who deferred to the secretary of war. "We were momentarily staggered by the amount, Mr. President. A price tag of that magnitude logically suggests that the information is of supreme importance. It also convinces one that the information that is the subject of such a demand is rock-solid, unimpeachable." Stimson glanced at Donovan next to him. "It is for that very reason we believe this to be a giant ruse. A misdirection, albeit a highly sophisticated one."

"Yes. Someone desperately wants us to believe whatever it is the contractors tell us.

"Which brings us to what, precisely, it is that the contractors—more accurately, whomever they are working for—want us to believe. Do we have any idea, any speculation what that might be, gentlemen?"

Stimson tilted his head deferentially to Donovan, who said, "We do not specifically, Mr. President. Except that they've cryptically said—and I'll quote as accurately as possible—that the outcome of the war itself will be driven by the events of the next few weeks, and without us having the information that is in the contractors' possession, the Germans will likely win."

The President drew his head back. "Well," he said slowly. "These contractors surely have a flair for the dramatic, don't they?"

"They did pull off a highly dramatic stunt with the entire Kapsky affair," Stimson noted.

"Yes, they did," Roosevelt said softly. He toyed with his cigarette holder as he thought for a moment. "Do our men in the field— Canidy and Fulmar, that is—have any idea what these contractors may be alluding to? Do *you* have any ideas? Any at all?"

Donovan and Stimson turned to each other and responded in tandem, "No, Mr. President, we do not."

Roosevelt smiled wryly. "Did you fellows rehearse your lines beforehand?"

"Mr. President," Donovan continued. "Our best assessment is that this comes from the Soviets, that this is something they want us to believe. Possibly misdirection."

"Upon what do you base such an assessment?"

"Admittedly," Donovan said somewhat sheepishly, "it's mere conjecture based on the Kapsky affair, but it's possible the contractors are again doing the bidding of the Soviets—that they are on their payroll. But we can't be certain. We don't have direct evidence. In any case, it would be worthwhile—and wise—to try to determine what it is they want us to know."

Stimson and Donovan sat silently as Roosevelt pondered the matter for several seconds. "How worthwhile?"

"One hundred thousand dollars, Mr. President."

Roosevelt's brow furrowed. "Not nearly as much as a million, yet . . . why so much?"

"For the same reason the Thorisdottirs—the contractors— demanded one million dollars. To make our interest seem genuine. Plausible. To make the Soviets, or whoever it is that wants us to think the information is genuine, believe our interest is genuine. That we believe the information to be real and true."

"Yes, I understand. The flimflam artist never believes he can be fooled. A figure that large leads them to believe *we* actually believe what they want us to believe."

"That's the idea. We're like a linebacker who knows the opponents' quarterback wants him to think the play is going to the right but is actually going left."

"The Soviets are not our opponents," FDR said almost mechanically.

"They are our ally, but they are indeed our opponent," Donovan said.

"All right," Roosevelt said. "One hundred thousand dollars. Tell our men. Make the necessary arrangements."

A tall young man appeared at the door. The President looked expectantly past Donovan and Stimson. "Yes?"

"Excuse me, Mr. President. Mr. Hopkins asked me to remind you that the press availability starts at eight forty-five." Roosevelt acknowledged the young man, who quickly disappeared.

"I trust you two to communicate to our men in . . . Where are they now?"

"Gotland, Mr. President," Donovan replied.

"Still? After two attacks?"

"We surrounded them with an overwhelming security force," Donovan said.

Roosevelt pondered the reply for a moment. "All right, then. When are they going to Tehran? Don't forget, I'd like those two in Iran."

"Yes, Mr. President. They will be departing shortly."

"Splendid." Roosevelt beamed. "I can barely wait to meet them. Everything you've told me about them sounds as if they should be in a Michael Curtiz film. My mind's eye sees Canidy resembling— what is that fellow's name? Errol Flynn. Anyway, you'll let them know about the one hundred thousand dollars. I'm off to once again bedazzle the press."

CHAPTER 30

McDermott was wiping the crumbs from the Glenfiddich-soaked bannock off his thick mustache when he heard the sound of a motor vehicle approaching the cabin. He rose from the kitchen table, opened the door to the front porch, and saw Sergeant Wood riding in a jeep driven by a redheaded corporal coming from the direction of the airfield. The vehicle came to a stop about twenty meters from where Canidy and Fulmar were doing push-ups and pull-ups.

McDermott went out to join them. Wood hopped out of the jeep with a smile, rubbing the back of his neck. "Do you ever stop doing push-ups?"

Canidy pointed accusatorily at McDermott approaching from the cabin. "That SOB has us running and doing calisthenics three times a day. Orders from the boss."

"We received a message for you by way of MI6 in London. It was coded, although I don't know why."

Canidy's face expressed disbelief. "You don't know why? After we almost got blown to hell?" He flipped a thumb between himself and Fulmar. "I thought we were the ones who got concussions, not you."

"Well, the message seems pretty innocent, if you ask me. Don't know why it needed to be encoded. But anyway, our guys decoded it. Can't figure out what it refers to, though."

"Well," Canidy said impatiently, "what does it say?"

"'Authority to one hundred thousand.' *What is that supposed to mean?*"

Canidy looked knowingly at Fulmar, who nodded.

Wood said, "Well, you guys seem to know what it means, and that's all that matters. Still, mind letting me know?"

"It means one hundred thousand," Canidy said.

Wood held up his palms toward Canidy. "Okay. I get it. I'm not supposed to know. If you tell me, you've gotta kill me, right?" He returned to the jeep and a minute later disappeared over the rise.

"Think that will do it?" Fulmar asked. "It's a hell of a lot of money, but it's only one-tenth what they demanded."

"One hundred thousand dollars. That's about forty times what the average man in America makes in a full year, so probably one hundred times what the average man makes in Iceland."

"A hell of a lot of money," Fulmar repeated in agreement. "But they said the outcome of the war would be decided by what they told us."

"They'll take it. It's the only offer they're going to get. They'll still be rich." Canidy began walking in the direction of the dock. Fulmar accompanied him. "We'll need to make arrangements to get the money to them. It's not as if there's a Western Union nearby."

"Again, assuming they'll take it."

"Care to make a wager?" Canidy asked.

"I say they hold out for two hundred fifty thousand dollars."

Canidy shook his head. "No way," he said emphatically. "They'll take the hundred thousand dollars and sail into the sunset."

"How much are you willing to bet?" Fulmar asked.

"You don't have anything I want."

"Good looks."

"Too Aryan."

The two OSS operators descended the slope toward the dock where the *Njord* was moored. The Thorisdottir twins were standing on the starboard bow drinking coffee, the morning sun reflecting off their almost white hair, making it appear as if they were crowned by halos.

"Look at them," Canidy said. "They look like they knew we were coming."

"That's not clairvoyance, Dick. We were bound to appear sooner or later."

Canidy and Fulmar stepped onto the dock. Katla waved them aboard and raised her coffee cup as an offer. Both men declined.

"You have a counterproposal from your superiors," Kristin said matter-of-factly.

The men clambered onto the boat and stood in front of the sisters. "We do," Canidy confirmed. "One hundred thousand American dollars."

The words were barely out of Canidy's mouth when Kristin said, "Two hundred and fifty thousand dollars."

The muscles in Canidy's jaw became taught and visible. His right hand rested on the M1911 at his right hip. "You're lucky you're even alive," he growled. "This is not a negotiation. It's one hundred thousand dollars."

"Everything is a negotiation," Kristin said calmly.

"Not this. One hundred thousand dollars for everything you know. And if anything you tell us is wrong—if you mispronounce the name of a person or place, if a time is off by one second—we will find you and we will kill you."

"Our apology, our contrition, was sincere, Major Canidy," Kristin said. "We regret the deception."

"Don't forget the attempted murder . . ." Canidy hissed.

Fulmar quickly interceded before the exchange escalated any further. "It's one hundred thousand dollars, ladies. That's it. That's more than enough to assuage your alleged remorse."

Both Kristin and Katla appeared stung by Fulmar's sarcasm. Neither man felt regret. Kristin transferred her coffee cup to her left hand and extended her right to Canidy. "One hundred thousand dollars."

Canidy ignored her hand. "You'll get the money when we get the money," he said flatly. "Tell us what you know."

Kristin sheepishly withdrew her extended hand and nodded. "Very well. We trust you."

"You shouldn't," Canidy retorted with a grimace. "So, what intelligence is worth one hundred thousand dollars?" he asked, his voice steeped with sarcasm. "How are the Nazis going to win the damn war and subjugate all of mankind?"

"They're going to assassinate Joseph Stalin, Winston Churchill, and Franklin Roosevelt."

Both Canidy and Fulmar stared silently at Kristin for several seconds before Canidy turned to Fulmar, who said nothing. Canidy turned back to Kristin. "Impossible," he said flatly. "Killing *one* head of state—of *any* state—let alone one of the three major Allied powers, would be next to impossible. Especially in a time of war. Killing three *is* impossible." Canidy put his hands on his hips in disgust and shook his head. "The U.S. is not going to give you one hundred thousand dollars for this load of elephant dung, especially after you tried to assassinate Kapsky and screwed us so badly on the notebook." Canidy became more agitated as he continued to speak. "You sail all the way from—whatever goddamn place you came from—ask for a million dollars, and feed us this crap? It's clear you think we—and apparently the entire U.S. military and its civilian leadership—are as dumb as a comatose armadillo. But really, you expect us to buy this? Hell, at least give us some credit for recognizing we shouldn't believe you two if you told us our names were Major Richard Canidy and Lieutenant Eric Fulmar. But instead you expect us to hand over one hundred thousand dollars for telling us the Nazis are going to kill—are even remotely *capable* of killing—not just one of the most heavily guarded men in the known universe, but three—"

"Dick's right," Fulmar interjected coolly. "That can't be done. Almost as important, our superiors would assassinate *us* for giving you one hundred thousand dollars. Hell, for giving you a *dollar* for that load of crap." He threw his hands up in exasperation. "*This* is what you sailed across the North Sea, the Baltic, to tell us? Even if they wanted to, they couldn't do it."

"Really?" Katla asked evenly.

"*Yes*," Canidy said. "Really. It would be futile to even attempt it."

"Futile?" Katla pressed.

"Hell, yes. Why is that so hard for you to grasp? The Nazis can't get to Stalin, or Churchill, or Roosevelt. Impossible."

Katla shrugged. "They were able to get Mussolini," she reminded them. "On a remote mountaintop surrounded by hundreds of armed guards who should have seen them coming from a hundred kilometers away. That was no less difficult than killing Roosevelt, Churchill, and Stalin. In fact, it's far easier to kill a heavily guarded person than it is to seize and safely escape with him."

Canidy's eyes locked with Fulmar's. Katla could tell they were reassessing their assumptions.

"Even if they could pull it off, it would be a strategic catastrophe for them," Canidy said.

Kristin tilted her head toward her left shoulder. "Please explain."

"I know my country. If they assassinate our President, it would enrage the population and prompt us to fight harder."

"Enrage you more than Pearl Harbor?" Kristin asked. "How is that possible?"

Canidy said nothing.

Kristin gestured toward Katla. "Clearly, we are not military strategists, but rage does not strike me as a strategy. Regardless, I repeat, the Nazis will decapitate the Allies and exploit the chaos, strategic confusion, and disinformation that will inevitably follow, however transitory."

Canidy placed his hands on his hips, walked past the Thorisdottirs to the leeward edge of the bow and back to where Fulmar was standing. "What do you think?" he whispered.

"This is a big deal no matter how you look at it," Fulmar replied. "The real questions for me are when and how. We need more."

Canidy nodded and turned to the Thorisdottirs. They looked at him with guileless expressions.

"We need more," Canidy said. "Specifics. Methods. Time and place that each is expected to be assassinated . . ."

"Of course," Kristin said. "You did not permit us to elaborate. What we know is limited, but it may be enough to thwart the attempt."

"Attempt? One attempt?"

"The assassination will occur in Tehran when Stalin, Churchill, and Roosevelt meet," Kristin said. "Whether when they are together or separately we do not know. But it will be at the conference."

Canidy and Fulmar glanced at each other.

"Is that sufficient for payment?" Katla asked.

Canidy ignored the question. "That place is going to be swarming with troops and personal security details." He nodded toward Fulmar. "We'll be there also. If they're planning on doing it there, it'll have to be a suicide mission. Still, getting close enough to shoot any of the three will be next to impossible, even if they plan never to get out again. And they'd have to be undetectable until they can get close enough to take action. It can't be a large group if they hope to remain undetected until they get close enough to execute," he said. "Do you know who or how many they're sending?"

"Likely Brandenburgers," Katla said. "We understand the Genius has deployed them to great effect. Have you ever encountered them?"

"We believe we've had the good fortune of *encountering* them twice. Delightful chaps."

"When can we expect payment?" Katla asked.

"You'll get paid," Fulmar assured her. "The United States of America fulfills its commitments."

"Yes, but when, specifically?" Kristin asked.

"Soon," Canidy answered. "It's just a matter of informing our superiors and they'll transport the money here. American dollars."

"Hours?"

Canidy shrugged. "I can't say, precisely. Probably longer than that. We'll contact them right now."

Fulmar stepped off the boat and onto the dock. Then he proceeded up the slope toward the cabin. Canidy turned to follow, but
was stopped by Kristin, who seized his left arm.

"You do not want us to leave."

"As I just told you, I don't know how long it will take for the
cash to get here. But I expect it shouldn't take long."

"It is not so much about the time of delivery, Major Canidy. As
furious as you are with us, you do not wish us to leave."

Canidy pulled his arm free and stepped onto the dock. "We'll be
back when the money arrives."

CHAPTER 31

It was not lost on Taras Gromov, formally still Major Taras Gromov, that Lavrentiy Beria had bypassed Gromov's immediate superior, Colonel Aleksandr Belyanov. Beria's aide had directly contacted Gromov to summon him to Beria's office. It wasn't clear that Belyanov was even aware of the meeting, although the seemingly ubiquitous Lieutenant Valeri Novikov, one of Belyanov's two top aides, passed Gromov in the hallway leading to Beria's chambers. At some point Belyanov would be sure to know about the meeting and be curious about its purpose.

Belyanov had a reputation for ruthlessly protecting his turf. Toward that end he deployed Novikov to be his eyes and ears in the internecine warfare conducted within the walls of the Kremlin. Novikov would identify officers who seemed to be finding favor with Beria, and Belyanov would identify ways to subvert them. He would permit no one to usurp his value to Beria and Stalin. That included fast-rising Major—soon to be Colonel—Taras Gromov.

Upon Gromov's arrival in the antechamber, a sternly efficient aide immediately ushered him into Beria's office. Beria was sitting ramrod straight behind the desk, his penetrating gaze fixed directly at Gromov as if he had known the precise second the assassin would walk through the door. Beria gestured for Gromov to sit, then motioned for the aide to remain.

"Has Novikov left?" Beria asked.

"He remains in the anteroom," the aide responded. "He is unsure whether you were through with him."

"I am in need of the cables, but I am no longer in need of his presence. Tell him to inform Colonel Belyanov that I no longer need to see him at noon, either."

The aide nodded once and left, closing the door behind him.

Beria again gestured to one of the chairs in front of the desk. "Sit, Gromov." Beria leaned forward, placing his clasped hands on his desk. "Your operators made contact with the Americans as you instructed and told them that the Nazis are going to assassinate Comrade Stalin, Prime Minister Churchill, and President Roosevelt."

Gromov smiled.

"Unfortunately," Beria continued, "the information did not have the desired effect. The Americans appear to be highly skeptical that the Germans will attempt to assassinate the Allied leaders. It appears they may think an attempt is a charade. Consequently, it is unlikely that there will be an increased urgency on their part to open a Western Front. They have not even confirmed a timetable for opening such a front."

Beria leaned even farther across the desk, as if for emphasis. "The Americans have a saying. In truth, it is not merely an American saying; it is universal: 'Words are no substitute for action.' If the Americans do not believe the words coming from your friends, then action is necessary, the type of action for which no one is better suited than you.

"Comrade Stalin has requested that you be personally involved, Gromov."

"I am, of course, ready to do whatever is necessary, Comrade Beria."

"If the Americans and British are not motivated by words, then we must motivate them by action. We direct you to go to Tehran and stage an attempted assassination of Comrade Stalin, Churchill, and Roosevelt."

Gromov could feel his heart beating forcefully against his sternum. Beria could see Gromov's normally implacable expression betray something resembling a mixture of astonishment and eagerness.

"An attempted assassination," Gromov repeated. "Not an actual assassination."

Beria flashed his macabre smile. "Correct. Obviously, none of the three can be harmed in the slightest. But it must be obvious to all that the Germans attempted to kill all three. Comrade Stalin, of course, will know every detail of the attempt but will feign incredulity. The other two must be put into fear for their very existence."

Gromov hoped that his facial expression wasn't reflecting his alarm. He initially began processing potential strategies and tactics to execute the assignment. But the enormity of the plan's ramifications rendered him nearly catatonic.

Precisely how to execute the assignment was less important than the consequences if he were to make a mistake. As the previous world conflict had shown, an attempt, however staged, on one world leader was cause for war. If the United States or Britain learned that the Soviet Union had staged an assassination attempt, even a fake one, on their respective heads of state, the consequences would be incalculable. And that was presuming no one got *hurt*. If Gromov made

the slightest mistake and someone in Churchill's or Roosevelt's entourage was hurt, alliances could be shattered that would affect the
outcome of the war.

Despite his eagerness, Gromov immediately concluded that the
plan was too risky. More accurately, it was idiotic, bordering on in-
sane. Yet Stalin and Beria were behind it. Gromov knew he could
never suggest that the plan, such as it was, might not be the smart-
est course of action. Although excited to be chosen, he felt trapped.
He had to execute Stalin and Beria's command and do so perfectly
or suffer the fate of anyone who questioned two of the world's three
greatest tyrants.

Gromov's thoughts were rattled by Beria's voice.

"You have misgivings, Gromov."

Beria had read his face. Gromov cleared his mind before answer-
ing. "Not at all, Comrade Beria. I am simply considering the opportunities and methods to execute the assignment."

Beria nodded understandingly. "Comrade Stalin and I do not
issue the command without a full and deep appreciation of its in-
herent risks. The decision was made after due deliberation and con-
sideration of all the plausible alternatives.

"Obviously, you must take extraordinary care not to harm any
of the three, particularly Comrade Stalin. Even the slightest injury
would have historic implications . . ."

The understatement of the millennium, Gromov thought.

"We have already begun preparing the groundwork," Beria explained further. "We have spread unspecific whispers of a Nazi
attempt to gather intelligence at the Tehran conference. We will
elevate the whispers to rumbles at the appropriate time to increase
Allied anxiety, interspersing kinetic activity closer to the actual

conference . . ." Beria grinned confidently. "We are unparalleled at causing random chaos.

"There will, of course, be the inevitable photo opportunity involving the three leaders—indeed, they will insist on it. That may be the opportune time to stage the attempt, but you may use your discretion as to precisely when, where, and how you do so, provided it is done in a way that makes clear it was the Germans who did it."

Beria paused to permit Gromov to absorb what he'd heard and to pose questions. When none came, he kept going. "You will not travel to Tehran with the official Soviet delegation, of course. You will go before everyone else arrives, except for several NKVD and SMERSH personnel, who are in Tehran already or soon will be. You will be provided with contact information so they may provide whatever assistance you may need. Of course, they are highly trained and understand the vital importance of there being nothing that can implicate the Soviet Union."

The mention of assistance eased Gromov's anxiety only slightly, but apparently enough that it showed on his face. Beria leaned back in his chair.

"Of course, I need not express our full appreciation for the crucial task we've assigned to you. Understand that you will have whatever support in terms of personnel, equipment, and authority that you need to execute this operation. We have anticipated all of the operational problems you are likely to encounter and have made provisions for them. Nonetheless, you know better than most that such plans and provisions have a tendency to dissolve upon contact with . . ." Beria paused and grinned. "Well, in this case, with our *allies*. Neither need I recite the potential for cataclysmic consequences if even the smallest detail of the operation misfires."

Gromov did not need the assistance of the NKVD or SMERSH, who, he feared, might even be a hinderance. He sat utterly still and consciously disciplined himself to project a confident, competent bearing. He was determined not to give Beria the slightest sense that he had any reservations about the plan.

"The attempt on their lives," Beria concluded, "will prompt outrage, not merely from Churchill and Roosevelt—and, Stalin, of course—but from the entire populations of the United States, Great Britain, and the world. Even if they were not otherwise inclined, the leaders of those nations will be compelled to, at minimum, open a Western Front against Hitler."

Still not completely convinced, Gromov gave a sage nod of agreement. Regardless of its wisdom or lack thereof, if this was Stalin's plan, Gromov was determined to be the one to execute it. Albeit with some amount of trepidation.

"To be certain, Comrade Beria, are the targets to be wounded?"

"That must at all costs be avoided," Beria replied. "You are more familiar with these things than I, of course, but it strikes me as extremely perilous to even attempt a wounding. A misjudgment of a few millimeters, an unexpected movement of the target, could turn an intended wounding into an unintentional kill.

"Members of the entourage are another matter entirely. It strikes me that if one or more members of the entourage was grievously wounded or killed, that would obviously signal that the true targets were one or more of the Big Three, and that would produce our desired result . . . Outrage that causes Britain and America to attack Germany from the west."

"Do you have a preferred method of kill? Rifle, handgun . . ."

Beria shook his head. "The only preferences are effectiveness and absolutely nothing traceable to the Soviet Union. Use whatever yields the desired result. Rifle, handgun, sharp or blunt instruments. Something that makes plain it is an attempted assassination by the enemy, the Germans. The more dramatic, it seems to me, the better. But I fully grasp that you must sometimes work with whatever options providence makes available."

"A rifle probably is optimal," Gromov said. "But it is best to plan with at least one option. A handgun or knife, of course, vastly increases the probability of capture . . ." Gromov paused, not wanting to even remotely suggest the slightest uncertainty or reluctance to perform the assignment.

"Comrade Stalin and I appreciate the magnitude of the risks involved in the assignment, Colonel Gromov. Risky to the continued alliance between the Soviet Union, Great Britain, and America; risky to the effort to defeat Germany; and risky to you and those who assist you. It is much to bear. That is why among the millions of patriots in the Red Army Stalin and I chose you. Comrade Stalin trusts you. After all, you have performed magnificently under the most difficult circumstances. You have never failed. On the contrary, you have a habit of surpassing expectations. Expectations that to most would seem unreasonable, if not impossible."

Gromov noted Beria's reference to "Colonel," although he'd yet to be officially promoted. Gromov was not so naïve as to think that Beria's flattery was not purposeful, but it remained gratifying nonetheless. "Is there anything else you need me to do?" he asked.

"In fact, there is. We have information that the two Americans you outmaneuvered to acquire the Kapsky formulae will be present in Tehran. Despite your having prevailed over them, they remain a concern," Beria noted.

There was a barely audible knock on the door—two raps—and Beria's sternly efficient aide cracked open the door.

"Excuse me, Comrade. Colonel Belyanov's aide has been waiting with the cables you requested."

"Comrade Novikov." Beria waved his hand. "Show him in." Beria turned to Gromov and smiled the macabre smile. "Colonel Gromov, children will read epics about you one day. Good luck."

CHAPTER 32

Immediately upon Skorzeny's arrival, the Oberstleutnant rapped on Canaris's door and opened it without waiting for an answer, ushering Skorzeny inside. Canaris gestured for Skorzeny to sit and immediately began speaking.

"The NKVD will stage an assassination attempt upon the Allied leaders in Tehran, the purpose of which is to spur Roosevelt and Churchill to immediately open a Western European Front against the Wehrmacht, which, obviously, would pose a significant problem for us."

Skorzeny sat back, astonished. "The NKVD would assassinate Churchill and Roosevelt? Has Stalin gone crazy?"

Canaris held up his hand, signaling Skorzeny to be patient. "Perhaps. Or perhaps crazy like a fox. It will be an 'attempt,' not a successful assassination. It will be a charade to galvanize the Western powers to attack our western flanks and relieve pressure on the Red Army to the east.

"Given the current situation with the Red Army's bridgeheads on the Dnieper and Vatutin's drive against Kiev, an attack from the west would be, to say the least, problematic for us."

"To say the least," Skorzeny noted.

"We assess that establishment of a Western Front is inevitable if not imminent," Canaris said. "But there is a vast strategic difference between such a front being established now as opposed to a year from now, the latter of which is a more probable American and British timetable. Among other things, the latter timetable would provide sufficient time for Kluge, Manstein, and Model to regroup and reestablish the advanced positions we held prior to the Donbas offensive, thereby freeing up manpower and provisions for our forces in France.

"The Führer has concluded that since the Russian assassination charade will, indeed, advance the timetable for establishing a Western Front, the charade should be made into a *reality*."

Skorzeny blinked several times. Canaris remained silent to allow Skorzeny to absorb what he had just heard. Skorzeny said nothing.

"The Führer," Canaris continued, "believes that a decapitation strike will significantly disrupt the Allied war effort and throw them into chaos, particularly in the Soviet Union, where there likely will be murderous battles among the leadership to succeed Stalin."

Skorzeny was tempted to ask, *But at what cost?*

"The Führer also remains concerned that the Allies will make use of strategically critical information, documents, and expertise acquired from a professor a short time ago." Canaris noted that Skorzeny's eyebrows rose. "You are familiar with this matter?"

"No, Herr Admiral. I had heard that Standartenführer Konrad Maurer was in search of certain documents. That is all."

Canaris appeared perturbed. No one outside a small circle within the Abwehr was supposed to know of Maurer's search for documents of any kind. Security and secrecy within the Abwehr were notoriously tight. The fact that Skorzeny was even tangentially aware that Maurer was searching for documents alarmed and angered Canaris.

"Did you know Standartenführer Maurer?" Canaris asked.

"By reputation only. I understand he was killed in action recently."

"He was," Canaris acknowledged. "He was killed in the process of seeking certain information for which the Americans, British, and Soviets were also searching. The information was of extreme importance to the war effort and for the postwar geopolitical balance. Each power sent their best to acquire such information. The Soviets sent an NKVD major, Taras Gromov. The British, Sergeant Conor McDermott. The Americans sent a Major Richard Canidy and Lieutenant Eric Fulmar. The Americans and British initially acquired the documents as well as the creator of said documents. But in the end, Major Gromov prevailed on behalf of the Soviets."

Skorzeny tilted his head. "Forgive me, Herr Admiral. I am somewhat confused. The Americans, British, and Soviets are allies. How is it that Gromov 'prevailed' over his allies?"

"They are allies in *this* war effort, Obersturmbannführer Skorzeny. But at some point the war will end and the world may look quite different. That, however, is not of present concern. What *is* our concern is that, quite serendipitously, our information is that Canidy, Fulmar, and Gromov all will be in Tehran. Each has been, is, and will be a problem. They undoubtedly will be an impediment to executing the Führer's orders in Tehran."

Skorzeny understood. "They are to be eliminated."

Canaris discerned the conflicted expression on Skorzeny's face as if he were struggling not to say something. "You have a question, Skorzeny? A statement?"

"Respectfully, Herr Admiral. It need not be said that I will carry out any order I am given, including this one . . ."

"But?"

"This operation consists of a series of assassinations. I am a soldier, not an assassin. I respectfully suggest this task is best suited for a sniper, someone with a demonstrated record for efficiency and accuracy. It may, therefore, be better to have someone such as Matthäus Hetzenauer or Josef Allerberger execute this task." Skorzeny held up his hands. "For efficiency and certainty."

Canaris smiled appreciatively as he rose from his desk and strode to the credenza along the wall to his right. He glanced at the wall clock on the other side of his office as if to confirm that it was now permissible to have a drink. He gestured toward a bottle of Black Forest Rothaus that sat in the middle of an array of whiskies. Skorzeny shook his head. Canaris poured himself a splash, downed it, and exhaled.

"The Führer insists it be you, Skorzeny. And, frankly, who can blame him? You are undefeated. You have executed magnificent operations that have awed even our enemies. It makes sense, does it not?"

Skorzeny chose his words carefully. He had heard whispers from Schmidt and others that Canaris was sometimes at odds with the Führer's agenda. But it was wise not to say things that might be misconstrued. "I am eager to carry out the Führer's directives. I am simply pointing out that there are individuals with skills better suited for the success of this operation. And who are not so easily recognizable."

Canaris poured another splash of whisky and presented it to Skorzeny, who nodded appreciatively but did not drink it. "Reasonable points, Skorzeny. I do not disagree. But I repeat, the Führer insists it be *you.*"

Canaris turned and walked back to his chair. As he did so, Skorzeny unobtrusively placed the glass of whisky on the floor next to his chair. "All is at your disposal," Canaris said. "We have asked for volunteers to assist you from a group of Brandenburgers. The best dozen. They do not yet know of the objective, but they leapt at the chance to assist you; I suspect they would march naked and unarmed into Stalingrad in the middle of winter for the opportunity to assist Skorzeny. But regardless, the Führer insists it must be you and he wishes to tell you this directly."

"Then clearly it shall be me," Skorzeny conceded.

"There are only a handful of individuals who know about the operation," Canaris said. "Obviously, Wolfgang Schmidt, who will supply all of your equipment." A look of disdain grew on Canaris's face. "The Führer also informed Himmler, who insists that McDermott and Canidy be eliminated before anyone else so that they do not, once again, compromise the outcome . . ."

Skorzeny caught himself rolling his eyes.

". . . and who further insists that Canidy and McDermott be eliminated no later than November 28."

"Why by that date, Herr Admiral?"

Canaris tried unsuccessfully to mask his disdain for the reason.

"Maurer was a favorite of Himmler's. Our information is that Major Canidy is the one who killed Maurer. November 28 is Maurer's birthday." Canaris sighed. "The official, and entirely logical, reason is that elimination of Canidy and McDermott by that date decreases the probability that they will thwart or interfere with the assassination of Stalin, Churchill, and Roosevelt."

Canaris said uncomfortably, "Do you have any other questions, Obersturmbannführer Skorzeny?"

"I do not."

"Very good. Wolfgang Schmidt will provide all the equipment that you and whomever you select to assist you will need. Good luck, Obersturmbannführer Skorzeny."

CHAPTER 33

The jeep careened down the slope toward the cabin, adjacent to which Canidy and Fulmar were once again performing push-ups under McDermott's supervision. The vehicle stopped ten meters from the pair. The driver, a corporal, remained in his seat as the passenger, a short, prematurely balding man in his thirties wearing a charcoal gray tweed suit coat and an affable expression got out and ambled toward the OSS agents with his right hand extended.

"Blake Wilson," the short man said, shaking first Canidy's hand and then Fulmar's. "Colonel Donovan sent me to brief you on your upcoming operation."

"I'm Canidy. He's Fulmar. And the sadist over there reeking of Glenfiddich and bannock is Sergeant Conor McDermott."

Wilson pointed to the cabin. "Can we go inside?"

"We can," Canidy said. "But perspiration and confined quarters don't make for optimal briefing conditions. Why don't we stay out here?"

"Lip-readers," Wilson replied.

Canidy's eyebrows arched theatrically. "Are you serious? Lip-readers?

Don't get me wrong. I just met you and you appear to be a fine man, but lip-readers?"

Wilson chuckled. "Not my idea. Colonel Donovan, or perhaps I should say General Donovan, insists that nothing be communicated in the open. He's a bit paranoid right now."

"He's a lot intimidating, too. If Wild Bill says we need to be on the lookout for lip-readers, I'll be on the lookout for lip-readers," Canidy said. "And just to be very clear: I'm not being sarcastic. I'm not second-guessing him. And by the way, he may be a general, but he prefers to be called 'Colonel.'"

Wilson grinned. "I wouldn't have said a thing, Major."

"Good," Canidy said, "because we're already in the doghouse. If just one wisecrack gets back to him, we're sunk."

Wilson looked puzzled. "That's not what I hear—you two being in the doghouse, that is. From everything I gather, General—Colonel—Donovan thinks you two are the best for the job."

Canidy laughed. "Maybe. I suppose it depends on the job. Mine-sweeper? I can see that."

Wilson shrugged. "Anyway, word is that you two are Donovan's favorites and he said you are perfect for this operation."

"You must be new to the Office. Donovan doesn't think any-one's perfect for anything. He's stuck with us and trying to make the best of things." Canidy began walking toward the cabin. "Come on. Let's get out of sight of the prying eyes of enemy lip-readers so you can tell us what the hell's in store for us."

Canidy paused and jabbed his right thumb in McDermott's di-rection. "What about him. Is he cleared?"

Wilson nodded. "Menzies and Donovan have discussed this. Mc-Dermott likely will be part of what this is about."

The four men walked to the cabin and arrayed themselves around the kitchen table, where McDermott's dish of Glenfiddich and crumbs of bannock sat. Wilson inspected the bowl but said nothing.

Canidy slapped the tabletop. "Well, what do you have for us?"

Wilson leaned forward in his chair. "As you've undoubtedly heard, the President is going to Tehran in a few weeks to meet with Churchill and Stalin. Naturally, we expect almost every spy in the world to be there also. There's no doubt the Soviets will have, literally, hundreds. We have to anticipate the Germans will have plenty of spies, too. Or at the very least, they'll try to have spies there.

"The NKVD has a young agent by the name of Vartanian who's been in Iran for quite some time. Apparently, they think very highly of him. He's told his superiors that he and his men have identified over one hundred Nazi Abwehr personnel in Tehran and in the surrounding region. In addition, he supposedly told his bosses that dozens of German commandos have parachuted into the Iranian desert. They're called Brandenburgers. Supposedly very dangerous. Real killers."

Canidy glanced at Fulmar, who rolled his eyes and said, "You're not telling us anything we don't know, Wilson. We're pretty sure we've already been introduced to those guys. More than once."

"They go behind Allied lines," Wilson continued. "Sabotage. Assassinations. That sort of thing. The Soviet guy says the Brandenburgers are there to prepare the environment for a strike on the Big Three by an even more elite team dispatched personally by Hitler himself."

McDermott grunted. "Doesn't really matter how elite they may be. I wager the Soviets, Yanks, and Brits will all have our own elite troops crawling all over that place. And regular army, too. Thousands, no doubt. Unless they plan to send the combined firepower of Rommel, Guderian, and Manstein to Iran, they're not going to get within fifty kilometers of that meeting."

"I was thinking the same thing when all this was explained to me," Wilson confessed. "But apparently the big brains in OSS think that it's at least a possibility."

"Let's face it," Canidy said. "We have to consider the possibility. Anyone gets any information that there's going to be an attempt on the President's life—*and* Churchill's *and* Stalin's—by the Germans, you've got to act like it's a given." He shrugged. "So what's our role, Wilson? If Rommel does show up with hundreds of Panzers, what the hell are we supposed to do?"

"I think our people don't believe a word of what the Soviets are saying. I could tell they were skeptical if not dismissive. But as you said, they really don't have any choice." Wilson shrugged and shook his head. "Your job, however, isn't to protect the President or anyone else. What you're supposed to do is keep your eyes and ears open. Donovan says every spy in the Northern Hemisphere is going to be at this party and he wants you two to keep an eye on the players."

Wilson fell silent, allowing the three to contemplate the mission. Canidy glanced at Fulmar, then McDermott, to gauge their reaction. He thought, if he was reading them accurately, that they were intrigued by the assignment.

"What are you looking at?" Fulmar asked. "This isn't optional. Of course we go wherever Donovan sends us." He pointed at McDermott. "What about this guy? Does he stay here stuffing his gullet with alcohol-soaked bannock or does he go, too?"

"I haven't gotten any specific instructions about Sergeant McDermott," Wilson replied. "I do know that Donovan has been coordinating with Commander Fleming on this matter and that McDermott will probably be part of this, so he's cleared to listen, at least, to our conversation."

"I suspect if I were going to continue babysitting these two I'd have gotten my orders by now," McDermott said.

"You likely will," Wilson opined. "When I've been assigned to conduct briefings in the past, it's always on close hold—only our folks.

"When it's time, you'll be flown into Iran. Our folks have confirmed NKVD information that German troops have parachuted into the desert west of Tehran. The speculation is that they're waiting there for a second force—likely more Brandenburgers—before making their way to Tehran for the meeting. The Office says it's best for you to shadow that contingent into Tehran and monitor them while they are there."

"Sounds too passive to be a Wild Bill plan," Fulmar said.

Canidy looked at Fulmar and shook his head. "Actually, it's not. It's pretty smart. Donovan wants to make sure we don't lose track of their forces. If we go into Tehran and wait for them, we won't know who's who or who's where. They could splinter off into a number of different teams, approach from several directions." He turned back to Wilson. "But, at the same time, even if that smiling Scotsman over there joins us, we're still too small to keep on top of multiple groups."

Wilson looked amused. "You know better than I do that Donovan—and Eisenhower—are going to have more agents and troops there. But you're supposed to be the freelancers."

Canidy, Fulmar, and McDermott looked at one another, each with eyebrows raised quizzically, to see if any of them had any further questions.

"When do we leave?" Canidy asked.

"The Brits sent a quartermaster over to the airfield. He's loading up your supplies and equipment. Not much from what I can tell. As soon as he's done, you'll be ready to go." Wilson snapped his fingers. "There's a satchel for you up there that will be brought down. Donovan made sure everyone who touches it—and that's limited to just the sergeant and me—signs off on its custody and whereabouts at all times. You're supposed to know what to do with it when you get it."

As Canidy descended the slope toward the dock, Kristin Thorisdottir emerged from the galley below and stood imperiously on the deck, hands on hips, as if expecting him. The weak rays of sun that managed to penetrate the light mist wafting across the coastline created a halo effect as they radiated off her white blond hair.

"How did you know I was coming?" Canidy asked, genuinely curious.

"I didn't," Kristin replied. "Just a coincidence."

Nothing's a coincidence with these two, Canidy thought. As he stepped onto the boat deck, Canidy took advantage of her near sightlessness to linger over her form a bit longer than he otherwise would have. Six feet tall, a figure lithe yet seemingly sculpted by an intense voluptuary.

Canidy placed the satchel of money at Kristin's feet.

"Thank you, Major Canidy."

"One hundred thousand American dollars," Canidy said.

"Yes, I believe you."

"Maybe you'd like to have Katla verify it?"

"No need, Major Canidy. Americans are always trustworthy. Unlike some."

"Even so . . ."

Kristin smiled. Canidy thought it appeared remarkably genuine. "You do not want us to leave," she said flatly.

Canidy struggled to say something clever and dismissive, something that would deprive her of the upper hand. Frustrated, the best he could do was "You continue to have an unwarranted opinion of yourself."

Kristin laughed. It sounded musical. "What is it Americans say? *Nice try?*"

Canidy became irritated. Not so much with Kristin, he realized, but with himself. Despite everything, she seemed to maintain the upper hand.

Katla appeared from below. She smiled and nodded at Canidy as she stood next to Kristin, who pointed at the satchel. She knelt and inspected the contents, but did not count the currency. "It appears to be the agreed sum," she said. "Thank you, Major Canidy."

"Major Canidy does not wish us to leave," Kristin told Katla.

"I see."

Canidy said evenly, "The transaction is complete, ladies. No need to stick around. You're free to go back to Iceland or Greenland or wherever it is that spawned you two."

Kristin smiled. Electric. She turned to Katla. "Do you see what I mean?"

"He does not want *you* to leave," Katla responded as she picked up the satchel and proceeded belowdecks.

"Goodbye, Major Canidy," she called over her shoulder. "You are a fine soldier and it was a privilege to meet you."

Canidy's face remained expressionless even as he ground his molars together. Kristin shook her head and stepped toward Canidy, placing her left hand on his right shoulder. Again, electric.

"Do not mistake Katla. She has always misunderstood American tone and idiom, so when she speaks it may sound to you as if it is sarcastic or taunting or belittling . . ."

"She is fortunate . . ."

". . . that she is a woman. Indeed. Someone such as yourself would not think to harm her."

"Wrong. I certainly would."

Kristin drew a step closer and kissed him on his right cheek, withdrew slightly, and brushed her lips against his. "For the reason I noted, I do not regret taking the Kapsky notebook . . ."

"Of course. Doing so made you wealthy," Canidy said.

"I sincerely regret the manner in which it was done and from whom it was taken. But as I said, it remained in Allied hands."

"Allies don't steal from one another . . ."

"Major Canidy, you are more experienced in these matters than I, so you know better than I that is untrue."

"Time for you to leave," Canidy said.

Kristin nodded. "You do not want me to leave. I suspect, however, that you have somewhere to go." She took a step back. "We will be on our way. But I expect this war to be a long one, still. And we shall see each other again." She turned and followed Katla belowdecks.

Canidy watched her disappear. He had a feeling she was right.

CHAPTER 34

Obersturmbannführer Otto Skorzeny had an uncommonly high threshold for fear and anxiety. It was one of the reasons he had successfully completed daring missions few others would contemplate. But he understood that he was best when in action. Adrenaline suppressed fear. Indeed, it exhilarated him, propelled him to take actions few if any dared to undertake. Common lore held that he did so with a smile, and in many cases the lore was true.

A confined encounter with the Führer, however, was another matter. He was mercurial and increasingly erratic, especially upon receiving less-than-spectacular news. And Skorzeny had learned that matters were becoming increasingly problematic to the east. Melitopol was expected to fall any moment after some of the most fierce fighting of the war. The Soviets were also said to be on the verge of executing a pincer movement that could encircle more than one million German troops in the Dnieper bend in the Crimea. The Red Army had severed the rail lines between Dnipropetrovsk and Krivoi Rog, leaving only one route of retreat. Skorzeny knew the situation was grave even without reading the intelligence reports. The German International Information Bureau had reported this morning that German forces had sieged Stampalia, liberating huge numbers of German prisoners. Skorzeny had long since understood that such propaganda nearly always masked an impending setback for the Wehrmacht. The Führer would, accordingly, be in a sour mood. There was little on this Earth, Skorzeny believed, more foreboding than that.

Skorzeny was sitting on the wooden bench outside the office contemplating the unfamiliar feeling of apprehension, when he heard the staccato click of boots on the marble floor. He looked up to see SS Brigadeführer Walter Schellenberg, one of the most powerful foreign intelligence officers in the Sicherheitsdienst, approaching rapidly. He had a broad grin on his face.

Skorzeny rose and saluted. Schellenberg grasped Skorzeny by both arms and shook him. "The Legend of Gran Sasso!" Schellenberg said excitedly. "It is good to see you again!" He lowered his voice conspiratorially. "The Führer, I should warn you, believes you to be invincible, indestructible. And why shouldn't he? The entire Reich believes it to be so."

Skorzeny's own smile was genuine. He had few reservations about Schellenberg's sincerity and none about his competency. He was exceptionally bright, having repeatedly and almost unfailingly outmaneuvered his British counterparts in counterintelligence. He had an open, almost childlike face, but a precise, exacting mind that some maintained rivaled that of the Genius, with whom the ambitious Schellenberg was good friends.

Skorzeny, towering over Schellenberg, took a step back and grinned. "You look well," he said. "The war seems to have no effect on you."

"We've compiled numerous victories," Schellenberg said. "We are on the cusp of legend." He laughed. "Why wouldn't I look well?"

Skorzeny understood this to be mere puffery. Schellenberg knew better than Skorzeny the details of the Dnieper encirclement. The Führer preferred only good news. He grudgingly tolerated stalemates. He punished failures.

"The Führer speaks of you endlessly. 'If we had a hundred Skorzenys the Reich would be unstoppable!'"

Skorzeny understood this to be not merely hyperbole but fiction, but nodded along nonetheless. Schellenberg, however, discerned Skorzeny's skepticism. "Truthfully, Otto, the Führer confides you are among our very best, if not *the* very best. Your record is the stuff of Homeric poems."

Skorzeny threw his head back and laughed. Schellenberg hesitated a moment, then joined Skorzeny.

"Sincerely," Schellenberg insisted between gasps of air. "Every nation needs heroes in time of war. You are that hero and there is no reason to be reserved about it. Come, he awaits." Schellenberg paused. "But first be aware that Goebbels prefers you not go on the assignment to be discussed. You are too valuable. He proposed Ernst Steiger perform the assignment instead." Schellenberg lowered his voice. "Steiger is a killer, vicious. He would kill for pleasure if there was not a war. He has quite an impressive record. But he is expendable. He is not Skorzeny."

The two strode toward the mammoth double doors to the Führer's chambers. Skorzeny, however heroic and indomitable, felt his chest and throat constrict slightly.

The anteroom to Adolf Hitler's chambers was occupied by several individuals, mostly young, efficient, attractive females. Skorzeny and Schellenberg, however, were immediately confronted by an imperious matron, who radiated an almost malevolent efficiency.

"What is your purpose?" she demanded.

Schellenberg grinned. "Frau Grunau, you are well aware of why we are here. You are well aware of the identity of the individual standing to my right. Now, kindly inform the Führer of our presence and immediately upon doing so get your prodigious hindquarters out of our way."

Skorzeny suppressed a chuckle as Frau Grunau's imperial expression wilted into compliance. Moments later, Skorzeny found himself face-to-face with Adolf Hitler.

Schellenberg and Skorzeny saluted. Hitler grasped Skorzeny's shoulders with both hands and beamed up at him with delight. "Obersturmbannführer Skorzeny! It is my privilege to meet you. The Fatherland is proud of your accomplishments."

Skorzeny, a bit embarrassed by the embrace, simply smiled.

Hitler waved the pair toward the chairs surrounding a low table before his desk. Hitler took the chair slightly elevated above the rest. "Admiral Canaris has provided the particulars to you. I do not have anything of real substance to add, other than to stress that at no time are you to acknowledge that the mission ever took place. At no time are you to acknowledge that there was a plan even remotely similar to this mission. And at no time are you to acknowledge that anything resembling this mission was ever discussed. Do you understand, Obersturmbannführer Skorzeny?"

Skorzeny replied swiftly. "I do, Mein Führer."

Hitler, in turn, nodded confirmation. "These injunctions apply now, during, and *after* the war. Whether the mission is successful or unsuccessful. Until death. Clear?"

Both Skorzeny and Schellenberg dipped their heads in acknowledgment.

Hitler tilted his chin upward. "If, at any time, inquiry is made concerning these matters, you are to respond that rumors of any such plan are just that: rumors, fiction without any basis in fact. Thousands of false stories spread in time of war. This is one of them. Understood?"

Once again, Skorzeny and Schellenberg nodded. Hitler stood suddenly. Both Schellenberg and Skorzeny followed suit. Hitler strode behind his chair, placed his hands on top of the backrest, and stood imperiously, ramrod straight. "Victory in the east is imminent. The Russians cannot match the quality of our men and equipment. They shall collapse before winter. Kesselring will prevail on a similar timetable. The Americans and British in Italy had good initial fortune. But once again, the quality of our forces is reasserting itself."

Skorzeny and Schellenberg stood silently at attention, their faces betraying no reaction whatsoever. Skorzeny had heard of the Führer's exaggerated assessments of strategic conditions and Schellenberg had been present for many of them. It was common knowledge that the Führer would erupt in rage if someone presented a less-than-glowing assessment of operational conditions or prospects. As a result, those briefing him increasingly provided glowing battlefield assessments and predictions of victory untethered to reality.

Hitler continued. "I am confident, of course, that you will successfully complete the assignment, as you have successfully completed all of your assignments, Skorzeny. But it is inevitable that at some point something out of your control will intervene. In case of such possibility—if you were captured, for instance—the reason for your presence in Iran is simple espionage, understood?"

Skorzeny answered dutifully. "Understood, Mein Führer."

"Weeks, months, or years from now, you may be asked about this matter. Historians may even interview you as you lie on your deathbed. You are to respond, without exception, that any story involving an alleged plan to assassinate Stalin, Churchill, and Roosevelt is fantastical, an attempt to enhance the reputations of those three. Clear?"

Skorzeny and Schellenberg responded affirmatively. Hitler smiled, his hands rapidly squeezing and releasing the backrest as his eyes rapidly darted between Skorzeny and Schellenberg. "Very good."

There was a light rap at the door. Hitler removed his hands from the backrest, clasped them behind his back, and raised his chin. "Come."

The door cracked open partially to reveal Frau Grunau's face. "Goebbels for twelve thirty, Mein Führer."

Hitler acknowledged the announcement and Frau Grunau disappeared.

"Everything is understood, then?"

Skorzeny and Schellenberg saluted affirmation in unison.

Hitler looked at them both. "When you return, Obersturmbannführer Skorzeny, we shall have a proper celebration and you will regale us with the details of your latest triumph." Hitler turned abruptly and faced the window behind him, standing with his hands clasped behind his back and chin raised. Schellenberg and Skorzeny obeyed the signal to leave.

The two proceeded out of the suite and into the cavernous hallway, where both stopped and stared at each other. Skorzeny opened his mouth, but no words emerged.

Schellenberg shook his head sharply once and whispered, "Say not one word."

CHAPTER 35

Strong headwinds buffeted the Douglas Air Transport Command C-54, its four Twin Wasp radial engines steady as it churned over the northeast Mediterranean toward the Dasht-e Kavir.

The engine on the right wing shuddered briefly. Canidy and Fulmar took it in stride. McDermott and Wilson, however, looked at once terrified and nauseous. While briefing them in Gotland, Wilson had told the other three that they'd be flying in a massive Boeing C-75 with four 900-horsepower Wright Cyclone engines, but the plane hadn't arrived in Gotland in time. Canidy had daydreamed about piloting the craft, checking the altimeter readings just as they approached the perimeter to the landing strip, wheels of the fixed main gear feathered gently down followed by the tail wheel, producing a wispy cloud as it landed. But he was disappointed upon seeing the C-54, an adequate but inferior craft.

Canidy clapped Wilson on the back. "You know, you didn't have to accompany us on the flight, although I admit that I'm impressed."

Wilson, looking as if were he to open his mouth vomit would precede any words, nodded acknowledgment. Donovan hadn't insisted that Wilson take the flight, only that Canidy, Fulmar, and McDermott be fully briefed before embarking on the operation. He left it to Wilson to decide whether he should accompany the trio on the journey to the Iranian desert. Wilson was determined to leave no stone unturned in his mission briefing and to answer any questions the team might have. More accurately, he was determined that any and all reports to Donovan of his performance would reflect nothing but his thoroughness, industry, diligence, and courage.

Canidy withdrew a flat silver flask from his tunic and extended it to Wilson, who declined with a shake of his head. Canidy gave the flask to Fulmar, then McDermott, each of whom took a taste of Dewar's before Canidy did the same.

Wilson tried to keep his left wrist steady as he examined his Hamilton wristwatch. "We'll be landing in a while—fairly soon. Your contact should be there with transport." He examined the watch once again, reconciling the time zones in his head. "In fact, he's probably there already. It will be either Lieutenant Ian Putnam or Sergeant Archibald Lewis. Both are in the region and have been for quite some time, but it will most likely be Lewis. He knows the area and knows the people. If you need anything—weapons, communications, food, medical—any supplies whatsoever, he'll make sure you have them. Also, don't be afraid to ask for instructions in case things go sideways."

Canidy smiled wryly. "Hell, I'm *certain* things will go sideways. Donovan sent us on this assignment as punishment for the Kapsky deal. He probably hopes that we'll get stuck in the desert and won't come back."

Wilson laughed. "Hey, I wasn't kidding. If Donovan thinks you're screwups, then you're the best screwups he's got. Besides, even though he's famous for keeping everything 'need to know,' somehow word is that your delightful presence was requested by FDR himself."

"Right."

"I'm serious. In some meeting between FDR and Donovan, FDR heard about some of your exploits and insisted you two be in Tehran. Apparently, he thinks you're not just effective but colorful, or something."

Candidy smirked dismissively. "The President doesn't think we're colorful. The President doesn't think about us period."

Wilson shrugged. "Suit yourself. I'm just telling you what I hear."

The plane shook, dipped, and rose, encountering several minutes of turbulence that threw Wilson against the bulkhead and made everyone slightly nauseous. Candidy leaned forward to look out the window. They were now over land.

"How much longer?"

"Not long," Wilson replied. "Assuming your contact is there when we land, it will take twelve, thirteen hours to get to the outskirts of the city."

"Do you expect we'll encounter any hostiles when we land?"

Wilson's face showed his concern. "Unknown. Germans are still supposed to be around, but it's a really big country. The odds would be like two mosquitoes colliding in the Grand Canyon."

Fulmar grunted. "So, yes."

"I can tell you this much. Our flight crew says they've been told to spend no more than five minutes on the ground from touchdown to takeoff."

"You'd think Professor Moriarty and the boys in R and D would have come up with something by now to make us undetectable," Fulmar said.

"I'm sure they have," Canidy replied. "But Donovan wants to make this as painful as possible for us."

Iranian Desert

1510, 24 November 1943

A short time later the plane began a final descent into strong headwinds and angled toward a makeshift runway in the Dasht-e Kavir. Canidy, Fulmar, McDermott, and Wilson all gripped their respective seats to stabilize themselves. Once the plane taxied to a halt, Wilson gave the trio a good-luck wave as they disembarked and in less than two minutes the plane was speeding eastward on the runway toward a somewhat ponderous ascent. As the three watched the plane climb into the wispy clouds, they were startled by the sound of the derelict engine of a Ford Mercury station wagon that had somehow approached from their rear without detection.

Out of the corner of his mouth, Canidy asked the other two, "Putnam or Lewis? I wager it's Sergeant Archibald Lewis."

"Lieutenant Ian Putnam," Fulmar said.

"Same," agreed McDermott.

The derelict car came to a halt in a swirl of dust a dozen feet from the three. A tall, slim redheaded man in civilian khakis jumped out, saluted, and said, "Sergeant Archibald Lewis. Everyone here calls me 'Archie.'" Lewis pointed first to Canidy, then Fulmar, then McDermott. "By your looks, you are Canidy, Fulmar, and McDermott." Shaking their respective hands in the same order, he added, "I'm to make sure that you have a pleasant stay in the Republic of Iran."

"Good to meet you, Archie," Canidy said, hoisting his bag onto the hood of the car. "How long until we get to Tehran?"

"At least twelve to fourteen hours of driving. Four hundred and fifty kilometers. Some of it a bit rough. Most of the terrain is somewhat flat, but the environment can be a bit tricky. Mountains, lakes, and deserts, and need to watch out for the lizards, wolves, and Persian cheetahs."

"What about the Germans?" Fulmar asked. "Any of them about? We were supposed to track them to Tehran."

"They don't tend to make their presence known. You'd have better luck spotting the leopards. I expect you've been briefed on the arrival of quite a number of them. Germans, that is. By parachute. Haven't seen them personally. Couldn't locate them. Clever little devils.

"The tribesmen also warn to steer clear of the desert spirits. They have a bit of a reputation for being downright malevolent. I haven't had the distinction, as yet, of encountering any of them. But both the Afshari and the Kurds say they're fairly abundant in the Dasht-e Lut, a bit south of here." Lewis smiled. "Fortunately for us, that's to our rear. And unless the Gerries block our path somehow, we've no reason to go there."

Canidy, Fulmar, and McDermott flung their respective bags into the rear of the vehicle and climbed in, Canidy next to Lewis and McDermott and Fulmar in the rear. Lewis hit the gas and the vehicle lurched forward, its rear tires taking a moment to gain traction in the sand. Within seconds, they were traveling nearly sixty kilometers per hour over less-than-smooth terrain, Fulmar and McDermott jostling violently in the back.

"For God's sake, man!" McDermott protested. "What's the hurry? The war will still be on when we get there."

Lewis slowed appreciably, but the backseat turbulence abated only slightly. McDermott and Fulmar resigned themselves to an unpleasant journey and compressed spines.

The din of the flathead V8 engines, combined with the noise from the tires covering rough terrain, made conversation difficult. In the first hour of travel, one of them would attempt to draw attention to some facet of the passing scenery, but their speech would be strained. Gradually, they resigned themselves to sporadic observations. Each, however, remained alert to any anomalies in the surrounding countryside. Although they saw few signs of human activity or presence, intelligence stated that Germans were alleged to be in the area and it was possible, indeed likely, they were equipped with faster, more maneuverable, and far deadlier transportation than the Ford Mercury. By varying degrees, each felt a persistent low-level anxiety throughout the trip. Most of the passing terrain was flat and wide open. They could be spotted by hostiles from at least ten kilometers on either side.

The conventional wisdom was that most of the Germans and their allies had fled Iran. But anyone who had worn the uniform of their country knew that conventional wisdom was often, if not invariably, wrong. An obscure recess of Canidy's brain persistently imagined a tank shell screaming toward them from the eastern horizon. The longer they remained exposed, the more likely bad things would happen. As far as Canidy and the other occupants of the vehicle were concerned, it was not a likelihood, but a certainty.

After riding uncomfortably for more than an hour they found themselves on smoother roads, which made conversation once again a possibility. Canidy was the first to take advantage of the situation. "This is nuts. I guarantee no one else is riding hundreds of miles over the countryside toward Tehran. Everyone else is going there, whether by plane or boat, more or less direct. More proof for my thesis that Donovan is punishing us."

Lewis looked perturbed. "No way, Major Canidy. As I understand it, this is to reduce the probability you'll be spotted by our mates in either the Sicherheitsdienst or the NKVD before you get to your flat. This way, you can spy on them to your heart's content when you're in Tehran."

Fulmar shook his head vigorously, as if doing so would increase the probability that his voice would be heard over the vehicle's engine. "The purpose is to flush out the Sicherheitsdienst and the NKVD."

Canidy shrugged. "Doesn't matter what the reason. Ours is definitely not to reason why. We're expendable rooks just doing what we're told."

Lewis grinned, turning his head slightly so that he could glimpse Canidy out of the corner of his eye. "Much too fatalistic, mate. I was told that you blokes are VIPs, that you're on some special mission that's of some significance to each of your countries. Given that, they—meaning your superiors—clearly do not consider you expendable."

They rode for several more hours, Lewis chattering away amiably about life in Britain while Canidy, Fulmar, and McDermott sat glumly, watching the passing countryside. Noticing the apparent boredom of his passengers, Lewis asked, "Baseball fans?"

McDermott shook his head. Fulmar didn't respond. Canidy shrugged. "Are you?"

"I was in the States a while back. New York. I got a chance to see the immortal Babe Ruth in pinstripes in his final season. I must say, it was something of a thrill."

Canidy perked up. "You saw the Babe in Yankee Stadium? Actually got a chance to see the Babe before he hung them up?"

"Certainly did," Lewis replied cheerfully. "Had the time of my life. Smashing city, New York. Even spent some time in Times Square. Had the whole American experience."

Canidy was roused. "You can't possibly prefer New York to London, now, can you, mate? Times Square to Piccadilly? I thought you Brits think that Yanks are barbarians."

Lewis laughed uproariously.

Unimpressed and irritated, Fulmar asked, "How much farther?"

Lewis cocked his head to the side as he estimated the distance. "Approximately two hundred kilometers, I'd say. We're making good time. At this rate, barring unforeseen impediments, we should be approaching Tehran in the next few hours."

Canidy persisted. "A Brit who prefers New York to London, Times Square to Piccadilly Circus. I suppose you're going to try to convince us you prefer the Statue of Liberty to whatever that memorial statue of Disraeli is called in the Shaftesbury Memorial Fountain."

Lewis laughed again. "I can't think of anything quite as dreadful as a statue of Disraeli!"

Canidy and Lewis laughed together. Fulmar and McDermott rolled their eyes. Canidy and Lewis laughed some more. Lewis pointed to a lone copse of trees a kilometer ahead. "I'm afraid I need to spend a penny. Anyone else?"

All three passengers nodded. Lewis pulled up next to the trees and turned off the engine. Everyone got out of the vehicle, stretched, massaged stiff muscles, and looked about. There were no signs of humanity in sight, not even an abandoned edifice. Only gray-brown terrain.

"Doesn't look like we needed any cover," McDermott said. "I don't believe any human beings have ever trod this ground."

Nonetheless, each observed the ancient male ritual of selecting a tree to irrigate.

For Canidy, the next five seconds seemed to unfold glacially over five minutes. Once each had taken his station, Lewis abruptly stepped to his left, withdrew his Enfield No. 2 from its holster, and leveled it toward the back of McDermott's head. A recess of Canidy's brain registered Fulmar catching the sudden movement, but both instantly calculated that Fulmar was too poorly positioned to react in time. McDermott was utterly oblivious to the weapon being raised to his cranium by Lewis.

Canidy wasn't conscious of his right hand seizing his M1911, raising it toward Lewis, and squeezing the trigger four times. Four .45 ACP rounds slammed into Lewis's chin and upper torso, propelling him toward the hard ground, the lower half of his face sheared from his head.

McDermott, chest heaving, stared at the corpse in disbelief.

"Whoever he was, he wasn't a Brit," Canidy said matter-of-factly.

McDermott asked Canidy, "You knew?"

"I suspected."

McDermott rubbed the back of his neck as if trying to reassure himself he hadn't been shot. "What gave him up?"

"The Bambino."

McDermott was flustered by Canidy's terse response. "The Bambino is . . . what, exactly?"

"I was a little skeptical when he said he saw Babe Ruth in pinstripes in his last season. Ruth spent his final season—a partial season—with the Boston Braves."

"*That's* what tipped you off?" Fulmar asked, incredulous.

"Not really. He's a Brit. Or at least claimed to be one. He shouldn't be expected to know every historical detail about the greatest player in a distinctly American sport. But he did make me pay closer attention."

McDermott's eyes widened with realization. "Piccadilly Circus, right? The statue in the fountain."

"Would you gentlemen kindly have mercy on me and tell me how you two sleuths figured it out?" Fulmar asked.

"First was how he lost track of the Germans we were supposed to follow. Flippant about it, like it was no big deal. Then he got the Babe Ruth story wrong. That and Times Square versus Piccadilly Circus. I asked about something anyone familiar with Piccadilly Circus would know, what any Brit would know: the fountain in Piccadilly Circus. Every Brit knows the statue is Eros, not Disraeli. Even our infirm friend McDermott here—"

"Hell, I did *not* know that," McDermott confessed. "I'm glad I kept my mouth shut."

"—so I kept my eye on him," Canidy continued. "And my finger just outside the trigger guard."

"If he's not a Brit, he must be German," Fulmar said. "Without a trace of an accent."

The three looked at one another quizzically. Canidy said, "We know who he *isn't*, but who the hell *is* he? Who sent him and how did they know where we'd be? Why were we targeted?"

"Damn few people know we're here," McDermott noted. "Fewer still know why. They wouldn't target us unless they knew both. That's a very small group of people . . ."

". . . a group that is both very small and very select," Canidy added. "So select that it consists only of three or four individuals in our respective governments and the flight crew on the plane that brought us here—and *they* didn't even know our names. So, how would he even know when and where to pick us up?"

Fulmar bent down and began rifling through the dead man's pockets, turning them inside out. He then removed the man's belt and examined it for any compartments. McDermott followed suit, kneeling at the man's feet and removing his shoes and searching his shoes and socks.

"Nothing," Fulmar said.

McDermott shook his head. "Nothing."

Canidy bent over and frisked the corpse and then removed every item of clothing, inspecting every fold and pocket. He then turned the naked corpse over to search for any skin markings or pouches strapped to the torso or limbs. He found nothing.

Canidy straightened and the three men looked at one another.

"Peculiar. No identification whatsoever. Not even fake identification. Whoever sent Mr. Lewis here didn't want any evidence as to who sent him."

McDermott blinked. "So?"

Canidy pointed at McDermott. "So, who do *you* think sent him?"

"One of a select rabble of kraut-eating SOBs." McDermott shrugged. "Probably the so-called Genius, Canaris."

"Why would the Genius care that we could identify the guy as a German? It doesn't take a genius to figure we'd assume he was the enemy, meaning a German. So he wouldn't even bother to cover it up."

Fulmar answered thoughtfully. "Not necessarily. What if we had asked him for his ID?"

"That makes my point," Canidy said. "Even someone with fewer brain cells than the Genius would have anticipated that and would have supplied the guy with fake identification. *Perfect* identification. Not *no* identification. No way. Someone doesn't want our man Lewis here to be traced back to them." Canidy took a deep breath and exhaled slowly. "And it's not the Nazis."

CHAPTER 36

Skorzeny was displeased but said nothing.

They were speeding across the desert spread among five Hill-mans carrying four men apiece. Too open and visible. Reckless. He couldn't imagine Canaris had planned this. Some functionary in the Abwehr would answer for this. Americans—cowboys—would do something like this. Not any operation associated with Skorzeny.

He put his irritation out of his mind and concentrated on the operation at hand. He believed he had more than enough support personnel to execute the assignment. Nineteen Brandenburgers, eight of whom were from the group he'd encountered in the gymnasium in Berlin. In fact, the Obergefreiter driving his car was Heinz Wagner, the Brandenburger he'd defeated ignominiously back in Berlin. Skorzeny had discovered that he was a delightful person: smart, tough, cultured, and disciplined. Very much like Skorzeny, but perhaps without the flair and daring.

Skorzeny had revised the plan countless times. He calculated that the odds of success were better than he'd assessed when Canaris first told him the objective. Still, even though Skorzeny assessed the chances of success as good, he'd determined that, at best, only one or two of them would survive. A suicide mission in the truest sense of the term. But then, several of his previous missions had been estimated to have under a fifty percent chance of success—some with no survivors. Yet each had far exceeded expectations, a few in spectacular fashion.

Skorzeny and the Brandenburgers were fortunate that they hadn't yet encountered any Allied troops. Although all of his men spoke nearly flawless English and were dressed as British civilians, they appeared too obvious. They were fortunate that the expanse of territory southeast of Namak Lake was fairly desolate, populated by Bakhtiari with little affinity for Westerners. Furthermore, they had a wide view. They could see adversaries approaching from kilometers away. Far enough to take effective evasive action without drawing suspicion. Indeed, Skorzeny's biggest concern had been parachuting into Iran. Experience had taught him that was when they were most vulnerable. They'd done so at night, but depending on the atmospherics, a nighttime drop had its own hazards.

The Brandenburgers seemed more than capable. There was an aura of menace and brutality about them, but they were clever and resourceful.

They would have to be.

Skorzeny had been skeptical about the mission from the moment Canaris had outlined it approximately a month ago. Skorzeny was a peerless operator, but he was not an assassin. He would perform whatever task was ordered; he was a soldier. But this was madness, both tactically and strategically.

Despite his serious misgivings regarding the strategy behind assassinating the Big Three, the tactical aspect was foremost in his mind. Assassinating the head of state of any nation was an immensely formidable undertaking. Just assessing the means and methods necessary to gain access to the security perimeter was enormously challenging. Then actually assassinating a leader was something of a suicide mission. And even if the assassination were successful, avoiding capture in the midst of an intense manhunt would burn through several lifetimes of luck.

All that was magnified several times over by an attempt on the leaders of three great military powers during a worldwide war.

"Zwei Stunden, Obersturmbannführer Skorzeny," the driver noted. Skorzeny nodded.

The Abwehr still had considerable resources in the area, both German and Persian. A small building had been secured for Skorzeny's team near the Soviet embassy in the name of a wealthy Persian businessman. Canaris, having studied their personalities and interactions, had deduced that the Big Three would spend the plurality of their time at the Soviet embassy. Several options for the assassination were examined: while the leaders were in transit; while they slept at their individual residences; while they met. The latter option was by far the most difficult to execute. Security would be at least triple that for the other two. The premises would likely be hardened against even an armored assault.

Yet Canaris judged that the meeting venue was the best option. Each of the leaders would be present, so only one assault was necessary. The Genius had determined that *three* independent assaults, in contrast, would have a diminishing possibility of success. Among other things, they would have to be executed nearly simultaneously so as not to forewarn the others, and the chances of discovery and interdiction, at minimum, tripled.

Beyond the location for the assassination, Canaris had given Skorzeny wide latitude as to the particulars. The Genius had insisted, however, that while preparing for the main event, Skorzeny and his men should take every opportunity to gather as much intelligence as possible. That instruction alone signaled Canaris's deep skepticism about the Führer's plan. Why bother gathering intelligence if a decapitation strike against the Big Three would radically alter, if not end, the war?

Skorzeny's musings were interrupted by the slowing of the vehicle. A kilometer ahead, a Red Army ZIS-5, likely a remnant of the Soviet-British invasion two years prior, sat in the middle of the otherwise desolate road. Several troops were milling about as if trying to figure out some sort of problem. A flat tire or perhaps an overheated engine.

"*Anordnung?*"

"*Nichtstun*," Skorzeny ordered. "*Bremsen.* They will believe we are allies unless we speak. No one talks. If they address us in any fashion, only I or Unterscharführer Richter will speak. Watch me and be alert."

Skorzeny turned to face the trailing vehicle and put a finger to his lips, followed by a slashing motion across his throat. A passenger in each of the trailing vehicles but the last repeated the gesture to the vehicle immediately to his rear.

Two Soviet Efreitors stood in the road and flagged Skorzeny's caravan. Skorzeny instructed his driver to stop. The closer Efreitor approached the driver's side of the car, somewhat warily but not hostilely, similar to anyone hailing a stranger.

Skorzeny spoke preemptively, in English. "What's the problem, *tovarisch?*"

The Efreitor threw up his hands in mock exasperation. "Not just one problem," he replied, also in broken but understandable English. "We have an overheated engine and it appears we're nearly out of gasoline. We've been here for several hours. We are on our way to Tehran."

Skorzeny said, "We can provide some petrol, but I don't know what we can do about the engine."

"There are six of us. Can you give us a lift?"

Skorzeny smiled and waved about the cars. "Unfortunately, as you can see, we have no room, really. Don't you have a radio?"

The Efreitor spat on the ground in disgust. "The radio, when it works, is only a little better than shouting—about the same range, but not as clear." The Efreitor examined Skorzeny's caravan more closely. "You have enough room if we sit atop one another. Uncomfortable, but not impossible. Otherwise, we will be stranded for the better part of a day."

Skorzeny summoned his best sympathetic look and hunched his shoulders in apology. "I don't believe we have the room to accommodate you, but you can be certain that upon arriving in Tehran, we will seek out someone to return and provide assistance. Just give me the name of your superior officer and where I might find him and we'll be certain that vehicles will be immediately dispatched to collect you. It will take no more, I am sure, than five or six hours."

The Efreitor threw up his hands. "How can you say that? It is a simple request and it would not be particularly difficult for you to—"

The rest of the sentence was aborted by a 9×19-millimeter round that obliterated the Efreitor's mouth. Before the Soviet troops could react, before the Efreitor's corpse had even collapsed to the ground, the other Brandenburgers began firing their pistols almost in unison, striking each of the stunned Russians multiple times before they, too, fell to the ground.

Skorzeny stepped out of the vehicle and walked among the corpses of the Soviet troops, gently nudging each with the toe of his

boot to confirm death. When finished, he turned to the Brandenburgers, who stood immediately behind Skorzeny's vehicle.

"Who gave the order to fire?"

Each of the Brandenburgers bore a look of incomprehension, if
not confusion. The driver of the vehicle shrugged nervously. "Obersturmbannführer Skorzeny . . ."

". . . did *not* give the order to fire," Skorzeny finished.

"You did not," the driver acknowledged. "It was assumed."

Skorzeny stepped closer to the team of Brandenburgers and
stood straight, taller than each of them but Wagner, with his chin
raised. "Listen closely. Understand." He paused for emphasis. The
only sounds were the random hissing noises from cooling engines.
Each of the fearsome Brandenburgers was riveted to Skorzeny with
almost canine obedience. "This operation is not business in the ordinary course. It is not simply a hazardous assignment. It is not
merely an extremely difficult assignment. Nor is it only the most
consequential assignment you or any German soldier has ever undertaken."

Skorzeny took a menacing step closer. He spoke slowly and with
almost painful precision. "This is the most dangerous, difficult,
and consequential assignment ever undertaken by any group of soldiers since Thermopylae. That is not a colloquialism. If anything, it
is an understatement. *In recorded history.* We *will* successfully discharge this assignment. But only because each of you will perform
precisely as I say. You must do *precisely* what I say you must do. *Precisely* how I say you must do it. And *precisely* when I say you must
do it. Any deviation by any of you at any time or in any way
whatsoever—no matter how slight, no matter how seemingly
trivial—may, and likely will, result in utter, unmitigated catastrophe. We have been charged by our nation with executing the leaders

of three of the most powerful nations in the history of mankind. They are protected by a nearly impenetrable cordon of troops and bodyguards who have shoot-on-sight and shoot-to-kill orders. The finest marksmen each of their respective nations has ever produced will be positioned in hides to which we will be almost oblivious and blind."

Skorzeny looked into the eyes of each Brandenburger in turn. "History . . . and mathematicians . . . almost guarantee none of you will leave Tehran alive. I know that is completely acceptable to each of you. What is not acceptable is failing to complete the assignment. Do not add failure to follow my orders to the interminable list of impediments to completing this assignment." His eyes blazed. "No mistakes."

Skorzeny motioned abruptly for everyone to get into the vehicles. He took his seat and signaled for the drivers to proceed.

CHAPTER 37

Gromov went slowly and quietly through the narrow lanes of Tehran's Farahzad and Shahran neighborhoods, familiarizing himself with as much of the area as he could. The more he did so, the more he could move instinctively to complete the assignment. He wouldn't have time to think, to calculate, to assess. He had to be able to move quickly and seamlessly, as if this were his backyard. The planning for the operation had been exquisitely detailed. Beria had assigned a team of NKVD officers and senior military strategists to reconnoiter the twelve-block radius surrounding each of the U.S., Soviet, and British embassies. They'd also traveled hundreds of kilometers along the various streets of Tehran, along the Trans-Iranian Railway, and along the perimeter of the city to assess the presence of security forces, whether Iranian or Allied.

Gromov had been briefed on likely avenues of approach and departure, as well as possible hides near each of the embassies. He'd dutifully scanned the reports, destroying each immediately thereafter, and sat patiently through the briefings. Admittedly, he'd learned some useful information about the city that would assist him in avoiding detection before, during, and after the assassination attempt.

Ultimately, Gromov would choose his hide himself, but the recommendations assisted his deliberations.

The actual choices were quite limited.

Yet each of the venues had vulnerabilities that could be exploited relatively easily. And each had more than a few avenues for retreat after the faux assassinations. Gromov had identified a large oil storage yard near the railway station along the outskirts of the city as a potential area to cloak himself if circumstances impeded a direct escape. But he wasn't particularly concerned that he'd be apprehended. Not only was he adept at evasive maneuvers but Beria had tasked several dozen NKVD officers with fomenting additional chaos in the vicinity of the Soviet embassy when the attempt occurred, affording Gromov an all-but-undetectable retreat. Regardless, Gromov would be prepared to eliminate any impediment to escape and evasion.

Beria had directed Molotov to use every means to ensure that at some point the three leaders would stage the obligatory group photo on the front balcony of the Soviet embassy. Although that wouldn't necessarily be where Gromov would make the attempt, it was one of the better options. The ambassador was working his channels to do so, mystified by how Beria was certain the leaders would meet at the Soviet embassy as opposed to the British or American.

The front deck was one of three embassy locations Gromov had assessed would afford an opportunity for an attempted assassination. The front balcony would no doubt be a location where a photo opportunity would be staged, and there were several vantage points that provided a relatively unobstructed view. Most likely, these vantage points would be covered by a combination of embassy security, NKVD personnel, and military guards. Beria had to keep those personnel in place so as not to raise suspicion. But their precise deployment would be adjusted so that Gromov's line of sight to the targets wouldn't be obstructed. Most likely, one or more of the security personnel would be struck—an unfortunate but unavoidable consequence of making the assassination attempt as believable as possible.

Gromov stopped instinctively in the desolate alley several blocks from the Soviet embassy and looked behind him. Standing ten paces to the rear was a hulking form, more than two meters in height and nearly 120 kilos in weight, without a discernible gram of fat. A broad chest and shoulders tapered to a narrow waist. The head silhouetted against the hazy glow from the streetlamp seemed carved from a block of stone: Serzhant Walter Garic; blond hair, blue eyes, Russian father, German mother. Gromov had not previously known him, but he was ostensibly to be Gromov's bodyguard and spotter. Precisely why Gromov needed a spotter to conduct a sham assassination attempt had not been explained, so Gromov surmised that Garic's true role—unbeknownst to him—was to take the fall for the failed assassination attempt. Something would be planted on him that would identify him as a German agent. It would be indirect and vague, but enough to cause investigators to conclude that Garic was an operative from the Abwehr or some other clandestine component of the Wehrmacht. Within seconds of the assassination attempt Garic would likely find himself surrounded by at least half a dozen NKVD officers, who would shred him with multiple rounds of fire before planting perfect counterfeit documents on him identifying him as a German intelligence officer. His corpse and the fake papers would be sufficient proof that the Germans had attempted to assassinate the Big Three.

A corner of Gromov's brain had, of course, entertained the real possibility that *both* he and Garic would share the same fate. It was possible but, he concluded, unlikely. Gromov, after all, was not an obscure Serzhant. He was a newly promoted colonel, imminently to be awarded the Order of Lenin. Were his corpse proffered as that of the assassin, British and American investigators would almost immediately determine that the attempt had been staged.

Still, though the possibility was exceedingly small, it was not zero.

With an intentional tone of irritation, Gromov asked, "What do you want, Garic?"

"I've been instructed to follow you wherever you go."

"Instructed by whom?"

"Colonel Belyanov." Garic shrugged as if everyone knew the answer. "Truthfully, nearly everyone who has given me directions about the operation instructed me to follow you. I am your spotter, your bodyguard, your valet. They said to make sure Gromov wants for nothing and is harmed by nothing."

Gromov became genuinely irritated.

"They, meaning Belyanov?"

"Everyone, Colonel," the giant said apologetically. "It was made clear that you are of great importance, as is your mission."

Gromov approached Garic. "We have not previously worked together," he said in a conciliatory tone. "And I generally work alone. I was informed you were to be my spotter. What else did they say, specifically, you are to help me with?"

Garic appeared slightly confused. "Everything, Colonel. Everything and anything you need to complete the operation. Supplies, spotting, protection—whatever else you may request."

Gromov grabbed Garic's arm in an expression of camaraderie. "This operation will be a success. We will work well together."

Garic smiled like a child meeting a famed athlete. "Anything that you require, Colonel."

Gromov gazed in appreciation at the soon-to-be-dead man. "You understand the assignment?"

Garic nodded tentatively. It was clear he *did not* grasp the assignment. Who would grasp a fake assassination attempt?

Gromov patted Garic's shoulder. "Do not think too much about it. You'll not be functioning as a typical spotter, but rather, my eyes and ears as I concentrate on the objective. Make sure I'm not interrupted before or apprehended after the objective is complete. Understand?"

Garic grinned, honored to have a role in any operation involving the revered Gromov. A part of Gromov wanted to warn Garic his time on Earth was rapidly winding down. Indeed, he had almost no time left. Gromov thought it might be wise to apprise himself of the same counsel.

"They have not told me the location or target yet," Garic informed him. "They told me you would do so."

"There is plenty of time for that," Gromov deflected.

He pointed in the direction of the Soviet embassy. "Come with me. Let me show you the potential hides. Keep in mind we need to retreat immediately and swiftly. Without detection."

While Garic grinned as they strode along the alleyway, Gromov withdrew his NR-40 from its sheath in the back of his collar and sliced it across Garic's throat all the way to the neck bone. The big man's body was suspended upright for a full two seconds, eyes wide, before collapsing to the pavement.

Gromov worked alone. Always. Garic would not have been a help but a hindrance. The marginal value he might have afforded in being the fall guy was outweighed by his possibly getting in Gromov's way.

Gromov walked quickly into the night, pondering whether there was one dead man in the alley or two.

CHAPTER 38

The very first American Canidy and Fulmar saw at the American legation was Lieutenant Michael Sandul, aide to General Hap Arnold. He was standing at parade rest in the vestibule just to the right of the main entrance. Canidy and Fulmar were waved in by the two Marines stationed on either side. Sandul was of average height with a powerful build and wide brown eyes that conveyed intelligence and seemed to absorb everything in a two-hundred-seventy-degree range of his forehead. He extended his hand to the duo.

"I know this sounds trite: You don't know me, but I know you. Both of you. At least by reputation."

Tentatively shaking his hand, Canidy rolled his eyes. "Hell, we can't be *that* bad."

Sandul chuckled and shook Fulmar's hand. "General Arnold and Colonel Donovan asked me to provide you with whatever you need while you're in Tehran—transportation, equipment, weapons—anything."

"Women?"

Sandul laughed again. "You won't have time for that. Colonel Donovan wants you around the embassy and around the city, using any intelligence we can provide or you can pick up to make sure there are no problems with the Big Three summit, and in the process acquire as much intelligence as you can."

"Anything in particular that we're supposed to look for?" Fulmar asked.

The smile faded from Sandul's face and he nodded. "Germans, Russians."

Fulmar's brow furrowed. "Germans I get. And I get that the Russians can be duplicitous. But why in hell should we bother ourselves with allies?"

"Donovan expects the Soviets will do everything they can to steal as much information from us—and the Brits—as possible. Anecdotal reports suggest that their intelligence services have blanketed the city. They outnumber us three to one. Maybe four to one. And if you encounter them, be careful. They play rough."

"They're supposed to be our damn allies, for crying out loud," Canidy grumbled. "It'd be nice if they at least *pretended* we're on the same side."

"Because they are," Sandul replied. "Donovan believes they wouldn't hesitate to kill one of us if it gave them an advantage," he added. "They'd just throw up their hands innocently and blame it on the Nazis."

Canidy's jaw tightened as he looked knowingly at Fulmar. "We've had some experience along those lines with them. They'll double-cross in a heartbeat."

Sandul put up his hands defensively. "Understand. They're great fighters. They will make, and have made, sacrifices most of us couldn't imagine. Nobody better to have at your side. But not behind your back. Even if you're an ostensible ally.

"A bit of advice. Look out for anyone Western-looking—Soviets, Brits, Americans. Anyone Western may, in fact, be German. Donovan—and from what I understand, the President—remains skeptical that the Germans are going to attempt an assassination here. That said, we're not taking any risks. We've got multiple levels of security around the embassies and all of the buildings housing our personnel."

"Speaking of which," Canidy interjected. "Where are we staying? I could use a bath or shower. The desert may be fresh in the springtime, but it stinks in the fall."

"We've got a bunch of flats for the entire Washington contingent—you're technically part of that contingent—nearby. I doubt you'll spend much time there. It's just a place to rest if you get any time to do so."

Canidy said, "Hell, we've had more than enough time to rest. Other than doing the infernal calisthenics and running ordered by Donovan, we've been sitting around a cabin recovering from a couple of injuries." He paused, a pensive look on his face. "But just in case we do have a bit of time, maybe you could fill us in on a couple things."

"Happy to."

"Have any maidens or ladies made it onto the traveling squad?"

Sandul burst into a laugh as if he'd been holding it in since he'd met them. "Your reputations, you'll be pleased to know, precede you."

A concerned look covered Canidy's face. "Donovan? Donovan told you that?"

"No, no. But a fair number of OSS people have made not-so-subtle references to your proclivities." Sandul rubbed the back of his neck. "I'm not sure what your preferences are . . ."

"Two eyes, two arms, two legs."

". . . but from what I've seen of the traveling squad, they'd make excellent bridge partners for your mothers. The youngest looks like she may have babysat for you when you were in diapers."

Throwing a thumb toward Canidy, Fulmar smiled. "Not necessarily a deal-breaker for this guy."

"You won't have time, anyway," Sandul said. "A pouch leaves the embassy twice a day. Donovan wants reports in every single one of them until the President returns to Washington."

Canidy grimaced. "That's not how we usually do things. Can't promise it will happen. Even if Donovan says so."

Sandul put up his hands in surrender. "I'm just conveying the message. I was told to brief you and I'm doing it. Also, Donovan says to be more alert than you've ever been. The city is now infested with nearly every spy and assassin on the face of the Earth. The Germans may or may not be here, but everyone else definitely is, and they're all pretty slippery, if not scary, characters."

"That's nice to know," Canidy noted. "But we're here for the Germans. Any word on them?"

Sandul nodded. "No doubt. We have to act as if they're here even if the story about the assassination is bull."

Canidy's eyes narrowed. "Any specifics?"

Sandul shook his head. "Speculation, but not specifics. I *abhor* speculation. Have you heard of the German superman by the name of Skorzeny?"

"Isn't every German a superman?" Canidy asked, elbowing Fulmar. "Even this guy thinks he's one."

"Skorzeny's the guy who Hitler sends to do the impossible. You've heard about the Mussolini operation, right? That was the most recent one by Skorzeny. Swooped into a massively guarded mountain fortress and plucked that fat bastard right out of there. Supposed to be like an Olympic athlete—Skorzeny, that is—with the brain of a rocket scientist and nerves of steel."

Fulmar shot an elbow into Canidy's ribs. "Sounds like this guy. But how does he fare with the ladies?"

"Donovan insists that if the Germans do send someone here, it will be Skorzeny or someone like him. Like the—I think they call them Brandenburgers. Commandos. Have you heard of them?"

Canidy glanced at Fulmar and then looked back to Sandul. "Heard, saw, and felt them. Hell, if I hadn't been blown off my feet by one of their explosives, maybe I'd even remember having smelled them." Canidy's face grew dark. "I think we've met them twice. Enough for me."

Sandul noted the expressions on the faces of Canidy and Fulmar. It was a mixture of hatred, determination, and dread, but with an overlay of fatigue. "You guys need some rest? Donovan insists that you be on alert throughout, but you'll be useless the way you look. I'll take you to your quarters. They're practically next door." He gestured toward their bags. "I'll get somebody to help with those."

Canidy shook his head sharply. "Come on, Lieutenant. Be serious. No one touches our gear. Office stuff. Not for regular military."

"Right," Sandul acknowledged. "I've heard about you guys. Any secret weapons in there?"

Canidy ignored the question. "How do we connect with a friend of ours? British military by the name of McDermott. He's with us."

"I'll get in touch with my guy at the British embassy," Sandul said as he gestured toward a side door. "You can meet him after you've settled. Just remember one thing: Tehran's like a beautiful lake in the middle of a jungle—interesting and wondrous. But it has a thousand ways it can kill you. And if it does, be certain it will be in a way that you could never have predicted."

CHAPTER 39

Obersturmbannführer Otto Skorzeny walked slowly along the desolate lane mere blocks from the Soviet embassy. He was dressed in clothing resembling a British civilian's, perhaps an errant member of the delegation that had begun arriving days earlier. He'd passed the nearby British embassy—less impressive than the Soviet embassy—several times.

Skorzeny had walked the same route nearly a dozen times since arriving in Tehran days ago. He'd also walked around the blocks surrounding the much smaller American legation located on the other side of the city.

There was significant and redundant security around each of the embassies. Everything within a one-hundred-meter radius of each had been evacuated and the perimeter completely secured. Hundreds of Western-looking men strolled casually around the boulevards, streets, and alleys surrounding each of the facilities, fooling absolutely no one, particularly Skorzeny.

For their part, the Soviets weren't even attempting to fool anyone. They all but advertised that the hundreds of dour-looking brutes milling about in a two-hundred-meter radius of the Soviet embassy were not merely security or secret police but merciless killers.

The softest target, by far, would be the American legation. It was small, with minimal security and several access points. Obviously, the Big Three would not meet there.

Skorzeny determined that to have the slightest chance of success, an assassination attempt on the Big Three would have to take place when they were together—using near-simultaneous shots in rapid succession or explosive devices. Killing one might be plausible, but thereafter killing the other two would be nearly impossible. After the first target was hit, the alarm would be sounded and security around the remaining two would be impenetrable until they were swiftly evacuated.

For that reason any attempt against the Big Three would have to be executed in rapid succession while they were meeting together. The lapsed time between the first shot and last, Skorzeny concluded, could not be more than five seconds, perhaps four. He had considered an explosive device, but getting one within any area where the Big Three congregated would be next to impossible. *But perhaps several devices . . .* thought Skorzeny. *Seriatim.*

The options were few. Skorzeny determined that for several reasons the most likely venue for the summit would be the Soviet embassy. Its sheer size allowed it to more readily accommodate the Big Three and their respective entourages than the other two locations. Furthermore, the scale of Soviet security forces was unmatched— troops, NKVD, even SMERSH. Also, the British embassy was nearby—only the American entourage would need to travel any appreciable distance. But the clinching reason was Stalin—he'd undoubtedly insist that the conference be held at the Soviet embassy, and he was even more unyielding than Churchill.

Skorzeny had done numerous circuits around each of the embassy grounds, although he abandoned reconnaissance of the American legation as soon as he concluded the conference had little chance of being held there. Though he was not a sniper, Skorzeny easily determined that neither the Soviet nor the British embassy had optimal sight lines for an assassination attempt. But the Soviet embassy sported a terrace that would be optimal for the group photograph that one or more of the Big Three would inevitably insist on. There were enormous pillars on either side of the terrace, but they were sufficiently spaced so that a sniper or snipers could have multiple angles toward the targets. Moreover, there were no railings or balustrades obstructing sight lines.

There were, however, numerous highly reflective windows along the terrace, behind the area where the Big Three would be seated for the photos. Skorzeny anticipated the windows would be optimal spots to post countersnipers.

There were several buildings within two hundred meters opposite the terrace where snipers could position themselves. None, at least in Skorzeny's opinion, were optimal, but that was the typical lot of a sniper. One didn't often get to pick the perfect hide. The area immediately surrounding the Soviet embassy that offered the best views of the terrace was interlaced with numerous lanes and alleys that twisted and curved. Good for evading pursuers in the short term but an impediment to a quick retreat.

There were three accomplished snipers among the Brandenburgers on Skorzeny's team. Gunter Kohl and Heinz Richter, each of whom had distinguished himself at Leningrad, Kursk, and Demyansk to the east; and Hans Macht, who had executed more than two dozen discreet assignments throughout France and Belgium. Skorzeny would trust, within broad limits, their expertise and judgment to determine the execution of the assassination.

But Skorzeny was skeptical that the kills could be accomplished with precision, that is, with single head shots or a shot or two to the chest. Based on what he had observed on his reconnaissance strolls, Skorzeny had anticipated that there would be aides, photographers, security personnel, and others who would be milling about, preventing clean, unobstructed sight lines toward each of the Big Three.

Rather, multiple rounds would likely be required to be sure. To be absolutely *certain* of success, a series of detonations would be required, both to penetrate security and to kill the marks. The usual coterie of diplomats, generals, and aides surrounding the Big Three would necessarily suffer casualties as well. Skorzeny and his men would rely on the ensuing mayhem to provide cover for the retreat.

Skorzeny assessed that the odds of a successful assassination of the Big Three were fairly high. Perhaps sixty to seventy percent. But he held no illusions about the probabilities of escape. Even in the smoothest, best-planned operations, in which enemy encounters were relatively limited, lives would be lost. An operation in what would be the most heavily secured six-block radius in the world guaranteed multiple casualties among his men, if not utter annihilation. So, he thought, if utter annihilation was all but certain, then why not simply use the method of execution that was all but certain?

Skorzeny's reconnaissance was interrupted by the muffled sound of footsteps several dozen meters down the lane. Four forms were silhouetted against the weak yellowish light of a streetlamp. They appeared to be male, shabbily dressed. Skorzeny could not distinguish any details except perhaps the most pertinent: as they drew closer, he could see that at least two of them appeared to be missing one or more digits on their right hands. Thieves, out for a night stroll.

The Walther P38 under Skorzeny's shirt would remain there.

Were he to discharge it so close to the Soviet and British embassies a mere two days before the summit, Soviet, British, and American security would become even more rabidly paranoid. More personnel would be deployed. The security cordon would be expanded and perimeter patrols would multiply.

Not needing or wanting confrontation, Skorzeny retreated in the opposite direction. He walked calmly but briskly, listening for a quickening of their footfalls or other signs of pursuit.

Fifty meters ahead two more figures appeared out of the cross lane, boxing him in. He could hear them talking to each other. He did not understand Farsi, but he easily grasped their intent.

Skorzeny raised both hands shoulder high to signal his desire to avoid confrontation. They continued to close until each group was no more than four to five meters from him. The tallest of the group of four extended his right hand, signaling Skorzeny should surrender his valuables without resistance. Skorzeny stood perpendicular to both groups so that all of them could remain in his line of vision. He adopted a body attitude of passiveness, surrender, and held out his hands to convey he had no valuables.

Irritated and disbelieving, the tall one scowled and lunged forward to seize Skorzeny's left hand. Skorzeny pulled the man inward and simultaneously thrust his three middle fingers into the man's trachea. A loud jet of air gushed from the man's mouth as he collapsed to the pavement, a panicked expression on his face. Before the minds of the remaining five had fully registered what had just happened, Skorzeny spun toward the two robbers to the rear and slammed his fist into the temple of the one standing to the left, caving in his occipital bone with a nauseating, audible crack that sent him to the pavement and the remaining four fleeing down the lane ahead of him.

Skorzeny assessed the two inert figures on the pavement and, concluding that they posed no threat, surveyed the surrounding area for witnesses. There were none. He walked casually in the direction opposite the one the robbers had fled in until he came to the end of the block. He then turned right—in the direction of the Soviet and British embassies—and resumed his reconnaissance.

CHAPTER 40

Canidy stood just outside the front entrance of the American legation watching various State Department personnel of indeterminate
portfolio and rank scurrying about the perimeter of the building
and into the lobby. The President was expected to arrive tomorrow,
and the War Department functionaries were preparing and dissem-
inating briefing papers and conducting small-group strategy ses-
sions in anticipation of the President's arrival.

Several dozen MPs were stationed both within and immediately
outside the premises. Augmenting the uniformed personnel were
countless plainclothes security officers who all seemed to wear
nearly identical expressions of officiousness and nervousness. Their
supervisors had drilled into them that they were responsible for the
life of the commander in chief in the most consequential summit of
Great Powers in modern history. They were told that they must act
as if there unequivocally *would* be an attempt on his life and that a
successful attempt would be one of the most cataclysmic events in
not just modern history, but world history. They would never in
their lives have a more consequential assignment. The slightest
mistake—a scuffed shoe—promised banishment to Outer Mongolia.

Canidy expected Fulmar and McDermott to arrive momentarily. When Canidy awoke in the tiny three-room flat where Sandul had deposited them the previous evening, Fulmar was gone. A note tacked to the door said he was out and would return shortly. And, sure enough, not more than ten minutes later he walked in the door carrying what appeared to be flatbreads with feta cheese, some kind of jam, and a bag of sundry items.

Irritated, Canidy asked, "Where the hell did you disappear to?"

Fulmar raised the bag. "Breakfast. Also, I took a look around, just as Donovan wants us to."

"And?"

"Not a hell of a lot to see, actually. Not that it's not interesting, but nothing unusual or suspicious at first glance. But I'm fairly certain the conference isn't going to be held at the American legation."

Canidy pointed to the bag. "Why don't we open up the bag and you can tell me why while we eat?"

Fulmar placed the bag on a coffee table in the middle of the room, which was one of only three in the apartment: a kitchen, a bedroom with two cots Canidy and Fulmar had slept on, and a tiny utility cabinet. A water closet was several doors down the hall. They sat on the floor. Fulmar pulled two clay cups of coffee out, handed one to Canidy, and then pulled out two rolls that appeared to Canidy like wheat pancakes filled with meat and vegetables. Fulmar handed one of the rolls to Canidy, who inspected it as if it contained explosives.

"What's this called?"

"I don't know. I just pointed to something edible and they gave it to me," Fulmar replied.

Canidy looked at the roll from multiple angles. "Smells okay." He watched Fulmar take a bite of his own roll. "How does it taste?"

"Not bad. I think it's lamb or something like it."

Canidy took a bite of his, grunted approval, and washed it down with coffee. "Why do you say the conference isn't going to be at the American legation?"

"Too small, I think, to hold everyone's entourage," Fulmar said between bites. "And it's on the other side of the city from the British and Soviet embassies. It's easier for one delegation to travel across the city than two."

Canidy nodded as he chewed. "Makes sense. But not as easy for Roosevelt to travel as it is for Churchill or Stalin."

Fulmar put up a finger as he chewed and swallowed before responding. "They're going to want to limit risk. Two heads of state traveling across the city present twice as many opportunities for assassination en route . . ."

"You're a cheery guy," Canidy said with a feigned groan. "How did it look out there in the light of day?"

"You'll see soon, but it's more of what we saw yesterday. It's not a modern city, but it's not backward, either. The problem for us is that it's very dense, at least in the parts I saw. There could be hundreds, even thousands, of Germans here and we might not detect them."

Canidy finished his coffee. "Be thankful we're not on the security detail. Those poor bastards have got to be at their wits' end."

Fulmar rose and gathered the scraps from the meal and placed them back in the sack. "Donovan expects us to surveil. We better surveil."

"I wish I knew what we were supposed to be surveilling. I haven't got the slightest idea what we're looking for," Canidy said.

"Sure you do. Germans. And Sandul says there are supposed to be lots of them, parachuting in like rain."

Canidy scoffed. "If there are so many of them, why hasn't anybody seen them?"

Fulmar put his hands on his hips. "That's precisely the problem. They don't *want* to be seen."

"I know this much," Canidy said as they headed toward the door. "I'll be perfectly satisfied not to see a single one of those Brandenburgers again."

"Can't say I'm eager to see them, either," Fulmar agreed. "But there's little doubt that's precisely who Hitler is sending."

Sandul cleared Canidy and Fulmar through security with a wave to the guards. Holding a slim leather pouch, he met the two OSS operators just inside the entrance. "This is for you," he said, handing it to Canidy.

"What's in it?"

Sandul shrugged. "I don't know. Wasn't told. Didn't look."

Canidy opened the pouch and retrieved its contents—a gray letter-sized envelope. Handing the pouch back to Sandul, he opened the envelope, which contained a single piece of paper with a short note and a photograph. A perplexed expression covering his face, he examined both as Fulmar and Sandul watched.

"What is it?" Fulmar asked.

Wordlessly, Canidy handed Fulmar the contents, generating a similar expression on the latter's face.

"Who gave this to you?" Canidy asked Sandul.

"A staffer—one of the State Department clerks. It arrived this morning."

Fulmar looked up from the paper and photograph and said to Canidy, "This is where it all came from."

"What came from?" Sandul asked.

Canidy and Fulmar ignored him, both of their minds fixated on the note and photograph.

Canidy spoke slowly and deliberately, analyzing the note and photograph, which Fulmar had given back to him. "This comes from the same two who told us about the alleged assassination attempt on Roosevelt, Churchill, and Stalin. They claim the man in the photograph is the man who paid them to tell us that."

Sandul began to ask a question, but Fulmar held up a finger, not wanting to interrupt Canidy's train of thought.

"We—and more important, the President and Donovan—believe it's probable that the assassination story is a Soviet ruse to generate urgency among the Allies to open a Western Front as soon as possible to relieve pressure on the Red Army.

"Quite apart from the ruse, the Thorisdottirs—the ones who told us about the assassination attempt—are manipulative backstabbers. We went through hell, lost men, getting Kapsky and his equations, and when we did so they betrayed us, stole the equations, and gave them to the Soviets.

"Then they sail all the way from Asgard or some such place to tell us they're sorry for their treachery." Canidy waved the photo and note. "And now they seemingly want to make amends by giving us *this*—presumably the man who's going to carry out the assassination or fake assassination."

Canidy looked at Fulmar and Sandul. "What do you calculate are the odds that this is another fine Thorisdottir–Soviet misdirection? Ninety-eight or ninety-nine percent?"

Fulmar shook his head. Pointing at the pouch, he said, "I'm still trying to figure out how they got that to the right people. If there was any doubt they have significant Soviet resources, that certainly puts an end to it. But the fact remains, we once again have to take it seriously, bogus or not. They know that once we have been given evidence someone is supposed to carry out an assassination of the

Allied leaders—even a fake assassination attempt—we *have* to ex-
pend time and resources on tracking it down, no matter how improbable. Donovan has been given evidence of who is supposed to
conduct the assassination. Whether fake or not. And he does nothing about it? In the one-in-a-billion chance there is an attempt, let
alone a successful one, everyone in OSS would be fried." Fulmar
snorted. "And that would be the least important consequence."

Canidy stared at the photo caption: *Colonel Taras Gromov.* He
looked inside the pouch again, finding nothing. "It would be helpful if someone from the Office told us precisely what we're supposed to do with this. Did anyone examine this before putting it in
a diplomatic pouch and sending it to us?"

"Seems pretty clear, I think," Sandul offered. "You're supposed
to look out for this guy Gromov."

"No problem," Canidy said acidly. "In a city of roughly a million
people, we should be able to identify a single guy from an undated
photograph. If he *is* supposed to do something bad, I'm sure he
wouldn't do *anything* to make it difficult for us to find and identify him."

"We should stay at the legation and wait for him," Fulmar added.
"He's probably going to want to introduce himself. Hell, he was
probably here waiting for us all night. Professional courtesy."

"German assassins and Russian assassins," Canidy mused. He
examined his watch. "What time does the President arrive?"

"Sometime tomorrow," Sandul said. "For security reasons, they
won't give us the precise time until an hour before."

Canidy elbowed Fulmar. "So, around twenty-four hours. We
should be able to track down an NKVD colonel, make sure he
doesn't make any waves, locate and neutralize an unknown number
of highly proficient assassins, and have time for a quick one before

the commander in chief meets with his British and Russian counterparts. Don't you think?"

"I think the odds of this turning out well are zero," Fulmar replied. "And just in case you had any doubts—I think the likelihood
we'll be killed, imprisoned, or court-martialed is only slightly above
one hundred percent."

CHAPTER 41

Several weeks before the invasion of Poland, the efficient minions of the Abwehr had purchased a small commercial building with offices that had been converted to four flats. What many mistook for the Genius's cleverness was actually meticulous preparation. Canaris did not concern himself with the distinction.

The building had remained unused until now. Skorzeny and his men used it for sleeping quarters and a base of operations. It would be abandoned once the operation was complete. A short distance from the building was a clothing merchant who supplemented his income by relaying information to the Abwehr. Until yesterday, he'd had little to relay. But upon Skorzeny's arrival he proved himself useful in obtaining a medium-sized Studebaker truck sufficient to transport Skorzeny and all of his men to the area surrounding the Soviet and British embassies.

Skorzeny had not yet received confirmation of the time or location of the conference. That wouldn't be a problem. Skorzeny was confident the location would be within the British or Soviet embassy, and almost certain it would be at the latter. He also was certain there would be a ceremonial photography session on the terrace. He had a short time to get his men familiarized with the area, but he'd been able to do so himself in very little time. His snipers were hardened veterans of multiple campaigns. They had performed under grueling conditions, often having to endure both artillery and countersnipers. The conditions here, by contrast, would be almost facile, *if,* that is, their expertise would even become necessary.

They parked the Studebaker several blocks outside the Soviet embassy security perimeter and walked the remainder of the distance, staggering their approach so as not to be noticed. Skorzeny had given his men a general description of the Soviet embassy and surrounding area, directing them to discreetly reconnoiter the area. He'd previously given them a detailed briefing of his own reconnaissance the night before and instructed them what to look for—particularly the snipers.

They scattered about the general area, conducting individual sweeps of the perimeter. Skorzeny assumed the British, Americans, and Russians had innumerable agents in the vicinity looking for anything and anyone suspicious. Although he presumed the Americans were relatively new at counterespionage, the British had centuries of experience and the Russians were both experienced and ruthless. Each of their intelligence services would be on heightened alert for the possibility of German agents. Accordingly, Skorzeny instructed all the Brandenburgers to return to the vehicle by no later than 5:00 p.m., after which they would return to their quarters and remain out of sight unless tactically necessary.

CHAPTER 42

Sandul drove Canidy and Fulmar to the British embassy in a surprisingly roadworthy black Peugeot that belched a dense cloud of gray smoke every quarter to half kilometer. McDermott greeted them just outside the grounds without his usual amicable expression.

"Who shot your dog?" Canidy asked.

"That's just about how everyone inside is acting," McDermott said. "All business. The big shots are arriving. Everyone is on best behavior. MI6 is approaching this as if doomsday were imminent. Not the usual British jocularity in times of stress."

"Any word on the final location?" Canidy asked.

"You must have mistaken me for someone who matters. I've heard bits of information. The PM apparently encouraged President Roosevelt to stay at the British embassy during his time in Tehran. That certainly will prompt Stalin to extend an invitation. Everyone's security services are acting as skittish as you would expect. I must have heard four contradictory security directives before noon alone. But even so, I think things are relatively under control."

"Any intelligence on possible German presence?" Fulmar asked.

"Not specifically. Lots of rumors though: Germans apparently parachuting in several teams of assassins outside of the city; Germans posing as Persian civilians all throughout the area. That sort of thing. All undoubtedly false, but it helps to keep the lads alert."

Canidy withdrew the photograph of Gromov from his pocket and displayed it close to McDermott's face. McDermott drew his head back to focus. "And what is this supposed to be? Someone we should keep an eye out for?"

"You're a quick study for a Scotsman." Canidy nodded. "He's Colonel Taras Gromov. Remember our sweethearts—the ones *you* introduced us to, by the way—who took us across the sea to Poland, rescued us from a rabid Nazi horde, and then double-crossed us by nearly killing the professor before stealing his keys to Armageddon?"

"I may have introduced you to them, mate," McDermott corrected, "but it was *your* Office that contracted with them."

"Well, those ladies sent this photograph to us by diplomatic pouch." Canidy raised his hand to ward off the question. "We have no idea how the Nordic goddesses pulled that off, but they do seem to be very well-connected and they are currently loaded with more money than all of us together will make in our lifetimes."

McDermott looked puzzled. "What does this Gromov have to do with anything?"

"We suspect this is more misdirection, but you have to give them credit. This is borderline diabolical . . ."

"It freezes us," McDermott agreed. "We can't take the chance that this assassination wild-goose chase is *just* a wild-goose chase.

Yet we can't possibly locate one man in this city in the next day and a half. Especially a man who doesn't want to be located."

Canidy grinned and put the photo back in his pocket. "The President of the United States requested our presence here. We've been given no specific orders. In fact, the only directive we've been given, reduced to its essence, is to keep our eyes open while we're here. That kind of imprecision is so unlike Donovan, it makes my head hurt. But I know one thing: if something bad happens, we're going to get the blame."

McDermott looked skeptical. "Do you think the Soviets—Stalin—would do something as crazy as actually going through with a staged assassination attempt? That they're not just spreading a rumor? Not even Stalin, not even a desperate Stalin, would do that. No, the risk would be unfathomable. If someone moves suddenly, isn't where they're supposed to be, or this bloke's not as good as advertised, the *staged* assassination will turn into a *real* assassination. And all hell breaks loose."

Fulmar nodded. "All true. But Stalin may have decided it's worth the risk. Or maybe he just doesn't care. As long as *he* isn't shot and no concrete evidence points to him. If anybody even raises a question, he will just act outraged and indignant and accuse them of being Nazi sympathizers."

Canidy exhaled long and slow. "People way above our grade have thought this through or will think it through. Hell, Donovan probably began thinking about it the Wednesday after he was born. We have a simple but hard job: keep our eyes and ears open and collect any information, even if we don't know what it means—and give it to the colonel."

"Simple enough," McDermott conceded.

Fulmar said impatiently, "Other than the fact that I have no idea what I'm looking for, I say we should start looking around. May as well do a couple laps around the Brit and Soviet embassies."

"I suggest we space apart," McDermott said superfluously. "Someone else may be looking for suspicious things and the three of us grouped together . . ."

"Right," Canidy said. "But stay within sight of one another. And don't try to be nonchalant. If you see something like this Gromov character, just yell."

The three took slightly divergent paths toward the Soviet embassy, eyes scanning as much of the surrounding area as possible. Each quickly determined that appearing completely inconspicuous was futile. They looked and walked like Westerners in Tehran. Fortunately, the residents were accustomed to seeing large numbers of Westerners and went about their affairs without an apparent thought about the trio.

Canidy's demeanor was that of a beat cop—seemingly casual and indifferent, but with suspicious eyes and his head on a swivel. Hundreds of people were going about their business in the periphery of the embassy grounds.

Canidy passed scores of individuals, the majority native but thirty percent appearing Western, and the majority of those looking like they were attached to one of the embassies. Indeed, subconsciously his mind was facilely, if not completely accurately, sorting them into British and Russian.

But within fifteen minutes he felt a vague prick of unease. Something about the environs was disconcerting, off. He continued walking around the perimeter of the embassy grounds, trying to appear casual, while anxiously trying to determine the cause of his nervousness.

Taller than most of the people in the area, Canidy swiveled his head about, locating Fulmar approximately forty meters to his left. Fulmar was looking directly at him. Even from a distance Canidy recognized that his childhood friend was feeling something similar.

Something's off.

Canidy swiveled his head around, searching for McDermott. *Shouldn't be hard*, Canidy thought. The Scotsman with the world's largest mustache should have stood out even if he weren't as tall as Canidy and Fulmar. His eyes darted anxiously about the crowd. Group to group, person to person. But the Scot was nowhere to be seen.

Canidy looked back to Fulmar, who was cocking his head toward a relatively tall man who had his back to Canidy. Canidy locked on the man for several seconds, hoping he'd turn around. The man kept walking. Canidy looked back to Fulmar and mouthed a question. "Gromov?" Fulmar shook his head impatiently, then nodded at another man who had his back to Canidy. Within seconds Canidy discerned the cause of his anxiety.

Scattered throughout the crowd were a number of distinctive-looking men. It wasn't that they were European—there were Brits and Russians and a smattering of Americans scattered among the crowd. It was that there were a noticeable number of unmistakably fit European males with hard-looking faces. They moved not so much like pedestrians but like predators. Predators that preferred obscurity but were compelled by necessity to be among the public. They were distinct from the Soviet and British plainclothes security personnel, who made no effort to conceal their identities or purpose.

Immersed in thought, Canidy was startled by the voice of McDermott, who asked simply, "What?"

Canidy looked around to orient himself. "Come with me."

The two of them wove through the crowd toward Fulmar, who was still scanning the crowd. Canidy craned his head to keep an eye on the whereabouts of the men who had pricked his suspicions. Mc-Dermott followed and within fifteen seconds they were next to Fulmar, who hadn't taken his eyes off a small group of men who were moving past the Soviet embassy.

Canidy grasped Fulmar's shoulder. "What do you think?"

"I think they look too much like the men who guest-starred in our nightmares a couple of months ago."

"Something about them," Canidy concurred. "They don't fit."

Fulmar kept his eye on several men retreating from the area east of the Soviet embassy grounds. "You're being unusually generous about them, Dick. Given the looks of this, I can't give them the benefit of the doubt."

Canidy, Fulmar, and McDermott continued to crane their necks to watch several men interspersed among the crowd of pedestrian traffic walk purposefully away from the Soviet embassy, feigning disinterest. Studiously nonchalant.

But each seemed to move a bit faster with each step.

"You think you and they might have a shared ancestry?" Canidy asked Fulmar.

Fulmar continued to track several of the hard-looking men as they snaked through the crowd. "They look too nervous to be innocent," he replied. "Too purposeful. A purpose that has nothing to do with everyday life in the city."

For no more than a fraction of a second, so brief that Fulmar wasn't sure the man had registered it, one of the men he was watching caught his eye. The man's pace quickened. Fulmar elbowed Canidy. "This is what Donovan sent us here to do."

Fulmar accelerated toward the tall man, followed by Canidy and McDermott. As they increased their pace, each sensed in their periphery a number of other individuals strewn throughout the crowd moving like fish against the current, moving in the same general direction as the tall man.

Canidy, eyes riveted on the first man, unconsciously felt his hip for reassurance: a fully loaded M1911. He was nearly oblivious to the smattering of indignant protests from civilians as he grazed past them, quickening his pace.

Canidy continued his pace, vaguely aware that he was being matched by Fulmar and McDermott, who flanked his sides. A good head taller than the majority of the crowd, he remained locked on the first man and the other hard men moving along his path.

The tall man glanced back at Canidy. It was a fleeting glance, barely a half second. But it confirmed Canidy's suspicion. The man and those moving in the same direction shouldn't be here. They knew that someone would recognize that they shouldn't be here. They were trying to retreat as unobtrusively as possible so that men like Canidy wouldn't be alerted to their presence. They preferred to operate clandestinely, without notice. Whatever their objective, being noticed was an impediment. Perhaps not a fatal one, but one that made a difficult objective even more so.

Canidy scanned his periphery. Although he couldn't identify each of the tall man's associates with precision, he estimated there were more than a dozen. Even though his mind was focused on the tall man, that told him something. Whoever they were, whatever their number, their objective wasn't innocent.

Intelligence gathering could be done by a few. It could be done by men with soft faces but shrewd eyes, by men who had never felt the doughy resistance of another man's flesh as it was penetrated by a serrated blade. These men weren't simply intelligence gatherers.

Canidy noticed the tall man glance back in their direction again. Just a civilian looking about, nothing calculated. Seconds later the tall man's pace quickened perceptibly. Canidy sensed the pace of the others in the crowd quicken also. A herd of sharks moving with a purpose. Canidy felt his hip again and his pace quickened. Longer strides. Fulmar and McDermott were slightly behind and to either side of him, their eyes also trained on the tall man. He was the locus. Whoever was with him, whoever shared his purpose, would be moving in the same direction.

Although Canidy was concentrated on the tall man, a small compartment of his mind tabulated the random bodies in the crowd moving in the same direction as the tall man and at similar speed. They also appeared alien. The fact that there seemed to be more than three times as many of them as Canidy, Fulmar, and McDermott, yet they were *fleeing*, indicated that they perceived themselves to be in a hostile environment.

Definitely Germans.

Probably Nazis.

Possibly Brandenburgers.

Canidy craned his neck above the crowd to keep the Germans in sight. He brushed by several civilians who muttered objections, punctuated by the loud curse of a younger man whom Canidy knocked onto his back. Canidy stumbled, causing Fulmar and McDermott to collide into his back, staggering all three. Canidy immediately straightened, anxious not to lose the tall man, who had quickened his pace in the brief moment Canidy had stumbled.

Now there was no pretense. It was a chase. The tall man was the first to break into a sprint, followed by the dozen or so sharks swimming within the civilian crowd. Their vector was toward a stone archway over the entrance to a narrow lane. That lane was one of many spokes emanating from the hub of the plaza three blocks southeast of the Soviet embassy. The closer they came to the lane and away from the plaza, the thinner the crowd got. Canidy's stride both lengthened and quickened, the sight of the men fleeing generating a reaction similar to that of a dog going after fleeing squirrels.

Canidy saw the tall man, flanked and followed by ten of the hard-looking men. They hurdled a broad stone bench at the edge of the plaza and disappeared into the shadows of the narrow lane.

Canidy was now at a full sprint, weaving among the thinning crowd as he approached the lane. In his periphery he could see Fulmar a half step behind him to the right. He couldn't see McDermott, who was trailing several steps behind: the difference between the infernal daily physical training and Glenfiddich-soaked bannock made manifest.

Canidy leapt over the stone bench as if it weren't there, but slowed almost immediately and came to an abrupt halt just outside the narrow lane, the buildings lining each side shrouding it in gloom. Were he to run headlong into such an obvious kill zone and be riddled dead by dozens of rounds of fire, Donovan would be sure to exhume his corpse and fire another six rounds into his lifeless remains for being so blindingly stupid.

Canidy, Fulmar, and McDermott stood just outside the lane. The stone pavement was flanked on either side by small shops and apartments. Canidy pulled his M1911 from his hip and held it in front of him at the low-ready, keeping it hidden from the crowd in the plaza behind them.

"Now what?" Fulmar whispered, instantly feeling foolish, as if the ambient noise of the crowd behind them wouldn't drown even a robust shout.

"I don't see one damn person," Canidy said, surprised. "Not even a civilian. Where in hell did everyone go?"

Fulmar said, "They were fast, but not that fast. It's as if they fell through a trapdoor and everyone else in the alley followed along."

Canidy peered into the murky lane, scanning the recesses, bays, and alcoves. No signs of activity. In contrast to the bustling plaza, it was desolate and quiet.

"It's as if everyone evacuated this place," he said.

"Do you think they're getting assistance from someone? Sympathizers?" McDermott asked.

Canidy shrugged. "Maybe."

"Well, if there was a question regarding German presence during the summit, it's been answered," Fulmar said. "Just as expected. But now we know for sure. We did our job. We kept our eyes open."

"I'm not completely sure we did," Canidy said. "I'd feel better if we'd caught or killed them." He kept his eyes on the lane as he began backing out. "We're not going in there without support. We need to go back to the legation and report this to Sandul, who'll get it back to the Office. Now that the German presence is confirmed, they'll triple security and do whatever it is they do to protect everyone—extend the perimeter, send troops out into the city."

"*They* will act, too," Fulmar said. "Now that they know *we* know, they'll make adjustments. They didn't come all the way here just to test our security, take in the sights, and go home."

"And we still have the matter of Gromov," McDermott reminded them. "I'd say we haven't solved anything. Things are even more complicated than they were this morning."

Canidy saw that something in the lane had caught McDermott's eye.

"Move!" McDermott shouted.

"What?"

"*Gun.*"

The three men spread out and ducked instinctively as a tongue of flame spat from a weapon protruding from an alcove between two shops down the lane. Fulmar and McDermott dove to the pavement as multiple fragments of stone from the building to their right exploded into the air above them. Canidy flattened himself against the wall to his right, placing a hand over his face to protect his eyes from the flying debris. He felt a sharp twinge of pain in the shoulder hurt during the Brandenburger attack in Gotland.

Even before the gunfire came to a stop, Fulmar and McDermott rolled toward the same wall on the left. Each drew his weapon.

Canidy glanced to his right, squinting against the flying debris. "They're four doors down!" he shouted. "On the right!"

Several more rounds tore stone and mortar from the walls above Canidy. He flattened himself against the pavement just as several rounds caused jets of stone to erupt like geysers from the wall where his head had been.

Squinting against the flying debris, Canidy saw several shadows darting from recesses on the right side of the lane. Canidy leveled his M1911 and squeezed a three-round burst at the shadows, unsure whether he'd hit any of them before he pressed his head hard against the pavement as several rounds of return fire sailed over his head.

Canidy yelled at Fulmar to lay down suppressing fire so that he could advance against the fire, but several more rounds screamed over their heads, causing Fulmar and McDermott to flatten once again against the pavement. Canidy cursed vehemently, fired a round, jacked himself up to his feet, and sprinted toward the fire in a zigzag pattern, Fulmar shouting angrily for him to get down.

Canidy fired another round toward movement he detected against the right wall. He saw bits of fabric spurt into the air followed by an eruption of pink mist. He dove to the pavement once again when a burst of fire screamed over his head. After a pause, he exhaled, braced, and began to propel himself forward, then dropped once again to the pavement and listened. Other than indistinct sounds from the plaza behind him, nothing.

He lifted his head slightly and scanned the lane in front of him. Nothing except the dissipating haze of gunfire. He remained still on the pavement, weapon trained forward, for nearly thirty seconds, listening. Then he turned to his left and looked behind him. Fulmar and McDermott lay a few feet behind to the left. They appeared unharmed.

Canidy shimmied to the wall on his right and slowly rose with his back against it. Fully erect, he stood still and listened and watched for another half minute. The only sensations he registered were the gloom ahead, the buzz from the plaza, and the faint acrid blue gun smoke.

"They're gone," Fulmar said.

"How?" McDermott asked.

"Hell if I know," Fulmar replied. "They were there and then they weren't."

Canidy continued to peer into the gloomy lane, cautiously looking for movement. "They must have had a plan," he said. "Just in case they were followed. They executed it with precision." He shook his head. "They just disappeared. Precise, disciplined, efficient. Sound like anyone we've encountered before?"

"But stupid," Fulmar said.

"I agree," McDermott seconded in a low voice. "There is no way in hell they wanted this to happen."

"No argument there," Canidy continued to stage-whisper. "Sure, the Allies secured the summit in case of German sabotage. But revealing that they are, in fact, here, with *gunfire* no less, clearly wasn't in their game plan. German heads are going to roll over this."

The three remained still for several minutes. Then Canidy looked ahead into the lane and announced, "Time to go."

No more than two seconds after they had begun to move, McDermott's upper-left sleeve tore open as a round grazed his triceps. All three turned toward the source. The tall man was sprinting down the lane, this time behind several other men, athletic and fit.

Canidy's instinctive reaction was to give chase, second-guessing himself as he did so. But he caught Fulmar and McDermott in his periphery doing the same thing and kept moving, while thinking that everyone in the lane was mad.

There are at least a half dozen, thought Canidy. *Yet, they are fleeing. At astonishing speed.*

The runners came to a small courtyard with a stone bench in the middle. Everyone, the pursued and the pursuers, leapt over the bench without breaking stride, resembling hurdlers in a steeplechase. The tall man and his companions broke twenty degrees to the right into an alley less than half the width of the lane. Canidy pivoted after them and took several steps before stopping abruptly. Fulmar and McDermott barely avoided crashing into his back.

As if waking up from a dream, Canidy said, "Let's get the hell out of here."

The trio backed out of the alley, keeping an eye on the gloom into which the tall man and his companions had disappeared. Once back in the lane, they retreated until they had returned to the brightness of the plaza.

"Instinct," Canidy explained between labored breaths. "Instinct can scramble your brains. Acting on instinct can get you killed."

"You weren't alone," Fulmar said. "All three of us reacted the same way."

"That doesn't make me feel any better," Canidy said. "Three out of four times that would get us killed, and the only reason it didn't this time is that they made a bigger blunder than we did. They drew attention to themselves by running. Then, apparently not satisfied with that, somebody takes a shot at us." Still panting, Canidy shook his head. "Somebody's going to pay when it gets back to their boss. Smart, efficient, and disciplined—isn't that what they would have us believe?"

Fulmar's eyes narrowed in thought. "Exactly. Being smart, efficient, and disciplined is their reputation. So we think what we just saw the last few minutes was a big screwup." He paused. "But maybe it wasn't a screwup. Maybe they *wanted* us to see them. To make us *think* it was a screwup."

Canidy smiled sardonically. "They don't pay us to think. We get paid to do. We get paid to tell the thinkers what we saw so they can take appropriate steps, like tripling security."

Canidy, Fulmar, and McDermott walked across the plaza toward the British embassy. They would report what had just happened: that they'd given chase to several formidable men; that they'd been shot at by such men, who'd seemed as if they wanted to be reported.

They did not know where those men, the enemy, were.

Perhaps just as troubling, they did not know the location of an ostensible ally, Colonel Taras Gromov.

CHAPTER 43

Canidy, Fulmar, and McDermott stood in the vestibule just past the entrance to the American legation, waiting for Sandul. Staffers were moving about, performing indefinable tasks; the imperative to look competent, efficient, and busy was paramount, since the President and his entourage were scheduled to arrive tomorrow. Canidy had seen a list of luminaries posted on the ornate easel next to the front desk. In addition to Franklin Delano Roosevelt, W. Averell Harriman, ambassador to the Soviet Union; General Hap Arnold of the U.S. Army Air Forces; Admiral William Leahy, the White House chief of staff; and Harry Hopkins were due to arrive. Canidy didn't recognize the other names on the display, but their titles all appeared to contain some version of "secretary," "deputy secretary," or "assistant secretary" of nearly every department in the federal government.

As opposed to the other collections of titled individuals, this one, Canidy thought, seemed warranted. This was not, after all, a meeting of county commissioners in a small upper-Midwestern city to decide the awarding of a sewer contract. The Big Three would be deciding the conduct of the greatest war in human history as well as the shape of the world in the aftermath. The lives of billions—many yet unborn—would be affected by the decisions made in the next few days. The presence of an extra brain or two from some obscure department wouldn't impede the proceedings.

Canidy was the first to notice Sandul walking briskly toward them.

"You probably know that Donovan won't be here," he said.

Canidy looked confused. "No, we didn't know for sure. But I didn't expect him to be. Was I wrong to have thought that?"

Sandul waved him off. "Doesn't matter. Donovan expects you to keep alert and vigilant. You're not protecting the President or any VIPs, but be alert for any and all opportunities to obtain information." He paused. "And I'm given to understand he *expects* information."

"Here's some information," Canidy offered. "Germans are here. And they seem to have made a point of letting us know they're here."

Sandul said, "Everyone would be surprised if the Germans *didn't* have people here."

"Right," Canidy said. "So why make a Broadway production of making it unmistakably clear?"

Sandul's forehead wrinkled. "Don't know. Maybe to distract us. Maybe to let us know they can do whatever they want to. Or maybe it was a mistake."

"These guys don't make mistakes. They know our security is vigilant. That it's here to prevent them from disrupting the conference or assassinating anybody. They want to cause *us* to make mistakes."

Sandul shrugged nonchalantly. "So, don't make any."

"Right," Canidy said. "I wish I'd thought of that." He eyed a tall woman with short blond hair, who cast a glance in his direction as she crossed the lobby. She wore a close-fitting *gimnasterka* and skirt and, Canidy thought, wore it very well. He jabbed a thumb in her direction and asked Sandul, "Friend of yours?"

"Alina Morozova, Soviet Ministry of Foreign Affairs. I don't know her title, but I do know she reports directly to Vyacheslav Molotov. She's been talking to Ambassador Harriman's people about having the President stay at the Soviet embassy so he doesn't have to travel across town."

Canidy began moving in her direction. "Maybe I should introduce myself."

Sandul grabbed Canidy's arm and grinned. "No chance, Dick. She's colder than Siberia in January."

Canidy retrieved the photo of Gromov with his free hand and displayed it to Sandul. "To ask about this." He pulled free of Sandul and intercepted Morozova before she reached the front entrance. Flashing a charming grin, he said, "Excuse me, Miss Morozova . . ."

Morozova stopped, turned toward the approaching Canidy, and imperiously looked him up and down. Then, to the astonishment of Sandul and to the amusement of Fulmar and McDermott, she flashed an inviting smile.

"I'm Major Richard Canidy. I'm hoping you can help me. I need to finalize certain security arrangements with one of your people, but I've been having a difficult time locating him and we really only have a few hours left."

Canidy displayed Gromov's photo. Morozova examined it and then looked skeptically at Canidy. "What is your name again, Major?"

"Richard Canidy, assistant to the undersecretary for management. There are several logistical items we need to finalize before the conference and we don't have much time in which to do it. My boss expects everything to be in order before our people arrive in Tehran, and I'm behind the eight ball."

Morozova looked quizzically at Canidy.

"I'm behind schedule and under pressure," Canidy explained.

Morozova took a closer look at the photograph and then examined Canidy's face. "The individual is not familiar to me, Major. If, however, you give me the photograph, I will inquire at our embassy. Given the urgency, I am sure he will be located and directed to contact you immediately."

Canidy held on to the photo. "Thank you, Miss Morozova. That's very kind of you, but I should really hold on to this just in case he appears, so I know it's him. I wouldn't want to be staring directly at him and not know he's my contact."

"As you wish, Major." Morozova turned on her heel and without politesse continued on her way.

Canidy returned to the group. "It's fair to say I've had better success with the ladies in the past."

"So, nothing?" Sandul asked.

"No." Canidy shook his head. "She recognized the photo. I can't say she knows him well, but she's seen him around. My sense is she's savvy enough to keep her mouth shut even if the guy's just the doorman."

"Gromov's a distraction, Dick," Sandul said. "You know the Germans are here. You know they are up to no good and they are brazen. Donovan wants you to watch out for *them*."

Canidy looked sharply at Fulmar and McDermott. "Donovan

wants us to keep our eyes open and to *think*. We know what the Germans are up to: no good. But what about the Soviets?"

Sandul exhaled forcefully. "Geez, Dick. They're our allies. Sure, Stalin's a manipulative, duplicitous son of a bitch, but we're fighting the same war, the same adversary." He nervously ran his hand through his hair. "And we can't have any incidents on the eve of the most consequential conference of the century. Can you imagine the consequences?"

Canidy looked about the area to make sure none of the diplomats, aides, and secretaries noticed his agitation. "Just a short time ago we had a bunch of Germans trying to take our heads off. *Those* are the consequences. And I don't see anybody from State or elsewhere doing a damn thing about it. Hell, they *can't* do a damn thing about it because nobody knows where the Germans are. Nobody knows what the Soviets are up to, either. I hate to break it to you, but they're not our friends. They double-crossed us on a pretty big matter just a couple of months ago. They were thinking four steps ahead of us. That's not going to happen again. Not to us. No more double crosses."

"You base all of that on a picture?"

Canidy leaned toward Sandul with an intense look in his eyes. "I base all of that on the fact that several people have been trying their best to kill us and have come damn close to succeeding. That tends to concentrate the mind."

"Donovan—"

Canidy cut him off. "Donovan expects us to use our brains. My brain says we cannot ignore a man's photo sent to us in a diplomatic pouch. Sent without explanation or elaboration. We were expected to know what to do with it."

Sandul took a step back and put his hands up. "Your call. Just trying to sort things out. What's next?"

"Back to that hovel you got for us," Canidy replied. "We're sure not going to get many chances for sleep in the next forty-eight hours, so we need to grab three or four while we can."

CHAPTER 44

Skorzeny stood before a chalkboard—like a professor quizzing his students—as the Brandenburgers stood in a semicircle several meters away. With a piece of chalk, he drew a rough map of the Soviet embassy, the plaza, and the lanes surrounding them. Then he turned to the men.

"Where did you first encounter them?" he asked.

The tall blond man approached the blackboard and pointed to the area of the plaza closest to the Soviet embassy. "Approximately here, Herr Skorzeny." He then traced his finger across the plaza to the lane into which the enemy had chased them. "When they identified us, I signaled to the men and we ran into the alley. The three men pursued us."

"Surprising," Skorzeny said.

"Yes, Obersturmbannführer. I merely sought to flush them out. I believed they would not pursue us into an alley. We outnumbered them and they could not know if we were armed. Not intelligent."

Skorzeny gazed at the sketch while putting a finger to his chin in thought. "Perhaps," he said. "But they were each in civilian clothes, correct?"

"Yes, Obersturmbannführer."

"You were flushing them out and identified three of them on the basis of movement. They were likely doing the same, even though they did not initiate the maneuver." Skorzeny turned to his left and pointed to a lean Stabsgefreiter with short white blond hair and pale blue eyes. "Wolf, please show everyone the sketches of the men."

The Stabsgefreiter held up a large sketchpad with charcoal drawings of three individuals.

Skorzeny asked the tall man, "How do you assess the accuracy of the corporal's sketches?"

"Very good, Herr Obersturmbannführer," the tall blond man said. "Acceptable for purposes of identification."

Skorzeny nodded agreement. He'd easily recognized the subjects. He pointed to each. "This one is American major Richard Canidy, this is Lieutenant Eric Fulmar, and this is British sergeant Conor McDermott. Everyone will study Wolf's renderings when we are finished here. Memorize them." Skorzeny turned back to the chalkboard and pointed toward two buildings across from the terrace of the Soviet embassy. "Unterscharführers Richter and Macht, you are comfortable with these?"

Macht and Richter spoke in unison. "Yes, Obersturmbannführer."

"How would you assess the degree of difficulty of hitting the targets within the agreed window?"

Macht glanced at Richter. "Striking all three targets is no more than a two, perhaps a three. That presumes the targets are arrayed on the terrace as presently anticipated."

Skorzeny nodded and pointed to a slightly taller structure south of the two buildings where Richter and Macht would be. "Benz and Kohl, how do you assess your difficulty?" Benz, a sinewy, hardened veteran of several nightmarish battles along the Eastern Front, turned to Kohl and back to Skorzeny. "Three, Herr Skorzeny."

Skorzeny nodded. "The probability that all will go according to plan, as you know, is near zero. That is precisely why you have been selected. For your demonstrated ability to adapt and improvise. I repeat once again, I expect the initial attempt to fail, so be prepared to immediately execute the second plan. Do not wait one second for my command. Immediately assault the western gate"—Skorzeny squinted at the sketch and pointed to the crude rendering of a gate—"here. Holtzman will be the first to get there. We estimate that he will approach it within ten meters of this entrance"—Skorzeny pointed to a triangle on the western side of the embassy—"before being cut down by NKVD guards. The explosives strapped to his torso that he will detonate before falling will provide cover for Spann and Deyling, behind which the remainder of you will advance at a distance of thirty meters. Conservatively, Spann and Deyling should advance to this point." Skorzeny pointed to an area adjacent to the Soviet embassy. "Likely farther because Holtzman's explosives should momentarily disorient the NKVD snipers, who will be arrayed throughout the complex. It is doubtful that we'll be able to locate them all before the event. Spann and Deyling will advance to just outside the terrace, or as far as they're able, and will immediately detonate their devices whenever they are struck."

Skorzeny paused and assessed the faces of the men. None revealed any emotion. He had seen this phenomenon before, most recently during the Mussolini extraction. It had less to do with character, training, or experience—all vital—than with fatalism. They were elite combatants. They expected to be here, at the fulcrum of the great war.

"Questions thus far?"

Nothing.

"The rest of you will advance as rapidly as you can, single file, ten meters apart, toward the terrace. Here you will execute the most difficult aspect of the operation: exercising restraint." Skorzeny traced a radius extending twenty meters from the terrace. "Advance as far as you can, or feel you can, before detonating your respective devices. Optimally, you will proceed to the base of the terrace itself. Your last conscious act should be—will be—detonation."

He turned to face the men directly. "Always have your hand on the detonator so that in the fleeting moment before death, you still have an opportunity to discharge. You have not been trained for this, but we are the most highly trained soldiers in human history. You have never failed. We have never failed. There is no means by which a protective service can guard against multiple highly proficient assailants who are prepared for annihilation."

Skorzeny saw only blank faces. No apprehension, no concern. Not even resolve. Inscrutable. Unsurprising, from a cohort who had witnessed the meat grinders of Stalingrad, Kursk, and Demyansk Pocket. Indeed, throughout the scores of reviews, walk-throughs, and map studies, not one of them had mentioned the one glaring omission: no discussion of any extraction plan. All intuitively knew no one was going home. Nonetheless, Skorzeny was compelled to quell any questions.

"Should Macht and Richter succeed, there will be no *need* to assault the compound. There will be no *need* for offensive detonation of your explosives." His jaw tightened with resolve. "*We will do so nonetheless.* There will be dozens of other high-level officials present. Ministers, secretaries, generals, admirals. The upper echelons of our enemies will be congregated, foolishly but propitiously, in one place. Never in the history of warfare has a combatant aggregated such a collection of principals in a single confined space. Our enemies will be staggered beyond belief. Yes, they will continue on for a period. At first ferociously, but ultimately flailing about, directionless, and dispirited. They will sue for peace and the war will come to a quick conclusion. The Fatherland shall prevail."

Skorzeny stopped. He understood he was beginning to sound like Goebbels, like someone who had never felt the sting of battle. But he also understood that these men looked up to him. He was not going to lead them into oblivion without at least a feeling of purpose and resolve. "Macht and Richter also will be strapped with explosives." Skorzeny chuckled. "This is not a statement on their marksmanship . . ."

The group laughed heartily.

". . . it is because all of us have the same stake in the outcome of this operation, including me."

There was a murmur that rose to a low rumble. "*You*, Herr Skorzeny? Why?" asked a Gefreiter.

"I am a soldier, just as you," Skorzeny began to explain, but resisted the impulse to say more. Instead, he returned to the tall blond man. "What is your assessment of the men you encountered?"

The man cocked his head to the right, thinking through the episode in the lane. "They are unconventional, obviously. Not just because they are not regular army, but because they seem to have been given permission—no, the direction—to think unconventionally. Following us into the lane was foolish, stupid. For a *conventional* soldier. But I think they did so precisely because they are unconventional. It is my assessment, Herr Skorzeny, that they must be eliminated."

CHAPTER 45

Canidy awoke with a start, disoriented.

He glanced quickly about and recalled that he was in the small apartment provided by Sandul. McDermott was asleep on a mattress across the room. The mattress between them, the one that had been occupied by Fulmar, was empty.

Canidy swung his legs onto the floor, braced himself, and thrust himself upright. He stood for a moment as if deciding what to do next. He was startled by McDermott's voice.

"What are you going to do?"

Canidy shook the sleep out of his head. "Where's Fulmar?"

"I don't know. I heard him knocking about. Maybe a couple of hours ago."

"He's probably out doing what I should be doing," Canidy said around a yawn. "I need to go out there and take a look around. We're on notice that the Germans are out there; Gromov, whatever he's up to, is out there, too."

McDermott yawned loudly. "Big city. You expect to just run into them?"

"I expect to have my head handed to me by Donovan if the day after the President is assassinated he asks me what I was doing the night before and I say, 'Sleeping next to a hairy Scotsman.'"

McDermott sat up, exhaled, and groaned to his feet. "I'll be going with you. After I pay a visit to the water closet."

The door to the apartment opened. Fulmar was silhouetted in the doorframe.

"Sightseeing?" Canidy asked.

"Nervous. We're missing something. I just walked around thinking I might run into it, whatever it is."

Canidy inspected Fulmar's face. He looked haggard. "I have the same feeling. I'm about to do a couple of laps myself. McDermott claims he's coming along."

Five minutes later they all were heading in the direction of the Soviet embassy. The night was eerily still. No sound, not even a breeze. Not the slightest indication that three of the most powerful men in the world would soon be arriving in the midst of the biggest war in history.

"A bit less than two miles from here," Fulmar said, "there's very heavy security around the perimeter. I estimate more than a thousand Red Army soldiers, assuming half are asleep right now. An equal number of rough-looking civilians, likely NKVD."

"No doubt that they're reliable and fiercely loyal to Stalin," McDermott said.

"No doubt," Canidy agreed. "Or they wouldn't be here. They'd be in a grave somewhere in Russia."

"Lots of British troops here also," Fulmar remarked.

They walked the rest of the way in silence, their heads on a swivel. It was remarkably quiet for a city of more than a million. Canidy surmised that the Brits, having had a robust presence in the country for some time, had prevailed upon the young shah Mohammad Reza Pahlavi to keep order. The presence of so many British, American, and Soviet security personnel no doubt had a sobering influence as well. Despite the calm, Canidy realized his right hand was resting on the stock of his M1911, thumb on the cocked hammer lock.

The trio slowed when they drew within four hundred meters of the Soviet embassy. Fulmar informed them, "We won't be able to get much closer here. We'll need to loop to our left and go over to the British side."

"What happens if we keep going?" Canidy asked.

"Not completely sure," Fulmar replied. "But I bet there's a fair chance they'd shoot first and interrogate our corpses later. These are Red Army troops and NKVD officers. They don't play nice. Hell, they don't play."

"Just a bit closer," Canidy said. "I need to get a sense of the layout."

"I doubt we'll see Gromov casually strolling about, if that's what you're expecting," McDermott muttered.

A short distance ahead, the trio could see regular Red Army troops at attention, along with a cordon of vehicles forming an extended perimeter around the Soviet embassy. A few officers were moving about the perimeter. The remainder of the troops appeared to be standing at parade rest.

Canidy, Fulmar, and McDermott stopped to examine the security perimeter. After more than a minute Canidy said, "*That* would be difficult to penetrate."

"Sheer suicide," McDermott agreed.

Fulmar nodded tentatively. "True. For a direct assault. Whoever tried it would be cut to ribbons, even if it was a fairly sizable force." He waved his hand in the direction of the boulevards approaching the embassy. "More likely, any attempt would need to happen on the approach to the embassy. With, say, an armored vehicle ramming the procession, followed by a squad or, even more likely, a platoon of soldiers with grenade launchers and Maschinenpistole .40s and the like."

Canidy nodded. "A force like that might be able to do it. But, of course, they'd be spotted a kilometer away. Hell, even well before that. The Brits and Soviets control most of the access points, including the Trans-Iranian Railway.

"But I bet there are still remnants of a sizable Nazi force out in the territories, purposely stationed there to ensure oil kept flowing to the Wehrmacht even after the Soviets invaded. Hell, the shah considers himself to be an Aryan; Hitler's pal."

McDermott pointed in the direction of the British embassy. "The protective cordon extends well beyond the Soviet embassy to the Brit embassy. That's a large area for any hostile force to penetrate before being cut to ribbons."

"Does the Wehrmacht do suicide missions?" Canidy asked.

Fulmar shrugged. "Don't know. Haven't heard of any. Although I bet the Germans at Stalingrad sure thought that turned into one."

Fulmar and McDermott followed Canidy's lead as he turned left to circumvent the perimeter of the security cordon. The number of men in plain clothes exceeded the uniformed presence. Canidy gestured toward them. "NKVD?"

"Most assuredly," McDermott said. "Stalin's pet dragons. They don't bother with observing the rules of warfare. I'm not sure they even recognize that there *are* rules of warfare. Best to steer clear of them."

Fulmar smiled. "I know what you were thinking, Dick. Be honest. You thought we were going to take a little stroll through the beautiful and placid streets of exotic Tehran and run into Colonel

Taras Gromov, didn't you? Maybe engage him in a discussion, per-
suade him not to do whatever bad things the Thorisdottirs anticipate he's going to do." Fulmar mimicked a patrician voice. "If we
could just *reason* with him, I'm sure we could reach a common understanding and avoid any unpleasantry or belligerency. After all,
that is the way of civilized nations."

Canidy withdrew the photo of Gromov from his hip pocket and
displayed it to Fulmar and McDermott. "Just in case."

McDermott took the photo from Canidy's hand and inspected it
closely. "The lying, thieving Thorisdottirs sent this to you," he said.
"The most manipulative beings God, in his infinite wisdom, ever
placed on this Earth. Whatever their purpose in doing so, gents, it
is not an honest one. Not one that helps the Allies. It is in service of
their interests and their interests alone."

Canidy took the photo back and put it into his hip pocket.
"Sure, it serves their interests. There aren't many pure altruists these
days. Maybe they owe him money. Maybe they're afraid he'll kill
them. But remember, we're here in part because of the story they
told. Whether the story is true, false, a double blind, or a double
cross, someone wants us to believe it."

"*Stalin* wants us to believe it," McDermott said dismissively. "He
wants us to believe Hitler is going to assassinate the Big Three."

Canidy nodded. "We're all agreed that's a crock. At least, that's
where the smart money is, without question."

McDermott stopped and faced Canidy, prompting Canidy and
Fulmar to stop also. "Look," McDermott said. "After all of the cra-
ziness we've been through in the last few months, I'm prepared to
believe a hell of a lot more than I would have before we rescued Dr.
Kapsky. The world you chaps live in—hell, the world *I* live in now—
is all deception, betrayal, and more deception. But just because it

benefits Stalin to have us think the Germans will try to assassinate the Big Three doesn't mean there's more to the story."

"But there *are* Germans here," Canidy reminded him.

"That doesn't mean they're going to attempt an assassination of the Big Three, and it definitely doesn't mean Gromov has got something up his sleeve," McDermott insisted. "The Thorisdottirs are sorceresses, witches who can get men to believe anything."

"You'll get no argument there," Canidy conceded.

McDermott twisted one end of his titanic mustache. "They're damn fine witches, I must say." He grinned. "I can't much blame you."

"The Office is different from regular military," Canidy explained. "Donovan anticipates not just the probables but the improbables and the variables. Then he sends us out, and we're expected to also anticipate the improbables."

Canidy stopped, noticing that they were drawing attention. The trio turned to their left and continued walking. They'd approached to within forty meters of a phalanx of dour-looking NKVD from whom they were getting close scrutiny.

"It's improbable that Gromov is here to do anything that will present a problem for the U.S. or Britain. Yet we can't be caught flat-footed if something unanticipated happens. Just because we're aware of Gromov doesn't mean we can't keep an eye out for the Germans, too."

"The Germans are the bad guys, as you are wont to say," McDermott emphasized superfluously.

"Yeah, well, those NKVD goons back there sure don't look like they consider us to be the good guys," Canidy replied.

The trio approached the west side of the Soviet embassy, where there was a portico backed by a half-dozen glass double doors. There were no railings along the center front, but a modest balustrade enclosed the sides and looped partially around the front corners. The three stopped at the same time, gazed at the portico, and turned to the rear. Canidy, knowing the others must have been arriving at the same conclusion as he was, said, "Degree of difficulty: between moderate and challenging."

"For most snipers, maybe," McDermott said. "But wouldn't you think they would send their absolute best?"

"They'd send more than one," Fulmar said. "Two, maybe three."

"Moderate, then," Canidy said. He gazed about the entire area, turning a complete circle as he did. "I've got to believe that same assessment was made by our people months ago, even before the President agreed to accept Stalin's invitation."

Fulmar exhaled forcefully. "You would think so, yet . . ."

McDermott raised both hands. "Wait a minute, please." The Scot put his right palm on his chest in concession. "I am skeptical regarding Gromov being some kind of a threat. I am not, however, skeptical about garden-variety negligence."

"The State Department approved Tehran as the venue for the summit," Canidy said. He pointed to the Soviet embassy. "They undoubtedly approved the embassies as possible sites for the summit. And since the Soviet embassy is the largest of the three, they had to assume it would host the summit. And if three glorified blisterfoots like us can figure that out, I'm pretty sure the State Department would have figured it out."

"Do you see any hides for countersnipers?" McDermott asked.

"Well, if I could see them, they wouldn't be very good hides, now, would they?"

Canidy returned his gaze to the buildings near the embassy and imagined himself a sniper, even though he had no training whatsoever and didn't have any idea what it entailed. Like any layperson, he supposed it required composure, focus, good eyesight, and, ultimately, shooting skills. He supposed that a highly proficient sniper of the caliber who would be tasked with the three most important targets in history would have certain criteria—a checklist—to maximize success. Among obvious factors—such as range, wind, and obstructions—would be likelihood of detection. Canidy's gaze shifted from the Soviet embassy to the nearby edifices and back to the embassy. Then he stared at the terrace for several seconds.

"Did Sandul say anything about the Big Three meeting on the terrace?"

Fulmar looked at Canidy quizzically, wondering where the question was headed. "No. I think it's assumed that at some point the historic occasion would be commemorated by a group photograph, and it seems the terrace is the natural spot for one. It therefore follows that a stationary group gathering would be an optimal place for an assassination attempt."

Canidy nodded slowly to himself. "It would, wouldn't it?" He stepped back from the buildings near the embassies and craned backward to take in the entire view. Within his field of vision there were hundreds of Soviet and British troops, NKVD officers, armored vehicles, and security personnel. Most were facing outward, with their backs to the embassies.

Canidy turned and looked at the Soviet embassy again—the terrace, the doors, the balustrade. He was irritated. Some idea buried in his mind was refusing to emerge. He tried to coax it into clarity, but couldn't quite capture it.

He was missing something. Their assumptions about an assassination attempt were off.

"What is it, Dick?" Fulmar asked.

Canidy shook his head so the question wouldn't interrupt his thoughts, but they evaporated before he could fully grasp them. He faced Fulmar and McDermott.

"How many Germans did you see yesterday, assuming they're Germans?"

"Ten, twelve?" Fulmar guessed.

"Eleven," McDermott said.

"Eleven," Canidy repeated.

Fulmar watched Canidy's face become lost in thought. "Whatever you're trying to figure out, do it fast," he said. "We only have a few hours until FDR, Churchill, and Stalin meet, and probably not much more than that to prevent anything bad from happening."

CHAPTER 46

They looked substantially the same as the last time he had seen
them, when they were escaping from the Germans on the *Njord*.
Perhaps a bit fitter, bulkier, and more toned. That was to be expected. After all, the last time he saw them—only a few months
ago—they had just made an arduous trek over much of northern
Poland, evading a number of Totenkopf patrols, with little food, no
sleep, and multiple engagements with a vicious and determined
enemy. They should be dead. And likely would be if not for him. As
they'd fled the Germans and scrambled aboard the *Njord* several
months ago, Gromov had picked off several of their would-be executioners. Candidy, Fulmar, and McDermott had been the beneficia-
ries of his proficiency at killing. And they continued to remain
oblivious to his presence.

Now, however, their lives were again in Taras Gromov's hands.
This time it was Colonel, not Major, Taras Gromov. This time it
was the imminent recipient of the Order of Lenin, perhaps even the
Hero of the Soviet Union. This time there was no reason to save
their lives, and several reasons to end them.

One of the reasons had nothing to do with his mission. In fact, it had nothing to do with the war. It was personal. It was not a major reason. Standing alone it would not have prompted him to kill. It did nothing to further his assignment or the interests of the Soviet Union. It had to do solely with his ego.

Kristin Thorisdottir had performed exceptionally well in deceiving the Americans. Her duplicity had secured the Kapsky notebook and, with it, Gromov's fortunes. But it was plain she was attracted to Major Richard Canidy. And that angered Gromov for the most basic of reasons: raw male competition.

Gromov conceded Canidy's attributes: he was tall, fit, and handsome in the American definition of the term. He was also cunning and daring. Despite that, he was inferior to Gromov in almost every way. Gromov was taller, stronger, fitter, and more masculine than the self-absorbed American. Gromov was also tougher, smarter, and more talented at their shared craft. Accordingly, Kristin Thorisdottir, Katla Thorisdottir, or *any* woman should have preferred Gromov to Canidy.

Gromov recognized the absurdity. He was not simply a professional. He was a professional killer. Petty jealousy was not a basis for killing and, in fact, it impaired a killer's proficiency. Gromov wouldn't permit anything to impair the operation, especially childish competition or jealousy. Rather, Canidy and his teammates fit perfectly into his assignment.

Beria had directed him to sow chaos at the conference, giving credence to the rumor that Hitler had ordered the Big Three assassinated. Canidy and his two teammates would be part of the chaos. They were integral to the plan: among the many who would die within the next forty-eight hours, Canidy, Fulmar, and McDermott were principal.

Gromov pulled his eye from the scope and looked about the

area. A few components of the plan still needed to fall into place. The summit had to be at the Soviet embassy. It would. There needed to be a symbolic gathering of the three leaders to photographically record the meeting for history. There would be. By force of his personality, Stalin would ensure it.

Then hell would be unleashed and Gromov would be the cause.

Skorzeny hadn't slept in more than forty-eight hours, but he was alert and energetic. He'd left their quarters while the men were asleep and spent the last several hours checking and rechecking the areas surrounding the three embassies. His initial conclusions hadn't changed—the Soviet embassy remained the most likely venue for the conference, and the terrace would be the location for the obligatory historic photograph.

The American legation wasn't grand enough, leaving either the British or Soviet embassy. Churchill and Stalin were forces of nature who would implacably insist that their respective embassies host the gathering. But Roosevelt, ever the calculating politician, would seek to placate Stalin and perhaps reduce the likelihood of postwar tensions between the emergent superpowers.

Skorzeny walked slowly past the plaza where his men had flushed out the three pursuers. They were undoubtedly Americans. Aggressive, but with questionable judgment.

His men would cross the plaza before approaching the outskirts of the embassy. This was where the exercise with the Americans proved instructive. The men had purchased local clothing and headwear. Otherwise they'd have been too easily detectable. The perimeters were impressively fortified but, in Skorzeny's judgment, ill-suited for the attack he had planned. The Soviets had hundreds of troops and security personnel, but it was plain to Skorzeny they were deployed so as to prevent a single invasive assault. Skorzeny's plan would sacrifice a limited number of men to breach the defenses for successive assaults.

None of his men would survive. He would not survive.

But it would work.

CHAPTER 47

Nervous energy had propelled Canidy most of the morning and had only grown in the early afternoon. Fulmar and McDermott had returned to the flat to catch a nap, but Canidy continued to walk among the embassies, watching the people and the traffic. By his third circuit around the Soviet embassy he'd become sufficiently recognizable to the dour NKVD agents that one of them waved. It was a somewhat derisive wave, a signal that they knew what he was doing. But a wave nonetheless.

On that same circuit Canidy saw someone who appeared to be a Westerner and who seemed more interested in the British and Soviet civilians than the other passersby. The interest appeared casual. The Westerner didn't strike him as suspicious. But something in Canidy's brain seized on the Westerner for further examination.

Canidy decided to follow at a moderate distance. The man was shorter than most of the other pedestrians in the area and had light to medium brown hair. His clothing was unremarkable. It wasn't identifiably Western or Persian or even something in between. But Canidy thought he *wore* it like a Westerner—a European at that.

Although he had no clues one way or another, Canidy didn't

think the man was part of the Soviet detail. Nor did he think he was attached to the British embassy. Canidy had no overt evidence to support his conclusions. It was simply a hunch, intuition.

Based on his previous wartime experiences, Canidy knew better than to ignore his hunches. So he followed him at twenty paces.

The man passed both the British and Soviet embassies without great interest, giving each no more than a casual glance or two. He approached the plaza where Canidy, Fulmar, and McDermott had given chase to the tall man. He stopped momentarily, as if deciding in which direction to go. As he looked to his left, then his right, Canidy could see his profile. A sharp nose, a shallow, crescent-shaped scar on his right cheek. The small man hesitated for a moment before slowly wading into the crowded plaza. Canidy followed, somewhat anxiously. The last time he'd followed someone into the plaza, it had culminated in a shooting gallery in one of the narrow lanes leading from the plaza.

Canidy remained at a distance of forty to fifty meters. The small man walked at an unhurried pace. His gait and body attitude were relaxed. He appeared oblivious to Canidy's proximity.

And Canidy knew it was an act. Canidy also knew he had no choice. He was compelled to follow.

The man continued to walk casually, almost as if he were baiting Canidy. *No*, Canidy thought. *He is baiting me, and he knows that I know he's baiting me and I can't do a damn thing about it. I have to follow him.*

When he crossed the plaza the man didn't enter the lane Canidy and his teammates had entered before, but the one immediately adjacent, which from Canidy's viewpoint appeared indistinguishable from the other.

And then the man broke into a sprint. Canidy took a deep breath, cursed angrily, and put his head down like a sprinter coming out of the starting blocks. He bolted into the lane, staying as close as he could to the buildings to his right.

The small man was agile and surprisingly fast. The unevenness of the pavement didn't seem to slow him at all. Canidy's larger size conferred only a slight advantage in overall speed, which was tempered somewhat by the small man's greater agility.

The man wove around several pedestrians and merchants startled by the chase. Alarmed, a few hugged the walls of the buildings flanking the lane, forcing Canidy to run down the middle of the pavement. He ran rigidly, his torso bracing for the possibility of gunfire.

Ahead, the small man dodged a pedestrian carrying a large wicker basket and continued running without the slightest pause. The startled pedestrian staggered in front of Canidy, who narrowly dodged a collision and continued his pursuit. He was gaining ground. His wind was surprisingly better than he'd been used to, thanks to the rigorous workouts on Gotland he'd despised as nothing more than simple punishment.

His quarry darted into an alley to the right. Canidy stopped abruptly. So far, there had been no fusillade, but Canidy suspected this was as likely a place as any for one. He pressed himself against the stone wall at the entrance and darted his head into the lane to check. No gunmen visible, only the small man pumping his arms as he sprinted down the alley. Canidy gave chase.

At the next intersection the small man collided with a merchant pushing a wooden cart, sending the cart, the merchant, and the small man sprawling on the stone pavement. The small man rolled and instantly sprang to his feet, yielding no more than two or three steps to Canidy, who hurdled the merchant in stride and kept sprinting. He was now less than ten meters behind. They ran for another forty meters before the small man leapt onto a wooden stairway that ascended a four-story ivy-covered brick dwelling on the right. Canidy jumped onto the third step and climbed the stairs two steps at a time, keeping an eye on the small man, who darted into an open window on the third level.

Canidy reached the third level barely three seconds later, flattened himself against the side of the window, and darted his head into the window frame and back. Nothing but silence and shadow. He held his breath, stepped inside onto a sagging wooden floor, and braced yet again—exhaling with relief upon not being cut to ribbons.

The ten-by-ten room was vacant. Canidy could hear the receding echo of rapid footsteps on wood and followed its source to an indoor stairwell. He caught a glimpse of the top of the man's head and shoulders through the banister as he descended two steps at a time.

Canidy dashed down the stairs without hesitation, sensing that if he hadn't been ambushed by now, he wouldn't be. The small man hadn't been baiting Canidy; he'd simply made a mistake.

Between the railings Canidy could see the small man careen into a portly man, who shouted what Canidy guessed were Persian profanities. Canidy bolted down the steps, causing the portly man to press against the far edge of the landing.

"*Oskol.*"

The small man dashed through the back door of the building's vestibule with Canidy slightly more than a flight of stairs behind. Canidy took the flight in two steps, landing next to the back door, where he hesitated. He quickly stuck his head out into the alley, scanned to make sure it wasn't a trap, and then burst through the door, following the small man, who was turning the corner to the right. Canidy pumped his arms as hard as he could as he accelerated, impressed that he still wasn't winded.

He turned right at the corner and instantly found himself in a small bazaar teeming with scores of merchants and patrons. A tall, scrawny man with a bushy black beard and horrid breath thrust poultry in his face and cursed bitterly when Canidy pushed him aside to get a clear view of the marketplace. Approximately forty meters to the right he detected a jostling in the crowd. Irritated if not angry individuals were gesturing and shouting at an invisible object. The jostling spread in the direction of a northeast spoke off the plaza. Head down and arms and legs pumping, Canidy quickened his pace once again, colliding with at least three shoppers before he reached the spoke.

Again he hesitated, darted his head into the desolate alley, and accelerated after the small man, who had momentarily disappeared. Canidy glimpsed a flash of a fast-moving figure darting around random people and objects in the alley. He straightened and ran upright to keep sight of the figure that flickered in and out of the crowd as he dodged individuals in the increasingly dense alley.

Canidy was gaining incrementally, but noticeably. Although he was panting heavily, he sensed he still had sufficient energy to overtake the small man, whose stamina seemed to be waning.

Thirty more seconds. He would have him. Maybe twenty.

The small man's strides were shortening. His arms were pumping harder and his torso was pitched forward. He didn't have a weapon. If he had one, now would be the time to use it. He couldn't fend off Canidy physically, even at full strength.

The small man glanced over his right shoulder. A telltale. He was near exhaustion. He couldn't continue much longer even at a slower pace. His strides were shortening and his head was thrown back.

The anticipation of overtaking the small man fueled Canidy. His stride shortened, but only because his pace had quickened and his arms were pumping like pistons.

The small man skidded as he made a sharp turn to the right and vanished. Not having been shredded by fusillades in the last several turns, Canidy kept sprinting until he broke into the lane after the small man and came to a complete stop, bewildered. It was as if the man had evaporated.

Although Canidy had a clear view for at least one hundred meters, the lane was completely empty. No pedestrians. No merchants. The buildings on either side seemed unoccupied. There were none of the ambient sounds typical of similar quarters.

Canidy slowed to a jog and then a walk, taking large gulps of air. He swung his head from left to right, up and down, right to left, and back again. No small man. No anybody. The lane seemed abandoned. Although there were plenty of signs of life—brightly dressed windows, freshly painted façades—there were no people moving about.

Canidy stopped and turned a full three hundred sixty degrees before standing absolutely still and listening for any movement, any noise indicating human presence. The utter silence was peculiar.

The last thing Canidy saw—a fraction of a second before feeling the impact of a blunt object to his head and losing consciousness—was the tall man emerging from a doorway on the left fifteen meters ahead.

CHAPTER 48

Obersturmbannführer Otto Skorzeny examined the detailed layouts of the American, British, and Soviet embassies that were depicted on three large chalkboards in the basement of the building.
The drawings were re-creations of blueprints provided by Group
III, the Abwehr's counterintelligence division, refined by Skorzeny's
personal observations from his surveillance runs over the last forty-
eight hours.

He stood with his chin in his right hand, giving almost exclusive
attention to the schematics of the Soviet embassy. Everything he'd
seen in the last two days confirmed his assessment that the main
conference would be held there. Even though the public statements
from the respective foreign ministries were equivocal about the location, the fact that the Soviet embassy bristled with several times
the security as the American legation and the British embassy combined confirmed Skorzeny's conclusion.

Although there were obvious infirmities with the plan, Skorzeny
believed it would work. Speed and violence usually did.

The robust security around the Soviet embassy was premised
on the expectation that any assassination attempt would be from a

gunman, most likely a sniper. It also assumed that the assassin would be concerned with his own survival.

Both premises were logical. And therein was the flaw. Skorzeny's operations defied logic. They were audacious, thought impossible until he actually executed them. Because of that belief, there would be a failure to prepare for the most obvious "impossibility." Skorzeny specialized in obvious impossibilities.

Skorzeny's concentration was disturbed by the muffled sounds of movement on the floor above. Moments later Obergefreiter Wagner came down the stairs looking sheepish and perplexed.

CHAPTER 49

A small man with short brownish blond hair and severe features walked down the stairs.

Skorzeny's salute was met almost simultaneously by that of the small man.

"Obersturmbannführer Skorzeny, your reputation precedes. I am Obersturmbannführer Ernst Steiger. Admiral Canaris sent me here to relieve you."

Skorzeny examined Steiger skeptically. He had never been relieved of any assignment, regardless of its import. This particular assignment was of such magnitude that any interruption invited suspicion.

Steiger walked slowly toward the chalkboard, hands clasped behind his back. He examined the embassy layouts for a few moments before turning to Skorzeny. "Transport is nearby to convey you to an airfield—more accurately, an area suitable for air transport—in Dasht-e Kavir desert. From there you will be flown back to Germany. I will take over command of this operation."

Skorzeny kept his composure, though his anger was evident to Steiger, who, after examining the drawings on the chalkboard, turned to face Skorzeny. "Admiral Canaris has convinced the Führer that your plan will succeed, but that you and your team will be annihilated in the process." Steiger traced a finger along the perimeter of the Soviet embassy before continuing.

"Reichsminister Goebbels has persuaded the Führer that no harm must come to the most famous soldier in the war."

Skorzeny approached to within a meter of Steiger and drew himself to his full height, nearly a foot taller than the visitor.

"I have not informed anyone other than the men in this dwelling what the plan *is*. Precisely how is it that Canaris concludes the plan will succeed?"

Steiger took a step back and pointed at the layout. "Obersturmbannführer Skorzeny, you are aware that our enemies frequently refer to him as 'the Genius'? I understand that you have met with him on more than one occasion. You recognize, then, that the name is not merely ironic.

"I wager he knew what your plan would be even before you did."

Steiger pointed to the drawing of the perimeter of the Soviet embassy and the dashed lines drawn across the embassy grounds toward the balcony. "Canaris knows the objective of your mission is, almost literally, impossible. He also knows you have never failed; you *will* never fail. There is only one way to accomplish the task. He has, accordingly, concluded that the operation will succeed, but you will die in the execution of same. That, my dear Skorzeny, the Führer finds unacceptable. You are not expendable to the Reich."

Skorzeny shrugged. "'A man can die but once,'" he recited. "'We owe God a death.' But what of you?"

Steiger smiled sardonically. "Clearly I am expendable." Steiger quickly held up his hand and grinned. "Be assured, I wish it were not so. There is, however, an infinitesimally small possibility that I may survive by hurling my explosives over the balcony rather than detonating them on my frame." *My plan is different*, Steiger thought. *I shall not use your explosives. I shall use a rifle, which will be delivered shortly. I will not die.* Steiger's smile turned into a chuckle. "Hope is eternal. Indeed, a short time ago I baited one of the men that our agents had identified as an American spy. A chase ensued. A test, if you will. He was, admittedly, tenacious and clever. And quite tall. But I prevailed."

Skorzeny struggled not to reveal his disgust. It was one thing to command men in war to sacrifice themselves for the greater good. He and his men had willingly undertaken the assignment with a full understanding of the risks. It was another thing to *compel* someone to take the place of someone who had *volunteered* to die.

Steiger recognized Skorzeny's disgust. The Führer's mercurial nature had unnecessarily sent many friends to their graves. "This was not a spur-of-the-moment decision," Steiger said in the Führer's defense. "The Abwehr sent a number of agents in advance to scout the area. They assessed troop deployments and security arrangements for the conference. And they provided detailed intelligence, including the diagram you have here."

Skorzeny raised his eyebrows with surprise and skepticism. "I have seen no evidence of such agents. Neither have my men. We have been quite thorough in our surveillance and countersurveillance. As such, we likely would have detected an Abwehr presence."

"Of course. That is the objective. One of our best men spent a number of years in America. He looks and talks like an American, although he might also pass for Germanic—blond hair, blue eyes, tall and robust. As I say, he spent several years in the United States before the war and has picked up their mannerisms." Steiger grinned.

"He is said to have American ties. I do not know his name. He reports only to one man: Canaris."

Skorzeny sighed and stared at the sketches. He recognized from his interactions with the men that they took pride in being chosen for the mission, to serve under his leadership. Their very selection confirmed they were among the most elite soldiers in the war. Indeed, in the relatively brief time he'd spent with them he had concluded the Brandenburgers were a match for anyone.

And then there was the matter of the American agents. "I assume you have been tasked with eliminating the two Americans?"

Steiger simply smiled again.

Skorzeny put his hands on his hips, scanned the diagrams on the chalkboards one last time, and then saluted Steiger. No pleasantries or salutations between the men. He turned crisply on his heel and ascended the stairs to gather his bag and climb into the vehicle waiting to take him to the desert.

He would miss the bloodbath.

CHAPTER 50

The disorientation Canidy experienced when he regained consciousness was gone, but his head still pounded. He'd seen several men a fraction of a second before losing consciousness and considered himself fortunate that he'd only suffered a blow to the head and a concussion.

A swarm of State Department personnel and military officers was moving about rapidly and purposefully throughout the American legation and the surrounding area in anticipation of the President's arrival. The maelstrom combined with the blur of movement was sufficiently disorienting that he didn't notice Fulmar and McDermott approach him until they were a few feet away. Both appeared alarmed.

"Where in hell have you been?" Fulmar asked. "And what ran over your face? You look like hell."

"Thanks for the compliment," Canidy replied. "But you don't have to worry. You're in my will."

McDermott was examining the left side of Canidy's head. "It would appear that you made contact with the enemy."

Canidy nodded. "Where's Sandul? I have a pretty good idea of the general area where the enemy may be. I also think there might be a lot of them."

Fulmar asked, "Lots of Germans? Here?"

"I don't know exactly how many, but one is too many. And I'm pretty sure there's more than one."

"I last saw Sandul back in that area," McDermott said, pointing to the management offices situated at a right angle to the entrance. "He was on a telephone."

Canidy brushed by them and strode rapidly toward the office. Through the window of the office door he saw Sandul on the telephone. Sandul waved him in. Canidy entered with Fulmar and McDermott behind him and motioned for Sandul to put the phone down. When Sandul hadn't done so in three seconds, Canidy strode to Sandul, pulled the receiver from his ear, and put the phone in its cradle. Startled, Sandul began to protest, but Canidy raised his hand sharply to stop him.

"Germans are here."

"How many?"

"Too many. And they're not here for the barberry rice."

Sandul saw the purple discoloration across Canidy's hairline. "Looks like you've had personal experience."

"We need to flush them out. For the second time now they've tried to flush *me* out, gauge my reaction, and—I don't know— maybe lure me in for the kill. They're pretty brazen about it. Confident. We need to find them before the conference begins."

Sandul tilted his head skeptically. "We—meaning . . ."

"Everybody we can get to find where these bastards are and kill them. I think I know the general area they may be in. Twice now they were heading in the same direction. We need to do a block-by-block, building-by-building search. I can lead the way."

Sandul raised his hands. A matador fending off a bull. "Whoa. Wait. Slow down a minute."

Canidy took a step forward and leaned into Sandul's face. *"Right now. Time to act. No waiting."*

Rather than flinch, Sandul also leaned into Canidy's face, surprising both Fulmar and McDermott.

"Don't try to boss me around like a kid just because I wear a suit and not fatigues. I'm not your enemy. I just don't have the clout to direct the military what to do. Especially because they're all on protective detail for the President and the diplomatic entourage." Sandul turned sharply on his heel and motioned for Canidy to follow. "But I know who does."

Canidy, Fulmar, and McDermott followed Sandul across the lobby as he approached two nondescript men in dark suits standing adjacent to the doorway. Sandul extended his hand to the man on the left, who grinned as Sandul shook his hand.

"Bowman," Sandul said, turning to Canidy. "Meet Canidy. He has something that the Secret Service should know about. Dick, this is Cedric Bowman, reports to Mike Reilly, Secret Service."

Bowman turned to Canidy. The gravity of Canidy's expression caused Bowman's grin to evaporate. "What can I do for you, Mr. Canidy?"

Canidy was blunt. "You can use whatever clout you have to get troops to the area outside the Soviet embassy district and find the Germans there who are going to disrupt the conference."

Bowman looked at once alarmed and bewildered. He responded calmly and deliberately, yet somewhat skeptically. "I take it you have credible information that there are German operatives nearby who pose a threat to the President as well as the prime minister and the marshal?" Bowman looked at Sandul, then back at Canidy. "Forgive me, but tell me again, who are you?"

In no mood for niceties, Canidy responded tersely, "Major Richard Canidy, Office of Strategic Services." He gestured toward Fulmar and McDermott. "Lieutenant Eric Fulmar, also of the OSS, and Sergeant Conor McDermott, detailed to British MI6. Fulmar and I report to General William Donovan, who reports to President Franklin Delano Roosevelt; McDermott reports to Stewart Menzies of MI6, who reports to Prime Minister Winston Churchill."

Canidy had Bowman's skeptical attention. Canidy continued. "We have good reason to believe that there are German agents in Tehran—"

"We are operating under that same assumption," Bowman interjected.

"This isn't an assumption," Canidy responded tersely. "This isn't speculation. This is certain. They're not—in my estimation at least—trying hard to conceal the fact that they're here. That alone should be troubling. What's more troubling is they don't appear to be intelligence gatherers, spies. They're belligerents. Combatants. They appear to be specially trained. We've encountered men like them a couple of times recently and it wasn't a pleasant experience."

"Specially trained? What do you mean?"

"Not ordinary conscripts. Not regular troops. They're specialized. But more than that, smart, fast, strong, mean. We can't wait for them to come here. To dictate the fight. We've got to go there. Find them and destroy them."

Bowman looked conflicted. Canidy understood. A guy he's never met tells him he's got to get troops to go hunt and kill Germans somewhere in Tehran before they get to the legation or the conference and kill the President of the United States. Hysterics and overreactions were not qualities that enhanced reputations in the Secret Service.

"Understand something, Bowman," Canidy said sympathetically. "No one wants to be the Chicken Little of the outfit. But if you don't get troops out there right now, the Germans will relocate, we won't find them, and there *will* be a catastrophe. And when the dust clears and the history books are written, somewhere it's going to say, 'Agent Bowman declined to send forces to destroy the threat and, as a result, Roosevelt, Churchill, and Stalin were blown to kingdom come in the most catastrophic assassination in world history.'"

Bowman's jaw jutted forward and his eyes became bloodshot. It took him only a few seconds to cross the lobby and disappear into a hallway.

"Hell." Canidy sighed. "I should have handled that better."

"I don't disagree," Sandul conceded.

Canidy asked, "Any ideas?"

Fulmar and McDermott shrugged. Sandul pointed out the windows next to the front entrance. Several dozen troops were gathered around an officer who was in an animated conversation with a civilian in a suit. The civilian pointed at something in the distance and the officer nodded. Then Bowman appeared next to the civilian, pointing in the same direction and nodding.

Canidy turned to Fulmar and McDermott. "Come on. They need direction."

The trio walked outside and approached Bowman, the civilian, and the officer, who paused in midsentence and looked curiously at Canidy, who dispensed with salutations. "Are you going after the damn Germans?"

Bowman said, "Lieutenant Braden, this is who I was telling you about. Major Canidy."

"Not if we don't know where to look."

"I can tell you, not far from here. They're likely in the neighborhood southeast of the plaza, east of the Soviet embassy. Approximately half a kilometer east. It's got two- and three-story buildings with shops and apartments."

Canidy thought Braden looked alert and bright, but extremely ambivalent, if not skeptical. "That doesn't narrow it down much."

"Best I can do," Canidy said. "So you better get going so you've got enough time for a thorough search."

Braden looked at him skeptically. "Maybe this is something for the Secret Service."

"Maybe this is something for the Secret Service and *you*," Canidy said.

"The Soviets are closer," Braden said. "They've got lots more personnel, too."

"We're not trusting the security of the President of the United States to the damn NKVD," Canidy said.

Braden glanced about anxiously. Canidy expected he was searching for a superior officer to make the decision. The nervous lieutenant didn't want to make the call and doubted he had the authority to make the call. He pointed to Canidy and said, "Wait here, sir."

Braden dashed into the legation. He was gone for no more than fifteen seconds before returning.

"Did you find someone who can make the call?"

Braden shook his head sharply. The look on the young lieutenant's face was at once full of fear and determination. He signaled to the group of men who followed him, and turned to Canidy, Fulmar, and McDermott. "Lead the way."

Young Lieutenant Braden has a set of cast-iron balls, Canidy thought. *I'm not sure even I would do something like this.*

He looked at Fulmar and McDermott, both of whom were looking at Braden with raised eyebrows. Fulmar tilted his head close to Canidy's and asked, "Relative of yours?"

Canidy turned to Braden. "Twenty minutes by foot," he said, a hint of admiration in his voice.

"Colonel Crockett will be back from the Soviet embassy in a little over an hour," Braden said. "We better be back by then."

Colonel Taras Gromov stood behind a concrete planter less than a block away and watched Canidy, Fulmar, and McDermott lead approximately a dozen troops heading east. The trio was oblivious to his presence, just as they had been in Poland a few months ago. Gromov could easily kill all three right now and fade into the city without detection. But that would disrupt the primary mission: creating havoc at the conference sufficient to convince Roosevelt and Churchill—and their respective countrymen—that Hitler had sent assassins to kill them. Killing Canidy now would cause the American, British, and Soviet embassies to lock down and cancel or at least postpone the conference until another location could be found. Any decision to open up a Western Front against the Germans would be delayed until then.

Gromov was patient. They had no idea what he looked like. He would have sufficient time and opportunity to kill Canidy during the disruption of the Big Three summit. To Gromov, the task of assassinating Canidy was not a directive, not an order. It was a luxury.

CHAPTER 51

The area east of the plaza near the Soviet embassy was quiet and dark. Canidy and Braden walked two abreast, followed by Fulmar, McDermott, and the remainder of Braden's platoon.

The darkness compounded Canidy's general unfamiliarity with the area, but he had no problem finding the lane that formed a spoke off the plaza. Braden signaled to his men, who split into two columns and hugged the walls to the buildings on the other side of the lane. There was little animation in any of the windows.

McDermott said, "If we can't find them, maybe we can still contain them. If we fan out and proceed eastward along three or four lanes, we might be able to contain them. Deter them."

Fulmar nodded. "At least it would increase the odds of encountering them. And even if we don't see them, they may see us and realize we'll detect them if they try to advance on the conference . . ."

". . . or, having seen us, they'll know how to avoid us," Canidy said. "Let's keep moving. Movement has a better chance of shaking things loose."

They moved slowly eastward, Canidy leading the way with Fulmar, McDermott, and Braden a few steps behind. The lanes were quiet and dark save for an occasional glow from a candle or lantern in a window. Canidy scanned the buildings along their right flank for the building to which he'd chased the small man. The surrounding darkness made them nearly indistinguishable. Their heights were nearly identical and their façades all consisted of a dark red brick-like material.

Canidy found the silence and lack of any activity whatsoever unnerving. It was late, but this was a large city with a teeming population, yet everyone seemed to be in bed by dusk. It was as if they were purposefully lulling the Allies into a false sense of security.

He turned to Braden and pointed at the building, when a grossly obese man with a thick black beard materialized in a doorway to their immediate right and raised a hand as if hailing a cab. The gesture was met with the rustle of a dozen M1 Garands being trained in the man's direction. Squinting at the obese man, Canidy raised his hand and said, "Hold it."

The obese man took a cautious step forward, then two more, so that he was within ten feet of Canidy. "You're searching for someone, yes?"

Canidy nodded.

"You are the one from earlier," the obese man said. "The athletic one chasing the short one, also quite athletic. You put on quite the display."

Canidy continued squinting, trying to discern the man's face. "You were there?"

"I was there."

"You're British?" Canidy asked.

"No, no. I am Assyrian. My name is Toma. My family sent me

to stay with relatives in Britain in my youth to avoid the Ottomans." The obese man put his hand down. "Though dressed as a civilian, you are an American soldier, yes?"

"That's right."

"Then you are precisely where you should be. I attempted to gain entry to the British embassy several days ago to tell them about the peculiar men housed nearby, but security for the conference is almost maniacal. I could not approach within one hundred meters."

Canidy took several steps closer, followed by Fulmar and McDermott. "What peculiar men? What were you going to tell the Brits?"

"They arrived several days ago at night. Very quiet. It was evident they did not wish to be seen, and they were not, except by me. I have bouts of sleeplessness, insomnia. So I am often awake when everyone else sleeps. I saw them arrive—approximately a dozen. Maybe two. Distinctive."

"Distinctive how?" Canidy asked.

"European, very fit, efficient. Hard men."

"And that prompted you to go to the British embassy?" McDermott asked.

"I observed one of their members walk about in the middle of the night as if he were a scout, observing. He was tall with dark hair and a scar across his cheek. Confident. Not arrogant, but someone who was used to winning."

Canidy raised his eyebrows. "You seem to come to pretty fast conclusions from mere observations."

"When your people have been the object of genocide, it is helpful to be observant."

"What did you plan to tell the British at the embassy?" Canidy asked.

"That there is a peculiar group here—on the eve of the conference among Churchill, Roosevelt, and Stalin. That they should come and see for themselves the men I just told you about. A peculiar group of Teutonic-looking men is something not to be dismissed."

Canidy looked at Fulmar, McDermott, and Braden. All three nodded. "Please show us."

Toma agreed. "Follow me, but I beg your indulgence. As an old fat man, my powers of locomotion are somewhat impaired."

Toma turned and proceeded eastward, waving for Canidy and the rest to follow.

"Hold it," Braden said. "How many are there?"

"I estimate between twelve and fifteen. Likely closer to fifteen." Toma shrugged. "But perhaps more. I cannot say that I've seen them all."

Lieutenant Braden looked at his men. Canidy knew he was making calculations. "No time to go back and get more troops, Lieutenant. They could be on the move any second. We need to be sure we get our eyes on them right now so we don't lose track of any of them before the conference."

Braden nodded agreement.

Toma began walking—waddling—at a surprisingly brisk pace. Braden turned to the men and said superfluously, "Stay alert." The Americans and McDermott followed.

They traveled east for approximately five city blocks before coming to an intersection with five spokes. Toma led them down the southeastern spoke, a lane slightly broader than the one they'd just left. It contained a mixture of commercial and residential buildings that were larger and taller than the ones in the lane. There were no lights in the buildings, making it difficult to see more than ten meters ahead. Canidy withdrew his M1911 and held it at the

334 W. E. B. GRIFFIN

low-ready. Everyone in the procession, including Toma, crept slowly and quietly.

They'd advanced steadily for nearly a half kilometer when Toma stopped and gestured toward a two-story brick structure fifty meters ahead to the right. Canidy pulled alongside Toma, who whispered, "That is where they came from."

"When was the last time you saw them?"

"I saw someone emerge from there a while ago. The impressive tall man with the scar. He departed in a waiting vehicle. I cannot be certain, but I believe I saw the man you were pursuing earlier enter a short time before that."

Canidy turned and faced Toma. "You sure know a lot, don't you?"

"When the majority of one's relatives have been exterminated, one becomes curious and vigilant regarding all manner of things. Everything and everyone must be presumed to pose a threat."

Canidy gestured for Fulmar, McDermott, and Braden to gather around him. "Toma estimates that there are twelve to fifteen men in there. Lieutenant Braden's got twelve men. Plus Fulmar, McDermott, and me. That's fifteen."

"Not enough to be sure," Fulmar said. "We need to be sure we kill or capture every single one of them."

McDermott agreed emphatically. "One or two of those bastards could pose a problem. We just didn't know letting any get away could be a disaster."

Canidy looked at Braden. "Lieutenant, is any one of you equipped with an SCR-300?"

Braden's look of incomprehension caused Canidy to rephrase his question. "A radio. Portable Galvin? Hell, seemed everyone had them in Sicily a few months ago."

Braden shook his head. "We aren't mobile. We're a detail to the embassy, not in the field, so we don't have need for one."

Though irritated, Canidy said in a measured voice, "We need support from the embassy. A platoon would be nice."

"We may be able to scare up a squad," Braden said.

"It'll have to do. But we need them as fast as possible." Canidy scanned the platoon. "Who's your quickest man?"

Braden turned to a short, wiry man standing a few feet behind him. "Morelli, do you know your way back to the embassy?"

Morelli's manner seemed tentative.

"You do or you don't?"

Morelli nodded vigorously. "Yes, Lieutenant, I know the way back."

"I need you to run your skinny ass back there as fast as you can and tell Sergeant Rohbach I said to get his squad up here as fast as he can. Understand?"

Morelli nodded vigorously again.

"Repeat it," Braden commanded.

"I need to run my skinny ass back to the embassy as fast as I can and tell Sergeant Rohbach to get his squad up here as fast as he can."

"If anyone gives you any shit, you tell them *Major* Richard Canidy said there are a bunch of damn Nazi assassins up here who are going to kill the President of the whole United States of America if they don't get here in ten minutes. *Now, go.*"

"It's more than a mile back," Fulmar said. "Let's pray his heart doesn't explode before he gets there."

Colonel Taras Gromov had completed several circuits of the British embassy, committing its features and dimensions to memory so that when needed he could act instinctively, without thinking. The difference between failure and success might be a fraction of a second.

His concentration now was on the American legation. At some point immediately after he manufactured mayhem during the meeting of Stalin, Churchill, and Roosevelt, the American delegation would return to the security of the American legation. Canidy would be among them. One of scores trying to bring order and security to chaos and danger. All energy would be directed toward the American President. Everyone else would be expendable and therefore vulnerable.

Gromov had identified several hides from which he could assassinate Canidy. In truth, he wouldn't need them. The general bedlam following an attempted assassination of the Big Three would be sufficient cover. Gromov's focus was on avenues of retreat afterward.

As Gromov completed his last circuit of the legation's perimeter he observed a blur of activity near the front entrance. An animated conversation between two American soldiers, a sergeant and a private, the latter of whom was gesturing frantically eastward.

The sergeant disappeared into the legation for several seconds. When he emerged he pointed to a squad of approximately eight men, who followed him and the private eastward at a rapid pace.

Gromov resisted a momentary urge to follow. He would wait until the chaos at the embassy. The chaos was the primary objective. He would kill Canidy, but at some point during or after.

Canidy, Fulmar, McDermott, and Braden's platoon formed a perimeter around the building to ensure that none of its occupants left undetected. The only sign of life they'd observed was a faint glow in one of the windows that seemed to come from somewhere in the center of the structure. Canidy was the closest to the spot where they'd first arrived so was the first to see Morelli return at the head of about eight to ten men, including a sergeant, who ran alongside him.

Morelli stopped next to Canidy and said, "Sergeant Rohbach, Major Canidy."

"Sergeant, here's the situation," Canidy informed him. "We're pretty sure there are a bunch of Germans up to no good in that building." He indicated toward Toma. "Our friend here says the men inside have been surveilling the embassies."

This wasn't algebra. He'd have to make sure they didn't take any action against the Big Three.

"Our best option, it seems to me, is to make sure they don't go anywhere near any of the embassies, either by containing them or, if it comes to that, killing them. Understand?"

Rohbach nodded.

"We think there may be about fifteen of them inside. If that estimate is correct, we may be able to contain them inside the building with the number of men we now have."

"How long do you plan on containing them?" Rohbach asked.

Canidy shrugged. "I'm not Doug MacArthur, but seems to me that's the logical strategy, at least until the conference ends or we can get more men up here."

"What we've got here is the most we can spare," Rohbach said. "The rest are on embassy detail."

Canidy clapped the sergeant on the shoulder. "Thanks for coming."

Rohbach smiled. "I'm probably cooked, but when Morelli told me the situation, I said, 'What the hell?' At some point you've got to make an executive decision."

The glow in the house lightened and shifted momentarily, suggesting movement within.

"Sergeant, go ahead and have your men support the men surrounding the building. Fill in any gaps in the perimeter. No one goes in or out without me saying so."

Rohbach nodded and did as Canidy requested. His men immediately moved to surround the building. As they did, the glow brightened again, as if another light had come on. Seconds later a figure obscured by shadow appeared at the front entrance and stood still. Although he couldn't see his face, Canidy suspected the figure was scanning the surroundings for options.

A few seconds later the figure began to move from the entrance and passed near a window, where the glow from the interior momentarily illuminated his face.

The small man, Canidy thought.

A second later the small man broke into a full sprint, catching everyone on the perimeter off guard. Within seconds he was past the perimeter, heading west down the lane from which the U.S. troops had come. Canidy immediately said to Fulmar, "Nobody leaves that building," before he bolted after the small man, grudgingly thankful for the physical torture he and Fulmar had undergone in Gotland.

Alarmed, Fulmar turned to McDermott and Braden.

"Nobody leaves this building. If they try, kill them all."

Steiger ran two blocks down the lane, when it veered slightly to the left, sufficiently that anyone following would momentarily lose sight of him; then he would run *away* from the direction of the

Soviet and British embassies. His pursuers would, logically, continue to move toward the embassies, and he would lose them.

He had seen the American troops surround the building and knew that he'd have no opportunity to get out when dawn broke. The mission would be thwarted. Indeed, the Americans might assault the building even before then. He calculated the odds that he'd be shot or captured as better than even. But the longer he waited, the likelihood of escape would continue to wane until it became zero.

Just before he left, he had ordered the Brandenburgers to remain put and not resist capture if it came to that. A fight between Americans and Germans a short distance from where the Big Three were scheduled to meet would likely lead to cancellation of the conference. And the opportunity to decapitate the enemy would be lost.

Canidy saw no sign of the small man. That, in and of itself, didn't concern him. He knew the small man was some distance ahead. Although there was always the possibility of ambush, Canidy remained more concerned about the safety of the embassy and the conference.

Canidy slowed to a trot and then to a fast walk. The Soviets had a massive security presence around the presumed site of the meeting. It appeared impregnable. But that, in Canidy's mind, was its chief vulnerability. The large number of troops and NKVD personnel understandably would cause almost anyone to believe security could not be breached. That, in turn, would lead to complacency. And complacency—even for a moment—was precisely what a premier assassin would be prepared to exploit.

Canidy knew the small man was that premier assassin. Hitler would send no other.

Fulmar had seen no movement in or around the building since the small man had emerged. He looked at the men nearest him. There were twenty. He had no idea if that was sufficient to contain the German troops in the building. But they'd have to do their best. Deterrence was the best weapon. *Avoid the fight with a display of superior firepower. Make the enemy think there are more of you and make them think they're outgunned, that combat is futile.*

And pray they aren't suicidal.

The silence was unsettling. A major metropolis on the verge of a monumental summit. Yet Canidy had encountered absolutely no one in the lane and seen no one in the alleys or at the intersections. Ideal circumstances for an ambush by a smaller man. Dark, no ambient light from the buildings. The small man's size would be an advantage. The blackness would more easily shroud his small frame. Canidy imagined him suddenly emerging from the gloom of a doorway or an alley and slicing Canidy's neck or impaling his back.

Canidy held his firearm at his side, index finger now inside the trigger guard. He resolved to fire at anything larger than a ten-year-old boy.

Steiger paused just before emerging from the lane into the plaza. The American was somewhere to the rear. He was an irritation and an impediment. Under the right circumstances, he might even be able to thwart Steiger's mission. The probabilities were low, yet still nagged at Steiger, distracting him from fully concentrating on the assignment: a mosquito buzzing around his ear or a jagged pebble in his shoe. It had to be addressed and eliminated.

The silence was broken by a sound, a footstep perhaps. Canidy paused, listened for a moment, then flattened himself along the exterior wall of the building to his right.

The lane ahead was vacant. The small man was out there, beyond Canidy's range of vision. He couldn't be certain of the direction from which the noise had come, but he believed it was from somewhere ahead.

He crouched and remained still. He saw nothing moving in front of him. Maybe it was the random sound of a structure settling or a noise from inside one of the buildings—something nonthreatening.

He waited approximately ten seconds before standing and training his weapon in front of him. He still saw and heard nothing. Given the narrowness of the lane, the sound of footfalls would be magnified and would echo. Canidy concluded that the small man must be farther ahead than he thought, so he moved forward rapidly. His eyes were wide to capture as much ambient light as possible and his steps were light, but he knew anyone within fifty meters listening closely would detect his approach.

Fulmar noticed the glow in the window shift and flicker as if objects were passing before its source. Moments later the front entrance of the building opened and a figure stood framed in the glow.

Fulmar nudged McDermott, crouched next to him, who nodded and nudged Braden, who, in turn, signaled and whispered to the man closest to him: "No one leaves."

The figure at the entrance took several steps forward toward the concrete planters in front of the building and turned his head slowly from left to right and back again. He didn't appear to be carrying a weapon, but he looked to Fulmar to be large and fit and able to handle himself.

The figure remained absolutely still, not as if he were listening for something, but as if he were purposely presenting himself as a target. His shoulders were back and his chin was up, defiant and fearless.

He reminded Fulmar of the nocturnal visitors to the cabin, when Canidy and he had been blown off their feet.

The plaza that teemed with pedestrians during the day was empty. Steiger walked briskly along the perimeter rather than across its center, which would be faster but would provide no cover.

The longer he walked, the more anxious he became, as if his reservoir of luck was diminishing by the second, grains of sand passing through an hourglass. A juvenile, foolish feeling, but it persisted.

He removed his Walther from his waistband and held it at his side, not from necessity, but for comfort. He glanced behind him. No one was following.

Fulmar kept his eyes trained on the figure in the doorway.

"What do you think he's doing?" McDermott asked.

"Testing," Fulmar replied.

McDermott nodded. "Right. Seeing if the coast is clear, if anyone's out there. Do you think there are any more of them out there?"

"You mean besides the guy Canidy went after?"

"Right. Is this the entire German contingent or are there more
like this around the city?"

Fulmar shrugged. "No doubt the Genius would *prefer* to have
several teams. But that would increase the probability of screwups
and detection, so it's probably unlikely." He paused for several seconds, thinking. "But if there *is* more than one contingent, we've got
a serious problem."

Canidy emerged into the plaza expecting to see the small man somewhere in its center.

He wasn't there. Canidy cursed under his breath.

He anxiously scanned the perimeter and glimpsed the small
man just as he entered another spoke on the other side of the plaza
and disappeared. Canidy's jaw muscles tensed and he startled himself, saying in a loud voice, "Just *kill* the SOB and be done with it,
Dick."

Canidy began to cross the plaza, but restrained himself and
moved along the perimeter.

The hulking figure in the doorway retreated into the building and
closed the door. The glow inside shifted and flickered.

Fulmar turned to McDermott. "This isn't going to work."

McDermott, anticipating what Fulmar was going to say, said,
"This is tactically unsound. We can't contain them from this distance without shooting them. And they'll be shooting back."

"And some will escape," Fulmar added. "We'll lose them. They'll be loose in the city." He turned to Braden and Rohbach. "You know your men. Give me your best assessment."

Braden understood and gave Fulmar a thumbs-up. "We have enough for a pincer. A squad goes to the rear to block any rear exit. Those planters look pretty thick and heavy enough for decent cover. We'll leave four men here for backup and the rest will advance to behind the planters. Nothing's going to penetrate them short of an artillery shell."

Fulmar said nothing for several seconds, thinking. Then he said, "The man in the doorway, those men in the plaza . . . they had the look of the men we had the pleasant encounters with in Gotland. Smart and highly disciplined." He exhaled.

"What does that tell you?" Braden asked.

Fulmar rubbed his neck. "We're in for the fight of our lives, or they'll stand at attention and surrender."

The edifice looked to Steiger as if it had been there for two thousand years and very well might have been. It was a small one-story structure, the exterior of which consisted of brown sandstone etched with intricate designs that he surmised had some theological significance.

Steiger glanced about to ensure he wasn't observed, then pushed open the heavy wooden door that, to his mild surprise, easily gave way without making a sound. He stepped inside and was engulfed by heavy, moldy air. There was a sound of slowly dripping water. The interior was utterly dark and he saw no evidence of light switches or candles. He'd been briefed on this, so he retrieved the box of matches from his pocket, struck one, and held it aloft to orient himself. Before the match went out he saw the rectangular stone table laden with several millimeters of dust. There were footprints in the dust on the floor leading to the table and multiple fingerprints in the dust atop the table.

The match went out. He dropped it, lit another, and saw the torch hanging diagonally from the wall. He put the match to it, it flamed brightly, and he dropped the match to the floor.

It was supposed to be beneath the floorboard under the table. Steiger shoved the surprisingly heavy table a meter, bent down, and lifted the floorboard that had the most fingerprints.

It was there as promised, in a nondescript wooden case wrapped in several layers of cloth that resembled a woolen blanket. He pulled it from the floor, laid it atop the table, opened the case, and unwrapped the blanket, kicking up a small cloud of dust.

His Mauser Karabiner 98k, along with two rectangular boxes that he surmised held 7.92×57-millimeter cartridges. Special delivery from Wolfgang Schmidt's shop.

Unlike Skorzeny, Steiger had no intention of sacrificing himself in order to kill the Big Three with explosives. That was for overrated heroes and Brandenburgers.

He bent closer to inspect the weapon and determined that it was spotless and oiled. The wrappings had kept the weapon free of dust.

History would record it as the weapon that killed Franklin Delano Roosevelt, Winston Leonard Spencer Churchill, and Joseph Vissarionovich Stalin.

McDermott and five of Braden's men circled behind the building housing the Brandenburgers to secure any rear exits. Moments later, Fulmar and Braden led the rest of the men to the front, where they used the concrete planters as cover as they trained their weapons on the front entrance. Fulmar waited a minute to give McDermott enough time to get situated. Only seconds later the front door opened and the Brandenburger who had appeared in the doorway earlier emerged. Fulmar said, "*Hände hoch.*"

"I speak English," the Brandenburger said calmly. "You speak German very well."

"Everyone out," Fulmar said, his voice hardened.

"You will get no resistance," the Brandenburger said. "I see your numbers and I am certain you have a number of men to the rear."

Fulmar's face didn't betray his surprise, yet the Brandenburger explained, "It is effectively done, finished. Once we are identified, we are impotent. Obersturmbannführer Skorzeny emphasized that our operation depends on anonymity, speed, and surprise. That is lost now."

Fulmar kept his weapon trained on the Brandenburger. "Nothing ever happens that easy," he said.

"We're willing to fight viciously, and to die, to the last man. But not for no reason." The Brandenburger then smiled slyly. "Regardless, it is not over yet."

A few people had begun to populate the area around the British and Soviet embassies as well as the plaza. Canidy hid his weapon under his shirt and stood at the west end looking in the direction in which he'd last seen the small man moving.

The small man likely was preparing for something related to the arrival of FDR, Churchill, and Stalin. Perhaps he planned to interdict one or more while they traveled to the conference site, but

Canidy still bet that any attempt would occur while they were together, and the most likely spot remained the Soviet embassy.

Canidy stopped at the northwestern edge of the plaza and asked himself what he would do if tasked to assassinate Hitler, Mussolini, and Hirohito in Tehran.

He gazed at the edifices to the west, nearest the Soviet embassy terrace, and walked warily in that direction.

Washington, D.C.

2045, 28 November 1943

Donovan cursed to himself as he reviewed the State Department reports relayed to him by the Military Intelligence Division, Office of National Intelligence, regarding the developments in Tehran. As he suspected, and as usual, they were superfluous, worthless. Diplomatic doublespeak devoid of detail and substantive analysis. What he craved but couldn't have was a report from Dick Canidy and Eric Fulmar. They knew what mattered to him and would provide a thorough accounting of such. The State Department personnel were consumed with the superficial protocols and niceties—not substance and consequences.

The OSS chief felt a sense of urgency born of years in the military and clandestine services. A sense that something calamitous was in the offing. He desperately needed information to evaluate the probabilities of disaster.

Donovan rose from the red leather chair in the den of his home off Wisconsin Avenue and poured a splash of Famous Grouse into a crystal tumbler. The chair had been part of the original office furniture when FDR had made him director of the Office of the Coordinator of Information at the National Institute of Health in 1941. In actuality, OCOI had been the predecessor to the OSS. Roosevelt knew Donovan admired the red leather chairs and couch in the office and insisted Donovan take them. Donovan declined, then relented and took one of the chairs, being certain to reimburse the Treasury for an amount twice its market value.

Donovan took a sip of the whisky and pinched the bridge of his nose as he reviewed the events described in the State Department report. FDR had landed on Saturday afternoon Tehran time, November 27. Stimson had been nervous about the President traveling down the narrow, filthy streets of the city with its open drains and sewers—and optimal opportunity for assassination.

The President had proceeded to the modest American legation with General H. H. "Hap" Arnold, Admiral William Leahy, and Ambassador W. Averell Harriman. Although the report made no mention of their presence, Donovan assumed Roosevelt had been met at the legation by Soviet foreign minister Vyacheslav Molotov and British foreign minister Anthony Eden.

Donovan cursed aloud when he saw no description whatsoever regarding the security provisions at the legation, although the report gratuitously mentioned that the British embassy was guarded by three hundred fifty men from the East Kent Regiment and the Soviet embassy was guarded by vastly more troops and NKVD.

Donovan grew briefly agitated upon reading that Molotov had informed Harriman of an assassination plot and extended Comrade Marshal Stalin's invitation to Roosevelt to move to the far more secure Soviet embassy. *Of course, the better to spy on him*, thought Donovan. Stalin might have been little more than a coarse Georgian peasant, but he was a supremely cunning and ruthless Georgian peasant. The good news, thought Donovan, was that the Communists wouldn't dare permit any harm to come to FDR while at their embassy.

The report contained no useful information about the private meeting among the Big Three on Sunday afternoon. Nor the plenary session later that afternoon. Any such information would be largely superfluous. Fresh off the Red Army's performance at Kursk, Donovan knew Stalin would dominate the conference and press for a commitment from Roosevelt and Churchill for a Western Front as soon as possible. Although both FDR and Churchill understood such a front eventually would be necessary, they'd temporize, promising a May invasion of France.

The report made reference to several ceremonial events interspersed throughout the proceedings: Churchill presenting Stalin with the Sword of Stalingrad; a dinner party celebrating Churchill's sixty-ninth birthday. There would be the obligatory photo session, Stalin likely wearing the uniform of Marshal of the Soviet Union; Churchill, who had held the rank of lieutenant colonel in the Territorial Army, would likely don an RAF commander's uniform. Roosevelt, resplendent in a light gray pin-striped suit and spotted azure tie, would undoubtedly outdo them both.

Donovan placed the report on the table and took another sip of whisky. He desperately wanted real information about what was happening in Tehran. The Germans were there. They were determined, clever, and resourceful. The military and State Department would be oblivious to their presence. Only Canidy and Fulmar would have an inkling of their intentions. As such, their odds of surviving the conference were low.

CHAPTER 52

Gromov felt the charge of anticipation. His objectives would soon be met.

President Roosevelt and his entourage had arrived. Accordingly, Canidy would be in and around the embassy and Gromov would avail himself of the first opportunity to kill him.

Creating mayhem at the conference was Gromov's primary assignment. Killing Canidy was not. It was primarily a personal indulgence, one that could not be permitted to interfere with or distract from his assignment. He would therefore discipline himself to achieve both.

Gromov would make Canidy part of the chaos. If not, Canidy would be killed at the first opportunity.

Canidy had lost the infernal small man. He had to be in the vicinity of the plaza, Canidy thought. Canidy hadn't been that far behind him.

Pedestrian traffic seemed to increase with every step Canidy took. It was still sparse, but the volume would soon make tracking a single person more difficult.

And that made Canidy increasingly nervous. The small man's actions suggested he was integral to the assassination of the Big Three. Indeed, based on his actions in the last twenty-four hours, it was likely he was the assassin. Canidy needed to locate him, see him. His instincts told him the longer the small man was unaccounted for, the greater the peril to the Allied leaders.

Canidy moved quickly past the troops outside the Soviet embassy and anxiously scanned the area opposite the terrace. The small man wouldn't be hanging around casually, presenting himself as a target. But nervousness compelled Canidy to examine every possible location that could conceal an assassin. The small man could not remain unaccounted for much longer.

Nervous energy drove Gromov to patrol first outside the perimeter of the American legation and then to travel to the Soviet embassy, where he scanned every millimeter of the perimeter for any anomaly, anything that appeared out of place, or anyone who appeared suspicious. In truth, he was hoping through sheer luck to spot Canidy. He would never permit personal pursuits to compromise his assignment. But optimally Canidy would be part of the chaos.

If he could dispense with Canidy first and still discharge his primary mission, he thought, so much the better.

Gromov watched as two military transports carrying approximately two dozen troops proceeded eastward from the American embassy. Another two empty transports followed. Given that each embassy had sufficient guards and didn't require reinforcements, he couldn't immediately think of a reason for the transports to be departing the embassy for anywhere in Tehran. Gromov desperately hated anything he couldn't immediately understand.

Steiger spotted Canidy, who hadn't spotted him.

Steiger proceeded along the west side of the Soviet embassy, using the multitude of troops and NKVD agents as a shield so Canidy couldn't see him. *Skorzeny's plan, though inspired, could never work*, thought the small man. Even if they had been able to breach the cordon, too many armed personnel would remain who could have killed the Brandenburgers before they got close enough to detonate their explosives. *Skorzeny's planning had been compromised by his ego*, Steiger thought. *So many were filling his head with assurances of invincibility that he was failing to think critically, failing to identify basic vulnerabilities in his plans.*

Steiger, on the other hand, stuck to plans and methods with a proven record of success. Perhaps his plan wasn't as inspired as Skorzeny's, but it didn't have to be. It was being executed by Steiger.

In fact, even though he didn't need it, Steiger had a backup plan. If he wasn't able to execute the assassination of FDR, Churchill, and Stalin together, he would kill Churchill and FDR as they approached the Soviet embassy. The hide he had chosen afforded him an astonishingly unobstructed view of the likely paths of FDR and Churchill toward the Soviet embassy. He would only be able to assassinate one of them, obviously, because once one of them was shot, the other would be immediately secured and rapidly escorted to safety along a predetermined and heavily fortified route.

But the effect, though not nearly as stunning as the assassination of all three heads of state, would be similar. The elimination of

Churchill or Roosevelt would cause a profound and prolonged disruption of the relevant nation's war effort. Moreover, it wouldn't necessarily galvanize the other Allies to open a Western Front.

Steiger looked behind him. He didn't see Canidy. He looked from left to right and back again.

Still no Canidy.

Satisfied, he looked for anyone who might be taking an unusual interest in him. Or anyone who might notice him moving toward his hide. He shook his head in wonderment. Not one of the nearby guards or NKVD agents seemed to take notice of him.

Three trucks, two jeeps, and twenty or more troops lined up outside the building housing the Brandenburgers. Braden's men formed two phalanxes and directed the prisoners into the truck beds.

Braden, at the direction of Fulmar, had ordered Morelli to go back to the embassy and tell them the situation and that Braden was requesting as many vehicles as they could spare. Fulmar, satisfied that the Germans were secured, turned to Braden. "I need one of your men to drive McDermott and me to the Soviet embassy. Right now."

Braden looked momentarily confused. *"American . . . ?"*

"No, the *Soviet* embassy," Fulmar repeated. "Canidy will be somewhere nearby and he'll need our assistance."

Braden nodded and waved to the driver of a closed-cab Dodge WC-51 who looked like a teenage James Cagney. The driver pulled the vehicle next to Braden and saluted. Braden pointed to Fulmar and McDermott and said, "Take these men to the Soviet embassy. Do you know where that is?"

"Yes, sir. We've made several runs between our embassy, the Russian embassy, and the Brit embassy."

Fulmar and McDermott thanked Braden and got into the back of the vehicle. Fulmar patted the driver on the shoulder and said, "Let's go. We don't have much time."

Canidy, having lost track of the small man, had moved in the direction of the Soviet and British embassies, hoping that he might catch sight of him. Canidy told himself that doing so was the most logical thing he could do, the only thing he could do.

Canidy moved at a quick pace, head swiveling from side to side. The Iranian civilians were easily distinguishable in style and manner from the small man. So, too, the serious-looking NKVD, of whom there seemed to be scores and most of whom appeared ready to shoot at the slightest provocation.

Canidy consciously tried to lower his anxiety by telling himself he was searching in the right place; if the small man was anywhere, it would be here.

But the effort was futile. Every minute that passed, his nervousness grew. The *President* wanted him here. In Tehran. The *President* believed Canidy merited being at the most consequential conference of the time, presumably because he believed Canidy to be a most capable intelligence agent and operator. Yet Canidy had lost—and was inept at locating—the most immediate threat to the President's life. As catastrophic as the loss of the Kapsky notebook had seemed to be at the time, it was insignificant compared to the loss of the commander in chief.

CHAPTER 53

Steiger appeared to look with indifference about the area surrounding the building before entering. In fact, he was intensely focused on everything and anything that could be a threat or impediment. Save for the guards and NKVD agents surrounding the Soviet embassy, there were no concerns.

The building consisted of six rooms. Steiger had paid the manager the equivalent of two years' pay to rent the top-right room and to keep the transaction to himself. The room was unfurnished and claustrophobic, and it stank of rotting food. The stench congested his nose, constricted his throat, and made his eyes water. The wooden floorboards were warped and creaked under the slightest pressure. He ignored all of that and proceeded to the closed shutters, through which fingers of dim light streamed and flickered. Steiger peered through the slats of the shutters and saw the security personnel surrounding the Soviet embassy. He examined the terrace and imagined Churchill, Roosevelt, and Stalin sitting there casually with their aides behind them. He wouldn't have to imagine much longer. Soon it would happen and history would be made.

Steiger knelt, placed the case on the floor, and opened it. He withdrew and examined the Karabiner once again. Then checked it again. And again once more.

The assassin took a deep breath and exhaled slowly. Again. Then a slight smile played on his lips.

He would begin the journey back to Berlin immediately afterward. The bedlam and confusion following the event would provide excellent cover, but impede a quick departure. He would leave his Karabiner behind, but would still have his Walther. He wouldn't need it. A small man such as himself would not stand out. He would proceed eastward in a Bayerische 321 presently parked not far from the building where the easily manipulated and distracted Americans had occupied themselves with the Brandenburgers. From there he would travel northwest to the desert, from which he would take a Junkers to Germany. He would be received by Hitler, Himmler, and Schellenberg as not merely a hero, but a legend.

The figure that had disappeared into the featureless building to Canidy's left may or may not have been the small man. Canidy hadn't seen his face, only the back of his head—light brown hair. Much of his body had been obscured by passersby. But he was small and he moved like the man Canidy had twice chased across half of Tehran.

Canidy scrutinized the area again, just in case it wasn't the small man. He saw no one else who resembled him. Canidy stood at the entrance to the building, looked around one last time, and took a deep breath before entering.

Fulmar and McDermott thanked the James Cagney look-alike, stepped out of the WC-51, and scanned the area.

Fulmar exhaled forcefully. "Too many people. We'll be lucky to find Canidy sometime in the next week."

"Then we better get started," McDermott said optimistically. "The odds shouldn't be that bad. Dick's nearly a head taller than almost everyone outside the Russian cordon. Anyway, what choice do we have?"

Fulmar nodded and the two proceeded to navigate around the western edge of the Soviet embassy grounds, looking for Canidy or anything that set off alarm bells.

Although his attention was largely directed at the Soviet embassy, Gromov scanned the area immediately surrounding it for any threats or impediments to his objective. Major Richard Canidy stood out like a blinding beacon.

Gromov sensed Canidy was hunting for something or someone. Gromov was distracted by the enticing target. But the imminent bearer of the Order of Lenin disciplined himself to concentrate on his assignment. It was the most consequential assignment of the war. He would execute it flawlessly.

Nonetheless, he assigned a compartment of his brain the task of monitoring the whereabouts of Canidy, his next quarry in the chaos that was imminent. As soon as Gromov's assigned mission was accomplished, he would shift his full attention to assassinating him.

———

Fulmar moved steadily yet quickly, his eyes darting around the area immediately west of the Soviet embassy. Canidy would be near the action, near whatever the potential problem would be. Finding Canidy would be the surest way of finding trouble.

"I tell you, I'm not as optimistic we'll find him as I was a few moments ago," McDermott conceded. "All I see are Persians and Russians."

"Keep looking," Fulmar said. "As you said, what choice do we have?"

"It's not a choice, really. Keep looking for Dick, but be alert for anybody who looks like they're up to no good. If they look German, so much the better," McDermott said.

"They may not look German," Fulmar said.

"Then we keep looking for someone who looks dangerous and like he's up to no good."

"You've just described Dick Canidy," Fulmar noted.

Steiger stood back from the window so he wouldn't be noticeable from the street. It was likely an unnecessary precaution. No one was looking in his direction. No matter. Steiger resolved to remain meticulous and exacting through completion of the mission. Although he saw no sign of them, he assumed there were Soviet countersnipers arrayed throughout the embassy compound.

He could see movement in the windows behind the Soviet embassy portico. Moments later three individuals emerged whom Steiger didn't recognize, but each wore officers' uniforms of the American, British, and Soviet militaries, respectively. High-ranking officers.

They were joined by men in civilian clothing. *Diplomats*, Steiger said to himself. Likely the highest-ranking from their respective governments. Some of them would soon be casualties.

Three chairs were brought onto the terrace by embassy personnel and arrayed in a semicircle. The officers and diplomats moved to the wings of the terrace in anticipation of the emergence of Roosevelt, Churchill, and Stalin. The animated conversation grew less so. Photographers swarmed on the steps leading to the portico.

Steiger took a step closer to the window.

A floorboard creaked as he did so. Then it creaked again.

Steiger immediately wheeled around and saw Dick Canidy appear in the doorframe. Steiger instantly began to raise the Karabiner, but Canidy lunged toward him, seized the muzzle and stock, and pointed the weapon at the ceiling.

Steiger, surprisingly strong, kept his grip on the weapon and thrust his right knee toward Canidy's groin, striking him in the upper thigh. The blow did little more than enrage Canidy. Using the Karabiner and his superior upper-body strength, he drove Steiger back several steps, pinning him against the wall. Steiger frantically tried to knee Canidy again and again, missing each time, but enraging Canidy even more. Releasing his grip on the rifle with his right hand, Canidy drew his fist back and slammed it repeatedly into Steiger's face, fracturing his jaw and right cheekbone.

The assassin maintained a grip on the Karabiner, but his eyes became glassy. Canidy slammed his fist into Steiger's face again and again, so hard that he could hear the sickening cracking of Steiger's facial bones. Steiger's legs wobbled and he began to sink toward the floor, hands still on the rifle, but his eyes glazed. Canidy's fist continued pumping until Steiger lay inert on the floor, blood from his nose and mouth forming a pool around his head and upper torso.

Canidy ripped the weapon from Steiger's grip and stood upright, chest heaving from exertion. After a few seconds, he reached down and felt the left side of Steiger's neck. No pulse—nothing but inert flesh.

Canidy stood erect and exhaled, adrenaline keeping his body tense and primed.

He looked out the window and saw the Soviet and British embassies. Directing his attention to the white façade of the Soviet embassy, he saw numerous individuals milling about the portico. He couldn't readily discern the identities of any of them, but they carried themselves with the self-importance endemic to diplomats and general officers. A mob of photographers was arraying themselves on the broad steps leading up to the terrace, some already taking photographs. Canidy felt compelled to scan the immediate vicinity for anything or anyone peculiar. He doubted he would see anything or anyone that would cause concern, but over the last several months multiple Germans seemed to have appeared out of thin air. He saw nothing out of the ordinary.

He took a last look at the small man's corpse, nudging it with his shoe in almost ritualistic fashion. Almost as if in retaliation he felt sharp pain in the hand with which he'd repeatedly struck Steiger; it was beginning to hurt.

Canidy avoided the blood on the floor as he left the room and proceeded down the stairs, out of the building, and into the crowded street. Donovan had charged him with gathering information in Tehran, and that was what he was going to do, until told otherwise.

Canidy's emergence onto the street seized Gromov's attention like a squirrel dashing in front of a dog. He watched Canidy pause on the sidewalk, looking in the general direction of the Soviet embassy. The assassin's eyes immediately noticed Canidy's right hand:

bruised, swollen, and covered with specks of blood. Canidy had found whomever it was he'd been hunting. Dozens of individuals were milling about, engaging in conversation at the embassy portico. Gromov recognized none of them, but clerks were not invited to summits. These were generals, admirals, and diplomats. Photographers crowded the broad steps leading up to the terrace, snapping scores of photographs. It would be a few minutes before Stalin, Churchill, and Roosevelt emerged onto the terrace; historic figures didn't wander about aimlessly engaging in idle chatter.

Gromov glanced down at Canidy again. He was craning his neck, looking at the embassy and the immediate vicinity to the left and right. Gromov glanced back to the portico. Still disorganized.

Gromov cursed. *This* would be his best opportunity to assassinate Canidy. Indeed, in the aftermath of the chaos Gromov was about to cause, he might not be able to find Canidy again, to make Canidy's assassination part of the chaos. Moreover, a live Canidy might yet interfere with the planned madness.

Gromov trained his weapon downward. The angle was impossible. Canidy was too close to the building. Gromov looked up again. The terrace was still disorganized. He estimated it would be several minutes before the Allied leaders would emerge, engage the attending officials, take their respective seats, and pose for obligatory photographs.

He touched the NR-40, his weapon of choice, inserted into the sleeve sewn into the back of his collar. He'd used it to great effect during the Kapsky operation.

He gently placed his Mosin-Nagant on the tar paper roof, glanced yet again at the terrace, and performed a rudimentary calculation: four minutes; two hundred forty seconds. More than enough time to create chaos. One hundred twenty seconds to reach Canidy, one hundred twenty seconds to get back to the roof. He felt a charge of excitement as he sprang to his feet, entered the door leading to the interior of the building, and descended the stairs—counting off the seconds. *More than enough time*, he thought.

He reached the front entrance to the building in forty-two seconds, peeked outside, and located Canidy standing barely a block away and facing in the direction of the Soviet embassy.

Too many people, thought Gromov. *This is a mistake. Two hundred seconds. Move.*

Gromov moved slowly toward Canidy, shouldering past street vendors and pedestrians. Canidy's gaze remained on the embassy.

One hundred eighty seconds. Sixty seconds to approach Canidy.

Gromov's excitement rose. He reminded himself that Canidy had never seen him, wouldn't recognize him as a threat. He would be on top of Canidy before he could react, insert the blade of the NR-40 into Canidy's right side just above the hip, and slice upward through the kidney toward the diaphragm. Quite painful. He would collapse to the pavement and bleed profusely. Dead within minutes. Gromov would have plenty of time to return to the roof. Stalin, Churchill, and Roosevelt probably wouldn't have even emerged to take their seats on the terrace.

Canidy began moving. Gromov cursed to himself. *Seconds added.* He followed Canidy unobtrusively as he walked across the street toward an alley in the direction of the Soviet embassy.

One hundred fifty seconds. Thirty seconds to kill Canidy.

Gromov suddenly quickened his pace, remaining behind Canidy and outside his field of vision. Canidy entered the narrow alley, the buildings on either side short but sufficient to obscure a view of the embassy. No pedestrians. Less than one hundred meters ahead, troops and NKVD ringed the embassy grounds. *One hundred thirty seconds. Ten seconds to kill Canidy.*

Gromov lengthened his stride, withdrew the NR-40 from the back of his collar, and closed the distance between himself and Canidy, who was oblivious to his presence. He drew his hand back to thrust the blade into Canidy's side, but felt the sensation of metal piercing *his* right side just above the hip.

Gromov's eyes widened with agony and astonishment as his trachea was sliced in half, preventing the air gushing from his lungs from making a sound. His body remained suspended upright for nearly a second.

The last thing on Gromov's mind before collapsing to the pavement was Yaron, the name of the peasant he'd killed in Estonia.

The sound of Gromov's head cracking on the pavement caused Canidy to spin around. Lieutenant Eric Fulmar stood over Gromov's bleeding corpse. He returned his M3 to his right hip and shrugged. "You owe me."

Canidy looked questioningly from Fulmar to Gromov's corpse and back to Fulmar.

"He was stalking you and was going to kill you," Fulmar informed him. "We noticed him immediately after he came out of the building. He had a look. In fact, I swear I've seen him before."

Canidy took a moment to absorb both the presence of the corpse and the presence of Fulmar. Fulmar filled in the blanks. "McDermott and I left the house in the good hands of Lieutenant Braden. We figured we needed to back you up." He pointed to Gromov's body. "I saw this guy following you. He looked familiar. Looked like trouble."

Canidy shook his head as if trying to sober up. "I know the face. From the Thorisdottirs' photo."

"That's it. Colonel Gromov. He'd struck both McDermott and me as someone we'd seen, too—somebody who might be a real problem. Gromov," Fulmar said, dropping next to the corpse. "Let's see what we can find."

Fulmar knelt next to the body, being careful to avoid the blood. He checked the pockets and said flatly, "No identification. No surprise." He then checked the waistband, pulling a pistol from the small of the corpse's back.

"Tokarev," Fulmar said as he continued to search. He then held up the NR-40. "Assassin's dagger, courtesy of the quartermasters of the Red Army. It's Gromov all right."

Canidy sighed. "Donovan never trusted our communist ally," he noted. "He believes we'll be fighting them next. But this . . ."

"Well, the President wanted us here," Fulmar said. "I think we've justified our presence.

"We've got a Soviet assassin dead here and Nazi assassin dead inside. All in less than twenty minutes. The conference will proceed without disruption. This *should* earn us a point or two. But we're talking about Wild Bill Donovan. I'm pretty sure he'll find that somehow we've screwed up and we'll be sent back to purgatory on Gotland."

Canidy grinned and clapped Fulmar on the shoulder. "Not this time. Only a handful of people will ever know, but even Donovan would agree we've earned our pay today. In fact, we may have earned a trip back home."

CHAPTER 54

The Führer's massive alpine redoubt in Bavaria sat atop the mile-high Kehlstein promontory. With trepidation, Schellenberg entered its cavernous oak-paneled meeting room with a western view of the mountain range. The two men seated therein notoriously hated bad news. And it was Schellenberg's misfortune to have to deliver it.

Seated to Schellenberg's left, his back to the massive window with its breathtaking panorama, was Reichsführer-SS Heinrich Himmler, his round wire-framed glasses seated on the bridge of his nose. He appeared perpetually irritated and this moment was no exception.

Seated on a deep-cushioned chair facing the window was the Führer himself. He appeared subdued, but Schellenberg noted that any room Hitler occupied seemed charged with electrical currents.

Schellenberg saluted and waited silently.

"Report, Schellenberg," Himmler commanded tersely.

"Mein Führer, I must report that the operation was unsuccessful. Stalin, Churchill, and Roosevelt remain alive. The conference in Tehran concluded with multiple bilateral and trilateral commitments, chief among them an understanding that the Americans and the British are to open a Western Front—a cross–English Channel invasion of France—with a time frame of May of next year. Contemporaneously, Stalin will launch an offensive on the Eastern Front. Our source indicates there were discussions concerning strikes in southern France and the Adriatic also, but the western invasion by the Americans and British was the principal point of discussion."

Himmler shifted in his chair, causing Schellenberg to flinch as if he were a child expecting a spanking. Hitler remained glum, motionless.

"The status of the Brandenburgers?" Himmler asked.

"All captured, save one," Schellenberg replied.

"One escaped?" Himmler asked.

"Killed, Herr Reichsführer."

Hitler stirred. "Steiger? Steiger is dead?"

Schellenberg nodded. "I'm afraid so, Mein Führer."

"So the Americans, then, have accounted for the entire team sent to Tehran?" Hitler asked.

Schellenberg's throat tightened. "Regrettably so, Mein Führer."

Adolf Hitler remained utterly still for several seconds that seemed to Schellenberg like minutes. Then he rose from his chair and walked slowly, hands clasped behind his back, to the large window with the breathtaking view. Schellenberg turned slightly to watch him.

Hitler gazed out the window for a few seconds before turning and looking at Schellenberg. "Do you know who killed Steiger?"

Schellenberg cleared his throat. "We are not absolutely certain, Mein Führer, but it is believed to have been one of the American soldiers. Most likely Major Richard Canidy or Lieutenant Eric Fulmar, U.S. Army Air Corps."

Hitler glanced at Himmler. "Fulmar," Hitler repeated softly.

"Yes, Mein Führer."

Schellenberg noted that Himmler nodded almost imperceptibly. "What do you wish us to do with them, Mein Führer?"

Hitler glanced at Himmler again, then turned to gaze out the window.

"Where are the two Americans now?" Himmler asked.

"At the American legation in Tehran, in the company of Admiral Canaris's two contractors who arrived there just a short time ago."

"The blond *Fischerin* from Iceland?"

"That is correct."

Hitler turned back from the window. Schellenberg detected hints of smiles playing on both Hitler's and Himmler's lips.

"Do absolutely nothing with them," Hitler said. "We will encounter them again, and I have a plan to use them to our advantage."

Moscow, Soviet Union

1122, 2 December 1943

The second-most feared man in the Soviet Union drank heavily sweetened tea as he sat at his desk studying the reports regarding Tehran.

The talented Colonel Taras Gromov was dead. A shame. Extremely formidable and useful, he had been scheduled to receive the Order of Lenin and in time would have succeeded Aleksandr Belyanov as head of the OKRNKVD.

Nonetheless, the objective of the Tehran conference had been achieved without Gromov, and thankfully so. The order to fire upon the conference—to sow terror among the Allied leaders in order to ensure opening a Western Front—could very well have ended in utter disaster.

Gromov's death remained baffling. He'd been found in an alley within a short distance of hundreds of NKVD, SMERSH, and regular Red Army troops. Although the alley was near the Soviet embassy, there was no view of the embassy from there.

Gromov, though highly proficient, wasn't irreplaceable. Beria would identify another proficient NKVD officer to be his primary assassin. Russians, after all, produced many such men.

Not only was the Western Front to be established, but intelligence operations were going even better than he'd hoped. Although Dr. Sebastian Kapsky was recovering in Western custody, the Soviet Union had his formulae.

Beria remained astounded, pleasantly so, that he had an informant in the Abwehr. The formidable Canaris appeared to be oblivious to the fact that the chief armorer for the Abwehr's most secretive and consequential missions had family in Soviet Kaliningrad, family whose lives could be extinguished with a snap of Beria's fingers.

Perhaps more astounding was the obtuseness of their ally, the Americans, who refused to believe that an *ally* would have a mole at the highest levels of their government.

Swiveling his chair, Beria turned to the credenza behind him and poured a measure of vodka into a blue crystal glass and drank it slowly as he contemplated the upper echelons of British, American, and German intelligence services. Menzies, Donovan, and Canaris were problems. They were smart, tough, and indefatigable. But he could manage them.

Soviet success in this war and beyond, however, required the immediate elimination of a Major Richard Canidy, USAAF.

ABOUT THE AUTHORS

W. E. B. Griffin was the author of seven bestselling series: The Corps, Brotherhood of War, Badge of Honor, Men at War, Honor Bound, Presidential Agent, and Clandestine Operations. He was invested into the orders of St. George of the U.S. Armor Association and St. Michael of the Army Aviation Association of America, and was a life member of the U.S. Special Operations Association; Gaston-Lee Post 5660, Veterans of Foreign Wars; the American Legion, China Post #1 in Exile; the Police Chiefs Association of Southeastern Pennsylvania, Southern New Jersey, and the State of Delaware; the National Rifle Association; and the Office of Strategic Services (OSS) Society. He was an honorary life member of the U.S. Army Otter & Caribou Association, the U.S. Army Special Forces Association, the U.S. Marine Raider Association, and the USMC Combat Correspondents Association. Griffin passed away in February 2019.

Peter Kirsanow practices and teaches law and is an official of a federal agency. He is a former member of the National Labor Relations Board and has testified before Congress on a variety of matters, including the confirmations of five Supreme Court justices. He contributes regularly to *National Review*, and his op-eds have appeared in newspapers ranging from *The Wall Street Journal* to *The Washington Times*. The author of *Target Omega* and *Second Strike*, he lives in Cleveland, Ohio.